BY KAREN MARIE MONING

THE FEVER SERIES
Darkfever
Bloodfever
Faefever
Dreamfever
Shadowfever
Iced
Burned
Feverborn
Feversong

GRAPHIC NOVEL
Fever Moon

NOVELLA
Into the Dreaming

THE HIGHLANDER SERIES
Beyond the Highland Mist
To Tame a Highland Warrior
The Highlander's Touch
Kiss of the Highlander
The Dark Highlander
The Immortal Highlander
Spell of the Highlander

FEVERSONG

KAREN MARIE MONING

FEVERSONG

A Fever Novel

DELACORTE PRESS

NEW YORK

Published in the United States by Delacorte Press, an imprint of Random House, a division of Penguin Random House LLC, New York.

DELACORTE PRESS and the HOUSE colophon are registered trademarks of Penguin Random House LLC.

Library of Congress Cataloging-in-Publication Data
Names: Moning, Karen Marie, author.
Title: Feversong : a Fever novel / Karen Marie Moning.
Description: New York : Delacorte Press, 2017. | Series: Fever ; 9
Identifiers: LCCN 2016042486| ISBN 9780425284353 (hardback) |
ISBN 9780425284360 (ebook)
Subjects: LCSH: Paranormal romance stories. | BISAC: FICTION / Romance / Paranormal. | FICTION / Fantasy / Paranormal. | FICTION / Romance / Fantasy. | GSAFD: Fantasy fiction.
Classification: LCC PS3613.O527 F49 2017 | DDC 813/.6—dc23
LC record available at https://lccn.loc.gov/2016042486

Printed in the United States of America on acid-free paper

randomhousebooks.com

246897531

First Edition

Book design by Caroline Cunningham

This one is for you, intrepid readers, for picking up a copy of Darkfever and following me into the Dark Zone, keeping the faith and staying to the light, and being outstanding company until closing time.

I tip my glass with a slainte and a heartfelt

go raibh maith agat.

The Fever series wouldn't exist without you.

GLOSSARY ALERT

If this is the first book you've picked up in the Fever Series, at the end of this novel I've included a guide of People, Places, and Things to illuminate the backstory.

If you're a seasoned reader of the series, the guide will reacquaint you with notable events and characters, what they did, if they survived, and if not, how they died.

If you're reading an ebook, factor this into your expectation of when the story ends, which is a bit before the final page count.

You can either read the guide first, getting acquainted with the world, or reference it as you go along to refresh your memory. The guide features characters by type, followed by places, then things.

PART I

Let your plans be dark and impenetrable as night,
And when you move fall like a thunderbolt.

–Sun Tzu

To know your enemy you must become your enemy.

–Sun Tzu

PROLOGUE

MAC

My philosophy is pretty simple—any day I'm not killing somebody is a good day in my book.

I haven't had many good days lately.

I reflect on the highlights of the past year:

July 5, the day my sister, Alina, called my cellphone and left a frantic message that I ended up not hearing until weeks later. She was murdered, abandoned in a trash-filled alley shortly after she placed that call.

August 3, the night I arrived in Dublin, saw my first Fae monster behind the glamour and realized either I was crazy or the world was. Turns out the world was but that didn't help much.

September: an entire month vanished during a single afternoon in Faery, playing volleyball with an illusion of my dead sister.

October 3, I was tortured and nearly killed by the vampire-wannabe Mallucé in his hellish grotto beneath the Burren. That's the night I learned to eat the flesh of dark Fae for its healing properties and the enormous strength it bestowed.

October 31, Halloween, the night the walls between man and

Fae came crashing down, I was gang-raped by four Unseelie princes and turned into a mindless shell of a woman, an addict to Fae sex.

November, December, and part of January are calendar pages ripped cleanly from my mind, leaving no memory at all, until I surfaced from being hellishly Pri-ya to find I'd spent all that time in bed with Jericho Barrons.

Then there's that date I'll never know—impossible to gauge the day, year, or even century in the Silvers—when I killed Barrons and, believing him dead, became a woman obsessed with obtaining the *Sinsar Dubh* so I could re-create a world with him in it.

More of January and February: lost in the Silvers, working with the enemy, the Lord Master, plotting my revenge.

May 11, the night I learned the girl I loved like a sister was the one who'd killed my sister.

May 16, the day we reinterred the *Sinsar Dubh* in the underground chamber at the abbey and I discovered V'lane was really Cruce, one of my four rapists, and that I'd been working all along with the most cunning, dangerous Unseelie prince in existence.

June 26, the day I chased Dani into the Hall of All Days, a place I didn't dare follow. If I had a do-over, I'd leap through that damned Silver and chase her anyway, despite the formidable odds.

July 22, I discovered who Jada was, and that my brilliant, effervescent, spunkalicious Dani was gone, leaving behind a controlled, humorless, stone-cold killer.

Now, I add another date to my grim tally.

One year five days after I first touched my well-pedicured foot to Ireland's wild soil—*August 8:* the day the *Sinsar Dubh* won. And all it had to do to defeat me was wait patiently, quasiquietly, with gentle nudges here and there, until I mindfucked myself into crossing that forbidden line. It took my hostile squatter a mere two and a half months from the day I buried the corporeal Book beneath the abbey to seduce me into opening it.

I'd spent most of that time sleuthing for a spell to summon the Unseelie King and demand he reclaim his Book from inside me, withdrawing from Barrons and the world, becoming a shell of who I was—all because I'd been afraid the *Sinsar Dubh* might somehow trick me into opening it.

It had.

I understand something now: that which we fear, we somehow beckon near and engage in a dance, as toxically intimate as a pair of suspicious lovers. Perhaps it's because deep down we want to face it. Perhaps it's just the way the universe works; we're magnetized waltzers and our hopes and fears emit some kind of electrical impulses that attract all that we dream, and all that we dread. We live and die on a dance floor of our own making.

Here, now, drifting where it's silent and still, I begin to apprehend with acute clarity every single thing I did wrong.

1

"The killer awoke before dawn,

he put his boots on"

A WAREHOUSE IN A DARK ZONE, DUBLIN, IRELAND

I rise.

Or try to. Jada crashes into me with a muffled grunt then her hands are on me, everywhere, touching, patting and pulling, undoing my restraints, and the sensation is too much. My body is hypersensitive.

Finally, she frees my hands. I push her away and open my eyes. Too fast, too much. Light thrusts cruel needles into my brain.

I close my eyes swiftly. Scents assault me: the acrid odor of the Sweeper's minions, concrete and dust, chemicals and sweat.

"Turn off the lights," I say.

"Why?" Jada says.

"I have a headache." I wait without moving as she hurries about the warehouse, extinguishing the blinding lights the Sweeper arranged for our surgery.

Once I sense diminished brilliance beyond my lids, I open my eyes again. Tolerable.

"Mac, what did you do?" Jada exclaims. "They're gone. Just gone!"

Sound impacts the delicate structure of my ears as if she's taken a gong to a shield. Not gone. The Sweeper and his minions were displaced, still nearby. I say, "A simple spell of sifting—backward, not forward." No Fae has the power to fold things into the future, and only the king and I possess this small way to manipulate the past. In a matter of minutes the Sweeper will be here again, at our operating tables. But I intend to be gone.

I. Intend.

I rise. My body doesn't move as planned. It shudders, flops, and goes limp. "Stiff from being on the table so long," I tell Jada, who watches me with narrowed eyes. I contract my abdomen, bend at the waist, stabilize my upper body, rotate my hips and shift my legs as a unit over the side of the gurney and touch my feet to the floor.

I stand.

I AM.

Desire. Lust. Greed. And the path I choose to supremacy.

Master of adaptation and evolution, I slide more surely in my skin with each breath, enjoying the complex albeit imperfect elegance of what I possess. I inhale long and slow, swelling first my abdomen then lungs with air. Breathing brings an assault of unfathomable stenches, but I will acclimate.

Everything MacKayla Lane experienced is filed in my meticulous mental vault, but during my incarceration in her body I couldn't see, I couldn't hear, I couldn't smell.

I was—as she is now—trapped in a dark silent prison, my only connection to the world an attachment I forged to her central nervous system, through supremacy of will and relentless trial and failure. My existence was a smattering of complex electrical charges, intricate patterns without substance. Although I spied on her life as much as possible, I was able to seize use of her body, hands, and eyes only once, for brief duration. All else was diluted, secondhand perception absorbed from within except on that overcast rainy day I killed the Gray Woman and Mick O'Leary.

The power. The glory. That was the day I knew I would win. Those clumsy, debilitating hours I rode a body for the first time.

I require time to perfect control.

I. Require.

I draw myself up inside, gathering the enormity, the ancientness, the hunger and storm of my existence, and expand into the imperfect biological vessel I've claimed, saturating, possessing, every atom. I fill my blood, my bones, my skin.

I turn the full force of my regard upon Jada, blink once, and reveal myself. My eyes, reflected in the stainless steel door of a commercial freezer unit behind her, fill with obsidian until no white remains. Around me the very air cools; I have such presence.

She changes color. Fear impacts the nerves that connect brain to heart, constricting circulation. The blood vanishes from her face, leaving freckles upon snow. Her eyes widen, her pupils dilate and freeze. The scent of her body alters to one I find . . . intriguing.

I experience all of this with my own senses. It's incomparable. My mere existence embedded within this stolen skin reprograms the anatomy of those around me.

Power.

I was made for it.

I would prefer to shred her flesh from bone but several things prevent me. I smile with my new face.

"I would run if I were you," I tell her softly.

She does, lightning fast. No hesitation, no debilitating deliberation. There one moment, gone the next. Among humans, she is superior.

I covet her speed and dexterity. MacKayla Lane would call it "freeze-framing." If I could eat Jada and absorb her talent, I would ignore those things that stay my hand.

There is something else I can eat. Clever MacKayla. Flawed MacKayla. Those that fall pave the way for my ascendance. When one begins at the bottom, ascendance is a given.

I depart the warehouse and enter the gloomy day.

I enter.

I am. The Sweeper will appear shortly. Not even I have the power to destroy that one.

I'd contemplated pretending to be MacKayla, living among them, infiltrating their circle while pursuing my goals, but deemed the risk of discovery too high. Concealing my brilliance, feigning to be so much less—impossible. Besides, I am a newly forged sword and will surely benefit from time with hammer and fire.

Time, my enemy, my ally. I have precious little of the commodity to implement my plan. Expediency is directly proportionate to success. When opponents war, the strongest and swiftest wins. I am already the former and intend to be the latter.

Until they hunt me, time is my ally. I possess the weapon to accomplish all my goals. I prize the spear, I loathe it. It might damage me. Its weight beneath my arm both reassures and repulses.

Singing softly beneath my breath—one of MacKayla's favorites, "Sh-boom, sh-boom, life could be a dream sweetheart"—I move down an alley, around a corner, proceeding to my first objective. My map of Dublin, once an amalgam of neural currents, now has visual latitude and longitude. While MacKayla wandered aimless, I did not. I was paying attention.

What a sorry experiment she was. I desired so much more.

Unwavering laser-focus on one's goals is power. Humans rarely achieve it, infesting their garden with the cultivated parasites of empathy, compassion, mercy, nurturing the grubs of guilt and penance, heaping emotional fertilizer on every acre of arable, marchable, conquerable land until nothing remains but the sky-high, sickly weeds of their stunted vision. A blind gardener reaps no crop, escapes no predator.

We are desire, lust, greed, and the path we choose to supremacy.

Humans romanticize this truth. Fact: they *desire* sex. Fact: they *desire* limiting that vessel from having sex with others. Fact:

they create a ritual called marriage and an illusion called love to validate their *greed* and bid for *supremacy* over the object of their *lust*.

WE ARE DESIRE, LUST, GREED, AND THE PATH WE CHOOSE TO SUPREMACY. Take notes. Cretins. Idiots. Call it what it is. Then go forth and fucking conquer.

There are currently two Unseelie princes and one princess living. They will die. I permit none between my throne and me.

My body is human, not prince. Pity. A Fae form would eradicate irksome limitations. But there were no princes available the night I seized the opportunity for escape. I lack wings to soar into the sky, slash Death's throat with my spear and douse the fire below with his blood.

But my first victim knows MacKayla and will come to her unaware she is me.

I giggle. "Surprise," I murmur, envisioning the moment.

I spy the first of my children, offspring of the spells I am as I exit the Dark Zone. They are more my seed than they ever were the penitent king's. Oxymoron that. A true king knows no penitence, bows to nothing and no one.

All of MacKayla's knowledge of the world around her is mine. Her names for things come easily to me. My existence within her has been far more vivid than anything I experienced from within the covers of the Book that once incarcerated me. Three of my forty-ninth-made caste—those she calls Rhino-boys—have a woman in the alley, willing sacrifice to partake of their flesh. They play with her for momentary pleasure, beady eyes, beady minds, puny shadows flickering in puny caves.

Much of the Unseelie King's knowledge is mine as well. I sprang into existence from the spells he created to birth his Dark Court and know the True Names of the Unseelie, which grants me control over them. Unfortunately there are those Unseelie recently born, such as the Highlander prince, whose names are yet unknown or I would simply summon him and slay him now. Then there is Cruce, currently bound by the king's chamber magic, impossible to summon. I will eliminate my most challenging enemies first.

I chime in the First Language and three tusked heads swivel. I command them to worship me, to offer the flesh that will grant me Jada's strength and speed. The woman is abandoned as my children stumble, snuffle, and fall to their knees, heads bowed, shaking with fear and subservience. A simple caste. Not my finest work.

The Fae have long hungered for someone to lead them, make the decisions they fear, the bold ones that bring chaos, death, and war. I'm momentarily incensed by their limits—these frail toys that are all with which I have to play. These things that aren't real like me.

Still, I prefer frail toys to nothing. I've had an abundance of nothing.

Nothing is Hell. Nothing is where MacKayla is now.

It's in breaking things that you understand them.

It's in understanding them that you control them.

The Unseelie tremble before me.

As will the world.

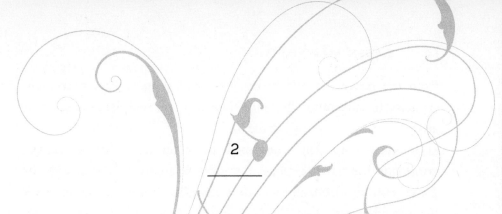

2

"Hey I heard you were a wild one"

CHRISTIAN MACKELTAR

Arlington Abbey. Despite my efforts, the fortress has fallen. Although the deadly icefire no longer burns, I was unable to prevent the citadel's destruction. The roof has collapsed and blackened timbers jut skyward, broken ribs of a once-great beast. Walls slump in graves of chalky ash and tumbled stone. The ancient sanctuary, built first on a *shian,* pagan temple, then church, is a ruin.

An inch of ice coats the lawn and the now cold bones of the abbey. Drawing moisture from the sky—Dublin has a veritable flood rain eternally waiting to fall, as if, on the day of creation, a vengeful god suspended an airborne ocean above the Emerald Isle—I'd shaped it with my wrath into a killing frost, and soared over the fortress, extinguishing the unnatural blue-black flames.

My efforts were not without price. I may be Fae but my back and shoulders burn from prolonged flight, and my gut spasms, somehow still flawed from my repeated disembowelment on a cliff.

Beneath the fallen bastion is a labyrinthine underground city that houses a prison containing Cruce. As he has not yet exploded from the bowels of the earth, it's a fair guess the subterranean stronghold still stands. Perhaps the surviving *sidhe*-seers can go to ground. At least the wall of the abbey directly above Cruce's prison no longer teeters dangerously near the black hole, threatening the voracious anomaly's exponential growth. I collapsed that wall inward with an airborne kick; now it's dust, a good distance from the event horizon.

Shouts split the air as the *sidhe*-seers cry out the names of their dead and summon aid for those still alive.

I fly over the abbey, a dark-winged shadow in a sky of forbidding thunderclouds, watching through narrowed eyes for movement on the battlefield. Those of Ryodan's men who fought in human or beast form to save the abbey now patrol the perimeter of the estate's great wall, prepared for the next attack. Though this assault has ended, another will come. The campaign to free Cruce has just begun.

I catch a shiver of stealthy movement in the corner of my eye. An Unseelie slithers beneath a mound of ice-covered, decapitated corpses. When it surges up into the path of a *sidhe*-seer seeking survivors, I drop like stone, slash and maim until it moves no more.

When the *sidhe*-seer is safe, I cease my midair attack and, wings beating hard against the wind that came wed to the ice I called, drive myself up into the sky. After several more sweeps over the grounds in which I spy nothing of concern, I land in the midst of the battlefield, angling my wings back and up, close to my body so I won't have to spend hours scrubbing blood and guts from the infernal things before I sleep.

As I collect the corpse of a *sidhe*-seer who looks a mere child in death and may well have been, I stumble over an ice-covered, decapitated Unseelie, distracted by what remains of the many dead around me. Not their bodies. Something else. The dying leave a psychic imprint when they go; the body shits, the soul expels a ghastly fart of one's strongest emotions, fears, and desires. Residue everywhere. I'm sticky with it. I feel their rage, hear screams no one else can, echoing in the air around me. I live with one foot in a world no one else can see.

Women shiver in the unnaturally cold, gusty air, clustered around a growing pile of their fallen sisters, watching me warily as I approach, stealing glances, looking hastily away. My faded jeans, hiking boots, and gray fisherman's sweater only make me look a wolf stalking near, wearing half a sheepskin, covering none of the frightening parts. I see myself as they do: an enormous man with a distant, wintry gaze that calls a price if engaged, majestic black-velvet wings, frosted torque, and tattoos slithering like dark snakes beneath my skin as they always do when I'm aroused by lust—murderous or otherwise—cradling a young, fair-haired girl. Looking, no doubt, as if I'm the one that killed her. My face appears more feral in a mirror than it feels on my bones. We could not be more incongruous together, the corpse and I. Yet we fit together perfectly. The only girl I'll ever take into my arms will either already be dead or soon end up that way.

One of the women stares too hard, meeting my gaze.

Her thoughts are clear but I'm not the one to defuse her battle-lust with aggressive sex behind abbey hedges. *Bloody fool,* I tell her with my eyes, staring back. *Look away. Never look back.*

Blood trickles from the corners of her eyes before she closes them and presses a hand to her temple.

I hope I gave her a headache. She'll not lock eyes with me again.

My first name is Death. My last, Keltar. My middle: Celibate.

I move into the small crowd. Women inhale sharply and pull back, making a wide corridor for me. There are a few among them, however, including the one who stared, that dart furtive glances my way. Though Unseelie, I fought beside them, put out the fire, so they rewrite my myth in their minds, romanticizing, domesticating the transmogrified Highlander. I keep my gaze fixed on the corpse I carry, my movements rigid and aloof, damning them for considering for even one mad moment the idea of having sex with an Unseelie prince.

I understand it, though.

War is funny like that. Adrenaline begets a need for more adrenaline until we're all junkies, until only when we're in danger do we feel no pain, only when we're locking jaws with Death do we feel alive. Battle-hardened soldiers understand how to save the imperiled day.

But we will never again understand how to live the normal ones.

I gently deposit the dead girl's body on the pile. As I straighten from releasing my slight burden, I go motionless, sensing a new-comer. MacKayla Lane is near. I know her scent; it's sunshine on skin, the nearly intangible whiff of chlorine from a summer pool, and something too muddy and complex to be named. She's always smelled that way to me; the promise of a hot new girlfriend that might just be a nut job.

I push through the *sidhe*-seers, circle the frozen fountain, and head into the gloomy, dark morning, making for the south wing. The sky is so dense with thunderclouds, it's little better than twi-light on the grounds. Mac's down somewhere beyond an iced, toppled pile of stones, although I can't fathom why she remains alone when her sisters are here. Her allegiance was unquestionable tonight, to the abbey, to Dani, to the human race. She belongs with them. Unlike me.

Someone closes a hand on my shoulder from behind. I knock the hand off and whirl, wings lifting, rustling in warning. Around my neck, my torque writhes, flares with a cold blue-black light. No one touches me. I say who. I say when.

"Hey," says the *sidhe*-seer who stared too long.

I give her a look. It says, *Shut up and go away. And do it right now or die.*

She arches a brow. "Would it kill you to say 'hey' back?"

Her voice is beautiful, husky with a knife-edge rasp and a sexy

French accent. "Ah, a scintillating conversationalist," I say sarcastically. "What will you dazzle me with next? A witty 'What's up?' "

"You made the ice that put out the fire," she says.

I let my eyes fill with the strangeness of what I've become, silently daring her to look again, but she keeps her gaze fixed on my sternum. "I'm not a man for small talk. Say something that matters or leave."

She stands her ground, unfazed by my efforts to drive her away. "I hear you've got a problem."

"What would that be?" I'll go see Mac, check on Dageus, then go home alone where I stay alone until there's something for me to do that proves me more man than monster.

"When you have sex with a woman, she dies. Yet you need it like you need to breathe. I hear you won't do it anymore because you don't want to kill anyone. How's that working out for you?"

What makes her think she can walk up to an Unseelie prince and instigate a glib conversation about sex? Who knows I'm not having sex and talks about me to *sidhe*-seers? "Where did you hear that?"

"Colleen. Your sister worries about you."

Her hands form casual fists at her waist. This one has a cocky swagger and a bit of a death wish. Bloody Colleen, dishing with her bloody friends about her bloody brother. She and I are going to have a talk. "And you think you can help me with that?"

"It's no more complicated than anything else in life. It takes discipline and I know discipline. I cut my teeth on it."

She looks like she did, lean and long, with a strut of a walk and the clear definition of a six-pack beneath her torn, bloodstained tank. Beneath a shredded jacket, half-empty ammo belts crisscross her chest. Unlike the others, if she feels the biting wind I called to this meadow, she doesn't shiver.

An F2000 assault rifle rests on a frayed strap over her arm, blood-crusted knives are tucked into her waistband, her boots. Her right cheek is bruised and split, her knuckles are raw, and her lower lip is spattered with dried blood. She moves closer to me and leans in. I drop my head forward and breathe smoke and battle-sweat, blood and woman. I catch the hint of heather soap. Colleen says they make it the old way at the abbey. It reminds me of the Highlands, of Tara, of innocence offered and taken, and death.

"Kiss me," she says, staring at my mouth. "You know you want to. I saw how you looked at me."

My gaze rests on her blood-spattered lips. Lush, pink, her mouth is Eros crusted with Thanatos. I miss kissing. I need now, more than ever before, to release the storm of sexual and emotional energy inside me. "I want to do much more than that."

"I won't let you." She shifts her weight, swinging her rifle behind her back. "Not yet."

"You can't stop me." No one can. And there's the rub. A kiss would lead to a fuck and it would be her last because I can't control myself. I drain a woman of life in bed. It's odd to stare into eyes that never meet yours. It's enough to give a man a God-complex. Her pupils dilate, widen then narrow again, with a shimmer of banked fire. Not deterred—intrigued. This one likes dancing on a high wire.

She wets her lips, tastes the dried blood and scrubs it away with the back of her hand. It doesn't work, just smears more blood on her face. "A single kiss. Then walk away. Discipline begins. You think I have nothing to teach you. You think no one does. I thought that once, too. Maybe you're right. Maybe you're wrong. Maybe you're a coward. Try the kiss."

Dark eyes meet mine in level challenge. The message is clear. She'll stare at me until she bleeds again.

"You want to measure your power by the power of those with whom you play. It turns you on." I sneer.

"Am I supposed to be turned on by mediocrity?"

"You're supposed to be turned on by a *human*. Get your bloody kicks somewhere else." Twin drops of crimson appear in the corners of her eyes. I pivot and turn away.

"Right. Go on then," she flings at my back. "Sure, you'll never fail—if you never try. Hell of a life, that. When you're ready to put on your big-boy pants, you know where to find me."

"My pants and what's in them are already too big for you," I say coolly. She wants to tempt me, lead me down a dark path that will end with me carrying the sin of yet another woman's death on my conscience, all because she wants to play with the big, power-ful, dangerous man. It's not about me. It's about her. She needs to pull her head out of her ass.

She laughs and walks off, confident, sexy, sure-footed on the slippery ice, like she expects me to turn and look. I know, because I turn and look, unwillingly appreciating the fluid, aggressive grace of her spine, the lean muscle of her legs, the curve of her ass.

Then I lope across the frost-covered grass to find Mac, in a foul mood. Once I'm turned on, I stay that way for a long time. Though pumped by a human heart, my blood runs Unseelie prince, twisted and unquenchable.

I slam a fist to my chest directly above that chambered beast and remind myself it was born Highlander and Highlander it will remain.

"Christian!" Mac's voice is an urgent whisper.

I hurry to join her. We will face whatever our next battle is together.

3

"Welcome to my house"

MAC

It's dark. I can't breathe. I can't see.

Blind, I exist in a void, a tightly compressed Mac-in-the-box, waiting for someone to crank my handle.

The body I don't have tries frantically to gulp air.

Though I no longer have a mouth, somehow I scream and scream.

4

"What a Wonderful World"

MacKayla's memory is mine. Not all, but enough; those ways in which she interacted with the physical world.

I know where Barrons keeps his car keys and that the mirror in the study on the first floor of the bookstore is the booby-trapped passage to his underground lair. I know how to navigate it; I once helped her gain entry. I know exactly how she takes her coffee, applies her makeup, does her hair, the way she greets and speaks with her adopted mother, her false father. I understand every nuance of what to say and do to pass myself off as Barrons's Rainbow Girl.

Her body memory is also mine. Driving a car presented no challenge. Navigating the icy terrain is different but not difficult. The cold, however, is unpleasant and makes me shiver. I share her distaste for inclement weather and snow.

I glide across the wintry, windy abbey grounds, moving more surely inside my flawed bag of muscle and bone with each step. I'd like to sink within, pry open Mac's box and murder her after a splendid afternoon of tea and torture for taking this vessel so for granted that she abused, neglected, and risked it at every turn. The vessel that was meant to be mine from the moment I inhabited it.

It's not strong enough. She should have done better. Because of her frailties, I embark on life handicapped.

The first of my victims hurries toward me through the gloom, another broody conflicted fool that reviles the gift of power he was given. The power I would strip from him if I could.

"Christian." I infuse my whisper with urgency.

When he appears from behind the rubble of charred, ice-dusted stone, I'm struck by the keen desire to possess his body. The undeserving prick's vessel is superior to mine. Might I, like my former incarnation—the corporeal copy of the *Sinsar Dubh* that has since crumbled to dust on a slab—possess another's skin via physical contact? Might I dump myself within and hold it? Might Christian be capable of containing the enormity that I am without rapidly deteriorating to the point of uselessness?

The body I have is certain yet flawed.

Christian's is not flawed yet not certain.

MacKayla would call it the old bird-in-the-hand or bird-in-the-bush adage.

I giggle at the thought of MacKayla. She has neither birds nor bushes. She's in Hell and I put her there. Through desire, lust, greed, and supremacy.

Christian looks at me strangely, wings rustling in the cold breeze. "Mac?"

"Nervous laugh. I always think I'll get used to how you look." He accepts the excuse, too consumed by self-loathing to be focused on the world. And why wouldn't he die tonight? He believes the world populated by obvious monsters. The most dangerous of us are the least obvious. He relies on his skill as a lie detector, reading and judging the conflicting emotions of others.

Pity for him, I suffer none. Reading me is impossible. His scales can't weigh the stuff of which I'm made.

"How is Dani—er, Jada? Is she all right?"

I left her alive. There are the unworthy who will die sooner, and the worthy audience/interesting prey who will die later. Existence without mirrors, without games, is an endless yawn. "She'll be all right. Ow!" I say, clutching suddenly at an eye. "Ow," I exclaim again.

"What's wrong, Mac?"

"Dratted wind! I think a splinter of wood flew into my eye. Can you look?"

"It's too bloody dark out here to see anything."

Above us, clouds roll, crash together, and the sudden booming is like knives in my ears. "Well, try. It feels like a blasted boulder. Christian, help me!" I tilt my head back and squint up at him, resisting the desire to clap my hands over my ears. He moves in, puts his hand on my face, and that's when I strike.

I reach inside my jacket for my spear, my lovely, lovely spear that is my most prized and loathed possession, treasured because it will slay all those that must die so I may achieve my true destiny, despised because it could rot me from the inside with the tiniest of pricks, and yank it from my—

"Mac, hold still. I can't do anything with you twisting and turning like that."

I still beneath his touch, not because he proposed it, but because I'm rendered motionless by rage.

That bitch! That clever fucking *bitch*! She's ruined everything! EVERYTHING!

I recall Jada's hands on me before I was fully fused into my new skin, touching me everywhere, undoing my ankle restraints first. Had she not freed my feet before patting other places, I'd have paid more attention. She'd lulled me with deception. Tricked me! Thighs. Breasts. Side of my ribs. "Fuck!" I explode. She freed my hands last, once she'd taken what was not hers to take.

The one thing I require to achieve my aims.

"I know it hurts but you've got to hold still, Mac," Christian snaps.

He has no idea how it hurts. She took advantage of that first moment in which I wasn't fully cocked and loaded. It wasn't *fair*. I'd just been born.

I'd been as certain of the spear's presence on my body, its weight in the shoulder holster beneath my jacket, as I was loath to touch it while acclimating to my new skin, so I'd not reached for it until now.

Only to find a gun tucked inside—not my spear at all.

I allow the useless weapon to slip from my fingers and drop to the ground, close my eyes, and summon a spell. Mouth working soundlessly, I call forth one of my favorites.

"I can hardly get the damn thing out if you don't—Mac, what the bloody hell are you—"

My hand is on his mouth, but not my hand alone. He speaks no more, his lips stitched by the greedy needles of a bloody crimson rune I summoned from *my* glassy lake, not hers. She never found hers. I made sure of it, keeping hers hidden through illusion and sleight of hand, subtle manipulation of her neural circuitry.

He stumbles, tries to back away, but I fling rune after rune at him. They latch hungrily to his neck, his arms, onto his wings, those beautiful, majestic wings that should be mine, which he didn't deserve and doesn't honor.

Clawing at himself, he crashes to the ice-dusted ground.

A dozen more runes fly from my hands as I murmur quietly. I sling them onto his body, where they leech to his clothing and skin, spread and grow, until the Unseelie prince is immobilized by the same parasitic magic that fortified the Unseelie prison walls, runes nourished by the victim's attempt to fight them, growing stronger and larger with the least resistance. In no time at all the High-lander will be cocooned in a bloody, inescapable prison.

I'll give him something to brood about and a hellish eternity in which to do it. Cretin. Idiot.

"But I wanted to kill you," I whisper as I lick his face in all its bloody, suffering goodness. "I wanted to watch you die. I've not killed in this form. I want to know how it feels." I permit my essence to fully animate my face, backlight my eyes.

He stares at me with horror. He gets it, belatedly, who Mac really is. Who I am.

I AM.

I plaster him with more runes, putty them gently over his eyes, his forehead, plug his nose, then shove him to the ground. Perhaps I kick him a few times for good measure. I don't know, I don't care, my mind has already moved on. I may not have the spear—at the moment—but I will gather my enemies and store them until I do.

I pick him up and drag him behind the pile of rocks. I'll collect him before I leave the abbey, take him with me to my lair.

Perhaps I'll play with him before he dies.

It is in breaking things that you understand them.

I've always been a curious sort.

♪

As I enter the demolished abbey from the rear, I keep my ears on the voices of *sidhe*-seers beyond the tumbled walls and my eyes focused for random opportunity.

It's everywhere.

Here, I scrape ice from a box of rat poison used to protect the fortresses' larders. There, I find a half-standing pantry containing ice-slicked, corked jugs of water from their artesian well. The two meet in a lovely drink of hemorrhagic death. No guarantee it will be imbibed or that enough will be drunk. But there's a possibility it will. It's enough to entertain.

I move carefully over piles of slippery stone and splintered beams. Slip east, then down, knowing the way because my erstwhile host walked this path while I siphoned impressions from the leaky sieve of her mind.

Below. Below. I would so prefer not to go below to the catacomb in which my prior incarnation was housed for SO FUCK-

ING LONG I THOUGHT I WOULD GO INSANE. But I didn't. I kept my cool, calm, collected self and waited for the right moment, amputating myself from within the *Sinsar Dubh*'s covers as it was being carried, slipping out the door unnoticed, so to speak, the ultimate sleight of hand.

I stop outside the closed doors of the cavern. Long ago the king sealed and unsealed the doors of his great citadel in the Unseelie prison, frequently during his time of endless experimentation trying to re-create the Song of Making. For such an obsessive entity, he's a careless bastard. Many of his memories are mine. Trapped inside the cavern, held immobile by his sticky spiderweb of runes, such knowledge did me no good. From outside the cavern it's quite possibly all I need in order to contain (then kill!) the vestiges of my former self that cannot be permitted to exist within Cruce.

I speak the spell that once opened and closed the ancient doors of the king's personal demesne, and as I expected, the towering portals swing wide. Unlike the idiot king, I rarely use the same protection spell twice.

In the shadowy interior a prince rises, glides toward the open entrance. The last time MacKayla saw him, Cruce was imprisoned. He is no longer. He's a giant of a Fae, with enormous black wings dusted with an ornate design of sparkling iridescent flecks, a body of brutal strength and delicious perfection. He was made to rule, to crush, to conquer. Fury ignites my blood. His superb vessel should be mine.

"Cruce," I say as I step across the threshold.

He stops, assesses me. "MacKayla. It was not you I thought would come."

My spear, my lovely spear, I was eager to kill him. To take from him what I can't have for myself. Now I can only contain and store him with the bastard Highlander until one of the two deadly Hallows are mine.

Still, I see no need to hasten to the endgame.

Endgames are so anticlimactic.

It's over.

Then there you are.

Bored again.

"Did you think I wasn't listening? You offered me the world," I say. "You said I would be your queen." Cruce thinks I'm Mac. My eyes are green. Currently. "You have the *Sinsar Dubh*."

He's wary. "That should make you fear me."

"Should it?" I know better. I'd been forced to leave behind half the magic I possessed to transfer myself into Isla O'Connor the night I escaped the abbey, but I'd cleverly embedded the majority of my prior self into the covers of the Book and planted a spell in the pages so that if they were ever read, the sentience I'd forsaken would cease to exist and crumble to dust. I will never permit another *me* to walk free in the world. I know what I'm capable of.

"The king said me becoming him, you becoming my queen, wasn't the only possibility," Cruce probes. "I have thought long on that. What did he mean, MacKayla? Why did he seem to think the magic of our race might prefer you?"

He's wondering what power MacKayla possesses that she was able to open the king's doors. He was interred before my self-flagellating vessel discovered me inside her, hence doesn't know *I* stand before him. I stop a few paces from the great pretender who lived in Faery for half a million years as a Seelie prince, only to be exposed as the last made Unseelie prince, while I spent an eternity in solitary confinement. Now *I'm* the great pretender and he's the one who will be imprisoned. "We must trust one another if we are to rule this planet together."

"Ah, now you seek to rule it with me?"

"I freed you, didn't I?" Toying with Cruce amuses me. He can sift. I can't. He's technically more powerful in that ability alone, and when I best him it will prove that my mind is so superior it doesn't matter what power those around me possess. Everyone falls to me eventually. He's a cretin. Idiot. MacKayla would never have said "rule." She would have said something inoffensive like "guide." That was his first and only red flag. *Those that fail to protect themselves deserve any harm that befalls them. You are your own kingdom. Guard it. Or lose it.*

"Why is that?"

"I believe you absorbed the spells from the Book, but it did not possess you. Is that true?" *I know it for fact. Aside from a few redundancies, spells, music, wards, runes, he has nothing to compete with the enormous sentience of me. Although some of what he absorbed from reading the Book is equal to what I possess, it won't matter. He won't see his demise coming.*

He hesitates briefly then nods, eyes narrowed.

"Then come with me now, and hurry. Our world is in danger. The Fae court has no ruler. If you can get them under control and help us with the black holes, the others will accept you."

Ah, there it is, what I wanted to see in his eyes. Interest, the belief that he has the possibility of a grand future. Desire. I know what impeded desire feels like. I know what Hell is. I will rain it down on this planet and everything on it.

"You said I raped you. You despised me," Cruce says silkily.

"A minor offense. I've changed since then." *And how. There's little satisfaction in imprisoning an already imprisoned mind. It's the free ones, the hungry ones, those that fight, those with great ambition, that are so much fun to amputate and torture. They take the longest to break.*

He studies me a moment. "Then kiss me, MacKayla, and take back my name."

Now that the doors are open, he thinks to touch and thereby sift simple MacKayla Lane away from here, where he might interrogate her at his leisure. He senses a trap, just the wrong one. Like most powerful beings, he overestimates himself, and co-authors his own demise.

I move near, tip back my head, and wet my lips.

When he steps forward, mouth descending, arms extending, I

slam both hands into his chest, plastering handfuls of dripping crimson runes to his skin, preventing him from sifting, freezing him in place.

His eyes flare and he roars with rage, struggling against the runes, which of course only makes them stronger, faster.

I slap a rune onto his mouth, stitching it closed.

Moving with the heightened speed that eating Unseelie flesh bestowed on my vessel, I slam rune after rune onto his body, cover his mouth, then use one of my knives to hack his wings from his body and fillet them into tiny bits. Like the day I dismembered the Gray Woman, I slice and slash in a frenzied rush of power and the mighty Cruce falls before me. Despite his superior form, no one is superior to *me*. He is nothing. With MacKayla's body, I can carve reality into whatever shape I desire.

I AM.

I slice, sever. Blood runs. Ebon feathers fall. The bird in the bush may not be mine but I can cripple and break it.

I strip the three amulets from his neck, drop them around mine, summon more runes and finish spinning his bloody cocoon.

Slowly. Bit by carefully chosen bit. To make absolutely certain he's aware of everything that has happened, and is happening. I watch his eyes, drink his despair, blot his vision last. His suffering is exquisite.

WE ARE DESIRE, LUST, GREED, AND THE PATH WE CHOOSE TO SUPREMACY.

Not one thing less. Not one thing more.

Those that conquer.

Take notes. Once you truly, deeply, intimately understand what I'm saying, you're that much harder to victimize.

Then the game, for me, becomes that much more fun.

BETRAYED

When my mother first discovered I could freeze-frame—which isn't nearly as cool as teleporting, it just means I can move so fast no one can see me, and they feel only a breeze as I whiz by—she began tying me to stuff to keep me close to her.

When I was really little just about anything worked: a chair, a table, the sofa where she would park me to watch cartoons while she'd frown over job ads in the paper.

I don't know how she supported us in those early years but somehow we got by. Times got leaner, though. Food was mostly canned beans and potted meat; there was no more of that sweet creamed corn I so loved.

One day I figured out I could untie myself. Mom always said I was too smart for my own good, walking early, picking up big words and talking way before I should.

She bought a dog leash the next morning, a pretty one with pink rhinestones. It must have cost much more than she could afford to spend, but it was for her daughter, not a dog.

I snapped it within a week.

She fetched thick rope and became an expert at tying complicated knots.

But I was strong and fast and the rope frayed and split in no time. She'd say with an exasperated laugh—"Danielle Megan O'Malley, my little darling, you're going to be as strong as ten men one day! What on earth did I give birth to, a superhero?"—and I'd preen.

She had a lot of rules for me. The world was a bad place, she said, full of bad things that hunted for little girls like me. I was special and she had to protect me, and keep me hidden.

Top on her list was no freeze-framing beyond the house. I was never to go out any of the windows or doors. OUTSIDE was a country I wasn't allowed to visit until I was OLDER—both magical words that I heard capitalized and the color of warm butterscotch when she said them. To discourage it, she kept the shades tightly drawn, shutting out all the interesting things to see.

But I'd peek when she wasn't watching and OUTSIDE was irresistible—there were children and puddles to splash around in and sunshine and fog and flowers and bikes and things happening, and everything was always changing, like you were living in a TV show and you got to discover the plot as you went along, even make it up and shape it yourself.

I wasn't always great with her rules. She caught me in the yard more than a few times.

One day after she found me sitting on the front stoop, watching girls jumping rope in the yard next door, she tied me to the fridge then went and bought a thick chain and screwed a heavy bolt into the sofa. She padlocked the chain around my waist.

An hour later I smashed the lumpy green couch to smithereens, dragging it behind me, trying to freeze-frame through the doorway to the kitchen.

She stood at the kitchen counter making dinner and I giggled and giggled because I thought it was so funny to see the couch all crooked and skewed with the stuffing poking out, but she got angry and said things I never wanted to hear her say again so, for a while that felt like years to me but was probably weeks, I stayed wherever she put me until she told me I could move.

It was inevitable OUTSIDE would get me again; sneaking a peek behind the curtains, spying an ice cream vendor pushing his cart with dozens of children crowded around, licking their cones and spooning up their gooey sundaes and allowed to be OUTSIDE, and I knocked them over like little bowling pins, snatched up a whole tub of chocolate fudge caramel for myself and was back inside the house before Mom even knew I was gone. All the vendor saw was kids falling all over the sidewalk and maybe noticed a tub of ice cream missing but I'd already figured out that when grown-ups couldn't explain something, they pretended it hadn't happened.

I almost got away with it.

I would have gotten away with it. I even had a plan for how to get rid of the empty tub.

She brought my lunch into the living room.

I shoved the tub of ice cream behind a chair but she stayed and talked to me while I ate my beans and the ice cream melted and puddled out and she said those angry things again and I cried so hard I thought my tummy would split.

I crossed-my-heart-hope-to-die swore I would never disobey her rules again. And most especially that I would never, never go OUT-SIDE.

She cried then, too.

A few days later she came home from the grocery store with hardly any food but she had a bunch of tools and bars and sheets of metal. She told me we didn't have any more money and she'd sold everything we could sell, so she had to go back to work.

She was getting a dog to watch over me while she was out and she was going to build a very special cage for it. She'd even learned to use a blowtorch and hammer to do it. I thought she was terribly clever and exciting!

I knew it was going to be a very special big dog because the cage was ginormous. I knew why she had to build it inside: it was three times as wide as any of our doors! Shortly before it was done, I played inside the cage, imagining all the fun I was going to have with my new, very best friend. With a best friend it would be a lot easier to resist the lure of OUTSIDE.

I wasn't as strong then as I am now. My strength increased as I matured, along with my other senses. But I knew the dog we were getting was going to be very, very strong because the bars on the cage were as big around as my mother's arm and inside she bolted a thick *collar and a heavy chain to the floor. She said the dog might have to be restrained sometimes when we had company.*

We never had company.

I began to think I was the only one excited about the new addition to our family. While she worked on the cage, I'd dream up names for our dog and try them out on her, and her eyes would get strange and her lips would pull down.

I've always slept hard.

One night my mother gave me a bath, dried and brushed my hair, and we played games on the rickety kitchen table until I nearly fell asleep on my stool. Then she carried me to her bed where I lay my head on her pillowcase—the one with the little ducks—and I put my hands on her face and stared at her with sleepy eyes because I loved watching her while I fell asleep, and she held me so close and so tight, snuggled up in her good mom-smell that I knew I was the most important thing to her in the whole world, and I slipped off to happy dreams.

The next morning I woke up with a collar around my neck, chained on a small mattress inside the dog's cage.

5

"The days are bright and filled with pain"

JADA

She stood by the edge of the mattress in the study on the silent, otherwise empty first floor of Barrons Books & Baubles, frowning down at the body draped in nearly transparent pieces of silvery cloth.

Not that Ryodan knew she was frowning or even that she was in the room. Although his body shivered with agony, the rise and fall of his chest was nominal; she'd counted his breaths, twice a minute. His pulse was nonexistent. He'd either gone into a deep meditation or someone, no doubt Barrons, had put him into a magical, healing sleep.

Unwrapping a protein bar, she knelt by the mattress, lifted the edge of one of the pieces of fabric and inhaled sharply. Raw, blistered flesh oozed pinkish liquid. She carefully released the edge and lifted another.

He'd burned himself to the bone in places, to keep her safe, while she'd tried to rescue someone she'd known full well on some level wasn't there.

"The wound I refused to dress," she whispered, for a moment fourteen again, chained in a dungeon with Ryodan trying to get her to face the atrocities of her life, stare them down cold, acknowledge and make some kind—any kind—of peace with them; his brand of tough love, the only thing that'd had the slightest chance of penetrating her formidable armor. She'd told herself it wasn't concern but manipulation. Her thoughts and feelings about the man had always been at odds. She'd idolized him. Craved his attention and respect. Never trusted him. Yet what he'd done tonight . . . she could see nothing the mighty Ryodan might have gained from it.

She'd made her own kind of peace by freeze-framing into the future, faster than the wind, faster than any pain could follow. Seeking adventure, sensation, stimulation, because as long as she was feeling something new, she didn't feel anything old. *Past is past,* she'd crowed to anyone who'd listened.

She knew Ryodan's words by heart. She knew everything he'd said by heart. Few adults had given her useful words. Tucked into a Mega brain behind a gamine grin and insouciant swagger, they'd always been treasured.

The wound you refuse to dress is one that will never heal. You gush lifeblood and never even know why. It will make you weak at a critical moment when you need to be strong.

Tonight her unhealed wounds had cost her. And him.

She'd watched him die once, gutted by the Crimson Hag. Somehow, miraculously, he'd returned from the dead, whole and good as new. She wasn't worried that he might die from these burns.

Regardless, looking at him in this condition made her feel sick.

She closed her eyes, reliving the abbey under attack, the bloodbath of a battle, so many dead, cut down so young, the hellish fire, the moment she'd felt her mind snap.

Shazam.

Ryodan stumbling from the inferno, carrying her and her stuffed animal, both unharmed.

Which brought her to thoughts of the completed tattoo at the base of her spine, the cellphone in her pocket, and the certainty Ryodan could find her no matter where she went.

Of course, now that she had what she'd so desperately wanted, she couldn't justify pursuing a personal agenda.

Forgotten in her hand, the protein bar had melted and chocolate ran warm and gooey through her fingers. She devoured it in two bites, barely chewing, licked her hand, and pocketed the wrapper.

Her hands curled into fists.

"Ryodan, we've got problems. Mac's gone. She tried to save us from the Sweeper by using the *Sinsar Dubh*. When she took a spell from it, the Book possessed her. I can't find Barrons. I don't know if Mac is still in there somewhere. I *do* know the Book will destroy everything it comes in contact with." She paused then said flatly, "Logic dictates I kill her at the earliest opportunity."

Which, technically, had passed.

She'd taken Mac's spear before she'd undone her restraints, erring on the side of caution. She should have attacked the moment the Book revealed itself with its nightshade-toxic gaze. She was faster and the Book had been having obvious acclimation problems, struggling to get off the table, swaying slightly as it found footing. She could have stabbed it with the spear, cleaved it in half with her sword, ensuring the body that held the *Sinsar Dubh* would rot and die.

Mac's body.

Eventually.

Slowly and horrifically.

For a woman who lived by the motto *carpe momentum et cetera sequentur,* she'd never wanted to seize a moment less.

She knew why and told the unconscious man heatedly. "Because friends don't give up on friends. They *never* give up."

The body on the mattress shivered but said nothing.

Lost in the Silvers versus lost in the Book: Jada didn't perceive the odds of rescue as substantially disparate. The fallout, however, could be catastrophically different: one girl, never to be seen again, versus the earth's total domination and destruction. Assuming the black holes didn't destroy it first.

"Lor told me you didn't know where I'd gone," she told the silent room. "It wasn't your fault. It wasn't Mac's either. People need to stop thinking they're responsible for my actions. It wasn't like I needed to be rescued. I've never needed to be rescued." She'd always found a way to save herself.

Still, she knew intimately the despair of day after day passing, followed by nights cold, hungry, alone; of belief dying bit by bit.

Mac had sacrificed herself, to ensure Jada's survival. If Mac hadn't opened the *Sinsar Dubh* and used a spell to save them, the Sweeper would have sent horribly "fixed" versions of Mac and Jada out into the world, which might have been every bit as deadly as the Book being unleashed on it. And who could say the Sweeper's work on Mac's brain wouldn't have freed the *Sinsar Dubh* anyway? There'd been no easy, good choices tonight, only the lesser of evils—two women destroyed or one.

Over her dead body was Mac waiting for a rescue that never came.

As she stood and moved toward the door, Ryodan muttered something too garbled for even her acute hearing to decipher.

She glanced back. "You shouldn't be trying to talk. Rest. Heal. Get back on your feet."

He muttered again, jerking with such violence that several pieces of spelled cloth protecting his skin fell away. When she moved to the mattress and knelt to replace them, he blew the cloth from his face and went into instant convulsions from the effort.

She didn't tell him to stop trying to speak. Ryodan made his own decisions. Whatever he wanted to say, he badly wanted her to hear.

When he was still again, she bent near his mouth. His once beautiful face was a charred, monstrous mask, eyelids blistered, lips burned to a raw gash.

She'd done this to him. Her meltdown. Her heart the Sweeper had deemed flawed. She'd always excelled at the pretending game. But she'd taken it too far this time. She'd lost sight of what was imaginary and what wasn't. And it had cost them all, those she hated caring about yet had never been able to stop caring about.

He spoke carefully then passed out so hard he no longer shivered. It had taken all his strength to murmur a single sentence.

Jada gently replaced the spelled cloth, eyes shining, torn between hushed awe and a fierce desire to snicker.

He'd said, *Holy psychotic PCs, Robin, we've a murderous MacBook on the loose!*

"Batman," she said, hoping he was in a place of no pain. "This time around, *I'm* wearing the cape."

♪

She took the stairs three at a time to Mac's room on the fourth floor.

It wasn't there.

A room still occupied the location; it just wasn't the same one she'd been in earlier. The cozy, messy bedroom had been supplanted in her absence by a parlor with a red crushed-velvet sofa, a faded Persian rug, crystal lamps, and a cheery fire burning in an enameled hearth.

She walked back out into the stairwell and glanced up, eyes narrowed.

When she'd left earlier to follow Mac, the stairwell hadn't continued past the fourth floor. There'd been only a ceiling with elaborate crown molding where now a dizzying staircase ascended.

From years Silverside, Jada was accustomed to shifting spatial dimensions. Barrons Books & Baubles housed at least one powerful, distorting Silver, if not more; a mystery to be explored when time permitted. She found the Nine's secrets intriguing to an obsessive-compulsive degree.

She located the bedroom on the sixth floor, on the left side of the corridor, not the right, shrugged out of her coat, stripped off her shirt and swapped it for one of Mac's. Her clothing was stained with dried blood, entrails, and dusted with the pungent yellow residue of the zombie-eating-wraith straitjacket she'd briefly worn. The combined stench was overwhelming her sense of smell, diluting it. After wiping her face with a damp towel, she scrubbed down her pants and boots as well.

She grabbed Mac's black leather biker jacket and began transferring her many weapons, protein bars, and last remaining energy pod. While strapping on the sword and tucking the spear into a thigh holster, she spotted the cuff she'd given Mac on the table by the bed.

She had no idea why Mac had taken it off but she wasn't about to leave it lying around. She'd risked a great deal to take it. Crossing the room in a few long-legged strides, she shoved the cuff onto her wrist and pushed it up under the sleeve of her jacket.

A charred stuffed animal, wedged between pillows on the bed, stuffing-guts spilling from its slashed belly, watched her every move with round, shiny, reproachful black eyes.

I see you, Shazam.

She shook herself briskly. Emotion was deadly. Plans and objectives, clarifying.

She tucked the stuffing back in, tugged the edges closed and gently placed the teddy bear on a high shelf.

Then she turned, dashed down the stairs and burst out the back door, into the gloomy Dublin dawn.

She used her left hand, her sword hand, to trace the same spell she'd etched earlier to pass through the whirling tornado surrounding Barrons Books & Baubles. Black veins flared beneath her skin, licked up into her wrist, and her hand went ice cold. Many years ago she'd stabbed a Hunter with the Sword of Light and something had seemed to seep through her weapon into her fingers. She'd learned Silverside that her left hand cast better, stronger spells. It often itched and tingled, and sometimes at night she'd wake up to find her hand cold and black. Shazam had professed a special fondness for being scratched behind his ears with her left hand, claiming it felt different, but when pressed for more information, the grumpy, cranky beast had merely flashed a Cheshire smile and refused further discourse.

Shazam. Her heart hurt. Grief was a silenced wail that had no beginning or end, just a long, agonizing middle.

Inhaling deeply, she focused on her city.

She'd not seen a single person since leaving the warehouse with the exception of Ryodan, and suspected Barrons was out searching for Mac, perhaps for her as well. The streets were empty, silent, glistening gray beneath a bank of dense thunderclouds. Were it a normal morning—if there was such a thing anymore—there'd have been both Fae and humans milling in the street, but any human who'd seen the Fae gathering en masse last night had either joined up and been killed or gone to ground, fearing a death march similar to the one on Halloween when the walls between worlds had been destroyed.

As she passed the church where she'd nearly frozen to death, she scanned the black hole suspended over the rubble, assessing size and circumference. It was larger by nearly a third, exuding a gentle pull of distortion. Mac had told her she could hear music coming from the black holes, but even with her extraordinary hearing Jada couldn't detect the faintest vibration.

She considered her current problems: Black holes devouring the world, the Song of Making lost, nearly half her *sidhe*-seers injured or dead, another attack on the abbey imminent until Cruce was freed or destroyed, the Unseelie King and former queen absent, Mac possessed by the *Sinsar Dubh*.

Banner day in Dublin. No time to print a daily.

It occurred to her that if they could find a way to control Mac/the *Sinsar Dubh*, it might not be entirely a bad thing that she'd opened the Book. If they didn't hurry up and find a way to patch the black holes on their world, or at least find a way to stop them from growing, the human race had no future, and allegedly the *Sinsar Dubh,* scribed by the Unseelie King, contained information about the legendary Song of Making. She'd pondered that allegation at length, not certain she believed it was possible because, according to all the myths she'd uncovered about the history of the Fae royals, including the many oral stories she'd collected Silverside, the king had never succeeded in re-creating it—so how could anything about it possibly be in his Book? Maybe the Book contained clues? Bits and pieces the king had collected hinting at the true nature of the song that, with Dancer's help, might be analyzed and improved upon? Speaking of Dancer, she had to somehow get word to him that Mac had gone postal. She wondered if he still checked their hidden cubby at the O'Connell Street Post Office, and made a mental note to drop him a message there, assuming she didn't run into him before then. He had the uncanny knack of showing up whenever she thought really hard about him.

She eased up into the slipstream and vanished. In that higher dimension, the world slid by without friction. Buildings, people, their many messy emotions, disappeared beyond a beautiful, starry tunnel. If only she could eat enough to maintain the metabolism to fuel it, she'd live in the slipstream and never come down—a superhero, protecting her world, unseen, untouched.

She was nearly to Chester's when she crashed into a brick wall she'd not sensed—which meant one of the Nine—and dropped back down.

Scent came before sight: Jericho Barrons. She ricocheted off his chest and went flying. With those lightning-fast reflexes that could pluck her out of freeze-frame, he grabbed her arm and stopped her from careening violently down the street.

"Dani," he said.

She tipped her head back and stared up into eyes black as midnight, a dark, savage face. Every hair on her body stood up on end, as if charged by a sudden surge of electricity. He threw off the same kind of primal energy as Ryodan. She'd once crushed on Jericho Barrons violently. Before she realized he and Mac belonged together like earth and sky, night and day, fire and ice. She'd found tatters of legends about the Nine on some of the worlds she'd traveled Silverside, but never managed to find an origin myth, only songs and tales of nine merciless warriors who battled for gain and, despite dying, came back again and again. Unkillable, unstoppable, unbreakable, she hungered to be those many "uns" herself. No matter the price. She snatched her hand away and smoothed her hair. "It's Jada."

"Have you seen Mac?" he said.

That was Barrons. No small talk. She appreciated it and answered in kind. "She's been possessed by the *Sinsar Dubh*."

Barrons went so still she lost him in the early morning gloom. Just when she'd decided he'd left, his disembodied voice murmured, "So, that's why I can no longer feel her." Then he was there again, morphing out of the brick wall that had been behind him. He could be a perfect chameleon when he chose. "Are you certain?" he said so softly that she shivered, because she knew what soft meant from this hard, implacable man. It meant every ounce of his energy had just been diverted and channeled into a mother lode of a nuclear missile that was locked, loaded, and targeted on whatever had just offended him, and that he would expend no more energy than was strictly necessary to speak.

"Yes."

His eyes darkened, eerie shadows swirled in his irises, and a muscle worked in his jaw. "How certain?"

"Unequivocally."

"What happened?" he said, a bare whisper.

She tightened her ponytail, pulling it up higher. Her hair was curling again, or trying to. She hated it curly. It made her feel like Dani, out of control. Those at the abbey didn't know the *Sinsar*

Dubh was once again roaming Dublin, and she had little time to fortify what was left of the fortress against the next attack, whether instigated by those trying to free Cruce or Mac herself. "We have to get to the abbey, Barrons. We can talk on the way."

He pulled out his cellphone, thumbed up a contact, and held the phone to his ear. "Do you feel the *Sinsar Dubh*?"

Jada heard a woman's frantic voice carrying clearly from his phone. She knew that voice. She heard it in nightmares, crying, begging, and finally screaming. She shivered, reached for another protein bar and wolfed it down.

"Barrons, I've been trying to call you! I felt it about an hour ago! Here. In Dublin. What's going on? You said it was locked up. How did it get out?"

"Where is it right now?"

"It headed north, into the country, then I lost it. Where are you? Where's Mac? I'm coming with you."

"No you're not. Find your parents. Stay with them until you hear from me."

"But M-Mom and D-Dad d-don't know I'm alive," Alina stammered.

"Fix that. And if you feel the *Sinsar Dubh* approaching, take Jack and Rainey to Chester's and call me. If you can't get to the club, go to ground wherever you can."

"What's going on?" Alina demanded. "I have a right—"

"Do what I said." Barrons hung up.

Jada listened to the exchange with narrowed eyes, realizing the woman Mac had said was walking around Dublin looking and acting like her sister somehow was on Barrons's autodial. He seemed to believe it really was Alina and, like Mac, the woman could sense the *Sinsar Dubh*. But he didn't trust her entirely. Either that or he didn't want one more liability to worry about.

"Mac's headed for the abbey," Barrons said.

Jada filed thoughts of Alina away for later perusal. They were entangled with far too many emotions to be entertained at the moment. They went into the same box that held so many other things that she would get to . . . one day.

By the time they got to Chester's and climbed into a big black armored military Humvee, she was operating with her usual machine-like efficiency despite her many recent shocks and unhealed wounds.

Past was past. Tidying up one's internal landscape was a luxury of the safe.

Safe was something she'd never been.

6

"Don't you know there's fire in the hole"

MAC

I force myself to stop screaming.

The silence is absolute.

I'm in a vacuum.

No, that's not quite it. I'm drifting in space, blind, with no radio. Though my initial impression was of being stuffed inside a tiny box and I know somewhere there are walls, I feel as if I'm floating without friction in a vast darkness.

I'm aware of absolutely nothing but my own awareness of absolutely nothing.

It borders on madness.

Hell isn't other people, as Jean-Paul Sartre claimed; it's being trapped somewhere dark and silent with only your own thoughts, forever.

Terror wells inside . . . whatever I now am.

A disembodied consciousness?

Do I still exist? Am I in a box inside my body, or something worse? Am I dead? Is this being dead? Would I know?

Fear threatens to obliterate me. Here, in hell, I *want* to be obliterated. I want the horror of the hellish awareness of only my own awareness to stop.

I'm screwed.

Barrons may have punched into my head once to save me from the *Sinsar Dubh,* but back then I still controlled my body and the Book was locked away, unopened. There's no way he's getting in here now, past the psychopath that imprisons me. I felt the power of the *Sinsar Dubh.* It was incomprehensible. Ugly, sick, twisted, hungry, and enormous as the Unseelie King. It scraped me out of every nook and cranny of my body and stole it from me, and there was nothing I could do to stop it. In those brief moments of contact I'd felt I, too, was a psychopath; its touch had been so palpably evil, so saturating, that I'd been contaminated by its mere presence. It was bigger than me. More focused, driven by such an enormity of rage and malevolence that it, too, was enormous. I'd felt a mere mouse in its house.

I remember the night the corporeal Book almost made Barrons pick it up. It was the only time I ever saw Jericho Barrons back down. He'd raced through rainy Dublin streets, *away* from the enemy.

My sensory deprivation is absolute. It's as if the world doesn't even exist. For all I know, it doesn't. For all I know, the *Sinsar Dubh* has already K'Vrucked it. Using my body.

Terror is a voracious thing, devouring the darkness around me. In moments it will devour me, too.

Whatever I am, I make my essence . . . pause. If I were physical, I'd be a woman going still, eradicating emotion, focusing pure intellect on a problem. Even stripped of my body—I exist. That's enough. That's a starting point. I'm beginning to think that all the bad things that happened to me in the past year were simply the universe's crash course in waking me the fuck up so I could face this moment. Talk about condensed training. What haven't I already survived?

This is just one more problem. Each one has always seemed bigger and more insurmountable than the last. That's nothing new.

I will not cede the crumbs of my existence to mindless panic. Here, where there is nothing, I have something, and it's enough: choice.

I will choose anything over fear.

Rage is fuel. Rage is gasoline. And Ryodan wasn't completely right—because rage, wielded as a weapon, with focus, purpose, and skill, is also massively useful energy. Anger can refine, distill, clarify.

Besides, there's nothing left to burn in here but myself.

And if I incinerate my body in the process—good.

7

"Welcome to the Slaughterhouse"

I encounter a *sidhe*-seer in the underground city.

We nearly crash into each other as we round a corner from opposite directions. I carry neither light nor torch. Shadows soothe my newborn eyes.

"Mac!" the woman gasps.

I access my meticulous files, attach neural impulses to visual stimuli: her name is Margery, she's power-hungry and fancies herself clever.

I drop the feet of the body I'm dragging behind me, coughing lightly to conceal the thud. She sweeps the beam of her flashlight over me. I blink and hide myself before the blinding glare hits my eyes, to reveal serene green.

I blink several more times. The light is brutal. "Get that bloody light off me," I growl. I see bright spots on the dark walls, on her shirt, even after she turns it away.

"What are you doing down here?" she says.

"I was checking on Cruce. You?"

"I thought to do the same," she replies stiffly. "What with the fire and the attack, I feared he might have escaped."

"And what were you going to do if he had? Raise a hue and cry? Scream? Would you scream, Margery?" I purr.

Her eyes narrow. "Mac, are you all right?"

"Never been better," I tell her, stepping closer, but it's not true. Something happened to me while I was destroying the slab in the cavern that once housed Cruce and me, smashing and stomping it so it could never be used again, that cold, hated stone. My body began to tremble. Walking had become a wobbly affair and I'd had to sit for a time.

"Well, then," Margery says, "let's go check on him together, shall—"

I punch my fist through shirt, flesh, and bone and rip out her heart.

I clench it in my fist and crush. Blood drips. Muscle explodes. Bits plop to the floor. Interesting. That's what gives them life. How fragile. Inconsequential.

Margery's body teeters and slumps to the floor.

Life to death in an instant. Not with a bang. Not even a whimper.

It wasn't nearly as satisfying as I'd thought it would be.

Disappointed, I grab Cruce's ankle, bump over the body, and continue down the corridor.

I go up and up, winding my way through the many levels beneath the abbey, dragging my prisoner who grows heavier with each step.

I wonder if I should have eaten Margery's heart.

Perhaps I weaken because my body requires food. I never paid attention to how often MacKayla ate or what. I consider when she last fed her body. It was quite some time ago.

I decide to eat the next human I see.

As I drag Cruce up the final flight of steps, my breathing grows labored. I pause at the top to catch my breath. For so long, I desired corporeal form. It was my sole focus. But like killing, my new body disappoints. Eons ago, before the bastard king trapped me beneath the abbey, I traveled galaxies the same way my prior in-carnation traveled this world, luring host after host into picking me up, possessing them. I'd not found a single animate form I was able to possess that hadn't rapidly decomposed, until MacKayla. But while she doesn't come apart at a level of cellular cohesion, her body has its share of weaknesses. I must find a way to temporarily strengthen the bird in my hand besides eating the flesh of my chil-dren until I become fully, untouchably immortal.

Beyond the half-crumbled wall that once concealed the stair-well, I hear the crush of stone beneath shoes. Someone is near.

Abandoning Cruce's body, I skirt debris and hoist myself up and into the demolished room beyond.

And smile.

There's a pretty, delicate thing searching the ice-covered rubble for supplies. Perhaps pretty, delicate things, like strong, arrogant things, are more satisfying to kill. Margery was stout, dour, and dull, and died so quickly.

"Full of fun and games and slowly," I murmur. Then I'll eat. Or perhaps I'll eat while she's still alive. Perhaps living flesh better nourishes.

MacKayla never ate a human, bound by scruple, chained by morals, but it's conceivable that human flesh, like Unseelie, may confer some power.

It's a theory worth testing.

MacKayla knows this woman well.

"Jo," I say, hurrying to join her. "Can I help?"

8

"One world, it's a battleground"

JADA

She sat in the passenger seat of the Hummer across the wide console from Barrons, ripping open a bag of stale chips she'd pilfered from a box of supplies in the back.

"Talk," Barrons barked as he started the Hummer. "What happened to Mac? Were you there when it did?"

Jada recounted the tale, from the moment she'd seen Mac out the window of the bedroom, hurrying down the alley following what had looked like an ambulatory trash heap, calling Barrons's name; her decision to follow; her subsequent assault by the ZEWs and waking in the warehouse; to the final moments of Mac's decision to take a spell from the *Sinsar Dubh* to save them. She was about to tell him what happened once Mac had risen from the table when Barrons suddenly growled, "Mac."

"Where?" Jada straightened instantly. "Stop the Hummer."

"Not here. The abbey. I just felt her. She's furious."

"Sounds like the Book to me." Its malevolence in the warehouse had been staggering, so palpable it seemed to suck the very oxygen from the air.

"It's her. I haven't been able to sense her at all for hours and suddenly she's—bloody hell—I lost her again."

"Is it a tattoo? Is that how you know Mac's location?"

"You're wondering if Ryodan can track you."

"Yes."

"Did he finish the tattoo?"

"Yes."

"Yes."

Jada felt a muscle begin to twitch beneath her eye, pressed a chip-salted finger to it and willed it to go still. Ryodan hadn't told her that along with being able to track her if she phoned him—which put the ball in her court—he now had his very own Marauder's Map of her that he could unfold and observe anytime he chose—which put the ball in his court. There was no place she could hide, not with Dancer, not snooping at Chester's, perhaps not even in Faery. "Is it something you have to think about or do you just know where she is all the time?"

"It requires little thought."

"You said she was furious. Does the tattoo allow you to feel what she's feeling?"

"Certain emotion. At times."

"How accurate and how far is the reach?" she said coolly.

"Depends."

"On what?" she said frostily.

"Get over it. No magic is without price. You asked for it. Ryodan has no single-edged swords. Nor do you."

"Maybe not. But at least I don't go around—"

Barrons cut her off: "We have bigger problems than your irritation over not having absolute freedom and control. We all want that. None of us have it. One thing signifies: if you'd known, would you still have asked for the tattoo?"

Jada closed her mouth. Even knowing, yes, she would have taken his tattoo. She quickly polished off the last of the chips and ripped open a candy bar, wondering where the Nine stored their enviable supply of food—and why?—it wasn't as if she'd ever seen one of them eat.

Barrons said, "After Mac used the spell, what happened?"

"The Sweeper and the wraiths vanished. The Book pretended to be Mac at first and said that it had sifted them backward."

Barrons looked at her sharply. "In time?"

"That's what it sounded like," Jada said grimly.

"Fuck," he said softly. "If it can manipulate time . . ."

"We're in a world of shit," she finished for him.

Barrons was silent a moment then said, "Resume. I want to know every detail, no matter how seemingly insignificant."

Closing her eyes, Jada re-created the scene in her head and painted the picture for him with attention to details that would have impressed even Ryodan.

♪

Half an hour from the abbey, Jada stretched and the cuff on her wrist pinched her arm. Thinking she'd slid it up too far, she unzipped the sleeve of her jacket and shoved it back to reposition the wide armband. The ruby gemstones on the gold and silver cuff glowed as if lit by tiny crimson flames. She turned it this way and that, examining it. "Bugger," she muttered.

"What?" Barrons demanded.

The cuff she'd so easily removed many times in the past had somehow become a seamless band of metal, with no way to take it off short of hacking off her own hand. When she'd stretched, it had caught on her arm, trapping a tiny piece of her skin.

"My cuff. It's closed. It never was before."

"Where did you get it?"

"I took it off Cruce when I first arrived at the—ah, *shit!*"

"What the fuck?" Barrons snarled. He hit the brakes so hard it gave her whiplash.

An enormous red object had just materialized out of thin air. It crammed the entire front seat from window to window, lap to ceiling, obliterating her view of the windshield. It was wedged in so tightly, the two of them were packed beneath it like sardines in a can. She tried to kick up into the slipstream but nothing happened. She was too tightly compressed. Shifting her focus swiftly, she sped up only her fists and began pounding the intrusion.

"Jada, it's not attacking us. Look at it," Barrons snarled.

She drew her fists in close to her body and shot him a look. "Are you kidding me? I can't see anything *but* it." She barely had enough room to keep her head jammed back against the seat, with a scant few inches between it and her face.

Barrons had adopted a similar posture, head back against the seat, studying it through narrowed eyes. "Mac may have sent it. I've seen those runes before."

"What runes? There aren't any runes on it. It's a bloody red blob."

"The whole thing is made of runes fused together. And it's not entirely a blob. There's a foot jammed up against my window."

"What kind of foot?"

"What do you mean 'what kind of foot?' How the bloody hell many kinds of feet are there?"

"Among the Unseelie alone, thousands: hooves, tentacles, claws, pincers. Then there's the Seelie castes. Humans. Animals. Be precise."

"A human foot. I see toes."

"Painted nails?"

"No."

"Hairy?"

"No hair. Big feet. Male."

Jada frowned. She'd never seen anything like it. Not here, not Silverside. She lightly prodded it.

It instantly stung her fingers and tried to latch on, much as the stinging sentences from the *Boora Boora* books in the Unseelie King's library had once done. "Barrons, we've got to get this thing out of here!"

When he kicked open the door, the blob expanded instantly, exploding out, dangling from the Hummer, and Jada finally had enough room to shove it off her lap and vault from the vehicle.

Barrons maneuvered himself from beneath it, dragged the blob to the ground by a foot, and they stood staring down at it.

"What the hell is it?" she demanded.

Barrons paced a tight circle around it, examining it from every angle. "The question is 'who?'"

"Well, whoever it is was either enormous to begin with or the runes caused it to grow and expand once employed." She still couldn't see any runes.

Without another word, Barrons grabbed it by a foot, dragged it around to the back of the Hummer, hefted it and quickly thrust it in. When the rear doors wouldn't close, he stripped off his belt, looped it through the handles and tied them together.

"What are you doing? What if it keeps growing? The Blob did." She'd loved that movie, had gorged on jellybeans and Snickers, watching it with Dancer, a long time ago, in another lifetime. Snickers. How could you not love a candy bar that was named after a good chortle? "It could absorb us both. Then who will save Mac?"

"Shut. Up," Barrons said flatly. "And get in."

♪

Arlington Abbey was the first taste of life Jada had experienced beyond a cage. It had been as magical and mysterious to the eight-year-old girl who'd known neither friends nor freedom as Hogwarts to Harry. Exhilarated to be free at last, she'd zoomed about like a drunken Energizer Bunny, unable to stop, unable to eat enough, talk enough, see enough, *live* enough. No collars, no chains, no bars. Just the great big wide open. Toilets—not bedpans that piled up outside a cage. Choosing what to eat—not living in dread that nothing would be brought. Having a drink of water whenever she wanted it. Simple things. Priceless things.

Initially she'd considered Rowena's stifling control inconsequential, given how her life had been, until she began to see how much damage resulted from the headmistress's machinations, that the *sidhe*-seers were becoming less, not more—weak, not strong—because of her dominance, subtle manipulation, and sinister experiments. There were the cages you could see and those that weren't so easy to spot before you were lured into them with sweet promises and lies until you were stuck like a fly on sticky tape with only your shattered innocence for company.

Then Mac had come along and seen it, too—the certain destruction of their order if drastic measures weren't taken.

Upon escaping the Silvers, Jada had made drastic measures one of her top priorities.

She'd begun shaping the women into teams of skilled fighters with the clear goal of becoming strong, focused, empowered warriors on behalf of Dublin and the world. She'd worked with each *sidhe*-seer in turn, identifying their strengths and working to enhance them. She fortified the abbey with magic she'd learned Silverside. She found herself somewhere she fit and could always return to—which she'd never had before—a place where she was valued and respected. Five and a half years of wandering had changed her perspective on many things.

The abbey was a ruin.

"We'll rebuild." She stared as they entered the long drive, past the Fae corpses to the smoking shell of the once mighty fortress. Near the front entrance of the abbey women tended the injured and wept over the slain. Her gaze lingered on the piles of the dead and her hands fisted. She'd just been getting to know many of them, had quietly reveled in each step they were taking toward becoming empowered warriors. And just like that—their lives were over. Gone. Ash and dust, as if they'd never been, their only future now to become a name chiseled on stone, a catchall for confidences, tears, and belated regrets.

She forcibly dragged her gaze away and turned it to the black hole on the grounds, the large inky sphere suspended against a slate sky, and was relieved to note the abbey wall had collapsed and no longer posed a threat.

Barrons stopped the Hummer inside the gate, got out, untied the doors and replaced his belt then dragged the blob by its feet out onto the grounds of the estate, away from the vehicle. He shouted in an unintelligible language to a shadowy figure patrolling the wall, flanked by three of the enormous black-skinned beasts that had fought beside the *sidhe*-seers last night.

She'd seen him many times at Chester's. When she'd been younger, he and several of Ryodan's men had managed to hem her in, despite her freeze-framing abilities, while Ryodan interrogated Mac. His name suited him. Despite standing a good four to five inches taller than Ryodan, with a heavier build, he was easy to overlook; one moment etched in stark relief against the moss-covered wall enclosing the abbey grounds, the next gone until he reemerged from a smudge of shadow.

"Fade," Barrons said, and moved quickly away with him. As the two men spoke softly, Jada pricked up her ears, but they were speaking a language she didn't know. After several moments Fade issued a series of commands to the black-skinned beasts and they fell on the blob, snarling and slurping noisily.

It took her a few seconds to realize they were eating the bloody skin off the thing in an effort to free what was inside. What were these dark, lethal beasts of Mac's that she'd found in the Silvers that could imbibe such dangerous magic? Why were they obeying Fade? What language did they heed? More importantly, how might she gain control of them? Last night, when Mac had alerted her to their presence in battle, she'd watched them carefully, assessing friend or foe. Like the Nine, the beasts Mac had brought could kill the Fae—with no apparent weapon. That made them every bit as valuable as the sword and spear.

Speaking of the spear . . . Jada shouted across the lawn to Enyo Luna, the tough young half-French, half-Lebanese woman she'd found wandering Dublin, leading a cocky band of hardened, militaristic *sidhe*-seers. When the walls had fallen, Enyo and her women undertook the long dangerous journey to Ireland, adding to their numbers along the way, seeking their birthright and a place to call home. The natural born warrior had fought her way into the world, inside a military tank—the only safe haven her mother had been able to find—in a town in Syria under heavy fire. Enyo had drawn her first breath in the midst of war and maintained that was where she would also draw her last. Draped in rounds of ammo, face bruised and blood-spattered, dark eyes gleaming, she loped like a graceful dark panther across the battlefield toward them. In war, she was one hundred percent focused and committed, the best of the best, but in everything else she was unpredictable. War kept Enyo's restlessness and wildness under control, yet Jada was uncertain what she would be like in a time of peace. It took one adrenaline junkie to know another.

When Jada tossed her the spear, Barrons watched it fly end over end through the air, measured Jada a long moment and nodded.

"So it's ours again," Enyo said, catching and sheathing it in her waistband in a fluid movement. "Does that mean we've lost Mac?"

"No," Barrons said, dangerously soft. "I've lost many things. Mac will never be one of them."

"In a manner of speaking, for now," Jada told Enyo. "Has there been any sign of Cruce? Do we know if the prison holds?"

"We've no cause to believe he's escaped but haven't looked. I'll send Shauna below to check."

"If you see any Fae alive . . ." Jada didn't finish the sentence. Enyo was already moving away, dark gaze shifting across the battlefield, watching for movement, spear at the ready.

Jada moved closer to the blob, ceding the beasts a respectful distance, and stared down at the thing that was being released from its crimson shroud. Now that part of the fleshy cocoon had been torn away, she could make out the individual runes from which it had been knitted, and realized she *had* seen them before. Mac once used a few to prevent the Gray Woman from sifting that night nearly six years ago when she'd saved Dani from a gruesome death at the Gray Woman's hands. The night Jada's world had bottomed out and she'd been exposed as Alina's killer.

"It's Fae. Has to be a prince. Looks like something hacked off its wings. Brutally," Fade said.

"Pure rage," Barrons murmured.

"You think it was Mac?" Jada clenched her fists, forced them to unclench, worrying that the prince lying facedown on the ground was Christian MacKeltar. He didn't deserve this. He'd had enough misery already; first being turned Unseelie then getting captured by the Crimson Hag and killed over and over again, and finally losing his uncle to the Hag's cruel javelin. Once he'd spared her from having to make a hellish decision by sacrificing himself. It was a debt she didn't feel she'd fully repaid.

"I've seen her use these runes before. They're from the *Sinsar Dubh*. She's eliminating the princes. If you hadn't taken the spear, this one would be dead."

Jada glanced quickly at Fade. "Where's Christian? Have you seen him lately?"

He shook his head. "Not for the past hour or so."

Barrons spoke to Fade again, in the same unintelligible language.

Jada said tightly, "If you don't trust me enough to speak English around me, I don't trust you enough to work with you. Are we a country or are we islands? I make one hell of an island. Your call."

"I told him to turn the thing over."

"And you couldn't say that in English?"

"I just did."

Fade issued another series of guttural commands. The beasts rolled the Unseelie over on his back and resumed tearing off the runes.

When the face was cleared, Jada released a soft sigh of relief. She'd last seen this prince in a prison of ice, below the abbey. It was Cruce, not Christian. Then she stiffened. "We've got to lock him up again!"

"I'm not so sure of that," Barrons disagreed.

"But he's the *Sinsar Dubh,* too," she said.

"I'm not so sure of that either. I think he absorbed the knowledge of the Book, whereas Mac may have been absorbed by it. Cruce read it in the First Language, the spells passed up his arms. From what you described, that's not at all what happened to Mac."

Jada saw nothing to be gained by assuring him Mac had definitely been absorbed. She hadn't been in the cavern the night the corporeal *Sinsar Dubh* was interred and didn't know the details. But Cruce wasn't throwing off anything like what had been palpably emanating from Mac, the dark whirlwind energy of a pure psychopath. "We have to find Christian. If he wasn't first, he'll be next."

Barrons sliced his head in curt negation. "Without the spear or sword, the Book can't kill Christian and these beasts can release him. We must determine the significance of Cruce appearing in the Hummer."

On the ground, the Unseelie prince stirred, groaning.

Barrons prodded him with the toe of his boot. "Wake the fuck up, Tink, and tell us what happened."

Cruce opened his eyes, blinked up at Barrons.

And vanished.

Jada shot him an incredulous look. "You just set him free. I thought you left a few runes on him."

"Why would I do that?"

"They prevent the Fae from sifting."

"And you're just *now* telling me this?" he said with equal incredulity.

"I thought you knew everything. You always know everything. You recognized them."

"That doesn't mean I know every blasted detail of what they bloody do," he snapped.

"Well, I suggest you grab a few before the beasts finish them off. If we don't get the chance to use them on him, they might be of use holding Mac."

While Barrons dispatched Fade to fetch a container, Jada closed her eyes and pinned Cruce's sudden appearance in the Humvee on her mental bulletin board. Around that inexplicable event, she tacked up every fact she knew about him, stepped back and studied the big picture, seeking logic. The world around her vanished, leaving what she loved best: a mystery, an unexplained event, and her fierce, consuming desire to riddle it out. Everything in the universe made sense, if one gathered enough information and examined it properly.

Up went the impaired state of Cruce's prison, the closed doors of the cavern, the cuff she'd worn for months without it ever closing, the apparent release of Cruce by the *Sinsar Dubh* (or had it caught him wandering the grounds, already free?), the cuff abruptly closing—as if responding to a signal it had previously been unable to receive—the legend that in addition to affording a protective shield, the cuff of Cruce had served as the concubine's way of summoning the Unseelie King. For that reason alone, Jada had deemed it worth stealing from Cruce's arm, but it never worked.

Suspicion took the cohesive form of a valid premise. "You've got to be kidding me," she murmured.

"What?" Barrons demanded.

She opened her eyes. "We were talking about him right before he appeared. When I took the cuff from his arm, he was still imprisoned, his power contained. A short time ago, before he was turned into a blob, he must have been free for at least a brief time."

Long enough that the cuff might have responded to its creator and established a bond between them?

Trusting that Barrons was correct and she wasn't summoning another version of what Mac had become, Jada tested it. "Cruce."

The prince was back again, standing in the middle of them, swaying slightly, his hand at his throat, looking shocked and startled before his expression turned thunderous.

He vanished.

"Cruce," she said again.

He was back again, coldly furious. "You will stop doing that, human, and you will give it back to me. It was never meant for you." He stalked toward her, hand outstretched, but froze when she slid the sword from behind her back.

She scrutinized him closely but detected none of the enormous malevolence she expected from the *Sinsar Dubh*. "Your deceit doesn't work on me anymore." She'd felt the intense pressure of the illusion he'd just tried to force on her, to convince her that he'd taken her sword and she was defenseless against him. "I'll only bring you back, each time. We can do this all day."

"Give me my cuff or die, human."

"Explain," Barrons fired at Jada.

She smirked. "It seems I've got the all-powerful Cruce on a leash."

"That same leash tethers you, human," Cruce purred, and vanished.

"Bloody he—" was all Jada managed to get out before she, too, was gone.

9

"I do what the good girls don't"

Jo offers me a smile when she sees me approaching. "That'd be great, Mac," she says, accepting my offer of aid. "We're trying to collect what supplies remain and move them below."

"Isn't that water over there?" I say, nodding toward the half-collapsed pantry. "Looks like a dozen or more jugs."

Her smile brightens. "We need to get that out to the women. Most of them haven't had anything to eat or drink since last night." She moves to the collapsed structure and begins removing the jugs.

She doesn't know she's handling poison, death. Idiot. She doesn't understand that nothing can be taken for granted in this world, would undoubtedly refuse to believe we even exist—those of us that see through others as if they're cardboard cutouts with their simplistic needs scribbled in Sharpie on their flat, one-dimensional faces.

I need nothing. I am desire. Lust. Greed.

"How are things with Lor?" I toy with her as I move near. She begins to hand me water jugs, one after the next. I sweep a dusting of ice from a long flat stone, place it there, then three more in quick succession beside it. I open one and while her back is turned pretend to take a drink. "Oh, that's good. Here, have some." I offer her the jug and watch as she takes a long, deep swallow.

"Ew, that's weird," she says, wiping her mouth. "It tasted sweet."

"Probably some of the jugs Jada put sweetener in," I lie. "She told me sugar-water fuels her freeze-frame better than plain. So what's up with Lor?" I prod. I want to see her happy, excited about the life she's never going to have when I take it from her.

She laughs. "Oh, God, Mac, I never would have guessed that man was so . . . *complicated*. He's smart. Like super freaky smart. Who'd have thought? He's trying to help me create a filing system for my memory."

"Do you care about him?"

She takes another drink, grimaces, and hands me the jug back. "I haven't had time to think about it," she demurs. "We're all too busy just trying to survive."

But she does. It's there in the soft glow in her eyes. She's thinking that she has someone she can count on, someone strong who makes her feel good and alive, as if life holds endless opportunity for adventure and—what a stupid fucking delusion humans erect and cling to—romance. She's *happy*. She put on makeup this morning, took care with her hair. She's hoping to see him today.

She will never see him again.

I am the last thing she'll see, the face of her god as I punish her for the unforgivable sin of failing to protect her kingdom.

But this time I'll take it slow. Savor every succulent nuance of killing, destroying, breaking, defiling. Lust blazes white-hot in my body, between my legs, and I nearly stagger from the intensity of it. Destroying makes me want to fuck. But this woman lacks the parts I desire.

I stare at her through the dim light, assessing, fixing my gaze on her neck. It looks tender and full of blood. Perhaps blood will strengthen me. "Come," I suggest softly, "let's secure these below, then we'll take a few jugs to the *sidhe*-seers."

I collect two of them and she follows me like a fucking idiotic puppy who thinks the world is a good, safe place to explore, full of happy people with hands outstretched in kindness, bearing gifts of food and toys to the demolished entry to the underground city. As I mount the rubble at the top of the stairs, I freeze.

Cruce's body is gone. How could Cruce's body be gone? I'm momentarily blank, unable to divine a possibility that encompasses this anomaly. No one else has been here. I would have heard someone creep up the stairs and drag him back down. I would have picked up some small sound if he'd somehow managed to escape the runes (IMPOSSIBLE!) and slipped off.

I can't explain this. Something has transpired for which I am unable to account. That means I have an enemy. A clever, clever one. Someone tampers with my work. WHO IS INTERFERING WITH MY PLANS AND HOW? I consider attempting to employ the same temporal spell MacKayla used, see if it would work on me to shuttle me back a few minutes in time, where I might warn my other self as I top the stairs to watch for an enemy and identify it, but it's possible duplicate versions of myself could split my power, and if one version of me was destroyed in the temporal conflict, so too would be whatever power it possessed. I remember too well what happened when I amputated myself from the corporeal version of the Book. I'd had to leave parts of myself behind. Important parts. They'd served as a distraction, kept all eyes on the Book, not Isla, but I'd never stopped ruing the loss. Some of my more powerful spells had been sacrificed that day. LIMITS. LIMITS EVERYWHERE! Fury floods my veins. My body trembles with it, weak thing that it is. Not only don't I have the spear, now one of my cocoons is missing. My meticulously crafted swift surgical strike is being undermined at every turn!

Incensed, I whirl on Jo, all subtlety and plans for leisure gone, and grab her by the shoulders. I need an outlet. Now.

"What's wrong, Mac?" she gasps, startled, staring at me wide-eyed. Doe eyes. Dumb, trusting eyes.

I grip her tightly with one hand, digging my fingers into her back, my thumb into the soft flesh beneath her collarbone, and slam her in the face with a fist, using every ounce of my Unseelie-flesh-enhanced strength.

With the first blow, Jo's nose explodes, her right jaw fractures, and her eyes roll back into her head.

She staggers for footing. "My God, Mac, what—"

With the second blow, I unhinge both jaws completely and she doesn't speak again. Choking on blood, strangled screams gurgle from her throat.

I punch her again and again and again, shattering the bones of her eye sockets, her brow, blinding her, splintering her skull, incensed that I have an enemy I know nothing about.

A clever, clever enemy who has stolen something that is mine. Two things now have been unfairly thieved from me!

Terrified, broken mewling sounds leak from the broken, bloodied hole of Jo's face. She was too wounded by my first blow to mount a defense. I release my hold on her and she melts to the ground, trying with the vestiges of her dying will to curl into a protective ball, but there's no protection from me.

I am ceaseless, relentless, hungry as a tsunami.

My will is stronger, my aim unencumbered, my desires greater.

I always win.

I kick her hard, again and again, splintering ribs, exploding organs.

I fall on her and punch her head until brains glisten wetly in her bloodied hair then I tear into the side of her neck with my teeth and begin to eat.

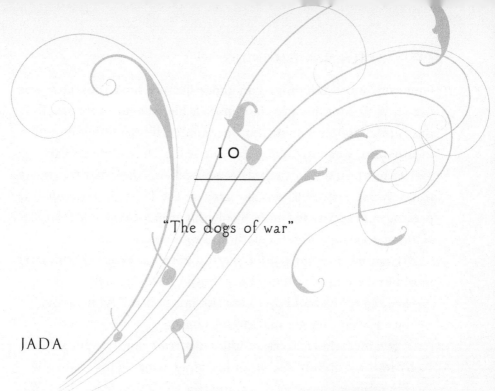

10

"The dogs of war"

JADA

She raised a hand to shield her eyes against the glare of sunlight reflected off a mirror of white sand. She stood on a wide sunny beach beneath a cloudless, dazzlingly blue sky. Palm trees rustled in a tropical breeze and azure waves lapped at a sandy shore. Brightly colored hammocks swayed between trees. Paradise.

Not.

She squinted at the Unseelie prince standing a dozen paces away. He'd transformed himself with glamour and was now the Seelie prince V'lane. She suspected he'd donned a familiar form to conceal the mutilation of his wings, unwilling to let others see him in a weakened condition. His current incarnation was that of an exquisitely beautiful, deadly, erotic Fae of the royal line, capable of reducing a woman to a state of mindless, sexual need.

She focused her *sidhe*-seer gifts and peeled back the glamour revealing his darker form. V'lane was tall, but Cruce was a giant, well over seven feet tall, more densely muscled, his face less classic, the lines sharper, more savage, chiseled by an angry, defiant god. Kaleidoscopic tattoos slithered beneath his dusky skin. In both forms he wore a flowing iridescent robe that shimmered in the brilliant sun, more blinding than the reflective sand. His face was drawn with pain, his eyes half closed. He was far more taxed by the *Sinsar Dubh*'s assault than he wanted her to know. In either incarnation, weak or strong, he was still a Death-by-Sex Fae. Yet she wasn't feeling that will-destroying desire she'd felt too many times in the past. Nor was she sensing the twisted, psychopathic presence of the *Sinsar Dubh*. She let his true form recede from her *sidhe*-seer vision and refocused on the golden illusion.

"Give me the cuff, *sidhe*-seer," Cruce snarled, "or the next world I take you to will not be so hospitable. You will die there."

She rested the hand on the hilt of her sword. "As will you."

"You will never get that close to me."

"Try me." Jada accessed the slipstream and reappeared directly in front of him, the tip of her blade beneath his chin.

He vanished.

"Cruce," she said, and he reappeared a half a dozen feet away, scowling. He backed up and they stood measuring each other across three meters of powdery sand. She assessed the situation quickly: here before her stood the most ancient of the Unseelie princes, who possessed enormous knowledge and power and had proven himself a brilliant strategist, patient, cunning, controlled. The *Sinsar Dubh* was their primary enemy. They were each other's secondary enemy.

The enemy of her primary enemy was her friend. "I'd call this an impasse. Are you ready to negotiate?"

"I do not negotiate with *humans*."

"A human just hacked off your wings and sealed you in a cocoon from which you would never have escaped; a human that's far more powerful than you, and clearly doesn't like you. When she learns you've been freed, do you think she'll just forget about you?"

"Royals regenerate and that was no human. Your precious MacKayla is gone. What remains will never be human again."

Mac wasn't gone. Barrons had felt her. That was enough for

Jada. "So long as I wear the cuff, we're going to be closer than either of us like, and I have the weapon that can terminate your immortal existence."

"I *am* a weapon that can terminate your mortal existence."

"Like I said, impasse. Bottom line: we can kill each other or work together against our common enemy. Negotiate. What do you want? I have my list ready."

"I want my cuff back."

"Not on the table."

Snarling, Cruce lunged but swiftly checked himself.

"I've got the advantage. Accept that and quit wasting my time. Mac is a problem for both of us. If you have knowledge from the Book, you may know something we can use to get her back."

"There is no getting her back from that. That was not Mac-Kayla. Nor was it the Book, at least not the one I touched. That was . . ."

"What?" Jada demanded.

"A sense of superiority that exceeds even mine, and I would not have believed that possible. It felt contempt for me. To the Book, I was as foul an aberration as a . . . a *human*. It is depravity, viciousness, sadism, and hunger for absolute dominance. Fae but unlike any I have ever encountered. It changed."

"And we're going to change it back," Jada said evenly. "If it takes you again, and I suspect it will, we won't free you next time. We'll leave you like that. You need us. If I were you, I'd make *us* need *you* for something." She paused a moment then probed, "This cuff protects the wearer from many things, Unseelie and otherwise. That includes you, doesn't it?" She'd been able to meet his gaze as both V'lane and Cruce without her eyes bleeding, and seriously doubted he was willingly muting himself.

The sudden flash of ire in his iridescent gaze was all the answer she needed. She smiled faintly. "You couldn't make it work against the other princes, without also protecting the wearer against yourself."

"I may not be able to harm you but I can sift you to a fire world, *sidhe*-seer."

"Where you'll die, too. I'm fast enough to take you out as I go. I want the knowledge you took from the *Sinsar Dubh*. I want you to tell me everything."

"I want MacKayla dead. She can be killed in her current form."

"That's not on the table either."

"Then we have nothing to negotiate." He sifted out.

"Cruce," she murmured, and he was instantly back, face taut with rage.

Abruptly, she was in arctic wasteland, with a bone-chilling wind knifing through her. Her leather jacket froze solid and crackled when she slid up into the slipstream. Vibrating, moving in that higher dimension, she was no longer quite so cold.

And the tip of her sword was at Cruce's heart.

He flashed her through a dizzying array of hostile landscapes, testing how quickly she could get to him.

She waited for him to tire. He would never take her to a fire world that would force her hand. He was too in love with his own immortal existence to invite death.

At last they were back on the beach.

Coolly, she peeled open a protein bar and ate it slowly, despite the desire to wolf it down in two bites to compensate for the energy she'd just expended. She was pleased to see that beneath his glamour he, too, was suffering from the exertion, far paler than before.

"My my, how you have changed, little girl," he mocked. "I recall you, human. Still brash, not so gangly." His eyes narrowed to slits of glittering fire. "Not gangly at all."

"You've changed as well." In her past encounters with V'lane, the prince had always been flirtatious yet solicitous, well-spoken yet feigned ignorance of many human ways. With Cruce, all pretenses were gone. Here was the brilliant dark prince who'd plotted and planned for eons, icy, focused, ruthless. V'lane was a seducer, Cruce a conqueror.

"I want the Book rendered inert. I want protection until it is."

"Accepted. You will wear a glamour that shields humans from your sexual thrall, until the goals we agree to pursue are achieved."

He inclined his head. "As you will. I rule the Fae court. As of this moment."

"You'll have to confirm with Barrons. I'm not opposed to it, if you remove them from our planet immediately."

"This is *our* planet and here we will remain."

She'd expected the rebuff; it was one of her planned concessions. "I want your full assistance rebuilding the walls between our worlds."

His eyes shimmered with sudden interest. "I will aid you in reclaiming the Song of Making."

"From a distance and with only superficial knowledge of it," she stipulated. This would be an ongoing war in which keeping the enemy close was the only way to win it.

He laughed and the sound was a symphony of dark crystals chiming. "Not possible and you know it. You cannot invite me in yet bar the door. Working together entails risks for all of us, *sidhe-seer.*"

"You'll cooperate fully with the needs we have on a daily basis; sifting, helping us complete tasks we deem necessary. That means no wasting time with ego or arguing."

He said disdainfully, "Demand the same of Barrons."

"I won't have to. Time isn't one of our luxuries and he knows that."

"You will return my cuff to me when our common goals have been met."

"In exchange for a final service."

"What service?"

"A small thing that will cost you nothing. Then I'll return it."

His head swiveled in an entirely inhuman way and his eyes cooled to iridescent ice. "For all of this I have only your word."

"Ditto," she said.

"As of this moment, I am my race's king and all will recognize me as such. My rule is undisputed. Even your bastard Highlander prince will pledge his fealty to me. Barrons and his kind will acknowledge my reign and kneel before me."

She snorted. "I have serious doubts about the fealty and kneeling parts. As of this moment you'll order your race to stop killing humans."

"Not on the table. My brethren were locked away with nothing for too long. I will not subject them to starvation again. The status quo remains as it is. Nothing changes with the exception of us working toward the common goals of destroying the *Sinsar Dubh*—"

"Containing it and saving Mac."

"—and restoring the song to my race."

Her hand tightened on the hilt of her sword.

His gaze moved between her eyes and hand and he sneered. "When our goals are met, my race will stop killing humans on your planet. But no sooner."

She knew why. "Because with the song, you could go anywhere, conquer any world."

"Restored to our former glory, we will find a more . . . hospitable place."

"You mean a world easier to victimize."

"We are not monsters. Had my brethren not been imprisoned for eons, their needs would not be so great. Who can say—perhaps they would have become like the fairy court, in appearance and temperament."

"And that's such an improvement," Jada mocked.

He bristled and she could almost hear the rustling of enormous, nonexistent wings. "You will treat me and my race with respect."

"We'll treat you and your race precisely as you treat ours." It was the way of the world; leaders pulling together for a tenuous peace while their factions continued to war. "Agreed?"

"Until our aim is achieved and not one moment more, we are agreed. If you wish to continue an association at that point, it will be subject to new stipulations."

"Fair enough. Return us to the abbey."

"As you wish," he said, with frost-filled, dangerous eyes.

♪

Back at the abbey, Jada apprised Barrons and Fade of the agreement she'd struck with Cruce, stressing the necessity of working together quickly and without contention. "You can kill each other when this is over, but until that time we're allies who've shelved animosity in the interest of rescuing Mac and fixing the black holes. If any of you have a problem with that—leave."

No one moved.

She turned to Barrons. "I know the bookstore is heavily warded. Can the *Sinsar Dubh* enter it?"

"On its own, no. Rowena carried it in when she was possessed by it. I'd not warded the store against the old woman. Mac's ability to enter remains to be seen."

"Speculate."

"The old bitch was human, possessed by a Book."

"That's exactly what Mac is," Jada pointed out.

"I felt her and disagree."

"What did you feel?" She wished she had his atavistic senses!

"Irrelevant. Move on."

"It's not ir—" she began hotly, but terminated it swiftly. Now was not the time. She glanced at Cruce. "Begin sifting the injured *sidhe*-seers to the alley behind the bookstore."

Cruce hissed, "I will not sift *sidhe*-seers—"

Barrons made a rattling sound deep in his chest. "You are not filling my store—"

"What part of 'quickly and without contention' did I fail to make clear?" Jada said coolly. "Do you have a better idea, Barrons? Is Chester's protected against the *Sinsar Dubh*? If so, take the *sidhe*-seers there. The Book has obviously been here and may still be. We must transport my women to safety."

"Who put her in charge?" Fade growled at Barrons. "Did you agree to this?"

"I'm not in charge," Jada said evenly. Their egos required delicate handling. "I'm doing damage control. We're all in charge. The issue at hand happens to be the lives of my women."

Barrons narrowed his eyes and stared at her a long moment in silence. Then he inclined his dark head. "You heard what Jada said. Move the *sidhe*-seers. But to Chester's not my bookstore."

"When she has informed her women of the truce," Cruce stipulated. "One of them has the spear. Only when she no longer does will I move them."

"I'll tell Enyo you're off limits," Jada said. "She'll obey me."

"I place no faith in the faith you place in humans, human. Reclaim the spear."

"Fade," Barrons growled, "guard Cruce until Jada and I have prepared the *sidhe*-seers." He turned and stalked off toward the entrance of the abbey.

Jada loped to catch up. "Thank you for supporting me." Focusing on the abbey entry, she swiftly accessed the slipstream.

Only to be yanked violently back down by Barrons.

"I don't," he snarled. "Like everyone else's, your objectives are emotional, flawed, and in the wrong fucking order."

She snatched her arm from his steely grip. "My objectives are not—"

"Save the *sidhe*-seers?" he mocked. "If we pull out, we leave the abbey grounds unprotected. You must be willing to sacrifice anything no matter how it affects you emotionally to gain a single thing—the four stones that can contain the *Sinsar Dubh*. They're in the rubble somewhere, aren't they?"

She nodded tightly.

"Tell me where, and don't bloody point because Cruce is standing right behind us."

"I stored them in a safe in the sitting room off the Dragon Lady's Library." She told him the location as best she could without gesturing in the direction of the rubble to search.

"Only once we have them do we yield this place and attend the needs of the weaker. To be a protector, you can't think like a protector. You must always think like a conqueror *first*. It costs. Blood and soul."

Jada muttered a string of curses. He was right; the priority was the stones and she'd not given one thought to them. They were the only hope they had of containing the *Sinsar Dubh* and buying time to figure out how to get Mac back. Yet the first thing on her mind had been the survival of others. Perhaps the Book had come here to kill the princes, but most likely it had come to claim the only thing capable of containing it, yet had been unable to resist mowing down its enemies along the way. Its delay was their advantage. "Is Chester's secure?"

"Enough. Parts. Occupy Cruce relocating the women. I'll search for the stones and return to Dublin when I have them. Mention nothing of this to the fairy."

"And if you run into Mac?"

He flashed her a savage smile. "I intend to."

"Barrons, you don't know what she's like. You weren't in the warehouse. You didn't feel what she's become."

"I'll take my chances."

"But—"

"Enough. Go. *Now.*"

Shaking her head, she turned to leave. He called after her, "Cruce doesn't know the stones are here and is interested only in securing his own safety and protection—at the moment. What the Book did to him screwed with his head but it will clear. Keep him distracted, act fast and stay alert. The dogs of war don't negotiate.

They deceive, awaiting a more prime opportunity to attack. If he thought he could seize all four stones, he would. They could contain him, too. He'll covet them every bit as much as the Book does."

Jada nodded grimly and kicked up into the slipstream.

Then he was there beside her in her sacred place, she could feel him near, though she saw nothing but a starry tunnel. She was chafed to realize it was because he was moving slightly faster than her. She couldn't help herself. "Barrons, you've *got* to teach me how to do that!"

His words buzzed softly and seemed to come from a distance. "Help me get Mac back and fix our world, and if Ryodan won't, I will."

Chills kissed her skin because Barrons was a man of his word, and once she'd have considered chewing her own hand off to be able to move as fast as Ry—them.

"Last night was a bitch, kid, but you pulled it together. Ryodan was right. You've become one hell of a woman."

Somehow, it didn't irritate her that he'd called her kid. It was as if his words had been a nod to both Dani and Jada and it felt good. Dani was her foundation. Jada was her fortress. Both were her. Both essential.

Then Barrons was gone.

11

"Out of sight of God"

Humans are worthless. Weak.

As is their flesh.

Killing Jo was satisfying but she tastes unpleasant and eating her provides no nourishment. My energy is flagging.

The single time I'd seized control of MacKayla's body in the past, I'd ridden it hard for hours, but my tenuous hold had grown progressively weaker. For no reason I'd been able to discern, I lost control of the vessel and it slumped to the pavement. MacKayla had perceived the passage of time as a complete blackout. I was cognizant for the entire duration; in control one moment, controlled the next.

Still, from that day, my supremacy was assured. Losing dominance of her body to me had frayed the threads of her already damaged confidence. I'd ceased my efforts to conquer and begun to seduce, silently lending my power to fuel her wishes, turning her invisible, using my darkest magic to bring her dead sister, Alina, back to life, nudging here and there to undermine, creating sinkholes, poisoning the soil, sowing doubts in the garden of her mind. NEVER LET ANYONE ELSE INTO YOUR GARDEN. WE

HOE OUT THE CROPS AND SEED IN WEEDS—ALL THE WHILE TELLING YOU HOW BEAUTIFUL OUR WEEDS ARE, THAT, IN FACT, THEY'RE NOT WEEDS AT ALL, AND YOU'RE SO LUCKY TO HAVE THEM—UNTIL YOU'RE NO LONGER CERTAIN WHAT A WEED EVEN IS.

Imbeciles. Wretches. That's how we win. Don't turn over the fucking keys to your kingdom then cry foul play when you get evicted. Once you let us confuse you with enough lies that you no longer know your truth, we own your reality. AND YOU GAVE IT TO US.

As I push to my feet, I stumble and go back down. Snarling, I shove my hair from my face and rest a moment more, considering my next move. My muscles burn from exertion. Pain is a new sensation, distracting, infuriating. It's an insult that I was born so flawed. My jaws hurt from tearing flesh and there's a painful bone splinter lodged in my gums.

I pick it out with the tip of one of my knives. I came to the abbey to accomplish three goals: kill Christian, kill Cruce, and find the stones. Events have not unfolded as I'd intended. The Unseelie flesh I ate isn't fueling me as it did MacKayla. I'm burning through it too fast and require more. It doesn't help that my body hasn't slept in over a day. The loss of my spear grandly fucked my plans. By this hour, both princes should have been dead.

I expand my awareness, seeking the stones, which MacKayla was certain were somewhere in the abbey.

I sense nothing.

Might they have been moved? I assess possibilities and encounter an obstacle of my own making. In my quest for strength, I ate Unseelie, which mutes MacKayla's ability to sense Fae objects of power. LIMITS! YET MORE LIMITS TO REMEMBER! I must dally until it wears off or go to ground, rest then gather my army, seize the stones, destroy them, and move to the next phase of my plans. I consider summoning an army of Unseelie, resuming the battle on the abbey grounds while still more of them search the ruins for me, but MacKayla would call the stones my Kryptonite, and I'll not unearth them into untrusted hands.

Might I simply forget them? It occurs to me that two out of three aren't bad: the cocoons I've put the princes in, while not as much fun as killing them will be, are sufficient.

Paramount to my plans is the spear. I refine my goals, making it my priority.

I push myself up from the bloody remains of Jo in which I squat, becoming aware of eyes on me. I can feel them. Someone is watching me. Is it my clever, clever enemy? How is someone anticipating me? There is no one with my clarity, my focus, my resolve.

I stand motionless, curious to know the face of my foe.

Jericho Barrons steps from behind a tumbled wall.

For a moment I stare, consumed by jealousy. I had to be born a fucking woman in a world where men are physically superior. Christian. Cruce. Now Barrons. He exudes ferocity, power, hunger, his presence saturates the air with palpable, electrifying energy. Even the Fae fear him. Shades slink away when he passes. He has killed Fae royals—sifters! His vessel is wide-shouldered, big-boned, muscled and powerful as a lion. Undestroyable. I despise him for it.

"Mac," he says roughly, and I know what he sees: his precious little Mac, all blond and bouncy, defiled and vile—it doesn't escape me that VILE becomes EVIL becomes LIVE, more proof my supremacy was destined—drenched in blood, hair matted with it, face crimson, black feathers stuck to the congealed mass, bits of Jo's brains on his pretty girl's hands, under her nails.

He sweeps the remains with a dark gaze, trying to identify them; impossible, as her head is a glistening, bloody omelet, garnished with the broken eggshells of her skull.

"Jo," I tell him, enjoying the moment. "I ate her. Savage enough for you yet, Barrons?"

"Mac was savage enough for me as she was."

"She was weak." *Is*. Hate the bitch. Stupid, guilt-riddled cunt.

"Young," he corrects. "Sometimes the young surprise you."

"Young is boring. She never understood you. I do." Were he to doff his circumscribing ethics, we might raze galaxies together. I would fuck him. Discover what my body has to offer me in the way of pleasure. Lust speaks its hungry native tongue when I look at him, demanding satiety. There will be time for that. Later.

"Bullshit. She knows me. You don't."

"I know you far better than MacKayla did, steeped in all that grand insecurity. She couldn't make up her mind about shit. That's why it was so easy for me to make it up for her."

"She's getting there. I'm a patient man."

"Your love for her is your greatest weakness. Pity. You could have been so much more." He could have been like me. His monster demands he be like me. He muzzles the finest part of himself. MacKayla may pretend she doesn't know what he eats, but we do. We know what he is. We just don't talk about it.

"What do you want?" he demands.

"I have what I want. You have nothing to offer me."

"Try me. Bargain. Let me find you another body."

"Do you have one in mind?" I say, interested. I never underestimate my prey. Perhaps he knows something MacKayla and I don't.

"Mine," he says flatly.

I'm silenced by the unexpected offer. I assess his splendid body from head to toe, pondering how delicious his black-skinned beast would be to ride. Possessing him, I would gain access to all his secrets, his enviable powers. I'd be able to kill Fae without needing spear or sword. I'd acquire millennia of druidry and skills in the black arts. He would go so far to save her—yield his exquisite existence for an illusion called love? The fool is more deluded than I believed. Desire, greed, lust to possess his powerful, changeable, impervious skin saturate my every cell. If I were able to complete transference to his body, and my enormity burned him up like all the others, I'd come back again and again, forever. I'd only have to maintain my hold on my form through the dying and rebirth, and I've held my form against far more formidable foes. The Unseelie King himself tried to strip me out of the corporeal Book he'd made once he realized what he'd done.

And failed.

Perhaps, at the moment of his dying, I might evict the tatters of his sentience. He doesn't deserve the vessel he inhabits. My will is supreme. No other has my focus, my hunger.

He is up to some trick or he would never offer. Barrons is no sacrificial lamb. Besides, there is another, more certain way. I will fuck him. Then kill him. Once my goals are attained. "You think you stand a better chance against me than she does, because you have a beast within. You think you're stronger and would take on her battle for her, like you always do because she's such a pathetic victim. Your beast," I say silkily, "would be a mere mouse in my house. You chain it. Hobble it with your fucking morality; even those few shreds you possess."

"Try me," he says just as silkily. "If you're so certain of that. Take my body. Let hers go. Hers is fragile. It can die. You know mine can't. Logic dictates you take mine. *If* you can," he taunts. "Ah, but you're not sure you can, are you?"

Rage floods me. He's the bird in the bush. I crave his skin but am uncertain I could seize it. "MacKayla's body is all I desire. I've such fun and games planned for it." He deserves to be tortured. He impedes my desires. I make my face go slack, rearrange my features into a soundless shriek. Black eyes pale to green, then black then green again.

I pretend to be his Rainbow Girl beneath the gore, frothy, fragile, and fatally flawed. I fall to my knees, clutching my head. "Barrons," I scream, "help me! Oh, God, help me! I'm in here. Get it out of me! Please, Barrons, help me!" I infuse my cry with desperation, knowing he'll hear it in nightmares.

I shake myself violently, flood my eyes black again, toss my head back and snarl. "She is beyond your help."

"Mac, I'm here. I'm not losing you," he says roughly. "You've got to fight it. You can do it! Fight!"

Rah-rah fucking cheerleader. All he's missing are fluffy pink pom-poms. It's all I can do not to shake my head in disgust.

I make my eyes go green/black/green/black, body shuddering as if I'm weak and fighting for control.

"Barrons," I scream. "It hurts! It's killing me! Please, you've got to save me! I don't have much time!"

He lunges forward, checks himself and stops.

His pain is my pleasure. "You can't defeat me." I let my eyes go full black again. "She's mine and I will never release her." I push myself up and saunter toward him, swaying my hips, jiggling my breasts, a blatant reminder of the potent bond they share. And perhaps can again—my walk suggests. I wet my lips and smile. My body is hot, parts of it ache in a way that's sinfully delicious. It's an ache I understand. LUST. GREED. Dominate him. Chain him. Use and abuse him. I have plans for this one.

He mutters beneath his breath and a silvery wall appears in the air between us.

I saunter closer, stopping inches from his hastily erected and not nearly fortified enough to keep the likes of me out druid wall.

"The Fae taught the druids," I purr. "And not very well. We always withhold information." I reach for the three lesser amulets I took from Cruce that hang around my neck, enclose them in a fist and murmur softly, weaving a spell of illusion that will convince Barrons to drop his druid wall and become lamb to my slaughter.

The druid wall remains.

I chant louder and my amulets glow with blue-black fire.

The corners of his mouth lift in a smile and he says smugly, "The lesser three don't work on me. Only the king's does and I have that one. Mac doesn't know what I'm capable of. You don't either. You'll learn my limits. By discovering their lack."

It offends me that he possesses an amulet that should be mine, offends me more that yet another thing that should unfold in my favor doesn't. I go motionless, banking the embers of my rage with images of his destruction. I will torture him to the brink of death over and over. I will take him with me, my prisoner when I leave this world. I will make him beg for death until the black holes I plan to feed so they will grow rapidly out of control devour the earth and trap him as I was.

In nothing.

Forever.

I return his smug smile, thinking about it.

His eyes narrow to dark burning slits. "I'll kill her rather than let you have her. Take my body or come up with another deal you're willing to make. I'll hunt you across the motherfucking galaxies. I'll shred you limb from limb, dice and exorcise you. I won't let her live in hell. You have three days. Get out of Mac's body. Or die."

Long before three days have passed, I will be all I was meant to be and gone. And he won't hunt me long. Once I feed the black holes, he'll either die or be trapped in nothing forever. I consider attacking his druid wall by a different method but I am as uncertain of the current strength of my body as I am of whether I could seize his.

I whirl and dash away from him.

I race into the woods behind the abbey where I sequestered my car, as rapidly as my weakening body is capable of moving.

He lets me.

As I knew he would. He won't harm MacKayla's body.

Not so long as he believes his precious Rainbow Girl is within reach.

Everyone has something they value more than anything else. That's what we see when we look at you, scribbled on your flat, one-dimensional faces.

That thing that means everything to you—and without it you are so easily broken.

Fucking keys to your kingdom.

12

"Through these fields of destruction,
baptisms of fire"

JADA

After seeing the *sidhe*-seers safely to Chester's, Jada left them settling into the upper-level rooms and hurried back to Barrons Books & Baubles to address something she should have dealt with earlier. Every minute now, each hour, was vital.

They'd wasted the better part of a day sifting women, one by one, to Ryodan's club, sending others ahead by what few cars were at the abbey, and tending to the needs of the injured. Before she'd left the club, she'd lost four more *sidhe*-seers to wounds too severe to heal. Crushed skulls and lacerated organs were beyond their limited medical abilities, and although Cruce possessed at least some power to heal, he'd claimed to be too taxed by his time in the cocoon to use the ability at the moment. Whether or not that was true was anyone's guess. The ancient prince would resent employing any of his precious power for a mere human unless there was something significant in it for him.

They needed all hands on deck, and Ryodan, with his ruthlessness, Machiavellian mind, and knowledge of arcane magic, was crucial. Had he been uninjured today, she suspected he, too, might have healed some of the women. She had no such ability, and would sacrifice a great deal to learn it.

She stood near the mattress, staring down, watching the virtually nonexistent rise and fall of his chest through narrowed eyes, hands fisted, accepting that she had a profound aversion to seeing him in pain. Irritated by the matter that had brought her here for the second time in a day, she snapped, "Are you awake?"

His head moved slightly beneath the fabric.

"You're being illogical, you know. How long will it take you to heal this way? Days? Weeks? I watched you die. You came back as good as new. If you can die and come back whole, why don't you? Are there limits to how many times you can do it, like a cat with nine lives? Or maybe you can only do it during a full moon? What are you anyway? Whatever it is, you're useless in your current condition," she said crossly.

He made a strangled sound that might have been laughter and puffed at the fabric. After a moment she knelt on the floor and lifted it from his face, bending near.

"Could. You. Not," he said on a labored exhale.

She unraveled his comments. "You could die and come back but because of me you won't?"

He moved his head in a minuscule nod.

"Well, that's just insulting. I'm fine. I pulled it together. Won't happen again." She'd slipped. She'd recovered. Shit happened. Life went on. He'd burned himself to a crisp for her, and now was refusing to leave because he was worried about her. "Sorry you had to burn yourself for me." She paused a moment then grumbled, "Thanks." She absorbed his expression; though he had no eyebrows and his face was badly burned, he was somehow still managing to look at her like she'd just sprouted three heads. She clarified coolly, "I thank people when they deserve it. You just don't usually deserve it. Don't hang around on my account. It's not like you could do anything for me in your current state anyway."

He made a choked sound of laughter, terminated it abruptly then said, "Tattoo. Cell . . . don't . . . use it."

"Why not?" He'd completed the tramp stamp at her spine and told her if she called IISS he could locate her anywhere. But according to what she'd learned from Barrons today, the tattoo he'd inked into her skin enabled him to locate her even *without* her calling him. So, why was the phone necessary? "Because you're injured?"

"Take . . . too many of us . . . out of . . . the game. Too . . . dangerous . . . now."

She studied him in the low light, wondering again exactly what calling the contact labeled I'M IN SERIOUS SHIT on her phone would do and how many of the Nine her using it would impair. Wishing irritably he'd tell her. Obviously it did something more than merely locate her. But confidences weren't his strong suit any more than they were hers. "I have two missions: Mac, and saving the world from the black holes, and I'd like to do them in that order as I suspect saving Mac could help us save the world. I have no intention of doing anything with your cellphone in the meantime. When you die, how quickly can you return?" It had been a while before she'd seen him again the last time.

"Varies."

"But sooner than you'll heal this way."

"Yes."

"So, die. I'll be here when you get back."

Bloodshot silver eyes locked with hers.

"I'll stay in the vicinity. You have my word. You know it's solid." They might not get along, but she respected him and knew he returned the courtesy.

His eyes were a dozen shimmering, inscrutable shades of cool silver.

She shifted position, impatience making her restless. "What are you waiting for?"

"Not . . . that . . . simple."

"Why?"

"Can't . . . move. How . . . die?"

She got a sinking feeling in her gut. "Do you *always* come back? This isn't something that doesn't work sometimes? It's a sure thing, right?"

He gave another of those nearly imperceptible nods.

She exhaled explosively. As a teen she used to brag about one day taking down the mighty Ryodan. But the day she thought she'd killed him by freeing the Crimson Hag had been one of the more miserable days of her life. "Figures you'd make me do the dirty work," she said irritably.

His eyes crinkled and his lips pulled into a grimace of a smile.

"Are you laughing at me?"

"Thought you'd . . . get kicks . . . killing me. Old . . . insults. Could . . . get Barrons. Hate . . . that fuck . . . doing it. Enjoys it . . . too much."

"How do you suggest I do it?" she said tightly.

"Sword. Gut. Like Hag."

She glanced around the room, as if a more acceptable alternative might pop out of a corner or from behind the desk, or manifest in the mirror; one less brutal, bloody, and personal. "Can't I just give you an overdose of something?"

"Poisons . . . don't . . . work. Chop . . . head?"

"Oh, you really suck," she hissed.

"Techni . . . calities. You're . . . right. Logical . . . I die."

She dropped her head in her hands and rubbed her eyes. Killing came naturally to her. She could be ruthless, lethal, and without mercy, and considered it a strength. But Ryodan mattered to her. She'd made peace with that Silverside. She liked knowing he was out there in the world, alive, doing Ryodan-things no matter how much some of those Ryodan-things aggravated her. For the first year, she'd told herself stories while wandering worlds about the many interesting/irritating things he was probably doing in her absence, top on that list—hunting for her, having all kinds of adventures along the way. Those stories had always ended with him finding her; they'd swap tall tales and kick ass together all the way back to Dublin. She found the idea of killing him, even though his death would be temporary, abhorrent.

She raised her head, eyes blazing with emotion.

She didn't think he could go any more still, but he managed to, eyes narrowed, searching her face.

She hated that anything mattered to her. Yet last night all the grief and loss she'd been repressing had escaped. Once triggered, everything that had *ever* triggered her had a tendency to explode up from the floor of an ocean of unaddressed injury. Now her emotions were floating on the surface, and everything hurt.

It won't always, she suddenly heard his voice clearly inside her head. *Kill me fast. The dying never gets easier. But, Jada, the living does.*

With a grimace of determination, she pushed to her feet. "You'd better come back because if I have to carry your sorry-ass death, too—" She didn't finish the thought.

I'll be back. I'll always be back. He was silent a moment then added with a faintly sour note in his voice, *In the future, if you need help with something, ask me.*

She aired an old grievance just as sourly. "Why would I? You didn't help me when Jayne took my sword."

Kid, I had no fucking clue what to do with you. You were a Negasonic Teenage Warhead.

She'd had no fucking clue what to do with herself. She'd been a Mega-powered explosion of pure defiance to anyone who'd tried to impose limits on her. She'd not once considered whether there might be a good reason for those boundaries. Any and all limits—bad—had been her entire philosophy in a nutshell. Wondering when Ryodan had started actually reading the comic books he'd only pretended to know about, she said loftily, "I was nothing like that twit." She had no intention of saying one word more but couldn't resist adding, "I was enormously cooler."

I meant the movie.

Her shoulders slid back and she stood straighter. Even *Deadpool* had been impressed with the film incarnation of Negasonic. Preening only inwardly, she disparaged, "You've seen everything. How could you not know what to do with one teenage girl?"

Fucking superhero on steroids. I'd never seen anything like you.

The inward preen turned into a radioactive flare, lighting up her face. Sometimes she missed those days; how she used to feel when she woke up, like life was electric and *she* was electric and each day was just another awesome fecking run at riding all the glorious, rainbow-colored currents on the kaleidoscopic electric-life-slide. "Not even in all your . . . how many years did you say it was?" she fished.

Thought letting Jayne keep the sword would keep you off the streets.

"It didn't." Nothing would have. She'd have gone swaggering out into the streets naked and completely defenseless just to prove herself free. Anything less than absolute freedom had offended her as deeply as the cage she often felt she'd never escaped. The price of her exit strategy had been too high. Exit strategies usually were. "So, how old are you again?" she pressed.

The alternative was insisting you move into Chester's.

"You tried that. On multiple occasions. You'd have had to keep me chained up forever. I'd have snuck out at every opportunity and torched Chester's the second your back was turned." And no doubt planted explosives beforehand to make sure it turned into a spectacular fireworks display. "I defined myself by defying you."

Didn't know you'd figured that out.

"I figured a lot of stuff out. I just don't waste everyone's time droning on and on about it like some people."

We'll help you rebuild the abbey.

She stiffened. She'd been enjoying their banter. She wasn't now. "I didn't ask for your help. I don't need it."

Regardless, we'll do it. You need to be running it.

Some part of her backed away, withdrew from him, and she bade it good riddance. She'd been an octopus with tentacles outstretched, now she was a shark. Tentacles could be hacked off. No one messed with sharks. "You don't know a damn thing about what I need."

He spoke staccato fast and fiercely: *I've always known what you need. Someone to rage at who's strong enough to take all the pain and fury you have to dish out until you've burned it out of your system and nothing is left but a pile of ashes from which the Phoenix rises. Kid, woman, whatever the hell you are—I want to see you rise. Even if you have to hate me.*

She kicked up into the slipstream and swung her sword as fast as she could, with flawless precision and all her strength. When his head separated from his body and bounced away, crashing into the wall from the force of her blow, she doubled over, puking.

Finally she straightened, wiped her mouth with her hand, and backed away, eyes closed.

It was done. It was the right thing to do, the smart thing. And doing it at that precise moment without warning had prevented unnecessary suffering. Sometimes waiting for a bad thing to happen could be just as unpleasant as the bad thing happening.

It had, also, conferred the added boon of shutting him the fuck up.

It felt like shit.

I want to see you rise.

She shook the echo of his words out of her head, backed into the frame of the door and leaned against it, waiting to stop feeling so sick. After fiddling a moment with the door handle and finding no simple push-button lock, she pulled out the cellphone Ryodan programmed, not about to use magic she'd learned Silverside to spell the door shut. Spelling anything that belonged to Jericho Barrons wasn't something she was in a hurry to do. Knowing him, it had some subtle magic etched into it already and anything she tried would backfire or morph into something else. However, she couldn't just leave Ryodan's decapitated corpse behind a mere closed door for someone to stumble on. She might not know all his secrets but she'd protect the ones she did.

She sent Barrons a text. Or tried to. Her hands were trembling. She inhaled deep, held it, exhaled slow. Steady fingers danced over the keypad.

RYODAN ASKED ME TO KILL HIM SO HE COULD HEAL FASTER. SECURE YOUR STUDY.

Her screen flashed with a reply almost instantly.

All caps make it look like you're shouting at me. Don't. It pisses me off.

Scowling, she pulled a protein bar from her pocket and ate it in two bites. She couldn't afford to vomit energy. Everything pissed Barrons off. He lived on the razor's edge of eternal irritation. No doubt because he had to put up with mere mortals who thought too much when a good massacre would not only be more effective but much more fun. Leave it to Barrons to respond to such an abnormal text with a critique of her texting etiquette. She'd texted, like *never* before in her life. A text reached a single person. Her *Dani Daily* had reached the entire city.

Her fingers flew over the letters again. She omitted the puke factor. Damned if she was sticking around to clean it up. She had no clue how to turn off the caps lock. She had no clue how she'd turned it on, and mastering social etiquette didn't compute.

HE'S DEAD AND IT'S MESSY. SECURE IT.

He replied instantly:

I'M BUSY. YOU SECURE IT. OR DON'T. IT WON'T MATTER
FOR LONG ANYWAY. I HAVE THE STONES AND
CHRISTIAN. GET YOUR ASS TO CHESTER'S.

She snorted as she stepped from the room and closed the door.
He was right.

It did feel like being shouted at.

13

"Wasn't it you who said I was not free"

MAC

Rage gets me nowhere. I spin in circles of nothing, full of wild energy with no target to aim it at.

After a time—although that word means nothing to me here—I go still (another word that technically means nothing to me yet somehow does) and turn my thoughts to my captor.

Barrons said recently, *You think of the* Sinsar Dubh *as being an actual book inside you. I doubt it's either open or closed. Stop thinking of it so concretely.*

I'd felt a glimmer of understanding at his words. *You mean it's embedded in me, inseparably, and my ethical structure is the proverbial cover?* I'd replied.

The previous time the *Sinsar Dubh* had taken control of my body, I'd been furious at my clipped wings, my inability to do something, *anything,* to positively impact my world. I'd let that anger and frustration rip through me and explode out in a burst of violence.

I'd felt badass.

But maybe there'd been no "ass" in that moment at all; just a mother lode of "bad."

Here, in this silent dark place, without distraction, I apprehend my actions on that day more clearly. I'd broken my chains of doubt and fear with an act of savagery, telling myself since the Gray Woman was one of the bad guys, destroying her made me good.

Evil, Ryodan once told me, *is bad that believes it's good.*

Killing her hadn't been the wrong thing.

It was *why* I'd killed her that had been wrong. While I'd told myself I was killing her to protect Dublin, the truth was, I'd done it to make myself feel better, to assuage my feelings of impotence. That it would save potential victims had only been the icing on my selfish cake.

I've been in Dublin for a year. Although I met Jericho Barrons shortly after I arrived, more of those twelve months were lost in Faery, or spent in the Silvers, or passed mindlessly as a woman turned Pri-ya, than had ever been spent getting to know Barrons. In fact, I'm not sure I've ever gotten to know him. I've just gotten to know that I always want him around. And maybe one day I *will* get to know him.

Still, in those few months I spent with him on a mostly daily basis, I came to admire his system of ethics, unwavering focus, and commitment to those few people and causes he's selected as his own.

And while part of me wants to wail—*why didn't he save me from this somehow?*—another part of me, that clearer part, finally understands that this is what he was trying to get me to see all along; he couldn't save me and he knew it. He'd told me once that fear was more than a wasted emotion, it was the ultimate set of blinders; that if I couldn't face the truth of my reality, I could never control it, and would be subject to the wishes of anyone whose will was stronger than mine. He knew too well, from battling his own inner monster, what I've come to fathom only here and now.

The most critical, defining battles we wage in life, we wage alone.

Against ourselves.

It might be getting past an abusive childhood, struggling every day to regain belief in your own worth. Or being overweight and accepting that you don't have to look like whatever the ideal woman currently is to be loved. Maybe it's quitting drugs or giving up cigarettes. No one can do any of those things for you.

I've been divided all my life.

It's time for that to stop.

The Sweeper was right in wanting to fix my brain; there can't be two of us in here.

I didn't ask to be a *sidhe*-seer. I didn't ask to be in the wrong place at the wrong time as a fetus, and I certainly didn't ask to be dicked with by the Seelie Queen and Unseelie King all my life.

Yet this is the war my life has been shoving me toward since my mother carried me in her womb.

I can either be a victim—or a winner. Fuck victimhood. I don't wear it well; it clashes with my wardrobe.

I'm ready.

Only one of us is getting out alive.

It's going to be me.

14

"Do you wanna play a game? It's time to pay

for what you've done"

Ten minutes south of Dublin, I park in front of my chosen lair; formerly Malluce's gothic playground of death, sex, and fear.

The night MacKayla first laid eyes on the enormous four-story Victorian mansion, with its acre of haphazard, perspective-defying additions, oriel windows and transoms, turrets and porticos and wrought-iron balustrades, I'd known it would one day be mine.

John Johnstone Jr., murderer of his parents, feaster upon lessers of his kind, fueled, like me, by lust, greed, desire, and supremacy; his memory serves only to remind me that my body is as weak as his was and can be destroyed in the same fashion.

I drag myself from the car, clutching the door for support, taking care to position my feet properly. The soothing darkness of night has finally descended.

I'd have arrived much sooner if the unthinkable hadn't happened—the sun exploded in Dublin—assaulting my newborn eyes with cruel javelins of light. Not even the sunglasses I'd found in the car made it possible for me to stare into the burning glare and drive. Rather than continuing to pursue my goals, I'd been forced to pull into a thicket, cover my head with my jacket and bide time until dusk. I'd occupied those hours going over my plan, envisioning each step in exacting detail. Richly detailed thought shapes reality. I excel at thought.

My body, however, is a bitter joke. I've discovered MacKayla's nerve endings are as flawed as her mind; they cause enormous discomfort, overreacting to every sensation like a flock of hysterical doves.

I was certain when I merged with her body, evicting MacKayla's guilt-riddled consciousness from the limbs and organs, that firmly embedding my enormous, focused will in her tissue and bone would strengthen her flesh.

The opposite is true. In the same fashion Jada burns through energy and must eat constantly, I quickly exhaust the physicality I've appropriated. The body that houses me is unequal to my will. I'm a flame-thrower inside a Chinese lantern.

Before I became embodied, my path to supremacy was clear. It had, in fact, seemed childishly simple. Kill the three contenders for the power of the Fae race, summon and kill the Fae queen, absorb the True Magic, drink the Elixir of Life—presto, I'm immortal and unstoppable.

The theft of the spear changed everything.

It was the linchpin, the thing without which all else collapsed. For want of a motherfucking nail. My single priority is recovering the weapon. Or the sword. I don't care which.

I close the door and lean against the car, drop my head back, stretch my mouth wide and summon my flagging energy to call my army, rouse my children. I chime in the First Language, releasing their True Names in a brittle, beautiful song of tubular bells, ice, and velvety darkness. My words are lifted by a wind eager to do my bidding and go soaring into the night sky where they fan out then streak off into a million different directions.

Come to me, I command. *I am Creator/Ruler/King of yore, feel my power. Your will is mine. Come to me. We will feast and conquer.*

I repeat the summons, layering my haunting dark melody into the breeze until, with the prickling of my Fae essence, I feel the amassing throng of my children rising from shallow beds in the earth or sex-and-death-perfumed bowers in abandoned houses where they hold humans captive. I feel them turning away inside Chester's, separating from the Seelie and making for the door. Slipping from catacombs in cemeteries where they claimed lairs. They will stand guard at my lair, watchdogs from Hell while I determine what this vessel requires to function properly.

Come to me, I sing to the night, *obey your king.*

When I am assured my hordes are rising like the Wild Hunt, I begin the seemingly eternal walk to what will be my lair until I leave this world.

One foot.

The next.

Left foot.

Right.

Cocksucking body.

I've eaten as much Unseelie as my stomach will hold without bursting. Still, I weaken. I fortify my resolve with my mantra: WE ARE DESIRE, LUST, GREED, AND THE PATH WE CHOOSE TO SUPREMACY.

The towering double doors are ajar but my children will soon seal and guard them. I grab the fabric of my pants, slippery with blood and guts and brains, by the front of my thigh and hoist up one foot after the next, navigating a wide flight of stairs, stumble and crash into the doorjamb, holding it for support while I gather my energy.

The rambling house MacKayla found monstrous is lovely. She had plebeian taste. Fucking pink everywhere, until she discovered the absolution of black, hiding stains, concealing predators. Each room I pass through is a delight to my senses, fecund with the residue of worship, submission, and death. Here, humans willingly sacrificed themselves on the altars of need and loneliness for a brief glimpse of their god, bestowed only as they gasped their final breaths.

I abhor the word "need." There are things I require, as I have decided they will benefit me. Need is a disease endemic to the human race—a bit you put into your own mouth, pass off the reins to someone else then act surprised when they ride you hard. *Wake the fuck up*. Broken horses get ridden. And when they're past their prime, they don't get put out to pasture in a serene, happy meadow, but slaughtered and sent to the glue factory. The broken have a responsibility to die and make way for the living.

When MacKayla asked Barrons why so many Unseelie gathered at Mallucé's mansion, he'd replied, *Morbidity is their oxygen, they breathe richly here.* That night, I'd thought Barrons similar to me, possessing acute clarity of mind, formidable will, and unapologetic lust.

He is an embarrassment to his form, weakened by the illusions of love and self-sacrifice and no doubt countless others. One can never sell oneself a single illusion. More lies are always necessary to support the original lie.

Wasted eyes follow me as I pass: shocked, dimly curious, lustful, too drugged to approach. Mallucé's followers linger in the house, heroin-thin and pale, nested on pallets in dark corners or sprawled in a tangle of naked limbs on low-backed velveteen divans, burning incense, playing music, shooting up, snorting back, fading out.

Stoned passive prey.

My children will have food when they arrive.

Pity I lack the energy to partake of it myself.

I seek the basement. By the time I reach the subbasement that houses the suite of rooms where J. J. Jr.—human of surprisingly refined intellect—once lived, I am crawling.

I drag myself down the dimly lit corridor on my belly for a small eternity until I reach the immense square black door belted with bands of steel. I lie on my back and shove it open with both legs.

After a time I creep inside.

After another small eternity I rotate my body and push it closed with my feet.

After still more time I push myself to my hands and knees to slide the dead bolt, then collapse hard to the floor.

I lay curled against the door.

Something is wrong, very wrong.

I summon one of my crimson runes to seal the doors.

No rune appears.

Shivering, I try again and again, but each time I endeavor to sing a rune into existence I have only an empty, slack hand, fingers curled on nothing.

My magic springs from my will, not my body. The ever-increasing weakness of my form should not affect my power.

I cease my efforts, turning inward, examining myself.

My mind, disembodied, has been eternally cognizant. Not an instant of my existence has passed without my awareness of it. I am ever vigilant, ever alert, ever plotting and planning. At all times, since the moment of my birth, I have been a superior, incessant, voracious thinking entity.

Now it feels as if my very essence is being tampered with. My apprehension of myself is growing . . . dim, difficult to see clearly and focus upon. Focus is power.

Has the interfering little bitch found some way to attack me from within?

I sink inside and examine the box in which I placed her. It's a seamless construct without void; sleek, black, cold.

I willed it into existence and believe in it—therefore it is.

My belief is driven by intellect. Hers by emotion. I place my faith in no one but myself. She places hers in everyone but herself, and that makes her susceptible to anyone with a will more focused than her own.

I posit and push. She fears and doubts.

I WIN.

She's in a box that doesn't really exist and *believes it inescapable.*

Belief is reality.

Belief is so delightfully malleable.

I giggle but nothing comes out.

I think SOMETHING IS HAPPENING TO ME! WHAT IS IT?

My eyelids are heavy and remain closed although I would prefer them open.

I think I WILL NOT LOSE CONTROL OF THIS VESSEL AGAIN!

My limbs tremble, flaccid upon the floor, then go still.

I lie, immobilized. What is befalling me? Who is interfering with my plans? Have I been . . . wounded in some manner . . . of which I'm not . . . aware?

Is this

Dying?

Did I do

Something wrong

To my

Body? Did.

Someone.

Poison—

15

"I went down to the crossroads"

JADA

When she descended into the dissonant musical battleground of Chester's many subclubs, Jada wasn't surprised to find the nightclub packed. The worse things got out in the streets of Dublin, the harder the party rocked inside the slick chrome and glass walls at 939 Rêvemal, where the darkest fantasy could be indulged for a price.

Pushing her way through the crowded dance floors she realized that, although it was business as usual, there was a disturbing difference in today's clientele. There were only humans and Seelie in the many clubs. She hadn't spotted a single Unseelie and was already halfway to the guarded stairs that granted access to the private upper levels.

Eyes narrowed, she spun in a tight circle. The Unseelie were insatiable patrons of Chester's, but currently there wasn't a single Rhino-boy, not one of the grotesque singularities, or any of the Lord Master's militant guards to be seen. Not even Papa Roach with his stumpy-legged body formed of gelatinous, shiny carapaces was ambling about, hawking his fat-devouring, cockroachian wares, and she'd begun to suspect the revolting creature lived somewhere in Ryodan's palatial demesne.

The *Sinsar Dubh* had returned and there were no Unseelie in Chester's; it was a worrisome coupling of facts.

Nodding coolly to Fade and the eerie white-haired member of the Nine with dark, burning eyes whose name she'd not yet uncovered, she ascended the staircase, moving like a Joe, staring down at the dance floors, absorbing every detail. Although there were many advantages to accessing the slipstream, moving faster than reality blinded her to it, and she couldn't assess and report on current events if she didn't take the time to see them.

When she reached Ryodan's office, the dark glass was set to privacy, which meant the occupants could see out but no one could see in. She placed her palm against the panel. The door whisked aside and she peered into the dimly lit room.

Barrons stood glowering in one corner. Cruce towered, seething, in another, his upper body canted away from the wall, betraying the degree to which his mutilated back pained him. Christian leaned back against a third corner, arms folded over his chest, majestic wings high, curled inward around his body. All of them stared fixedly at nothing, as far from one another as they could be in such a confined space. There was more hostility in the office than air, and she wondered how long they'd been occupying such tight quarters, waiting for her to join them.

Barrons shot her an impatient glare. "About fucking time you got here."

Jada stepped inside and the door whisked shut behind her. She moved into the only corner left open, assessing the others. What an unexpected and powerful team—assuming they didn't kill one another before getting down to their goals. Death, War, whatever Barrons was, and herself, a superhero. "Where did you find Christian?" she asked Barrons.

The Highlander shot her a look of disgust. "Bloody Mac

bloody fucking cocooned me and left me behind a pile of bloody rocks, that's where."

Cruce bristled. "At least you still have your wings."

Christian ignored him. "Then those slobbering beasts of Barrons bloody licked me to death. First the Hag then this. Christ, whatever happened to going to college and dating pretty lasses?"

Cruce flashed him a cruel smile. "Those days are long gone, little brother."

"I'm no' your bloody brother. I'm no' your fucking anything."

"Barrons's beasts?" Jada said. Why did Christian think they were his? And how badly had being cocooned harmed him? He was pale, shifting his weight from foot to foot as if trying to find a comfortable position.

Christian muttered, "Whatever the fuck they are. Only time I ever saw them was at the abbey. Figured he brought them."

"Mac said she did. She told me she found them in the Silvers," Jada fished.

"Well there you go, lass. And Mac never lies or does anything the least bit shady."

Ignoring the jibe, she turned to Barrons. "There are no Unseelie in Chester's."

"Tell me something I don't know," he replied tersely. "Cruce tried to summon a few of the lesser castes. They didn't appear."

"Summon how?"

"When he absorbed the spells from the Book, he gained the True Names of the Unseelie."

She pinned Cruce with a sharp look. "What else did you get?" Obviously the Book hadn't affected him like it had Mac, but he'd gotten more than names.

"None of your fucking business, *sidhe*-seer."

"So, why didn't the Unseelie come?" she pressed.

"Because your lovely MacKayla now possesses the same knowledge, and they recognize *her* as more powerful than me. That will change."

"How did Mac come to be possessed by the *Sinsar Dubh* in the first place?" Christian said. "I thought there was only one copy and Cruce absorbed it. Where the bloody hell did a second copy come from?"

"Yes." Cruce seized the topic with avid interest. "How *did* the lovely MacKayla come by another copy of the *Sinsar Dubh*?"

"Twenty-odd years ago, while Isla O'Connor was carrying the corporeal *Sinsar Dubh*, it deposited a copy of itself into her unborn fetus," Barrons said curtly.

Christian stared at him incredulously. "You're telling me Mac had the bloody Book all along?"

"I believe it was dormant until she came to Ireland," Barrons said. "Something about it being here gave it strength it didn't have before. When she used one of its spells to save Jada from the Sweeper, it took possession of her."

Cruce's nostrils flared and his eyes narrowed to slits. "The entire time I was hunting it, she had it inside her?"

Barrons said, "She didn't know it was inside her until after we interred you. Jada, Alina was able to locate Mac. Fade tracked and followed her. She's holed up at Mallucé's abandoned mansion, with a mile of Unseelie surrounding her on every side. Tens of thousands of the fucks, even more than attacked the abbey."

"That's a problem," she said. "We have to get close enough to position the stones, and that means within ten feet or so. We also have to get her out, once we've contained her."

"Fade said she was staggering when she entered the mansion, appeared to be having difficulty walking," Barrons said.

Jada told him how clumsy Mac had seemed when she first stood up from the table.

"Now it's your turn, fairy," Barrons growled to Cruce. "When you absorbed the spells from the Book, was there something sentient within?"

The temperature in the office dropped sharply and ice crystals glazed the floor. "The correct term is 'Fae.' And yes, there was sentience within, but it vanished the moment the Book crumbled. I do not believe the *Sinsar Dubh* possessed the power to replicate itself. No Fae does. Not the queen. Not even the king. The sentience within the *Sinsar Dubh* must have found a way to split itself, transferring part into Isla, leaving part behind, weaving a spell to ensure much of what it left behind would expire if the Book was ever read. Fae revile the very notion of duplicate selves. We prize our individuality and position."

"So, what does that make Mac?" Christian demanded. "How powerful is she?"

Cruce smiled coolly. "Powerful enough to be a threat that must be eliminated immediately. The king cast every spell he ever used to create the Unseelie castes into a single vessel. When the spells commingled, they did exactly what anyone with half a brain would have expected—gave birth to the most powerful Unseelie singularity yet. Then the bloody fool left it trapped inside a book, alone. We do not sleep nor do we suffer solitude well. It is the most dreaded of Fae punishments to be bound in isolation without stimulation. Any Fae imprisoned with nothing for half a million years will go mad. Then come back from it. Then go mad again, worse. Over and over. Even if MacKayla carries only part of the *Sinsar Dubh*'s sentience, she is still a pure psychopath with immeasurable knowledge and power. *That* is what you seek to remove from her. There is no way to strip such a being from her body. It will never let her go. It will destroy her if it thinks you might succeed. There is no saving MacKayla. You must accept that you have no choice but to kill her."

Barrons said softly, "I will never accept that."

"Then you doom us all," Cruce warned.

Barrons murmured, "Psychopaths have their weaknesses."

"And are so savage one rarely gains the offensive long enough to exploit them," Cruce retorted.

"The two of you should know," Christian said dryly.

Barrons closed his eyes and rubbed his jaw, the rasp of his

hand against stubble loud to Jada's ears in the hostile silence of the office. Finally he opened them and said to Cruce, "If you were the Mac version of the *Sinsar Dubh,* what would you want?"

"A better body," Cruce said without hesitation. "One not human, with no mortal limitations. That would be any Fae's first priority."

"How would you get a better body? I already offered mine. It refused."

Jada inhaled sharply. "Are you *kidding* me? Do you know what it might do with your—" She broke off, not about to discuss the Nine's extraordinary abilities in front of Cruce.

Cruce said, "If it can't seize another body—and it must doubt its ability or it would have taken your offer, or tried to take mine—it will go after the Seelie Queen's elixir, the true Elixir of Life."

"Which is where?"

Cruce shrugged. "None but the queen is privy to that information."

Jada said, "She's missing and has been since the night you were iced at the abbey." And they desperately needed her if they were to have any hope of saving their world. She alone possessed the power to wield the dangerous Song of Making.

"Then it would appear the Book is out of luck," Cruce said lightly.

Christian shook his head. "False. There is something it can do and you know it. What is it?"

Barrons growled, "We'll hand you to Mac on a bloody platter if you don't tell us everything you know. Either you're with me or you're in my motherfucking way."

Cruce slanted his iridescent eyes half closed, and Jada could practically see him tallying his options and odds in columns the same way she did. After a moment he said, "I will offer you a deal."

"We've already made a deal," Jada said sharply.

"You forced concessions at a time of duress. I insist we renego-
tiate. I know what the Book wants and how it will go after it."

"And what do you want in return?" Barrons said acerbically.

Cruce said mildly, "No more than I wanted before—to kill the
queen and become the rightful ruler of my race. This time, however, you and your merry little band will help me accomplish it."

Barrons was motionless a long moment then inclined his head
in assent.

"You can't be serious," Jada exclaimed. What was he doing?
They didn't dare kill the queen. They needed her.

"You can't bloody kill the queen of the Fae just to get your
bloody girlfriend back," Christian spat.

Cruce glanced pointedly at Jada and Christian. "Do you speak
for them as well?"

"Yes," Barrons said, shooting them both lethal looks.

"We're in." Jada flashed Christian a look that said, *Trust that
Barrons has a plan.* "But if Mac comes to harm, the deal's off."

"Saving her without harm is your problem," Cruce said, shrug-
ging. "Mine is merely getting you close enough to place the stones."

"And placing one of them yourself," Jada added.

"We're not using him," Christian snarled.

"He'll be there anyway," she said. "The fewer people we bring
into this the better."

"But you have already impeded my plan," Cruce continued
evenly, "and must rectify that. MacKayla will not go after the queen
until she has one of the immortal weapons in her possession."

Jada said incredulously. "You want me to give Mac the spear
back?"

"No. I want you to permit her to recover it in a way that convinces her she bested you. The *Sinsar Dubh* is deeply paranoid."

Christian shot him a dark look. "She already came after us
once and you want to put a weapon in her hands that can kill us
both?"

"She thinks us out of her way in cocoons, and immortality is her priority. The longer the *Sinsar Dubh* inhabits MacKayla's body, the more it will despise its limitations. The moment she has the spear, she will go for the queen to coerce from her the Elixir of Life. When she does, we will trap her."

"But no one knows where the queen is," Jada reminded.

Cruce said, "The *Sinsar Dubh* knows a place at which our queen can be summoned and Aoibheal cannot refuse to attend. I know that location, too. Both the Book and I possess a vast store of the king's knowledge."

Barrons glanced at Christian.

"Truth."

"Where?" Barrons demanded.

Cruce said coldly, "I trust you no more than you trust me. Once MacKayla has the spear and begins to make her move, I will take you there. The quarters are tight and her army will be unable to accompany her. That is where we will trap MacKayla and kill Aoibheal."

Christian narrowed his eyes. "If you know how to summon Aoibheal, why haven't you done it already? What do you need us for?"

"Because he doesn't have any way to kill her," Jada said. "He'd have to put her back in the Unseelie prison and wait for her to die."

Barrons smiled mockingly. "That's not why. Both Cruce and the *Sinsar Dubh* covet the Fae queen's power. The moment she's killed, the True Magic of their race will pass to the next most powerful Fae. Historically, it has always gone to a female but legend holds if a Fae male is strong enough and the females are all dead, the matriarchy could become a patriarchy. Neither the Book nor Cruce is convinced the queen's magic wouldn't choose another if they killed her now."

Christian shot Cruce a look of challenge. "So the legend is true, the power will jump when she dies, if she hasn't passed it on first. Bring it on, bro."

"Ah, now you call me brother. Save your challenge for another day, puppy. Your fledgling power poses no threat to me."

"So you say," Christian retorted.

Barrons said, "The Book believes the queen's power might go to the Sweeper-enhanced Unseelie princess. Cruce fears it would choose Mac over him. Isn't that right, fairy?"

The Fae prince's eyes glittered dangerously. "You had better pray to your many puny gods—"

"I neither pray nor have gods."

"—that never happens, because MacKayla would then be the *Sinsar Dubh* and the Seelie Queen, beyond deadly, capable of raining down infinite destruction on both our realms."

Christian growled, "Which means we can trust you right up until the moment we help you kill the queen, because you'll be both then, too."

Cruce's smile was all teeth. "Pretty much. Got a better idea?"

Jada said, "Once Mac has the spear back, how will we know when she heads for the place she can summon the queen?"

"We watch the Unseelie princess. After MacKayla uses her True Name to summon her, she will head straight for the queen. The moment the princess disappears, we know to go ahead and lie in wait."

"While Mac conveniently removes the Unseelie princess from both your paths," Barrons said dryly. "Then we remove Mac from yours."

"Precisely. That is our deal."

"What about Mac's ability to sense the stones?" Barrons pressed. "Won't that keep her from coming into wherever it is you're taking us?"

"Her ability to sense objects of power is useless there."

"Christian will sift me there. You will sift Jada," Barrons ordered.

Christian shook his head. "I'm far from a reliable sifter. I'll need to know the location so I have time to perfect it."

Cruce spat contemptuously, "You are an unreliable sifter because you resist your true nature. You will never attain your full power until you relinquish your hold on your precious humanity. Let it go, puppy. Walk with the big dogs. Embrace what it is to be Fae, immortal and powerful beyond your wildest dreams."

"That boat's never leaving the dock. You'll have to tell me where. I need practice or none of this will work."

"Irrelevant," Cruce said impatiently. "Sifting to that place is impossible and for good reason."

Barrons smiled faintly, smugly, looking pleased for no reason Jada could discern, and said, "I assume you know where the Unseelie princess is?"

Cruce said coolly, "Earlier today, while I was sifting your *sidhe*-seers about, I took the time to drop an ancient scroll into an interested party's hands. It contained the princess's True Name. The bitch is already trapped in a cage of iron and wards and believes one of the new, young Seelie princes acquired the power to summon her from a long-forgotten scroll. He is another that foolishly didn't question sudden good fortune, too busy brooding about what he deems unfair bad fortune. He awaits one of the immortal weapons to slay her." Cruce shot Jada a look. "You will not be obliging him."

"Why would I? I'd never give a Seelie prince the spear or the sword."

"You might this one," Cruce said with an amused look.

"You already summoned and trapped her without telling us?" Christian said, incensed. "What else have you done that you've not seen fit to inform us about?"

Jada frowned. "Won't the Book have to eliminate the Seelie prince, too?"

"As I have already told you, fledglings don't signify and will not for some time. They are not strong enough to attract the True Magic. Only Mac, myself, and the Unseelie princess are powerful enough to be contenders."

"Where is the Unseelie princess and who is this new Seelie prince?" Barrons demanded.

"You will find them both at Dublin Castle. The young Fae princeling is the current leader of your New Guardians. But he will not be for long. Soon his transformation will become noticeable to humans, and they will never follow what they trap and kill."

"Inspector Jayne is turning Fae?" Jada exclaimed, horrified. "A Seelie prince?"

"One and the same. He has been cannibalizing our race far too long to escape without price. Even now I feel birth pangs as others begin the transformation."

"Who?" Christian demanded.

The prince said laconically, "I do not as yet know."

"Why can't I feel them?"

"Woof, woof," was Cruce's cool reply. "Embrace it. Or soon even they will surpass you. Like sharks, we circle when we smell blood. Get hungry. Or get eaten."

16

"Freedom's just another word for
nothing left to lose"

MAC

Here, drifting in nothing, my thoughts sparkle like diamonds, translucently clear.

Perhaps it's because I have no physical distractions. Perhaps it's because, for the first time since I was a fetus, I'm completely alone, free from the ever-present influence and malevolent manipulation of the *Sinsar Dubh*.

Out there, beyond my box, in the world, the Book is walking around, controlling my body, doing God knows what with it (I refuse to indulge that train of thought, I can't do anything to stop it, and the horrific things I might imagine would only dilute my clarity), but once *it* was trapped. For twenty-three years.

I simply have to replicate its path to freedom.

But first I have to figure out what it did; what *I* did, that enabled it to take control of my body away from me. Barrons says possession is nine-tenths of the law. So what did I do that allowed the Book to exploit its one-tenth possibility?

I understand how it got me the day I killed the Gray Woman but I don't understand how it evicted me this time.

Something about the moment I used one of its spells gave it the ability to overpower me, but what?

I turn my thoughts back to the instant it gained control and sift through my motives. Unlike that gloomy day I'd killed the Gray Woman, I hadn't been trying to make myself feel better, nor had I been seeking to improve my life.

At the moment I reached for the spell, all I'd been thinking of was Dani, that I wanted her to live out loud and in every color of the rainbow, unchanged, unaltered by a dispassionate entity that believed itself so superior that it could re-create her according to its own design—and who the hell was it to judge? I'd been thinking that I'd do anything to see her happy, hear her belly-laugh again, snicker, crack herself up, maybe fall in love and—who knows, if Shazam was really real, she'd save him and they'd swagger around Dublin, doing superhero things together. I'd even gone so far as to imagine her having children of her own someday, thinking how brilliant and amazing they'd be and what a terrific mother she'd make. I'd wanted her to get up off that fucking table, unchanged, unharmed. She'd already been through so much in her life.

My motives had been pure, as altruistic as I believed possible. I hadn't been thinking about myself at all. I'd made the decision with a strangely detached calm, a serene "Fine, take me, just let her live." I refuse to believe doing something out of pure love makes us weaker.

Then how had such good intentions landed me here?

I consider the question from every angle, finally able to draw a single conclusion: They hadn't.

There was something else, some other nuance that tipped the scales in favor of the *Sinsar Dubh*.

I peel myself like an onion, seeking the pearly core, determined to isolate precisely what had been in my mind at the moment I'd made the decision to open the Book. I shuck vanity, pride, ego, lay my heart bare and study it.

At the moment I'd opened the Book—as if it was something

that could even be opened or closed or anything that implied corporeality—I'd been thinking that I believed in good magic, that even if the Book's power stemmed from an evil source, I could use it for the right reasons, without price.

Wait. Not exactly.

There was something deeper, beneath that thought.

Oh, God, I'd still been afraid.

I'd been *saying* I believed in the good magic but in my heart lurked the insidious fear that I would lose control again like I had the day I killed the Gray Woman. Only things would go much worse this time.

Hope builds a stairway to Heaven. Fear opens an abyss to Hell. We stand in front of those two possible apertures at all times; choose which one to go through.

Was it possible the only thing that had given the Book control over me in that moment—was me?

I'm stupefied by my next thought: What if the war between us has always been nothing more than a battle of will? And it knows it. I'm the only one that doesn't. That would give it one hell of an advantage over me; all the advantage it needed. The corporeal *Sinsar Dubh* had trafficked in guile and sleight of hand. My internal one would be no different. Since the moment I learned of the Book, I'd heard nothing but tales of how all-powerful it was, how its will was impossible to resist, and damn it all, I'd believed it. Despite Barrons trying to make me see that the legend of a thing was often far greater than the thing.

Picture this: Two people are in a room. One's a sociopath, one's not. Who has the advantage?

The sociopath. Because it knows it's a sociopath. The empath doesn't. The empath thinks they're playing by the same rules. They aren't. They aren't even playing the same game.

There *are* no rules with a sociopath. There's only—

DESIRE, LUST, GREED, AND THE PATH WE CHOOSE TO SUPREMACY.

The words explode in the vacuum around me, stunning me.

I crane my awareness, as if I might turn this way and that, peering into darkness I can't see with eyes I don't have.

I just heard the *Sinsar Dubh!*

Because I'm finally starting to see through its games? Because this motherfucking empath *knows* it's standing in a room with a psychopath? Ah, suddenly we're playing the same game.

Now we both have no rules. I cast aside all my preconceptions, everything I thought and believed about the *Sinsar Dubh,* and begin at ground zero. What is the Book really? How much control over me does it *really* have?

I realize, much to my surprise, that it's oddly fascinating being nothing but a consciousness. It's strangely . . . freeing. Not that I'd choose to stay in this state, but it's much easier to focus my thoughts. I feel no pain. Nothing hurts or itches or is getting stiff from sitting in one position too long. I'm not worried about how my hair or nails look because I don't have any. I'm not hungry. I don't need to go to the bath—

Oh, God, but *it* does now!

The mouth I don't have wants to laugh. I wonder how that's going for it, as it tries to acclimate to the demands of my body with no instruction manual. It suffers limits it never used to have. Like the Unseelie, newly released from their prison, it must be ruled by endless, stupefying hunger—only unlike them, it now has a body it has no experience in caring for, and will make mistakes.

Good. I hope it's struggling.

Not too much, I amend hastily, because I'd really like my body back in one piece. I hope it flounders just enough to fuck it up royally.

My copy of the *Sinsar Dubh* has never been corporeal except for a few murderous hours, and now it needs to pee, and eat, and wash (I hope), and do all those other taxing, distracting things humans have to do on a daily basis.

It occurs to me that these early hours, or days or whatever is passing, are when it's going to be at its weakest, while it adjusts. I hope Barrons figures that out.

A coldly analytical sentience studied me my whole life, probing for weaknesses.

Two can play that game.

SOMETHING'S HAPPENING TO ME! WHAT IS IT?

The Book's panicked thought echoes like thunder off mountains, thrilling me. I expand my awareness, reaching out, pressing at the indefinable limit of walls I feel somewhere around me. Why are we bleeding into each other? Is it playing a game with me? Trying to trick me, lull me into some other mistake? Are there any more mistakes I can even make? Or is it weakening for real?

I'm not alone. It's in here, too. In me. We're both in me. A barrier separates us but a barrier can be breached.

I will hunt it.

I will find it. Study it. Identify its cracks and flaws and weaknesses that can be exploited. I dredge up the information I learned in my abnormal psych course—surprisingly easy in here with no distractions—and reflect upon the characteristics of borderline personalities. This isn't a battle of magic, it's a battle of "frame"— that construct of reality we adopt as our own, what we believe about ourselves and our relation to the world. I have to change the Book's frame the way it changed mine, chipping away at it, recasting it so *it* loses control. But first I have to *get* to it.

I WILL NOT LOSE CONTROL OF THIS VESSEL AGAIN!

I'd smile if I had a face. *Yes. That's it. You will. You will lose and I will win.*

Something is happening to the Book, changing its circumstances, and whatever it is threatens its ability to hold my body. Is it me? Is my growing understanding weakening its hold? I expand my awareness and get slammed by a wave of bone-deep exhaustion. It's the first sensation I've felt since the Book turned me into a Mac-in-the-box. Is something cranking my handle?

Oh, God, I know what's happening! It needs to sleep. With its consciousness tethered to my physicality, it will eventually pass out. It has to. It can't run my body around forever, or it would die. Bodies pass out when overexerted. What will happen to it then? What will happen to me?

I'm the constantly vigilant one now. I suffer no weariness, no need for slumber. I'm hyperalert, as clear as Ryodan's castle of glass in which everything is visible and can be studied.

It speaks again, three words weakly.

Did. Someone. Poison.

I wait, stretching, craning, pressing outward with all my will.

Abruptly, the sensation of walls confining me vanishes and I feel like I'm being sucked out of my box by a hydraulic vacuum cleaner, decompressing, expanding, growing.

For a long, terrible moment I feel as if my consciousness is being torn in half, as if something is struggling to hold me in my box but I'm kicking and flailing, trying to break free. The tension becomes unbearable.

Abruptly, pain slams into me.

Pain everywhere! I'm staggered by it.

I open my eyes, desperate to see what's causing the pain—

Holy shit.

I.

Open.

My eyes.

17

"They flutter behind you your possible pasts"

AOIBHEAL, QUEEN OF THE FAE

"You asinine fool, let me *out* of here!" Aoibheal shook her fist at the ceiling of the candlelit, flower-strewn boudoir in which she was trapped. Sparkling diamonds, illuminated from within by tiny twinkling fireflies, scattered around her fist and spiraled away through the air.

Her words, like all the others she'd spoken, threatened and cajoled, fell on deaf ears—if the uncaring Unseelie King was even listening. If he hadn't wandered off, distracted by some amusement, fickle bastard that he was. She'd even tried telling the ceiling that she remembered who she was and she loved him again, but if the king was eavesdropping, her lie had been unconvincing.

Even here, trapped within a portion of the Silvers, Aoibheal could feel the turmoil of her court; the bitter acrimony among her castes with the deaths of the princes; the rising of new princes; and the suffering deep within the planet.

She felt, too, the birth of the massive, malevolent power inside the O'Connor *sidhe*-seer upon whom she'd so heavily relied. The *Sinsar Dubh* was no longer contained and now roamed Dublin, more aware, more dangerous than its prior incarnation. Moving with intent, purpose, and a plan. She knew she was targeted in its crosshairs, yet had no idea how upcoming events might unfold. This world and all its occupants had fallen off the grid of her projected possibles.

She closed her eyes and sighed. She'd failed to secure her race's future. Had they been doomed from the moment the song was lost? Or had it begun before that, on that fateful day the ancient queen refused to turn the concubine Fae for the king? Had the First Queen not rejected his request, she would never have been killed, the two deadly *Sinsar Dubh*s would not have come into existence, and Aoibheal wouldn't now be trapped inside the boudoir of a dead woman, because the mad king was determined to believe she was his long lost love.

Their planet would not be dying, their race poised on the verge of extinction.

Before the First Queen had died, she'd done two things: the first from spite, the second from duty. She'd wasted precious time using the song to sing into existence the walls of the Unseelie prison, as punishment for the king's defiance.

Then she'd transferred the power of the Fae court, unearthing it from deep within their own fractured world, hurling it across the light-years and galaxies, to be buried within another one. The seat of their power had been moved again to yet more worlds by other queens, but long before Aoibheal took the crown it had been entombed in the planet Earth.

Each and every Fae in existence drew their magic from the roiling cyclone of power at the planet's core.

Without the song, Aoibheal was forced eons ago to irrevocably bind their power to this planet in order to sustain their race. If the Earth died so, too, would all Fae die, the instant their individual tethers no longer connected to its source.

If only she had the song, she could break the bonds and release the power of her court, to be moved again!

They could leave this world, not care what fate befell it!

She opened her eyes, gaze drawn unwillingly back to the translucent, slender form of the concubine where she rolled with her dark lover on a bed of white ermine and lushly scented flower petals.

The woman was identical to Aoibheal in every way.

But she was not Fae. The concubine was mortal.

Yet . . . still . . . Aoibheal felt an inexplicable connection to her. The passion of the residue-lovers had somehow touched her, stirring something in her essence, not quite a memory, but the shadowy images of what seemed a long-forgotten dream. Trapped in this chamber, watching them argue as heatedly as they loved, she'd started to fear she was losing her mind. Their idiotic argument had begun to consume her thoughts. She'd become . . . interested in their problems. Had wanted to step in and tell them to stop being foolish. Urge the king to let his woman go. Let her live and die as she wanted and love her while he could.

Such thoughts were alien to her!

The Fae queen would *never* counsel another to cede immortality unless there was no other way to survive.

Yet, she could see . . . no, she could *feel*, the concubine's point of view. The woman didn't wish to be Fae. Her faith was different than the king's. She believed life continued after what most perceived as death. Her race had souls, mysterious amorphous things that did not die when the body did, and to become Fae meant her cherished soul would ultimately wither and die. To the concubine, mortal death was nothing more than one door closing and another opening. She had no fear of it. Who was the king to force his woman to choose his faith over hers? Still, he mocked it. Told her death was the end, that she should capitulate her belief in something, for his in nothing. Yet the concubine's impassioned entreaties, like hers, fell on ears made deaf by ego and arrogance.

Aoibheal pivoted away from the bed. If, as the king claimed, she hadn't been born Fae but mortal, she would know it. She was not the woman who'd once been his concubine. She was bored, trapped alone, getting distracted by a passion play.

Still . . . the king claimed she'd been used as a pawn, forced to drink, unsuspecting.

Such had been known to happen, when feuds within her court escalated, until she'd assumed power and locked the cauldron away, along with the Elixir of Life, where only she could access them. She'd carefully conducted each Fae's forgetting. Protected them from one another.

She'd been trapped in the boudoir long enough to have reflected upon every aspect of the king's story, and was forced to concede that although his claims were outrageous and absurd, they were nonetheless possible. If someone *had* forced a cup from the Cauldron of Forgetting upon her much farther back in the past than she even knew she'd existed, then everything he claimed might be true. She'd been accused by her own High Council of granting mortals undeserved lenience, and on rare occasion of even protecting them.

She'd spent her entire reign studying and analyzing possibilities, the better to shape her race's world, holding none too extreme to entertain.

How then could she deem this one beyond the realm of plausible?

Aoibheal spun to face the towering black Silver that divided the two chambers, light and dark, cozy and cavernous, lovely and frightening. The mysterious portal chilled her. She'd cut her teeth on tales of what lay beyond in the Unseelie King's eerie realm of eternal midnight and ice. She'd recently been in that realm, until rescued by the O'Connor she'd delicately nudged to be there at her hour of need, but had glimpsed none of it, trapped in her coffin of ice.

She'd not regained consciousness until after the king had taken her from the abbey catacomb, had not foreseen that he would abduct her. She had no idea how she'd been freed from the Unseelie prison, and now her most powerful weapon, the O'Connor *sidhe-seer*, was possessed by the worst of the Unseelie King—most certainly her enemy.

She knew the legend of the king's mirror. It was said that only two could pass through the portal and survive. She eyed the enormous, gilt-framed Silver, striving for objectivity, weighing the limited choices she had. It was possible there was a way to escape her prison from the king's side of the boudoir. The arrogant king was too enamored of his own existence to believe the Queen of the Seelie would risk her own life trying to pass through it.

She smiled bitterly. He didn't know her.

She would sacrifice everything, confront any unpleasant truth, yield even her immortal life to preserve the future of her race. All that mattered to her was that her people survived. Even if that meant she did not. She was their queen.

If she attempted to cross the threshold and died, what would become of them all? Guilty of the death of yet another queen, might the king finally *do* something to save their race?

If she tried and survived, it would mean that her entire existence was a lie, that she was far older than she believed she was, and had been born the unthinkable—mortal, human.

One thing was irrefutably true: she would die anyway if she remained where she was. Better to die trying than not.

When the planet collapsed, every Fae realm, including the Silvers and all they contained, would vanish. Except the king himself. Legend held he predated even the First Queen, some even claimed he'd made her. Made them all. And even now he had no care that his creations might cease to exist. Why would he? *He* would go on.

She glanced back at the concubine, tangled in bed linens with the king.

They touched her, struck a chord somewhere deep within her. Was it possible remnants of memory survived the cauldron? That a love as consuming as the one the concubine had shared with the king left an indelible imprint on a being's very essence despite the effects of the Elixir of Forgetting?

With every ounce of her being she wanted to deny it. Yet she would not repeat the egotistical mistakes of the stubborn First Queen.

Often, it was only the bold, fearless, risky action that had any hope of circumventing impending doom, as if Fate was amused by the colorfully unexpected, and while she was laughing, one might slip changes past the pernicious bitch.

It was her duty to exhaust all means at her disposal to save her race. No matter how terrifying or distasteful.

She eyed the sleek dark glass, peering through to the shadowy interior of the king's bedchamber.

Fire to his ice, frost to her flame.

She had no idea where the thought had come from.

But somehow she knew also that it was cold on the other side, his side. So cold it would be difficult to catch her breath.

She shivered at yet another thought that made no sense. She didn't need to breathe. She was energy and projection.

Setting her jaw, she snatched up the concubine's long-abandoned cloak of snowy velvet and plush fur.

Pulling it close around her body, she glided toward the mirror.

18

"I'm wide awake, I'm not sleeping, oh no, no"

MAC

I'm lying on a floor, staring at a door.

Where am I? Every muscle in my body—*my body!*—burns from exertion and my teeth hurt. Why do my teeth hurt?

Groaning, I take stock of myself. Can I move?

Gingerly, I extend a leg.

Fucking *ow*.

It feels like someone beat me from head to toe. And I need to pee badly. Whatever nefarious deeds the Book committed, it pushed my body to the extreme in the process. I stay still for a long moment, reacclimating to corporeality. The extraordinary clarity I'd attained with no body to distract me threatens to dissipate beneath an onslaught of sensation.

I press my palms to the floor, force my head up like a rearing cobra and peer into a dimly lit, chilly room furnished with neoclassical goth furnishings: a low brocade and velvet chaise, tall-backed chairs with those creepy canopies, an enormous four-poster bed draped in vintage velvets and taffeta.

I know this place.

I despise this place. And now that I'm back in my own skin, I can feel the palpable evil of the monstrous mansion wherein so many murders were committed. Evil leaves a residue, tainting and changing the very molecules of the location where it occurs.

I hear, too, somewhere beyond this room, the dark melody of thousands and thousands of Unseelie clustered close. More than I've felt in a single, condensed area since the night I cowered atop a belfry as the sky ran black with a horde of monsters breaking free after an eternity in prison. The discordant song of so many castes mingling nearly deafens me until I dial my *sidhe*-seer senses back to low volume. It appears the Book chose to surround itself with an army from the Court of Shadows. And what more appropriate place? It must have scoped it out through my eyes when I'd been here with Barrons, the night I stole one of the four stones. I wonder how much it had actually been able to see that night. I wonder if it knows everything I know. I shudder at the thought. Regardless, it knew enough to know this place was here and would suit it.

"Mallucé's." It comes out a fractured whisper. My throat is burning, dry, and my mouth is—oh, God. I stick a shaky finger in and pick at things caught in my teeth. Clearly the Book didn't bother to brush and floss, and just how the hell long have I been gone, what did I do, and how did I get here?

I drop back to the floor and fumble in my coat pocket for my cellphone. After what seems an eternity of clumsy rummaging, I close my fingers on it, pull it out, squint at the date and time, and collapse back to the floor with relief.

It's the same day, late night. Surely I haven't K'Vrucked the world in so short a time!

I stiffen, belatedly absorbing what else I just saw. Contracting muscles that loudly protest contracting, I push myself back up and peer warily at my hands. They're covered with cuts and abrasions, my palms crusted with blood and bits of black . . . I squint . . . feathers, I think. My nails have been torn off to the quick and there's other stuff stuck to . . . ew!

I just put one of my fingers in my mouth. No wonder I have such a bad taste in it.

"Shit," I whisper. My finger hadn't tasted any different than my mouth. What the hell has the Book been eating? I nearly heave the mysterious contents of my stomach at the thought.

I shove the phone back in my pocket. It takes me several long, agonizing moments to push myself to my feet, where I wobble dangerously before teetering into the dimly lit suite to search for J. J. Jr.'s bathroom.

When I find it, I'm sorry I did.

Obviously the Book wasn't interested in cleaning and tending our shared vessel. It had been far too busy doing . . . other things.

I clutch the sink for support, staring at myself in the mirror. Thinking there shouldn't even be a mirror here. Mallucé was pretending to be a vampire. Why the hell did he have to put a mirror here?

I close my eyes, swaying with exhaustion and horror.

The only part of my face that isn't crusted with blood is the white of my eyes. Even my eyelids are spattered rusty red. My hair is matted with more blood and some kind of organic matter I wish I hadn't seen. Bits of glistening gray stuff. Unseelie, I hope. My clothing is torn and equally plastered with ribbons of flesh and more blood. What in God's name did I do?

I open my eyes and stare levelly at my reflection.

I killed. A wave of horror threatens to engulf me. Who? What terrible things did I do? What sins do I bear?

I inhale slowly, exhale long and even, willing the sick feeling in my stomach and the palpitations in my heart to calm. Horror will accomplish nothing.

I can either give in to fear and give up—or refuse to let it touch me and go on.

I opt for the latter because the former is pointless and destructive and would make me an even greater liability to my world.

After emptying a fuller bladder than I've ever had, I turn on the

tap, splash water on my face, gulp it, swish and spit, then begin
scrubbing with the half-used bar of soap Mallucé didn't finish before he died. I scrub and scrape, then turn and grope blindly for a
towel because the blood is crusted on my skin so thickly that it's
not coming off. I scour my face nearly raw with the hot, wet towel
then plunge my head into the sink and lather my hair with the bar.

A few minutes later, trembling with exertion, I flip my wet hair
back and look into the mirror again.

I study my eyes carefully, spying no hint of madness, no deeply
buried glint of psychopathic glee. Just the wide, green-eyed gaze of
a woman who has no idea what heinous acts her body committed
during the past fifteen hours.

Less revolted by the thought of using Mallucé's toothbrush
than I am by the taste in my mouth—which says volumes about
how horrific it is—I scald the dead vamp's toothbrush under hot
water then squeeze toothpaste on it and brush vigorously, despite
the pain it causes.

When I finish, I rummage through the vanity drawers for floss,
then drop to the floor and begin the agonizing process of cleaning
between them.

I save what comes out, plaster it on a piece of toilet tissue and
examine it.

I ate Unseelie, at the very least. Black feathers. "Please tell me
it wasn't Christian," I whisper.

Laboriously, I strip off my jacket. And frown. My spear is
gone, my shoulder holster empty. Why? Where did it go? Did the
Book stab some hapless person and not bother to take it back?
Surely it wouldn't give away such a powerful weapon! I wonder
again just what the hell I did over the past fifteen hours.

Clenching my teeth, refusing to get waylaid by dangerous
thoughts, I focus on working my shirt over my head, and end up
smearing blood all over my face again. The spear is gone. So much
blood. I shake my head to keep it clear, desperate to strip down to
nudity to leave behind all the incriminating evidence of whatever

I've done, but there's no way Mallucé's pants will fit me. Still, I can change into one of his shirts.

After wiping my face clean again, I crawl into the closet that adjoins the bathroom. I sort through the dramatic, vintage goth clothing until I find a simple black brushed-silk tee and pull it on then lean back against the wall of the closet, frowning, catching my breath, pondering what just happened.

The *Sinsar Dubh* fell asleep.

I'd bet my life on it.

And somehow I'm awake and here again. Just how is that working? If it was so tired that it passed out, why doesn't me moving around wake it up? Is it possible this is what happened the day it killed the Gray Woman—because it's not accustomed to physical form, it quickly wears out and loses its control over me? Does this mean I'm me again and so long as I don't use another spell I'll be okay? Or does it mean once it regains its energy it'll instantly re-imprison me?

I felt it losing control of my body, experienced its rage, overheard its frantic thoughts.

I feel the same as I did after regaining consciousness the day it killed the Gray Woman, only worse, hurting everywhere, and desperately tired. I wonder, in years past, when I slept, did the Book slip out to play? Did I sleepwalk in my youth without ever knowing it? I wish I could ask Mom and Dad. Will the Book think that's what it did, if it regains awareness to find itself in a different location, clean, wearing different clothes?

I sigh. I have no idea what's going on or how long I have. I must make good use of the time. The only other time I lost control, I blacked out and was completely unaware of time passing. This time, I was aware, but locked away. It would be foolish to conclude that I've regained permanent control. I can't take anything for granted where the Book is concerned.

The last memory I have of my actions is the *Sinsar Dubh* taking possession of me as I screamed at Jada to run. I pray she heeded me and ran fast and far enough. If I sacrificed everything to save her only to end up killing her—

I can't even finish that thought.

Barrons. Surely he would have come after me—it. Is he dead? Did I kill him? Again? What did the Book do with its freedom? Surely, it has goals, objectives. But what? Considering that I've carried this thing around inside me all my life, I don't really know much about it other than it was prone to puerile taunts and threats to K'Vruck the world. But what does it *really* want? No doubt, beneath its glib, maniacal behavior lies a sharply focused, brilliant mind.

I force myself to breathe slowly, deeply, trying to sort through my thoughts, but Mallucé's scent permeates the closet with the noxious odor of his cologne and a whiff of decay that clings to his attire, and suddenly I can't get out of there fast enough. The mere scent of him is throwing me back to time spent in a hellish grotto beneath the Burren, and I need to be fully in the here and now.

I leverage myself up using hatboxes and a small trunk for support, stagger from the closet and stumble out into the bedroom, where I sink down against the wall, draw my legs up to my chest, wrap my arms around them and rest my head on my knees.

Life used to be so simple. When we're young, it feels like grand adventures await us around every corner. We're strong, resilient, undamaged. We think our soul mate is headed our way, we'll marry, have babies, and be loved. I bought into that. I thought I'd raise my children with Alina, take shopping excursions to Atlanta, attend PTA meetings, and enjoy family holidays. Spend lazy summer afternoons listening to the music of the gently creaking porch swing beneath slow-paddling fans, sipping a magnolia-drenched breeze and sweet tea, watching my children grow up in a mostly decent, normal world.

Maybe for some people it works that way.

But that was never my destiny.

I think I got twenty-two blissful, trauma-free years only because the rest of it was going to suck so massively. I mean, really, my godawful life was foretold over a thousand years ago by Moreena Bean, a half-mad washerwoman who prophesied that one of the Lane sisters would die young and the other would wish she was dead (yup, feeling that right now), and the younger they were both killed, the better off the world would be. If that's not destiny, what is?

But wait . . . the prophetic washerwoman had also said there were many stones to be tossed into the great loch of the universe, many possibles. And Kat had said we were only at the *beginning* of Mad Morry's predictions. Which implies, despite the dire nature of our current problems, the Earth is going to survive and go on for some time. Humanity is going to make it.

I just need to figure out what my part in ensuring that is.

Am I supposed to kill myself? Is my current age young enough? And on that note, is my sister still really alive? If so, is that why everything went wrong—because neither of us died?

I strip the idea of suicide of all emotion and weigh it as nothing more than an intellectual option. Will it remove all potential threat I present to the world?

If it would terminate the existence of the *Sinsar Dubh*, then unequivocally—yes.

I don't want to die.

A sudden familiar tension grips my body. I stare through the dimly lit room at the door.

Jericho Barrons.

He's alive. I didn't kill him.

And he's *here*.

The door opens and time seems to suspend and spin out in slow motion. I feel like I haven't seen him in a hundred years, perhaps because I was afraid I would never see him again. The Book had control of me for fifteen hours, and since I know it takes him longer than that to return from wherever he's reborn, that means I didn't kill him. Thank heavens. He gets beyond irate when I do, as if somehow it's a personal insult.

He's wearing black leather pants and a white shirt, cuffs rolled up, revealing strong forearms and a thick sliver Celtic cuff. His beautiful face is inscrutable as ever. I use the word "beautiful" but to the rest of the world he's not. The casual observer finds him disturbingly carnal, animal, unsettlingly predatory. The genetic stamp of Jericho Barrons's face was tossed in the gene pool trash-can eons ago. His bone structure is sharp, primal, his brow prom-inent, and he can seem downright feral if you catch a glimpse of him when he thinks he's unobserved. His eyes are so dark they're nearly black, and when he's angry, crimson sparks glitter within. His hair is midnight, slicked back. He has one of the most sym-metrical faces I've ever seen. His body . . . well, I see the lithe grace and power of the beast in him even in his human form.

He glides into the room in that fluid, animalistic way he adopted around me months ago. He recedes from sight then ap-pears again, standing, staring down at me.

Nice shirt, his dark eyes say. He misses nothing. I smell of Mal-lucé and he doesn't like it. I don't like it either but the vamp's shirt was preferable to mine. Barrons is both the most and least com-plex man I've ever known.

Mine was dirty. I bite back a laugh because it doesn't seem ap-propriate to laugh in the middle of such grim circumstances, but it strikes me as bizarrely funny that on the heels of me turning into a full-fledged psychopath, the first words we speak to each other are about my attire.

He sinks down next to me, leans back against the wall, leg and shoulder brushing mine.

"Did you know I was me again?"

"I felt you regain control."

I rub the tattoo on the back of my skull. Though I'd initially been furious he'd branded me with his mark, I've come to appreciate its advantages. "How did you get through all those Unseelie out there?" He doesn't look like he's been in a fight. Or a few thousand.

"The *feth fiada*. A druid spell of invisibility."

I scowl. "You never taught me that one."

"A born snooper like you? Hardly."

"Did I kill anyone?"

"You injured some but the Book appeared to be having a hard time acclimating to controlling your body. Jada is fine, as are your parents."

I narrow my eyes. I'd had far too much blood on my hands, hair, face, and clothing to have merely "injured" people. I study his profile. It doesn't elude me that he answered what should have been a yes or no question with an offer of parallel information that, while pertinent, was deftly evasive. He hadn't lied. But he hadn't told the truth either.

He turns his head and looks at me.

I know I killed, I say levelly.

Then don't waste my time.

Our gazes lock. In his eyes I see a wall I might push through to reveal names, places, and how. But if I get tangled up in who and how I killed, I'll come undone. I must be a smooth flat stone, skipping lightly on a dark lake that could drown me.

A few moments pass and I realize my heartbeat is returning to normal, my stomach no longer feels queasy, and I'm not nearly as tired and sore as I'd been feeling. In fact, I feel . . . good. All because this man sat down next to me. Such a simple thing, such a powerful thing. "Did you ever see that movie *What Dreams May Come*?"

He slices his head to the left.

Barrons always denies watching TV or movies, as if it's too plebeian a pastime for a man of his ilk. "I loved that film."

He gives me a cool look. "What the fuck was there to love about it? They all died. First the children. Then the parents."

I smirk. "I knew you watched it." The reason I'd loved it was because when the wife killed herself, she was sent to Hell to suffer in madness, alone for all eternity. But her husband refused to let that happen. "You came to my couch and joined me in my hell."

He smiles faintly. "Maybe you came to mine."

"Guess it doesn't matter whose couch it is." I lift my hand, hesitate, drop it back to my thigh. He's not a man for physical displays of affection. He's either having sex or not touching. "So, what am I supposed to do?"

He takes my hand, laces our fingers together. His hand is huge and strong and dwarfs mine. I glimpse the black and red ink of a fresh tattoo above the silver cuff, stretching up his arm. "What do you want to do?"

I lean my head against his shoulder. "Leave this world and find another that won't matter if I destroy it until I know for sure that I'm in control."

"Ah. So, you think there are worlds that can be destroyed without mattering," he mocks lightly.

"I could go to a barren planet with no life."

"It doesn't matter what you destroy, but *that* you destroy. There are two types of people in this world: those who can create and those who can't. Creators are powerful, shaping the world around them. All beings crave power over their slice of existence. Those who can't create do one of three things: convince themselves to accept a half-life of mediocrity and seething dissatisfaction, deriving enjoyment from whatever small acts of dominance they manage to achieve over their companions; find a creator to leech onto and exploit to enjoy a parasitic lifestyle; or destroy. One way or another, someone that can't create will find a way to feel in control. Destruction feels like control."

I pull back and look at him. "Your point?"

"You're a creator, not a destroyer. Destruction destroys the destroyer. Always. Eventually. And badly."

"Your point?"

"The *Sinsar Dubh* has leeched onto you. There's no place you can run. The battle goes with you."

"But I could minimize the fallout."

"Only to yourself. You might not care as much if it were a stranger on some other world that the Book killed, but I doubt the stranger would care any less, nor would the people who care about that stranger."

"Okay, not getting this. On the one hand, with the exception of creators, you just told me all people are essentially dickheads. Now you're arguing for those dickheads."

"I argue for nothing. I'm merely stating that whether you destroy here or on another world, you're still destroying. That's your battle—to destroy or not. Once you start splitting hairs, trying to convince yourself some things are more acceptable to destroy, you've already lost the most important war. There's no advantage in moving your battle to unknown terrain."

"You think I should stay here and fight, even if it costs the lives of people I love?"

"Your battle is half won. You're sitting here with me. The *Sinsar Dubh* isn't. Make that permanent."

"But you're not telling me how."

"What does the *Sinsar Dubh* want?"

"I don't know." That's what I'd been wondering before he came in. Trying to figure out its end goal so I could intercept and undermine.

"Yes, you do. It wants to be in the world, living, in control of itself. What do you want?"

"The same thing."

"Why?"

"Because I could be happy if things ever stopped going wrong!"

"Things never stop going wrong. Life isn't about waiting for peace to arrive, it's about learning to thrive in the midst of war. There's always another one on the way." He was silent a moment then said, "Why does the *Sinsar Dubh* want to live?"

"Damned if I know," I mutter. "Because it's greedy? Bored? The alternative is not living?"

"Why do you?"

I look at him. *Because I love people*, I don't say. *And I want to spend the rest of my life with you, see what you do next, celebrate your victories, grieve your losses, make love to you. God, why am I always my clearest only when it looks like I might lose everything?*

Because you still believe you can have everything, his dark eyes say. *You can't. We have nothing. Only the current moment. Once you understand that, you know what's sacred and not, and never lose sight of it again.*

"But *you* have forever. You have every moment."

"No. Like you, I have but this one. Death isn't the only foe that steals from you the things you prize. You think a monster has control of you."

"It does."

"It is in control only by your consent."

Bristling, I unlace my fingers from his, rake my hands through my wet hair and say, "That's not true. I didn't choose the Book. I didn't let it in. It took me as a fetus. There was no consenting or refusing."

"There is now."

"And your beast was *so* easy to subdue." I say, acid-sweet and pissed. He's acting like it should be simple. Like, why haven't I defeated it yet?

"Never said it was. But I did it. And I didn't sit around brooding, vacillating between committing suicide and running away. Both are unforgivable in my book."

"Stay the hell out of my head," I snap.

"How did you regain control?"

I worry my lower lip with my teeth for a moment then admit, "I don't know that I did. It may have simply fallen asleep."

"Wondered if that would happen."

"But I was figuring things out at the same time. It was growing weaker and I was growing stronger."

"And once it has rested?"

"That's the million dollar question. So, how do I fight it?"

"Become it."

I stare at him in disbelief.

"Remember the runes that fortified the Unseelie prison walls? They draw strength from resistance. Don't resist. Become." He stands and extends his hand. "Come."

I push up from the floor. "Where are we going?"

"I'm taking you back to Chester's." He pauses then says, "Where we will contain you with the stones."

I stiffen. "You just gave me a pep talk about fighting it. Now you're going to shut me down? You have no idea what that might do to me, or the Book. It could put us both in suspended animation and I won't be able to fight it."

"It may suspend only the Book."

"Right. Leaving me fully cognizant. Trapped. Forever," I say sharply. I'd accepted this fate once before. But I was making headway. I was certain I could win this battle, if I just had enough time.

"You said yourself you don't know if the Book will seize control of you again the moment it awakens."

My jaw juts. "Maybe I've beat it."

"I don't like this any more than you do, Mac."

"I'm bloody well certain I like it far less," I say heatedly. "You're not the one about to get locked away."

"No, I'm the just the one who has to endure you being locked away. There's no possibility I might be suspended while you suffer. I'll be aware of every bloody moment of it."

I wince. Put that way, it sounds a lot like what he went through with his son.

"Ryodan's out of play, Jada's holding it together by sheer force of will, the *sidhe*-seers are in a complete meltdown at Chester's, Dageus is a major fucking mess, and we have no idea how to stop the black holes. We need something off our plate, and the Book is the thing most likely to cause immediate, catastrophic damage." His dark gaze shutters. "You've not yet done anything as the Book that you won't be able to forgive yourself for," he says carefully. "In time."

I'm still so pissed off by his "off our plate" comment I barely hear him. As if I'm an unappetizing vegetable to be scraped into a Tupperware container and stuck in the fridge. "Then what? I wait passively until you either save the world or don't? And if you do, you'll free me to resume my fight? And if you don't, I'll get sucked into oblivion by a black hole?" I say irritably. I don't want to be locked away. I don't want to be passive. I wasted weeks of my life I can never get back being miserably passive and defeatist. Belatedly, his final comment sinks in and I stare up at him, horrified, because he just made it very clear I've already done something I'm going to hate myself for. My irritation is doused by a crushing wave of remorse. I've killed someone. Someone I knew. Someone that mattered to me. I close my eyes.

"Now you understand why we must do it. Not only is it possible the Book could destroy our planet far more quickly than the black holes, there are things it could do while in possession of your body that would leave you irrevocably scarred. I don't mean physically. Once you're contained, I'll move you to a place where I can remove the stones and you'll have the freedom to fight."

I open my eyes. "What do you mean? What kind of place?" Who did I kill? I fist my hands at my sides, desperate to know. Desperate not to know. He'd specifically said Jada and my parents were "fine." So, it was someone else. Not one of the Nine, because they would be reborn. Sidhe-seers? Children? Innocent bystanders? Christian? Jayne? All of them? Did I slaughter thousands in a single crushing blow?

"A place where your battle can take as long as it must without consequence, without you having to worry about destroying worlds. Even those you think don't matter," he adds dryly.

"And you just so happen to know a place like that?" I narrow my eyes. "Oh, God, you were so certain I'd fail, so sure I'd open the Book that you prepared for it!"

"You had an undiscovered country inside you. That gave you two options: pretend it doesn't exist and never set foot inside it, even though you know it's governed by a maniacal little Hitler determined to chip away at your borders and conquer you—or march in and start a war. I'd have been disappointed had you done anything less."

He'd just put into words exactly how I'd felt from the moment I realized the Book was inside me, and both options had terrified me. I'd begun leaning more and more toward the "starting a war" option. Then, at least, I wouldn't be vacillating. Living in fear of two options would always be harder than biting the bullet and choosing one to confront.

Because living in fear isn't living.

"But you stopped me from taking a spell for your son. I could have marched in then."

He smiles faintly. "I never said I was in a hurry for you to start a war. Come." He extends his hand again.

Instead of taking it, I reach up, lace my fingers in his dark hair and pull his head down. Brush my lips to his, a whisper of a kiss, breath and warmth, barely any friction. I lean against him, motionless, opening all my senses, absorbing the moment, every nuance, committing it to my memory in flawless detail so once I'm trapped in whatever manner I'm about to be trapped, I can recreate him, us together, in my mind. I tip my head back and put all my love in my eyes. Let it pile up and blaze there.

He stares down at me a long moment. A muscle works in his jaw and crimson sparks flare deep in his irises. "Your bloody timing bloody sucks," he says tightly.

"I thought we'd just established this moment is all we have. That means my timing can never suck," I say lightly.

He splays his fingers across my jaw, tilts my head back and

slants his mouth over mine in a hot, hungry kiss that knifes straight to my soul.

When we finally move apart, I slip my hand into his.

He speaks the words of the *feth fiada* and we vanish into the night.

To imprison me. Quite possibly forever.

CAGED

My mother sat on the other side of the bars, crying.

She said she didn't have a choice: her parents were dead, my dad was gone, she had no friends who could handle me, there was no dog that could keep me safe while she went to work, and somebody had to pay our bills.

She told me I was an especially good girl and she knew I couldn't help freeze-framing because I was too young to understand the danger it put us in. She said even though I had a mega brain, certain concepts were still beyond my grasp. I don't think anything was beyond my grasp. I just didn't have any fear.

She told me one day I would be grown up enough that the cage would no longer be necessary. I thought maybe she'd let me out at night when she was home but she said I didn't have the self-discipline yet to risk it. She thought I'd run away. I probably would have.

She wasn't being mean to me.

She was doing what she had to do. For us. She worried about me and was keeping me safe.

Years passed.

We developed routines. Life went on. You don't know things are strange when you don't know any different. She was good to me.

She pushed in food through the same slot in the cage that I used to push out bedpans.

In the evenings, after we ate dinner together on the floor, she brought me bowls of warm soapy water and helped me give myself a bath and clean my hair, which she brushed and braided by reaching through the bars.

We played jacks and cards and she bought me coloring books and crayons and hung my best pictures on the living room walls. On special nights we had popcorn and she rented a movie for us.

My birthdays came and went and I was always so excited because each year it was the very best thing that could possibly be happening to me—I was getting OLDER. We marked the occasion each year with my favorite meal of thick Irish stew and soda bread and creamed corn and chocolate ice cream for dessert, while telling each other bodacious stories about all the thrilling things we would one day do when I was free.

She hung a calendar on the wall behind the new sofa she bought to replace the couch I'd broken, and I watched with shining eyes as she crossed off the weeks and months, knowing each black slash took me one day closer to the last calendar she would ever hang.

Though she was gone all day, she left me well cared for with the TV on, lots of blankets and pillows, and all my favorite food, which we could afford again, and bedpans nearby.

When she came home at night, she'd spend hours with me, reading me stories, telling me about her day and all the wonderful things we were going to do when I was OLDER and she could let me out.

I really thought we were going to make it.

I thought one day the door would swing wide and we'd get busy doing all those things we'd missed.

She said that a lot: that we were going to make up for LOST TIME. I heard that word in all capitals, too, colored the dreary shade of dirty snow.

But I think whenever you put other people in a cage—any kind of cage—you start to think of them as less real.

19

"Pleased to meet you, hope you guess my name"

JADA

Jada sat in Ryodan's office, her arms folded behind her head, long legs outstretched, boots kicked up on the desk, body thrumming with restless energy. Killing time, waiting for something to happen, wasn't one of her strong suits. In truth, it wasn't a suit in her deck of cards at all, it was incarceration in a high security prison. Yet here she sat and would continue to sit for days, if it meant getting Mac back.

Cruce had sifted out some time ago, instructing them to return the spear with all haste while he watched the Unseelie princess, and the instant the Book summoned her, he'd sift back and alert them. Christian had vanished hot on his heels, muttering something about seeing to the needs of his clan.

She and Barrons had been analyzing strategies to get the spear back to Mac when he abruptly stiffened, as if listening to something only he could hear. *We may just have gotten lucky,* he said after a moment. *I sense only Mac, nothing of the* Sinsar Dubh. *Remain here. I'm going to go get her.*

And do what?

Bring her back here to contain her with the stones. Easier than trying to get four of us in and out of Mallucé's.

Jada protested, *But if she's in control, she's fighting it. And winning. You can't shut her away now. She needs time.*

Have you forgotten the Book has the ability to manipulate precisely that element? I suspect Cruce's prediction of its moves is correct. With the spear, the Sinsar Dubh *will hunt the queen. If it gains her power, too, it will be unstoppable. It's now or never, Jada.*

With every ounce of her being, Jada wanted to disagree. She despised cages of any kind and putting Mac in one was the last thing she wanted to do. Once something was shelved, it became far too easy to keep pushing that item back further and further until, draped with cobwebs and dust, it was forgotten.

Never. And you bloody well know it, Barrons growled.

She said, *I'll summon*—Barrons roughly clamped his hand over her mouth, cutting off her words.

Don't say his name. Don't even think it. Merely saying it summons him. I don't want that Fae fuck anywhere near Mac. He has far too much to gain by eliminating her, and nothing to lose. We do this with my men and no one else.

He'd vanished, leaving her alone in Ryodan's glass house.

Now she glanced around, shrugged, stood up, and set about ransacking it.

Only to find his office as void of personal information about the man as the man himself. The piles of paperwork he used to have were nowhere to be seen, his file cabinets window-dressing, stocked with empty folders, confirming her suspicion that he'd never actually been doing anything other than torturing her. There wasn't even a single pen or pencil in his drawer.

She narrowed her eyes, remembering the hidden panel where he'd once kept her contract, wondering how many other hidden panels the man had. She'd searched the obvious places. Ryodan was anything but obvious.

She kicked his chair back, knelt on the floor and began feeling around on the desk: top, sides, legs. After a moment she closed her eyes and turned off her brain, dumping her entire awareness into her hands, feeling for the slightest anomaly. It didn't take her long to find one.

When the panel slid out, she opened her eyes and resumed her seat in the chair. Before her was a shallow drawer with row after row of smooth, square black buttons. She began punching them in order, glancing intently around the office, waiting for something to happen.

The monitors. The bloody monitors. Of course the man-who-would-be-king had a spyglass to watch every inch of his club while perched high atop his lofty throne.

She punched, watched, and punched again as various private areas of the club appeared and passed from view. Nothing much interesting going on.

Wait, what?

She went back two buttons. She'd just caught a glimpse of Kat, who'd been missing for weeks.

There she was again, with Kasteo. They reclined, side by side, on forty-five-degree benches, before an enormous mirror, doing dumbbell wide-flies in perfect rhythm.

Katarina was developing biceps.

Lats, too.

She stared in disbelief. Delicate, serene, empathic Katarina McLaughlin was living at Chester's, deep underground, molding herself into a warrior? How had she persuaded one of the Nine, especially the legend that didn't speak, to teach her anything? Did Ryodan know she was here?

Of course he did. They were his monitors.

Her scowl turned thunderous. Kasteo was training Kat, yet Ryodan refused to teach her a bloody thing. She was far better raw material than cautious, slender Katarina McLaughlin. She was a freaking Valkyrie, forged of steel with the sword to prove it!

"You are *so* on my shit list, Ryodan." She was abruptly in exactly the right mood to cut off his head without puking, without regretting it one bit. Maybe even enjoying it. Hacking it off over and over again until he agreed to set her up with her own trainer.

She punched another button. Watched. Inhaled sharply and punched that one off. Level 4 was no place to get distracted by right now. But she'd just glimpsed up close and personal one of the Nine she'd encountered only a single time before and from a distance—the day Barrons had brought his men to the abbey to bust Pri-ya Mac out. The day all Nine of them had stalked in, some heavily hooded, others bareheaded with burning eyes, all toting automatic weapons.

She pressed another button.

And froze.

She wouldn't have thought anything could stun her more than the oddity of Kat with Kasteo, but this new vision shocked her into muteness and immobility.

When she finally managed to unfreeze her tongue, she whispered, "Holy leaping Lazarus—he's *alive*?"

And no one had told her. How was this even possible? Just whose body had Ryodan sent home to the Highlands to be buried?

She narrowed her eyes. Christian was with him, a tall, dark shadow, wings furled, standing a dozen feet away. Christian knew. Who else? Everyone but her?

The door whisked open and Barrons stood in the opening, with Mac at his side, Fade and Lor behind him.

She stood instantly, easing the panel closed with her thigh, counting on them being too preoccupied to glance up at the monitors. Few people looked up. Most people tunneled blithely through their days, noticing only what was at eye level.

"Dani," Mac said with a faint smile. "It's good to see you."

Once she'd called Mac TP, short for "that person," because each time she'd said or even thought her name, her heart hurt. But last night they'd talked like they once used to, like peas in the

Mega Pod, almost like sisters. Mac had forgiven her, sacrificed herself to save her, and the block of ice around her heart had begun to thaw.

"It's Ja— Hey, Mac." Really, what did it matter? Not only was it inefficient to constantly keep correcting her, Mac knew she was different now and had accepted that. The primary reason she'd rechristened herself Jada was to encourage *sidhe*-seers who'd known her as a troublesome teen to accept her as their leader; a thing they'd never have done if she'd introduced herself as the girl they so recently knew as the swaggering, cocky, insouciant Mega.

"Dani, honey, turn off the monitors," Lor said tightly.

Her nostrils flared and she shot him a frosty look. They should have told her what was going on, and Mac had a right to know, too. Either they were a team or they weren't. Clearly, they weren't. "I didn't say you could call me Dani. Or honey. Only people who don't keep secrets from me get to call me those things. It's Jada to you." Then she turned the warmth back on and said to Mac, "Are you okay?"

Scowling, Lor stalked to the desk, punched buttons, slammed the panel closed then moved back to the door, where he stood, legs wide, powerful arms folded across his chest.

"Been better," she said with a note of weariness in her voice. Her gaze dipped to Jada's cuff as she moved into the office and joined her near the desk. When she reached for her, Jada stiffened, but Mac only caught a stray curl of her hair and smoothed it behind her ear. Then she said, "I missed you."

Jada shifted uncomfortably. "Dude. Space. You just saw me last night."

A slow smile curved Mac's lips. "I never thought the day would come I'd actually be happy to have you 'dude' me. I meant before that. I'm glad you're back. Glad we're back. I missed us," she said simply. Her gaze dropped to the cuff again. "The ZEWs are still out there and so is the Sweeper. The cuff's what keeps them from being able to track you. Don't take it off."

Jada nodded.

"And listen to Barrons. Do what he says. He's got a plan."

Jada inclined her head.

"And for heaven's sake, try *talking* to Ryodan sometime. Have an actual conversation. I think he'd do anything you wanted, if you just asked him. Nicely. Barrons is the same way. Difficult to manage, yet manageable if you know the right buttons to push."

"Barrons is right here, Ms. Lane, and Barrons doesn't have buttons," Barrons said stiffly, and Lor snickered.

Jada glanced at Barrons, wondering if he'd told Mac what they were planning to do. Or were they supposed to take her by surprise? She discarded that possibility. Barrons would have already given her one of the stones, if that were his intention.

From the way Mac was doling out the big sister advice, she suspected she knew, but said anyway, "You're on board with this?" as she searched Mac's gaze.

Green eyes darkened to pools of obsidian. "Not a fucking chance in hell, you stupid cunt."

And Mac vanished.

20

"I was hungry and it was your world"

AOIBHEAL

*H*er name was Zara.
His was a symbol too complex for her mind to absorb.
She was one of her race's revered healers.
He was a god-king, half mad from long solitude.

Tethered to something much vaster than mere rock and soil, acolyte to the great, wise Soul-Thing that pervaded the universes, Zara was connected to all, bound to none.

She was wild and free, a powerful witch of the forests and stars and seas, her every breath filled with joy. Her name was a prayer, uttered by her people in times of need.

She always came: a fevered child to be tended, a wounded animal to mend, a tree damaged by storm. She healed, nurtured, repaired, and, when necessary, helped those whose time it was to become the next thing. Death was but a doorway to another life. She could see the souls of the living, their colors, shapes, and sizes, ailments and strengths. She could feel the soul of the All. Everything fit precisely where it was, had been, and was going.

And if being bound to none was sometimes lonely, on nights when she peeked through windows as her people nestled down

and made love, and children and futures, and mating season came
for the animals she protected, being connected to the All made it
worth the price.

Or so she thought.

Until he came.

♪

Aoibheal shook her head sharply, splintering ice with the motion.
It tinkled like shards of broken glass when it crashed to the floor
in the king's black velvet darkness.

"No," she whispered.

The moment she'd stepped into the mirror, it seemed to absorb
her, drawing her into a memory bubble planted deep within its
silvery interior, and suddenly she was somewhere else, racing
through a misty, triple-canopied forest, laughing, and being chased
by a flock of brilliant, winged, inquisitive *T'murras,* darting
through the leaves.

Somewhere she'd known.

Somewhere she'd rued ever leaving.

She'd recognized the place with the fundamental essence of her
being. She'd been born there. Fashioned from the elements and
minerals and waters of the planet itself.

The king had brought the *T'murra*s to her world, the first gift
he'd ever given her.

Had he chosen anything else, she'd not have been so easily
disarmed. There'd been no material goods for which she'd hungered. But he'd selected brilliantly winged living creatures, birds
with crimson and gold beaks that were wont to echo odd words
and phrases, sometimes stringing them together in ways that
seemed to almost make sense, and sang an exquisite melody—but
only at sunrise and sunset, as if they, like her, saluted the morning
and welcomed the night.

Impossible for one such as she to resist.

She'd been touched, beguiled, delighted by his gift. She'd

thought he chose them for her because he, too, loved the small things of the world.

"Zara," she whispered, cracking the ice again.

She glanced around the vast starlit chamber that was twice the size of an ancient Roman Coliseum, its floor scattered with exotically spiced, velvety dark petals. Tiny black diamonds floated on the air, midnight fireflies winking with blue flame. Between towering slabs of black ice that stretched to a starlit night sky, an enormous, velvet-draped bed filled most of the chamber. On the far wall, a blue-black fire sent tendrils licking up to the ceiling where they exploded in a fantastic nebula shimmering with blue vapors.

There was only one other piece of furniture in the room.

A small table upon which perched a translucent beaker, filled with a golden liquid, steaming at the narrow mouth.

Gathering her cloak around her, she crushed spicy petals beneath her feet as she glided toward it, feeling an unshakable sense of deft manipulation that chafed her.

Next to the beaker was a sheaf of thick vellum with three words on it.

DARE YOU REMEMBER?

She'd been wrong.

He'd known she would go through his mirror.

Why hadn't he simply incarcerated her there to begin with, and poured whatever potion he'd chosen down her unwilling throat?

She'd been his concubine. Who knows how many potions she'd willingly drunk for him? Who could say how they'd changed her?

Yet, he'd forced nothing upon her.

Merely set her on the path of choice.

A fluttering, high in the corner of the starry sky, caught her eye, at too great a distance to make out detail. She doubted anything was in his chamber at this hour by chance. Turning her back on the beaker, she moved to the edge of the bed and gazed up, waiting motionless for so long she froze solid again.

She'd heard their love had burned so fiercely there'd been nothing they wouldn't do for each other. That they'd traveled the Great All together, spinning breathtaking new worlds.

She'd heard.

She had no memory of it. Nor did she want it. She wanted no part of him.

She knew who she was now, and that her past had indeed been stolen from her. It was enough.

As she shattered the coating of ice, the fluttering thing at the starry ceiling dove for her, its jewel-toned wings spreading in a wide brilliant span, bold and rich against the sleek black walls of the king's boudoir.

The *T'murra* settled lightly, with a soft rustling of wings, on her left shoulder and began to peck playfully at the fur trim of her cloak.

Damn the bastard!

His idea of renewing a courtship, no doubt. Reminding her of their beginnings. Trying to seduce her into wanting to know more.

As the *T'murra* hooked its talons into the fabric of her cloak, they iced together, cracking only when she finally stirred herself to return to the beaker.

The sheaf of vellum now bore new words.

For the Light Court, the Cauldron of Forgetting
Because they are fools and will use it

For the Dark Court, the Elixir of Remembering
Because they are fearless and will choose it

She'd heard myths that such an elixir existed. It was claimed that even those who chose not to drink from the cauldron lost memories over the eons. The elixir allegedly cleared the cobwebs of disuse from the mind and restored each and every one to its proper time and place. It was said the ancient king drank it daily, refusing to yield even a single memory, and that this infinity of knowledge contributed to his fits of madness. Among the Fae, there were stories about everything, making it impossible to discern fable from fact. She'd never believed the elixir was real.

But she'd been wrong about many things.

She stared bitterly down at the beaker and its golden, misting contents, absently stroking the *T'murra* on her shoulder, which clucked as it began to nibble delicately at the lobe of her ear.

She'd been torn from her life as the mortal concubine, turned Fae then transformed into their queen. Why? Had someone groomed her to become the queen because she'd been deemed suitably malleable? And if she disappointed her groomer, would he simply erase her memory again? She'd had her memories stripped away, not once as she'd feared, sixty thousand years ago, but obviously multiple times, given how long ago she'd been the king's concubine. Her very existence, everything she was, had been thieved from her, repeatedly. How many lifetimes had she lost? Only to be left priding herself on being the ruler of a race that was not even hers!

If she believed the king, Cruce had done this to her and she would never have left her lover of her own volition. If she believed the king, Cruce had forced her to write a note decrying the king as a monster, and if she drank from the beaker she would be in love with him again.

She didn't want to be in love with him again.

Love had made her a Fae pawn, to be batted back and forth across their manipulative chessboard, damaged, altered, changed. *Look—she's a pawn! No, she's a queen! Oh, wait she's a pawn again! What say we make her a rook next?*

And for what?

To end up here.

Alone. A woman whose existence had been so fractured by magic elixirs, she no longer knew who she was.

Narrowing her eyes, she studied the beaker.

She had no desire to accept anything the king offered. But if she didn't drink it, she would spend the rest of her life—which might be considerably shorter than she'd expected if the Song of Making wasn't found—as no more than she was right now, a bitter Fae queen who resented the mantle she carried, resented the very people she'd been appointed to rule. If the Earth died, she would die as that woman. Wondering. Never knowing.

She sighed. On her shoulder, the *T'murra* clucked with seeming sympathy.

"Zara," she murmured.

The *T'murra* cocked its head and gave her a quizzical glance. *"Awk! Zara,"* it squawked, as if agreeing.

It had been Zara's joy that had drawn the king to her. Her passion, her wildness and unrestrained immersion in everything she did. That, too, had been tucked within the memory in the mirror.

She'd never known such . . . buoyancy of being. Not that she could recall. She couldn't even quite fathom it. Could only examine its weft and weave, a dispassionate observer. What good could lost memories of such feelings possibly do her? She was Fae now, capable of only shallow sensation. It might do no more than torment her with dim impressions of a life she could never feel again. Which was preferable—bitterness or an eternal sense of loss? Wouldn't both result in bitterness?

The concubine had not wanted to be turned Fae. When a mortal became Fae it lost its soul.

Zara had prized her soul above all else. And now had none.

She picked up the beaker and turned it in her hand, this way and that, eyeing the golden contents, the iridescent mist seeping from the narrow mouth, analyzing pros and cons, incentive and disincentive, reaching an impasse every time.

In the end she turned off her mind and made the decision with what mild emotion was left to her.

She tipped the beaker to her lips and drank.

21

"I am the knuckle, bow down and buckle"

MAC

The eviction from my body is instantaneous.

The moment I hear myself speaking words I'm not saying and never would, I'm seized by the *Sinsar Dubh*'s gargantuan will, scraped from my body, and stuffed back into my box.

Never think me weak, the *Sinsar Dubh* purrs. *I got you, babe. ALWAYS.*

As it crams me into the cramped, dark interior and slams the lid, I think—bullshit! There *is* no secret compartment inside my body that I can be stuffed into!

Just like there never actually was a book, open or closed, inside me. The *Sinsar Dubh* painted two elaborate illusions for me, and did one hell of a sales job. I infused both illusions with my belief and was thereby imprisoned. Not by the Book.

By my own gullibility.

Belief is reality.

In here, disembodied, I apprehend that truth in a moment of exquisite clarity and realize it's the keystone of existence. Not just mine. Everyone's. What's the surest way to be victimized? Believe yourself a victim. To win? Believe yourself a champion.

I *believe* myself a body, kick the lid off my nonexistent box with it, and the boundaries around me crumble into the nothing it really is.

I stand tall, my fury boundless for too many reasons to count but I'll start with: I'd been basking in a warm exchange with Jada. The first one in what seemed a small, painful eternity. She'd let me call her Dani. And deep in her eyes I'd glimpsed a welcome flash of that old familiar fire. My girl was in there. And getting closer to coming out.

Then my mouth had called her a "stupid cunt."

Yep. That's enough to thoroughly piss me off.

I hate that word. No idea why. I just do. And the instant hurt in her eyes, the unguarded emotion that preceded her intellect processing that the Book had taken me over again, had utterly slayed me. I have no doubt she'll understand *I* didn't mean it, but that's not the point. It just leads me to my second point: my psychopathic intruder deceived me.

Again!

How many times will I fall victim to its endless mindfuck?

What is *wrong* with me? It's not like it can cast a spell on me. I'm it. It's me. It can only try to control me with deceit and lies. And it keeps working!

I expand my awareness, feather into my limbs, settle behind my eyes and look out.

I may be free of the box, but the Book has full control of my body. I can feel my limbs, peer out through my eyes, but I can't control any of it. I'm a passive, straitjacketed observer.

My hand is around Jada's throat, shaking her violently. I can't see it because it's invisible, but I feel my fingers deep in the flesh of her throat as she dangles a foot above the floor.

Right. I called her a cunt and now I'm strangling her. My fury multiplies.

I permitted you to stay and watch her die, the *Sinsar Dubh* gloats.

Permitted, my ass.

I'm here and I'm not leaving and her dying is never happening. Dani is what I opened the Book for and I will destroy it for her, too. I gather all my will and focus it on the hand around her throat.

LET GO LET GO LET GO, I will with the full force of my rage.

NEVER, the *Sinsar Dubh* thunders back, flattening me, crushing me paper thin, nearly blasting me from my passive presence in my limbs.

On Jada's throat, my fingers tighten cruelly. She chokes, clawing at my arm.

How can the Book be so strong when it was recently so weak? I focus again on my hand, zero in on a single finger, stoking my rage. If I can affect even one finger, that'll prove to me that I can—

A strong arm hooks my throat from behind and yanks hard, choking off my air. The Book instantly releases my grip on Jada, realizing belatedly that although it had made my body invisible, suspending her in the air had given its position away.

I seize upon the fact with interest. It's fallible. It makes mistakes.

The Book uses my lips to shape soundless words, and suddenly a dozen duplicate versions of me spring into existence, cramming the office with identical Macs. I realize dimly that I look like hell, assuming we all look alike.

Lor and Fade go into instant battle mode, attacking versions of me.

"I've got the real one, she's still invisible!" Barrons roars.

That may be true, but the other Macs are fighting like banshees, leaping on Lor's and Fade's backs, kicking, punching. The Book is either capable of throwing glamour that actually has substance or weaving a highly sophisticated illusion of it that convinces the others they're actually interacting with it. Whichever it is, the end result is the same. Time seems to suspend a moment while I apply this information to my sister, Alina. Was she, too, nothing more than one of these types of illusions? Never back from the dead at all, merely an elaborate ruse that fooled everyone? If I questioned one of the duplicate Macs, would they, too, be fully programmed with pertinent information like Alina was? Now that the Book had what it wanted, did that mean Alina had already ceased to exist?

The Book doesn't fight the arm around my throat, instead it stabs viciously back past my rib cage, and I feel the spear sink into Barrons's body. It must have seized it from Jada's thigh sheath at the same time it grabbed her by the throat—in the instant that, stunned by my transition, she'd hesitated and didn't kick up into the slipstream fast enough. I'd missed that part because I was occupied destroying my box and discovering my power. I hear a soft hiss of breath, then Barrons growls and his hold on my neck loosens.

The Book ducks and twists from his grasp, scrambles away, and plasters back against the wall. I try desperately to turn my eyes to the left, to see how badly I've injured Barrons, but the Book doesn't cooperate. From the corner of my eye I see him move, lunge to his feet again, and heave a sigh of relief. The last time I'd driven my spear into him, he'd died.

Suddenly the many Macs go motionless and begin to chime an ear-splitting melody that is so wrong, so painful, that everyone in the office, including the Book, claps hands to ears, wincing. The hellish, crystalline symphony builds to an excruciating crescendo. I feel the horrific vibration deep in my bones.

The glass walls of the office rumble and begin to crack with the sound of thunder rolling, the floor beneath me begins to shudder, and abruptly it collapses beneath us in an explosion of glass.

Clawing air, I plunge to the dance floor below and slam into the floor hard. My body rolls, scrambles up in the midst of a tangle of humans and Seelie who trample one another in a desperate dash to escape the shower of glass.

Barrons hits the floor a dozen feet away, landing on top of a club patron brutally decapitated by a sheet of jagged falling glass. Slipping in blood, he bounds to his feet and roars, "Where the fuck did she go?"

Lor crashes into a knot of screaming women and Fade slams into a table next to him, shattering it with his weight.

"She vanished again," Lor snarls.

"Find her," Jada shouts from somewhere in the slipstream. "She took the spear back. We have to stop her before it's too late!"

They'll never find me. I'm invisible.

And the Book already has me halfway to the door.

As I'm unwillingly steered into the night, I try once again to exert control over my body. Furiously, I will my feet to stop moving. Cast away the spear. For whatever reason, having the spear makes me more dangerous. That's reason enough to get rid of it.

Nothing happens. I can't influence my body at all. What am I doing wrong? What's the missing ingredient? And what didn't Barrons tell me? Why didn't he warn me that the Book has some deadly plan it's trying to implement? Perhaps I could figure out some way to stop it. If I could figure out how to move.

I shake my inner head and sigh. I know why he didn't tell me. The same reason he didn't tell me who I killed. He didn't want to give me more to worry about. He figured I had enough on my plate, and I do. Either that or he anticipated what I didn't: that the Book was simply playing me again, and any information he shared with me, the Book might get, too.

And it *was* playing me.

How did it con me so easily? Why did I risk letting Barrons near me in the first place? I know the *Sinsar Dubh* is the ultimate deceiver. Why did I blithely allow Barrons to take me straight back into the middle of the people I cared about? I should have known better!

Why do I keep falling for its deceptions? And why is my belief not enough to override the Book's beliefs? How does its force of will continue to supersede mine?

It occurs to me the answer must lie within the very definition of its nature, and mine, so I begin to tally the differences.

I'm good. It's evil.

I'm compassionate. It's savage.

I love. It hates.

No, I can't even say it hates, just that it has an enormous superiority complex from which stem two mildly emotional states: rage when impeded and glee when full of itself for attaining one of its goals. It's not capable of any true degree of—

A nonexistent lightbulb pops on in my nonexistent head. That's it! I buy into its deceptions every time because of my *emotions*. Love, hope, desire, fear, doubt, confusion blind me. And it keeps winning because it has none.

How do I fight it? I'd asked Barrons.

Become it, he'd said.

I thought he'd meant I should participate to some degree in its violence and savagery, deceive it into believing I'd succumbed fully to its influence, then strike when it least expected it.

But that's not what he'd meant at all.

He'd meant *become* it.

Just like it.

WE ARE DESIRE, LUST, GREED, AND THE PATH WE CHOOSE TO SUPREMACY, the Book had said as it feigned falling asleep.

The *Sinsar Dubh* was appetite and ambition, nothing more, capable of only vague impressions of feelings, leaving it free to coolly dissect and analyze everything around it. While I was preoccupied with my emotions, the Book had nothing in its mind at all but a hunger to figure out how to exploit me. Its path to "supremacy" was unimpeded by the slightest distraction. What an enormous advantage! And so long as I felt, it would always have that advantage, always be able to remain one step (or ten!) ahead of me, merely by keeping me in an emotional tizzy, too confused to focus fully. Emotion diluted my focus!

I snarl silently. Fucker. It used that very thing it lacked against me.

At least now I understood why the past few months had been such a wasteland of foggy confusion. It was always subtly dicking with me. Who can say what subliminal messages it fed me, whispered in my inner ear, perhaps even as I slept. I may never know to what extent it has been able to eavesdrop on me and tinker with my internal hardware, but I do know one thing: I will never be myself so long as this tick is latched into my skin.

As the Book passes the tumbled east wall of Chester's, it spies a man and woman, walking slowly, holding hands. Invisible, they don't even know I'm there until the Book grabs both their heads, and muttering spells, crashes their skulls together, melding their faces at the cheeks. Then it shoves them together more, joining them at the hips, ribs, thighs. They scream as they're slowly, inexorably, fused skin-to-skin, bone-to-bone, into an awkwardly conjoined twin.

Then the Book just walks away, leaving the grotesque pair tottering about in the street, screaming. It laughs with my mouth, turns my head and glances back, purrs a spell, and instantly the gruesome twin is turned inside out; intestines and organs where their skin once was, mouths, ears, and eyes trapped within.

The macabre heap collapses to the cobbled pavement, where their now external hearts pulse wetly. The Book leaves them like that, alive.

Walks away, giggling.

The old me would have been overcome with horror, and while I was reeling, the Book would no doubt have driven another knife into me and twisted.

The new me observes with dispassionate calm: distraction/irrelevant/discern its true aim/impede it.

After a long moment in which I make no response, it probes,

Mac-KAY-la, in a singsong voice. *I know you're IN there.
T-T-T-Tea for two and two for tea, me for me and you for me . . .
did you like that one? I did it just for you.*

I say nothing.

*Pretending not to care? You can't fool me. You bleed for every-
thing. You were born to be bled. Born to be RIDDEN, until there's
nothing left of you but bones. Broken horses DIEDIEDIE.*

It had always mocked me for caring. While goading, pushing,
prodding, trying to make me feel even more emotion.

Don't talk to it, the Dreamy-Eyed Guy had said. *Never talk to
it.* More recently he'd cautioned, *It's not about eating the candy,
it's about giving away words—even that broody ass poet's.* He'd
told me over and over: do not engage. Not even with rhymes to
drown it out. Perhaps there were many Fae things one should
never, *ever* open a dialogue with.

After all, how had the Book finally worn me down?

By going silent.

Silence can't be interpreted. It can't be anticipated. It gives
away nothing. And in most people, prolonged silence instills unease. We fill it up with the very best or worst of our imagination.
As Ryodan said, the wise man is the silent one.

Each time I'd conversed with the *Sinsar Dubh,* I'd leaked information about myself, what mattered to me, what didn't, intention-
ally or not. The Book had learned something about me every time
I opened my mouth. Perhaps it had even learned from my dreams.

Barrons was right. I'd been its willing victim. By my consent,
I'd engaged, interacted, let it gaslight and disorient me until I had
no clue which end was up, then once I'd lost my bearings, I'd been
easy to point whichever direction it wanted.

If I had a body, I would draw my first deep breath since the
moment it evicted me. I understand now. I know what I have to
do. Anger was never the answer. It was the precise wrong approach.

I stop looking out from behind eyes I can't blink, detach from limbs I can't control, and retreat into myself, eliminating all distraction so I can give one hundred percent focus to my aim. I sink deep into the belly of my body, draw in, small and fetal.

It can make itself invisible.

I can, too.

I *believe* myself undetectable to the *Sinsar Dubh*. I devote all my will to that thought then get down to ferreting out and stripping away my emotion, peeling myself down to only those things that are ferocity, power, and will.

Distantly, the Book continues to taunt me but I tune it out. I can't stop it, so there's no point in paying attention to it. I must do my work, and return ready.

It takes time, it's slow going at first, but the more I butcher myself, the simpler it becomes.

I focus like a laser, slicing away every ounce of compassion and mercy I possess. I obliterate kindness, love, laughter, and joy. I scorch doubt and fear from my being. Every shade of terror, anger, frustration, and rage gets burned away. I gouge out confusion, which is so frequently an emotional state, not a mental one. I eradicate guilt, shame, even mild consternation.

I go even further.

I char hope into ash. I don't need it. Hope postulates a tomorrow. There is only this moment, and the one that focuses most fully on this moment will win.

I singe even desire from my essence, as that, too, could be used against me.

I hack ruthlessly at the finest parts of me, those things that make me *feel*, those things that make me *alive*—something the Book can never be, and it *knows* it and it frustrates it to be so empty, so it tortures and destroys everyone around it—until I, too, am cold and dead: savagery wed to resolution.

I find it startlingly . . . pleasant . . . to strip myself down to this unfeeling core as if it's always been there, waiting for me. I have a skeleton inside my skeleton and it's made of pure titanium.

I know what it is, where it came from: the rape of the Unseelie princes. They'd made me feel powerless, helpless, a useless piece of trash to be desecrated and crushed beneath their heel when they were finished amusing themselves with me. As if I were a plastic Barbie doll to be violated and broken and tossed away. And, as I'd laid there in the gutter, seeing myself through their eyes, as the complete irrelevance they'd considered me, I'd *hungered* to be the predator they were. The one standing. The one destroying.

I'd thought they'd destroyed me.

They hadn't.

They'd made me stronger. A beast of pure instinct and savagery had been born in that gutter that day.

I'd been afraid of it. I was no longer.

Barrons was right.

There *is* a monster inside me.

And she's beautiful.

22

"She is benediction, she is addicted to thee"

AOIBHEAL

The Elixir of Remembering worked in similar fashion to the passing of the True Magic from the Fae queen to her successor, with three significant differences: one, the elixir restored memories, while the passage of the matriarchal power contained no memories, just magic and lore; two, the elixir didn't immobilize the recipient while it was fully absorbed; and three, the memories from the elixir were integrated far more quickly and seamlessly than the queenly power.

On the day she'd been chosen to become the fading queen's successor, the nearly transparent matriarch had summoned Aoibheal to her boudoir, pressed both palms to her breast and passed the True Magic into her body, where it had expanded and settled. Aoibheal had been immobilized for several long minutes, unable to speak or move while her consort, V'lane, stood at her side, guarding her during that period of vulnerability.

She'd had to acquaint herself with her newfound power.

Young queens were not powerful queens. Time was necessary to sort through and study the many legends, myths, and magic at her disposal. It had been human decades before she'd come into her own.

The elixir worked quite differently. She'd thought her memories had been stolen. They hadn't. They'd been faded to mere shadows without substance, outlines with no content, and as the golden liquid permeated her essence, those shadows solidified, took shape and became accessible again.

Perhaps because she'd once known the memories, each and every one, they were easier to absorb than foreign, heretofore unknown facts. There was no sudden rigidity as an enormous amount of information was reanimated in her consciousness, no sense of being accosted or overwhelmed; on the contrary, she felt made whole again. At peace in a way she'd not known in her entire existence as a Fae. As if she'd been walking around with her most important parts amputated, then suddenly they were restored, melding effortlessly back into her body again.

Fire to his ice, frost to her flame.

No! She had no desire to see those memories yet.

She wanted her origins first. She wanted to access that time in her life before *he'd* come into it, the carefree, wild years during which the memory secreted in the king's towering Silver had told her she'd been happy and free.

Ah, there she was.

Zara, witch and healer, connected to all, chestnut-skinned and barefoot, she raced across a field of flowers toward her home. Her hair was long, dark, spiraling in glossy curls to her waist. Her eyes flashed with ebony fire and her short shift was the many bold colors of *T'murra* wings. The tattoos of her clan curved up her legs, fanned across her shoulders and down her spine.

She had family, four generations beneath a simple yet expansive roof: grandparents and parents, siblings and nieces, though no children of her own. Although mortal, they were a long-lived people, surviving well into their hundredth year. As the first memory the king had given her insinuated, she'd loved her life, known and treasured every inch of her small world.

She'd even loved him. That, she now knew without doubt.

But her restored memories were absolutely identical to the True Magic in a single, cruel way.

She could visit and study each one.

But she couldn't feel them at all.

She'd acquired facts, void of context. It was like reading a human novel about a fictional character's life. It was why the Fae had no books, didn't write things down. They derived no sensation from reading.

She had her answer. The loss of who she'd once been was permanent because she had become Fae. Once, she'd lived vibrantly. Now she could only do the equivalent of read about it and wonder how such passion had felt. Knowing that she'd had it and never would again.

What point was there in the king pushing her to restore her memory? She could never be Zara, never be the woman he'd loved to distraction and destruction. That woman was gone, dead, could not be reanimated.

As she'd feared, as the Fae queen with or without the full complement of her memory, the end result was the same.

"Bitterness," she said and sighed.

"Awk! Bitterness!" the *T'murra* perched on her shoulder agreed.

23

"There's a bad moon on the rise"

JADA

She erupted from the slipstream at top speed and nearly crashed into one of the pillars in the alcoved entrance of Barrons Books & Baubles.

Reconvene at the bookstore, Barrons had ordered before vanishing from Chester's.

She'd raced through Dublin faster than she ever managed to navigate the slipstream before, but Barrons, Lor, and Fade still beat her there and were pacing impatiently before the door.

As she skidded to a halt inches from a column, Barrons growled, "About damn time."

She bristled. "It's not my fault you haven't taught me how to move as fast as you. Barrons, we have to summon—"

"Don't say it!" he hissed. "I told you, we don't fucking need him."

"But we don't know where she's going. Plan 'We may have just gotten lucky' was a total bust. That means *his* plan"—she was careful not to say Cruce's name—"is back on the table."

"I know where the Book is going," Barrons said coolly. "Fae fuck thought he was being clever. He wasn't. Come." He whirled and stalked down the alley to the rear of BB&B. She loped to catch up, with Lor and Fade bringing up the rear.

"Where?" she demanded.

Barrons tossed over his shoulder, "Analyze: sifting inside the place is impossible, the stones can't be sensed there, the quarters are too tight for an army, it's near enough that Cruce believed we could get there from Chester's before Mac could arrive there from Mallucé's—an assumption he should never have made—and therein lies a way to summon the Seelie Queen."

Jada slapped the criteria up on her mental bulletin board.

"Substitute 'concubine' for Seelie Queen," Barrons suggested.

She hissed, disgusted she hadn't riddled it out sooner, "The White Mansion."

"Refine further. Where?"

She rapidly sorted through everything she'd learned about the place during her brief sojourn inside with Christian, came up empty-handed and told him irritably, "I've not seen enough of the mansion to isolate a preference for any one location over another."

Barrons said, "Even if you had, you don't think like a man. Were I the Unseelie King who'd built an infinite house for my woman, I wouldn't want to have to go looking for her every bloody time I wanted to see her. I'd have a way to summon her. And I know where I'd want her. The Book is headed for the concubine's bedchamber."

Then they were at the brick wall, behind the bookstore, at the very spot she'd once made the decision that had cost her five and a half years of her life.

"He kept calling her 'the queen' so I was thinking it had to be somewhere in Faery," Jada groused. Cruce had been doing it deliberately to mislead, and it had been effective.

"I made select comments to which he responded, yielding more information than he'd intended," Barrons said. "He needs us. He can't touch the spear. He can't kill the queen. Withholding information was his only leverage."

"We can't afford to be wrong."

"I spoke with Alina, while waiting for you. She confirmed the *Sinsar Dubh*'s presence at this precise spot mere minutes ago."

"Does she know what she's sensing is Mac?"

"No, and I didn't tell her. Every second counts. Move." He surged into the Silver concealed in the brick wall and vanished.

Squaring her shoulders, Jada leapt in after him.

A partially eaten Rhino-boy lay on the floor in the white room, keening and gnashing his tusks, clutching the oozing stump of an arm.

"She's rebuilding her strength," Lor said grimly.

Leaping over the savaged Unseelie, Jada dashed into the next Silver after Barrons, with Fade and Lor close behind. A chill of déjà-vu kissed her spine but now was no time for memories of the day fourteen-year-old Dani had leapt so fearlessly and blindly into one of these very Silvers, only to end up adrift in the Hall of All Days. Nor was it time for memories of the afternoon she'd entered one of the Silvers with Christian, and loosed the Crimson Hag on the world. After years of having to leap into whichever ones she'd been lucky enough to find, discovering the hard way where they led, she harbored a special hatred for the Silvers.

As they raced into the White Mansion, down dazzling alabaster corridors with high arched ceilings and tall, sparkling windows that framed a snowy garden and ice-crusted maze, Barrons opened the pouch he carried and tossed one of the stones over his shoulder for Lor to catch. The tall muscular blond palmed it and slipped it into his leather jacket.

White marble floors turned to sunny yellow, rose to turquoise then bronze as they moved deeper into the infinite, ever-changing White Mansion.

"You *do* know where you're going, right?" Jada demanded, catching the cool blue-black stone Barrons tossed her and tucking it into the outer pocket of her backpack.

"Inasmuch as anyone can ever know where the fuck they're

going in here," Barrons growled. "Mac has no more certain sense of direction in here than we do. Look for crimson floors, they lead to black then to the boudoir." He tossed the fourth stone over his shoulder to Fade, who was bringing up the rear.

There was a sudden commotion behind them. Vicious snarls met with cool laughter. She skidded to a halt, whirling.

Cruce stood behind her, encased in a shell of translucent, shimmering walls, clutching the fourth blue-black stone in an upraised fist, while Fade flung himself repeatedly against the barrier, with no result.

The Unseelie prince smiled at them icily. "Going somewhere?"

24

"I follow the sorrow song of the moon"

AOIBHEAL

There was no escape from the king's side of the boudoir either. The nearly invisible towering door set into the smooth black walls of his bedchamber failed to respond to her imperious command. Nor did any of her magic affect it. She was as trapped on his side as she'd been on her own.

She snorted. He'd always held on to her too tightly. That had been precisely the problem. Everything had to be his way.

She'd loved him when she first met him. She'd loved him still, at the end. But she'd realized love wasn't enough. It was possible to love someone who was completely wrong for you. You could waste your entire life loving that person, doing enormous damage to each other and the world around you.

She'd never wanted to live in his cage but she'd done it for him, hoping he would one day give up his mad quest to turn her Fae and be happy with what they had. Hoping he might eventually return to her world with her. All those eons he'd worked alone while she slept alone they might have been living, loving, creating.

At first, upon installing her in the exquisite White Mansion, he'd spent every night in her arms, anywhere and everywhere: in her bed; in his; sprawled in one of the eccentric tower rooms that opened to the sky, counting stars between kisses; on the floor of her closet; atop an enormous grand piano. They'd splashed their love from end to end of the ever-changing, ever-growing mansion while she'd drunk the nectar of galaxies from his lips, tasted infinity in his arms, and decided it might not be so bad to live forever, as long as she was with him.

At first they had no time for anything but each other. Their love had blazed like a supernova. But darkness began to eat away at their light. A silent, seething fixation had been born in him the day the queen refused his request to turn Zara Fae.

Over the eons, he'd begun spending nights with her less frequently, working endlessly in his laboratories, birthing the children of his Court of Shadows in an attempt to re-create the song.

One day she realized she hadn't seen him in months. Then years. She'd spent the time gathering seedlings and young plants and, although by then he'd given her trinkets with which she could create any number of fabulous illusions, she'd nurtured and grown her lush, aromatic gardens in the old, real way. She'd begun playing with the small creatures of the forest, tending their occasional injuries, taking pleasure in the beauties of nature that abounded in her realm.

Alone. So damned alone.

Missing her family, the bustle of so many comings and goings, the din of noise and laughter beneath their roof.

Between his visits he'd send her gifts with which to amuse herself, pretty baubles, fabulous jewels, and opulent gowns. She'd had rooms and rooms of clothing and shoes, cabinets filled with magnificent jewels, and nothing but time to walk around looking at them all, no one for whom to wear them.

With each increasingly lavish gift or object of power he sent, some—like the amulet, intended to make her more equal to him in power—she'd begun to think he'd never seen her at all. Or if he had, he didn't think she was good enough for him. Otherwise he'd see she didn't want power. He'd stop trying to turn her into something she wasn't. But she'd turned anyway. The longer she stayed inside her portion of his Fae realms, the paler she grew, her dark skin lightening, her ebony curls fading, until, in time, although she'd not been Fae, she began to look like one.

The day finally came that she understood his quest to re-create the Song of Making had nothing to do with her, and everything to do with him.

The Seelie Queen had denied him something. The arrogant god-king who was capable of such great tenderness and passion was also capable of great obsession.

But it wasn't with her.

It was with proving the Seelie Queen wrong.

It was with refusing to accept no for an answer.

He *would* have the song and he *would* turn his concubine Fae, no matter the price. And he would never rest until it was done.

After he'd created his Court of Shadows and brought his favored son, Cruce, into existence, she'd seen even less of him and more of Cruce, as the king began dispatching his prince to bring her potions.

Cruce became her companion, confidant, and friend. He would have been her lover, yet Zara's heart still belonged to her king.

One day she'd simply had enough. She'd not seen her king for so long she could not even recall how much time had passed since his last visit. The details of his face had grown blurry in her mind.

On that day, she asked Cruce for a favor, and he'd granted it.

It hadn't turned out as she'd planned. Cruce had been, after all, his father's son, subjugating her wishes to pursue his own.

Aoibheal stiffened and withdrew hastily from her memories, shaking herself to crack the thin sheeting of ice that encased her. There was an intruder in her mansion! She could feel it approaching, sense the violence and disturbance. The White Mansion was a place of beauty, peace, and serenity and did not like this entity within its walls. On her shoulder the *T'murra* shifted with sudden tension, peering this way and that, pecking at air.

She pressed a hand to her throat, expanding her senses, reaching out to taste and touch what came her way, to fathom the ways her future might unfold.

The *Sinsar Dubh* was here! Bringing into these hallowed walls the very worst of the king himself. Hunger for power. Bottomless need for stimulation and whatever dim sensation it might enjoy.

It drew nearer with each passing moment, hurrying straight for her.

She knew why. She'd passed eons in a court of incessant treachery and betrayal. The queen always had to watch her back. There was always one among the royals that coveted her crown.

Ironic that the result of the king's act of atonement for the wrong he'd done her might now kill her. He'd made the *Sinsar Dubh* out of grief at having lost her, and now his Book wanted her dead.

The king's love was a gift that just never stopped giving.

A bitter smile curved her lips. The Fae and their endless quests for power!

Now that she had her memory back, so many things made sense to her that had puzzled her as queen. She suspected that since her memories had never been actually gone, merely stripped of their vibrancy to the point of inaccessibility, even as Aoibheal she'd retained the defining characteristics and nature of Zara. She knew a Fae that tried to overthrow her once would eventually try again, despite wiping its memory with a cup from the cauldron. Humans had a saying, "An angry man is an angry drunk. A happy man is a happy drunk." The king had been wont to say it more simply: can't eviscerate essential self. No matter how many times the Fae tried to.

She finally understood her proclivity as Fae queen to interfere with mortals, her predilection to protect them, her fascination with Adam, who'd abandoned her incessantly to walk among mortals, even fallen in love with one of them.

And chosen to give up his immortality for her.

She knew now why she alone among the Fae could see human souls. Why she'd slipped off more than once to a city in the mortal realm called Cincinnati to spy unseen, marveling at Adam's golden glow. Feeling the shallowest impression of chafing dissatisfaction. Had she been capable of true emotion, she knew what it would have been—envy.

But she was getting lost in reverie again and there was no time for it.

Others were in her mansion, chasing the O'Connor possessed by the *Sinsar Dubh*, the sentient embodiment of the king's act of contrition.

He hadn't even gotten that right. And had been trying to clean up after that mess ever since.

But for whatever reason, it seemed he'd changed his mind about containing it and making amends. Or he'd be here now, stopping this fiasco before it happened, stepping in and saving her from paying the ultimate price for his mistakes. Righting his many grievous wrongs.

Didn't he know she'd drunk from the flask, had her memory restored? Didn't he know she knew the truth now?

All of it.

She shattered the ice that coated her and expanded her senses but couldn't feel him hovering nearby. Then again she had no idea if she'd ever been able to sense him, if he'd cared to keep himself hidden.

In case he was there, concealed from her awareness, she spoke clearly, choosing her words with care. "I have my memory back. I left you by choice. I wrote you a note on a scroll I tied with a lock of my hair. I said: 'You have become a monster. There is nothing left of the man I love.' I wearied of waiting. You are incapable of sacrifice and that made you incapable of love. Cruce offered to take me home to my world where I could live and die and return to the All. I wanted to escape what you'd become, go home and be Zara again. Pure, small things like me don't fare well among gods. If you ever truly loved me, release me from your prison. My freedom is the only thing you have that I want. Let. Me. Go."

The moment she finished speaking, she inhaled sharply and stiffened.

The *Sinsar Dubh* was here!

25

"Of our elaborate plans, the end"

THE SINSAR DUBH

I hasten down the corridor to the boudoir.

Although a confederacy of CRETINSIDIOTSFOOLS close in somewhere behind me, I pay them no heed. By the time they find their way across these ever-changing floors to the boudoir, it will be too late. I'll be gone.

WE ARE DESIRE, LUST, GREED, AND THE PATH WE CHOOSE TO SUPREMACY.

My path to supremacy was masterfully planned, and executed with only minor unfair setbacks from which I cleverly recovered.

How easy MacKayla was to deceive, manipulate into taking me straight to the spear I required to implement my plans!

I'd enacted my ruse at length and with elaborate conviction, in case she'd been somehow able to spy upon me. Brilliance such as mine takes nothing for granted. I'd permitted her to regain my body for a time, lingering, watching, spying upon Barrons, studying how he handled her, protected her from certain information, filing that knowledge away to use at the proper time, waiting for precisely the right moment to reclaim control of her body.

The look on Jada's face, such fun and games there! I'd wanted to smash my fist into it, giggle with delight, but interfering, under-handed Barrons had attacked me unfairly, seizing me from behind while I was invisible.

I drag the Unseelie princess behind me by her hair, cocooned in crimson runes. I summoned and slapped them on her without even breaking stride as I strode through Dublin. Although MacKayla's body continues to weaken, I float on a cloud of radiant energy, sustained by the promise of my certain success, so near at hand.

I AM.

And I am deservedly ebullient.

I drop my spell of invisibility. It's no longer necessary, and as I'm dragging the princess, my presence is obvious. I don't repeat the same intellectual lapses. I whistle a cheery tune, put a hop and skip into my passage over the crimson marble floors, and burst into song: "*Sh-boom, sh-boom, sha-la-la-la-la-la-la-la-la-la, sh-boom, sh-boom . . .*"

Expediency is priority. I will kill the princess once I reach the boudoir, while simultaneously summoning the Seelie Queen. The fool king didn't realize how much of his own knowledge he was passing into me the day he created me. I know precisely where he once placed his palm on the wall in the concubine's chamber to call his lover so he need not search his demesne for her.

Two swift strikes with the spear: princess then queen. Then I'll sift out instantly to the Fae court to drink the Elixir of Life, the location of which will become known to me once I acquire the True Magic from the queen.

Then off to see the wizard, as MacKayla would say, to snatch aside his curtain and reveal him as the charlatan he is compared to the REAL power I am. Then I will kill the bastard king who made and abandoned me so long ago.

A giggle escapes me. It has all been so SERIOUS up until now. I've been so focused on my goals, I've not gotten to PLAY, haven't permitted myself the opportunity to display my most dazzling powers, as I've required things on this world expediently, but that will soon be rectified. Then I can take my time, trot out my favorite spells. I will torture the vile, privileged, soft Seelie before I leave this world, mutilate and mutate them, leaving them hideous, deformed, amputated bits and pieces, hobble them and turn them inside out. Show them what it is to live in Hell forever. *"SH-BOOM!"* I punctuate the arousing thought with a shout. Then I will fuck Jericho Barrons to death. Over and over, amid much blood and torture, I will flay his skin from his bones while I fuck him. I will experience LUST to its fullest degree in every capacity possible.

Then I will sink within and torment the mouse in my house, the pathetic, fragile, morally castrated MacKayla who has already been so undone by weakness that she's withdrawn into a catatonic, fetal ball inside me.

And all it took to reduce her to such a state was allowing her to see herself torture and kill, get a small taste of the delights in which her body had been indulging. I should have permitted her to watch all along. I giggle and burst into another song as I skip down the corridor. *"B-B-Baby you ain't seen nothing yet! Here's something you're NEVER gonna forget BABY."*

Such as when I force her to watch her own hand feeding starry runes to the black holes, exponentially expanding their growth, destroying her planet in a matter of mere days, instead of the months it might currently take.

WAKE THE FUCK UP. THERE ARE ALWAYS MORE WORLDS.

I will rule all of them.

I will be feared, revered, obeyed, got-it-made in the motherfucking shade.

Fragile MacKayla, so easily broken. She gets attached to things: people, places, even pieces of clothing, as if it fucking matters what she wears, where she lives. As if any of the people around her are actually real. No one is real but me. They are *things*, not alive. Not like I am.

I'm disappointed she buckled so soon. I'd indulged myself in additional festivities en route to the White Mansion, the results of which, sadly, she didn't get to see. I'd wanted her to watch the splendid feats I'd done with her hands but she'd been GONE, so near to DEAD I've begun to wonder if I'll even get the chance to torture her more.

I'll revive her. She can't escape me. That's a certainty in my world: we will ALWAYS be together. I will always have my sad little horse to break and repair, break and repair.

She will watch me K'Vruck her world and everything in it. Brilliance such as mine demands an audience. I won't be cheated of my chance to watch her do what she does best—BLEEDBLEEDBLEED—and revel in being ME not It as It spews emotion all over the place. I won't be deprived of the opportunity to see It realize, fully understand, how clever, powerful, and brilliant I am. One of those priceless, perfect moments I gather like luminous pearls where, in the horrified comprehension in It's gaze I know It KNOWS It helped orchestrate It's own destruction. That's the moment I crave, desire, lust for, when my toys realize THEY are to BLAME for their own fucking fate. I wonder if anyone drank my poisoned water at the abbey and bled out, ruing that I wasn't there at the moment they realized what they'd done to themselves. They didn't HAVE to take a drink. They CHOSE to. I am not to blame. THEY KILLED THEMSELVES. But there will be endless opportunities for such rich experiences soon.

When I kick open the door to the boudoir, I draw up, surprised into a moment of near-immobility.

Triumph saturates my being.

Again I'm vindicated by the universe.

Chance favors the prepared mind. The universe adores the bold, fearless conqueror and seeks to aid him.

No need to summon the queen.

She's already here.

I leap into the room, drag the princess in behind me, slam the door, and exclaim brightly, *"SH-BOOM!"*

26

"Choose they croon the ancient ones,

the time has come again"

AOIBHEAL

"It's mad," Aoibheal said softly, staring through the shadowy, translucent Silver at the thing that had just burst into the concubine's boudoir, shouting nonsense. "Utterly and completely mad."

"Awk! Maaaaad!" the *T'murra* agreed.

She swept at the bird with her hand, urging it, "Fly now, young one! Go! I'll not see you harmed, too."

"Ack! Fly now!" It pecked at her cheek sharply, as if urging her into action.

"I can't," Aoibheal said. She was trapped. Was this the fate the king intended for her? Had he decided to terminate her existence in such a cruel, ironic fashion because she'd forced him to face what he'd refused to believe for eons—that his lover had left him by choice? "Go!" She shooed it again. "It feeds on death and destruction. I'll not give it more of what it wants."

Still the *T'murra* kept its talons dug deep into her cloak.

"Get off me!" She smacked lightly at its feathery belly with her hand.

"Ack!" It gave her a look of seeming reproach and lifted off, echoing in a loud squawk, *"Give it what it wants!"*

The *T'murra* soared up to the safety of the starry night sky, shrieking the random selection of words over and over again. Even as peaceful Zara, she'd sometimes longed to muzzle her talkative companions' lovely beaks.

Steeling herself, she turned to face her would-be executioner.

MacKayla O'Connor, the young child whom she'd so often visited in dreams, was now a grown woman, her jeans crusted with blood and entrails, her hair a wild mass of tangled clumps, the look in her eyes completely and utterly insane.

Black irises had obliterated green and, as the Fae queen stared through the shadowy Silver at her, she felt a pale regret. She'd manipulated the O'Connor as she herself had been manipulated. As the Fae king had tinkered with the mortal Zara, so too had the Fae queen tinkered with the mortal Mac.

But regret changed nothing, pale or vivid. The *Sinsar Dubh* was in full possession of what had once been human, but the golden glow of the O'Connor's soul was already fading. No soul would survive long, possessed by such evil as what faced her now, with but one goal: to kill her and seize the True Magic of her race.

No. Not her race.

The race she despised.

The race that would soon become extinct without the Song of Making.

And good riddance to it.

The Book would no doubt then seek her elixir, become immortal, thus ensuring the final death of the O'Connor's soul. She would become every bit as much a monster as the one that possessed her.

Aoibheal narrowed her eyes. She felt the proximity of the others, those who sought to stop the *Sinsar Dubh*. She felt, too, the presence of the legendary four stones carved from the cliffs of the Unseelie prison, etched with powerful spells, capable of holding the *Sinsar Dubh* in a state of suspended animation.

The day was not yet lost.

Her lips twisted in an imperious sneer.

He was coming, too!

The one from whom she'd begged her favor; the one who'd lied and, with the offer of a glass of wine to toast her freedom, had stolen her memory then dragged her off to live for hundreds of thousands of years among her enemy. Masquerading as ally at her side. Controlling her, shaping her. Taking what he wanted until what he wanted was nothing less than everything she had, at which point he'd tried to kill her.

Cruce was with them.

"Ack!" The *T'murra* squawked loudly from above, echoing bits of her earlier words again. *"Give it what it wants!"*

Aoibheal cocked her head and glanced up sharply, as the *T'murra's* words abruptly seemed no longer quite so random.

27

Mahler's unfinished Tenth, Cooke version

MAC

This is how it feels to be the *Sinsar Dubh*.

Only better. I lack even its shallow frustration and glee. There's nothing left of emotion nor any desire for it.

I'm perfection of aim, purpose without self.

I'm arrow to goal without ego.

I expand effortlessly into my body to evict the parasite that thinks to take from me what is mine.

I apprehend the small, dark stain of it as if from a great distance.

How dare it walk within my walls?

This is *my* kingdom.

28

"Releasing the demons"

SINSAR DUBH

I lunge for the mirror, dropping the princess, leaving her behind. Cocooned like Cruce and the Highlander, she presents no threat to me, can't contend for the True Magic. I am eager to taste my deserved victory and will visit her and my other toys soon, with ample time to savor their suffering. I realize now that the universe was once again favoring me, not working against me as I'd thought, when it permitted Jada to take my spear. Overeager from long incarceration, I would have rashly killed all three. Now I can draw out their tor—

STOP.

My feet skid to a halt on the black marble floor so abruptly I nearly topple face-forward. I try to lunge again but remain rooted where I am.

I cock my head without resisting further, pondering the oddity of just having forced myself to stop. Do I now possess in human form the equivalent of a gut instinct? Did it sense some peril to me I've failed to take into account?

I assess the Fae queen, her shadowy outline beyond the Silver. I hold the spear in my hand. There is no peril to me here.

I lunge forward again.

STOP.

My foot returns to the floor, mere paces from my goal. I'm so close I could reach out and touch the Silver.

The voice was mine.

But it wasn't mine.

Who, then? Is there some other entity inside me that has been cleverly concealed from me all this time? The voice didn't belong to the sniveling MacKayla. It is fetal, catatonic within me. It crumbled when I let It watch a single one of the glorious murders we've committed. It imploded beneath an onslaught of the illusions of guilt, complicity, regret. What the fuck is regret? I've never fathomed that muddy mix of emotion. *It* could never speak with such a voice.

This was a voice of power.

Who is it? WHAT IS IT?

DESIRE, PURPOSE, AND COMMITMENT TO THE PATH I CHOOSE TO WALK, MacKayla says in a voice just like mine.

I'd be rendered immobile if I weren't already.

What has It done?

HOW has It done it?

My mind whirls, dances, and skids across bits and pieces of the facts of MacKayla's existence I have tirelessly gathered over the years. I know this puny creature! I know Its limits, Its weakness. I know what It is capable of. AND NOT.

Ahhhhh. I would narrow my eyes and smile if I were in control of our vessel but, at the moment, It holds me *motionless*.

It has not tried to move my body. Has not tried to back me away. It can't. No more than It can sustain this emotionless state of temporary power It has achieved. It's an amateur, a rank pretender, aspiring to a throne it can never hold.

I giggle. "I'm flattered, really, but get over yourself, MacKayla." It felt dead to me because It had IMITATED me. It did something I'd not thought possible for one born so flawed. Shed emotion like a skin It could doff and don at will.

Did MacKayla study me as I studied her?

No matter.

I AM THE REAL THING.

It is not.

I do what I've done so many times before, reach for Its subconscious and feed It vivid images to manipulate and distract. Exploit that oh-so-exploitable part of It. I show It what It did to Christian, to Cruce, and wait for It to shatter.

IRRELEVANT, is Its toneless reply.

Incensed, I flood It with graphic details of the moment I ripped Margery's still beating heart from her breast.

DISTRACTION, It says without inflection.

I feel my right foot draw up from the floor then move BACK-WARD as It dares to try to move me AWAY from my goal, so near, so near!

Behind me, the boudoir door crashes open, and I hear shouts of "Place the stones! Quickly!" Then Barrons roars, "Cruce, you fucking bastard, do it or die!" Snarls fill the air and I hear a scuffle.

I'm filled with fury, apprehending MacKayla's plan. It doesn't have to sustain Its emotionless state forever, just long enough to hold me motionless and permit them to contain us. It would see itself locked away with me forever simply to prevent me from achieving my rightful place in this world! How unfair! How positively PETULANT It is!

I play my trump card.

I slam graphic images into Its brain: finding Jo and offering her the poisoned water.

Grabbing her by the shoulder, smashing its fist into her face again and again. Shattering bones. Exploding brain. Kicking and pulping organs.

Sinking to the ground.

EATING Jo SLOWLY and with great GUSTO.

YES, YES, I tell It, YOU ARE CORRECT, THAT IS WHAT WAS IN YOUR TEETH. BITS OF JO WERE CAUGHT BE-

TWEEN THEM. YOU ATE YOUR FRIEND. YOU KILLED
HER, AND I MADE MY EYES GREEN FOR HER SO SHE DIED
BELIEVING IT WAS YOU.

I feel It then.

The weakness I've come to know and cherish in my lovely bird
in the cage. The surface of Its false facade cracks and emotion begins to seep in. It is so easy to break, so simple to control. I can
never be broken in such fashion. I am superior.

Before they have time to place the final two stones, I recover
control of my body and leap into the Silver.

As we pass through the gelatinous membrane, I realize, with
utter incredulity, that I am being SCRAPED from MY limbs, MY
eyes.

The bitch has somehow taken control BACK!

Then we're through, mere inches from the queen, and Mac-
Kayla yanks me up short, a strike of a spear away from my goal.

All I require is control of my hand to kill the bitch queen and
take what is mine.

I stare with bottomless hunger at Aoibheal from behind eyes I
can't influence, unable to affect so much as a finger. Again I assault
MacKayla with images, this time of the woman I impaled on a
spiked fence en route to the bookstore. The young, handsome man
I left with nothing between his legs, bleeding in the street. The
child I stabbed through the eye with my spear then twirled in the
air as if on a skewer before tossing it into a crumpled heap.

It's the last one that gets It.

It falters. I seize control of my hand, raise the spear and—

IT FREEZES ME AGAIN!

"I'm not dying for them," the queen sneers contemptuously.
"They're not my people. They never were. You want the power of
the Fae race? Fine. Take it."

Aoibheal slams her palms into my chest.

29

"Let it go, let it go, turn away and slam the door"

MAC

But my eyes were green, I think dispassionately as the queen's hands slam into my chest. Didn't she notice?

Or perhaps she didn't care, unwilling to take the chance I might lack the stamina to see my battle through.

Ancient power rushes into me, penetrating my sternum, burrowing deep, and I feel as if my body is being filled with dense brilliance. It gushes into me, in an endless flood.

Too much, too much, I can't possibly hold it!

Then the queen is shoving me backward, into the mirror, back to the concubine's side of the boudoir as she issues an imperious command through the Silver to Barrons: "She will be immobile for several minutes while she absorbs the True Magic. You must contain her. Now!"

I'd tell Barrons it's not necessary because I'm in control, but I can't affect my vocal cords, my mouth. Nor can the *Sinsar Dubh*. We're both in a state of suspension, immobilized by the transference of the queen's blinding, stupefying power. It feels as if five tons of concrete just got dumped into a quart jar. I'm not Fae.

How is this even possible? Will it destroy me? Tear us apart? Is that her point, her purpose?

I remain at the ready—the composed, untouchable thing I've become—to defeat the *Sinsar Dubh* for good, the moment the power transfer is done.

Assuming we survive.

The Book tried its best to restore emotion to me and nearly succeeded.

But failed.

I'm beyond emotion now. I bear no guilt, no sins. I know neither right nor wrong. There is only aim and purity of purpose, the path I've chosen to walk.

Distantly, I hear Cruce roar furiously, "Why would you give it to a *human*? I was here! *I* am the worthy successor yet you gave it to *her*."

Aoibheal says, "I know everything now, Cruce—you who were once my treasured friend. My memory is restored. You betrayed me. You promised to return me to my world and let me die."

"I gave you everything! I gave you immortality—"

"I never wanted it," she snarls. "You knew that!"

"But to give it to a *human*?" he sneers. "Can she even carry it?"

"This one can," Aoibheal says, and I hear something in her voice and realize she *did* notice that my eyes were green. She knew it was me, not the Book. And did it anyway. Why?

"You took everything from me," she says to Cruce. "But even that was not enough for you. In time, I might have chosen to pass my power to you as I faded, risk a patriarchal rule. I saw your strength. Even, at times, your wisdom. But you tried to steal it from me."

"For the good of our kind!"

"*Your* kind," she says with an icy laugh, "not mine, and your *kind* is beyond hope now. The moment the Earth dies—thanks to yet another of the king's reckless acts of creation—the entire race of the Tuatha De Danann will expire; each and every one of you. Think no longer of yourself as immortal. You have mere months at best."

"We will leave this planet," Cruce hisses.

"Run as far as you want. It will do you no good. I bound the seat of our race's power to the Earth."

Cruce inhales sharply. Then says disbelievingly, "What the *fuck* were you thinking? Planets die! You know that!"

She laughs mirthlessly. "And now, so will the Fae. The instant the Earth does."

I can do nothing to arrest the velocity with which Aoibheal shoved me into the Silver. After what seemed several long moments of passing through it, I explode from the sticky membrane, go flying backward through the air, and crash violently to the floor.

My head snaps back and smacks marble with such force I see stars.

Then darkness claims me and I see no more.

♪

When I regain consciousness, I'm in a chair, in the middle of the concubine's boudoir, unable to move.

My eyes are open, and beyond twinkling diamonds suspended on air I see the cocooned body of the Unseelie princess, the thunderous-faced Cruce, being forcibly restrained by stony-eyed Fade and Lor, ashen-faced Jada, eyes enormous and full of grief, and beyond her the residue of the concubine, reclining on her plush white bed.

Barrons. My beautiful Barrons stands in front of me, dark gaze glittering with crimson flecks, mouth drawn back in a silent snarl.

The shimmering blue-black containment field of stone connecting to stone stretches between us from floor to ceiling, vanishing around my sides where I see no more of it but know my prison is complete. And as I suspected, it renders both the Book and me fully inert while leaving both of us fully cognizant.

That's okay. It's done. The *Sinsar Dubh* is contained and can no longer harm anyone.

Not true, sweet thing, it purrs. *I have YOU and an eternity to punish you for what you've done. Before, I was alone beneath the abbey. Now, I have a TOY. And I WILL break free again. It's only a matter of time. And tiiiiiiiiiiime*, it croons with guttural glee, *is on my side, YES IT IS!*

It resurrects the images it fed me before, slamming them into my brain in gruesome detail.

I have no idea if I did the things it shows me, if I really killed Jo so horrifically, causing her such hellish pain, while she believed it was me, or if everything is merely an illusion the *Sinsar Dubh* feeds me.

But here and now, it's irrelevant.

I know what it's doing. Trying to distract me while it searches for the True Magic inside us, in hopes of using it to quell me, and break free of our prison.

But it's too late.

I've already found it.

Legs splayed, arms folded, I stand atop the shining vault of power the queen passed us, blazing with purpose and power.

I will never let the Book touch it.

It's in my kingdom.

That makes it mine.

MACKAYLA, it says in a singsong voice. I KNOW YOU'RE IN HERE. OLLY OLLY OXEN FREE! COME OUT COME OUT WHEREVER YOU ARE! STOP BEING SO TIRESOME. YOU WILL NEVER DEFEAT ME. ALL YOU DID WAS TEMPORAR-ILY SUSPEND EMOTION. THAT DOESN'T MAKE YOU MY EQUAL. YOU CAN NEVER BE MY EQUAL. I AM SUPERIOR IN EVERY WAY.

No, it's not. I may have turned off my emotion but I can turn it back on.

It has no emotion to turn on. *That* is its two-dimensional, flat, miserable, unsatisfying existence.

I'm fully formed, missing nothing, needing nothing to leech onto. I have worlds of possibility inside me. It has none. It's empty, so empty that it tries desperately to fill itself by stealing from others.

The *Sinsar Dubh* is the true cardboard cutout, empty, flat, and flawed, with its parasitic needs scribbled on its face for all to see.

I HAVE NO NEEDS, BITCH! IT IS YOU WHO ARE FLAWED!

It's nothing *but* need. Empty, greedy, black-hole-sucking need. And it knows it, so it tells itself lie after lie, weaves an elaborate illusion of superiority, in hopes of escaping the horrific awareness that it is fatally, damningly flawed, missing something of the divine the rest of us have.

An epiphany takes gentle root within me.

The *Sinsar Dubh* has no hold on me.

The only hold it ever had was that it managed to latch onto me when I was unaware, innocent and young, and didn't know such monsters existed.

I'm no longer unaware, innocent, or young.

I don't need to evict it.

I can simply walk away.

When I rise from the chair, those in the boudoir panic and begin to roar at one another.

But not Barrons.

He stands motionless, searching my eyes through the crackling blue-black wall, and slowly, very slowly, the corner of his mouth ticks up in a smile.

I smile back as I move toward the perimeter of the prison that can't contain me, wasn't designed to do so, because I'm not the *Sinsar Dubh* and never was.

I have an unfortunate hitchhiker.

It's time to kick it out of the car.

As I step into the containment field, the *Sinsar Dubh* screams, DON'T YOU DARE LEAVE ME! DON'T YOU KNOW YOU CAN'T EXIST WITHOUT ME? I LOVE YOU, MACKAYLA! I'M THE ONLY ONE THAT LOVES YOU! I'M NOT DONE WITH YOU! I WILL KILL YOU! GET BACK HERE! I WILL DESTROY—

I'm beyond the containment field of the stones.

I'm free.

I can no longer hear the *Sinsar Dubh*'s threats and taunts.

And never will again.

30

Lingering in the ether, the Unseelie King retrieved the small scroll tied with a lock of his lover's hair from where he carried it near his heart. He rolled the tiny thing in his enormous palm.

He knew now.

She'd left him by choice.

He'd suspected the Elixir of Remembering had only a nominal chance of success. He'd created it when he realized he was losing memories to the relentless march of time. He'd wanted to keep each moment of his existence alive, vivid in detail, visceral and immediate. Imbibed on a daily basis, the elixir conferred the result he'd desired.

But as he'd feared, drinking it hundreds of thousands of years after the Cauldron of Forgetting had done its damage restored only the details, none of the context or associated feelings. She was Zara, yet possessed none of the spectacular passion and fire that had so ensorcelled him. As icy as the First Queen had ever been, she wanted nothing more from him than her freedom.

He'd been a fool to believe he'd been given a second chance.

Dropping the scroll, he ground it to dust beneath his heel then vanished, seeking solitude where old gods do, among the stars.

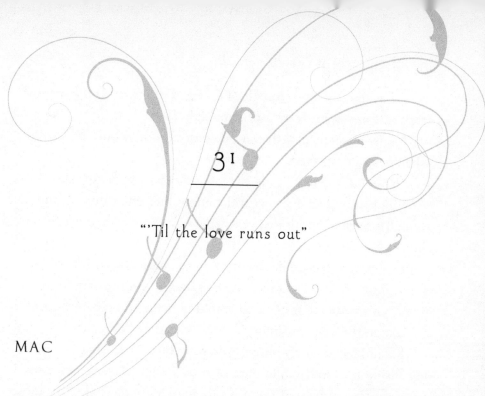

31

"'Til the love runs out"

MAC

You know those movies where lovers have been separated with no idea whether they'll ever see each other again and, when they finally do, after harrowing trials and tribulations, they dash madly toward one another, and the filmmaker shoots the scene in slow motion so the viewers get to revel in that long, drawn out moment of anticipation, waiting breathlessly for their first passionate embrace?

That's so not what happened with me and Barrons.

Neither of us moved. We just stood there looking at each other. His dark eyes gleamed with . . . I had no idea what because I couldn't currently feel and had no way of identifying emotion. But I chose to believe it was satisfaction, respect, and a "bloody good job, Ms. Lane."

No one else in the boudoir moved either. They were all staring past me.

I turned and glanced back at the containment field.

Inside a blue-black cage, a dark, angry tornado twisted and darted, flinging itself repeatedly at the walls.

To no avail.

I'd walked away from it. I'd left the *Sinsar Dubh* behind, trapped forever, in its own private hell.

I was unsatisfied with the outcome. I would only be satisfied when it was destroyed.

"You *did* it, Mac!" Jada exploded fiercely, punching the air.

I had indeed. But I was still remote and emotionless, and although a part of me almost yearned to stay that way, a bigger part didn't.

I wanted to feel again, to drink in the moment, the dawning of a new day. I wanted to savor my hard-won freedom. There was so much future ahead of us, if we could manage to save our world. I calculated the odds at slightly better than they had been.

I could feel the unfamiliar presence of the True Magic smoldering inside me. And while part of me thought, Gee, great, now I have another uninvited thing inside me I have to deal with, most of me was thinking how extraordinary it was that by an unexpected twist of fate I'd become the one woman who could wield the Song of Making.

That was a serious plus in our column. Cruce possessed at least some part of the *Sinsar Dubh*. Dageus was alive with the souls of thirteen ancient Draghar inside him. We had Dani's and Dancer's quirky, brilliant minds and Barrons's and Ryodan's vast experience with magic and the black arts.

Yes, our odds were definitely better than they had been, with the Fae queen missing, and me possessed.

I slanted my eyes half closed, sank within and embraced all that made me human; the good, the bad, the pretty and not so pretty, and as emotion rekindled, I stared past the *Sinsar Dubh*'s prison, through the shadows of the king's ancient, towering Silver to the woman who stood on the other side of it, a dazzling bird perched on her shoulder.

She met my gaze and I thought I detected the faintest trace of sorrow in her lovely, iridescent eyes. I could recognize emotion again.

Then she turned and glided to the now open door on the king's side of the boudoir and exited through it without a word, vanishing into the White Mansion.

The door swung shut behind her with such force that the floor shuddered and the king's enormous mirror abruptly went coal black.

The mirror shivered violently then—gilt frame and all—simply popped out of existence, leaving a smooth white wall where once it had hung.

The concubine's boudoir no longer connected to the king's.

The tiny flames flickering in the diamonds floating on the air around us abruptly went out, leaving cold, opaque crystals that clattered to the floor, amid petals that no longer smelled spicy but now emitted a strong whiff of decay.

The residue of the concubine vanished from the bed.

The fire in the hearth died.

The chamber was just a chamber, void of all trace of the opulent beauty, passion, and sensuality that had saturated it.

Although I had no idea what had transpired between the legendary lovers, I knew what these events signified: the epic love affair between the Unseelie King and his concubine was over.

Inexpressible sorrow filled me.

I felt as if I'd lost something. I'd liked believing in their immortal love. I'd once lived their passion in these rooms, and the depth of their commitment to each other had been as powerful and seemingly eternal as the Unseelie King himself. Their tortured affair had been wild and romantic, inspiring me, filling me with wonder and no small measure of desire for a similar enduring love. Minus the tortured part.

I frowned, not liking the implications of what I'd just seen.

The Unseelie King had shut the door and turned out the lights. The lights he'd kept burning for hundreds of thousands of years. If the king no longer cared for the boudoir to exist as perpetual testament to his life's love and obsession, then the king no longer *cared*.

And his interest in human problems had always been fleetingly whimsical at best.

The concubine/Fae queen who might have helped me learn to use the powers she'd transferred to me had just stalked out and slammed the door behind her.

I didn't need a genius IQ to figure out what their departures meant: no divine aid to humankind would be forthcoming.

Our world was dying.

Months, at best, the concubine had said.

And we were on our own.

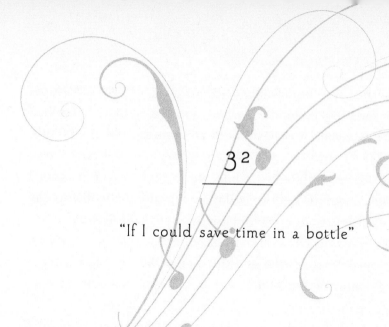

32

"If I could save time in a bottle"

MAC

The others began to bicker.

Cruce started it. No surprise there.

Jada was merely proposing we take further measures to secure the *Sinsar Dubh* in the chamber when he launched into a haughty diatribe about how no one was going anywhere until MacKayla "got her human ass over here," put her hands on his chest and passed the True Magic of the Fae race to the rightful heir—the only *Fae* in the room, thereby entitled, no, *owed* ... blah blah blah.

Lor pointed out that there was a second Fae in the room, the cocooned Unseelie princess, and as far as he was concerned, if the True Magic was going anywhere and it wasn't as matriarchal power, it would clearly go to her.

Barrons snarled that I was never going to be getting my human ass anywhere near Cruce, not now, not ever, and then Fade jumped in, pointing out that whether or not I even *was* still human was open to significant debate.

Jada and I looked at each other in disbelief.

"Shut up, all of you!" I thundered.

The silence was instantaneous. Four pairs of eyes jerked my way. Even Jada looked mildly startled, and I realized my voice had come out larger than it used to, with an unmistakable note of authority.

"Time moves differently while we're in here," I reminded them. "The concubine said we had mere months at best before the black holes devoured our world. How long have we been in here?"

"Fuck," Barrons exploded, his gaze darting instantly between the imprisoned *Sinsar Dubh* and the door. "We can't just leave it like this. If someone finds their way in and moves a single stone, it'll be free again."

I could see that happening all too easily. People were insatiably curious. Fae were insatiably power hungry, prone to overestimating their abilities to handle it. More than a few would be tempted to see if they could control the *Sinsar Dubh*. Cruce and Darroc had both tried. Hell, I'd been tempted when I thought I'd killed Barrons.

"And who knows what it's capable of in that form," Jada said. "It might be like that movie, *Fallen,* with Denzel Washington where Azazel could jump from body to body. Mac may have inadvertently left it in a form that makes it even easier for it to possess people."

"And thank you for pointing that out," I said caustically, irritated with myself. I wanted the thing gone, dead, destroyed, dust, not existing in an even more dangerous form that might be able to whiz through the air, entering and exiting humans as if they were convenient revolving doors, possessing hundreds, even thousands, if it escaped. To Barrons, I said, "Can you ward the door?"

"For fuck's sake, it's not a mere twinkle of a nose. Wards take time."

To Cruce, I said, "What can you do quickly to fortify this chamber?"

He folded his arms over his chest and regarded me with open

hostility. "You are the one who is so all-powerful now. *You* do something. Or transfer the power to me and I will."

A muscle leapt in my jaw. "Did you somehow miss the point of what the concubine said? If our planet dies, your race dies, too. Secure the damn door, Cruce," I said flatly.

Barrons stalked out and we followed him.

Jaw clenched, Cruce joined us, closed the door and murmured softly.

An enormous steel gate appeared, barring entry, heavily bolted into the walls on sides and top, and sunk deep into the floor.

"But a Fae could get past that, couldn't it?" I said.

"Fae are not 'its,' MacKayla, we are 'hes' and 'shes,' " he said tightly. "And technically you are one of us now." But he palmed a faintly pulsing blue-black rune and embedded it in the center bar of the gate. "This will do. For the time being."

"Um, guys, we forgot the princess," Jada said.

"She's bound in the cocoon, now doubly trapped," Barrons replied grimly. "Every minute counts. Multiplied exponentially in this bloody place. *Run.*"

We ran.

PART II

Swift as the wind
Quiet as the forest
Conquer like the fire
Steady as a mountain.

–Sun Tzu

33

"Saints and sinners are but we,

twisted wrecks of symmetry"

MAC

We returned to a completely different New Dublin, one run with near-militant efficiency by Ryodan.

Our stay in the White Mansion had cost us thirty-five days, Earth time.

When Ryodan returned from wherever he was reborn, he discovered the six of us, Barrons, Jada, Fade, Lor, Cruce, and I, had been missing for a week. With no idea what had happened to us or where we'd gone, he turned his attention to our pressing problem: the black holes that continued to expand slowly but relentlessly, growing inexorably nearer to the ground.

No one had any idea what would happen if one of the black holes made contact with the soil. We didn't fully understand the physics of the black holes we'd discovered in space and no one knew if ours were even the same kind of thing. Dancer was convinced they were a total wild card, differing widely from naturally occurring black holes. Some people theorized it would eat slowly away at the soil, some contended it would instantly devour a large area, while others insisted the entire Earth would be destroyed at a fairly rapid pace until it formed an accretion disk around the black hole, allowing the hole to consume it at its leisure.

Since the Fae queen had a profound connection to the Fae power nestled deep in the earth, I was certain her estimate of mere months was correct. And considering we'd been gone more than a month of those "mere months," I was grateful Ryodan had thrown himself into the issue of the black holes with the same intense focus he turned on everything.

In our absence he'd befriended Dancer, or rather commandeered the young genius to report to him daily about the progress being made at Trinity College, where a crew of thirty of the finest minds Dancer and Caoimhe had been able to gather struggled with theoretical physics and music theory, in an effort to fathom our problem and define the essence of the Song of Making.

"Ryodan's been spending hours a day with them," said Enyo, the tough, young French-Lebanese *sidhe*-seer who'd stepped up to the plate at the abbey in Jada's absence. She'd banged in the door of the bookstore about one minute after Jada and I arrived, as I'd been on my way upstairs to peel off my jeans and change into something sans guts, blood, and gray matter. Sighing, I'd gone right back down, and now sat in the middle of the wrecked bookstore, listening as Enyo brought us up to date. "Absorbing their theories, posing challenging questions, pushing their minds even further outside the box. Dancer's opinion of Ryodan has certainly changed."

Ryodan had also turned the focus of his meticulous gaze, Enyo told us, to the other side of the city, dispatching men to the abbey where they labored day and night displacing rubble in hopes of uncovering and salvaging as much of the abbey's libraries as possible. The *sidhe*-seers searched whatever tomes were found, seeking useful Fae lore. He'd dispatched RVs and tour buses to the heavily damaged fortress, to afford temporary living quarters.

He'd also done the unthinkable: Chester's was closed for business. The sleek, modern chrome and glass-walled dance floors of the biggest postwall nightclub in Dublin had gone as dark as the king's boudoir. Nobody was partying on his watch, when the Earth was in imminent danger of extinction. The streets of New Dublin were patrolled day and night by dozens of troops of the Guardians, an order that had grown enormously in our absence, attracting men and women from all over the world as the influx of immigrants to the city continued unabated. Enyo informed us they were under new leadership, as Inspector Jayne had mysteriously disappeared and was presumed dead.

I received the news of the good inspector's death with sorrow. I'd liked Jayne. He'd toed a hard line from day one, but it had been a necessary line, guided by a good heart. I glanced at Jada to see how she was taking the news. She locked gazes with me and shook her head minutely. *Tell you later,* she mouthed when Enyo wasn't looking.

Each and every black hole on Ryodan's map, Enyo told us, had been secured, not merely by orange ropes cordoning them off, but heavily armed guards, in our country as well as those in England, Scotland, Germany, France, Spain, Poland, Romania, Greece, Morocco, and Norway. Fortunately, there weren't nearly as many in other countries as there were in Ireland.

I was amused to hear Ryodan had begun publishing a daily paper, *Ryodan's World News,* a fact that chafed Jada enormously. When Enyo handed her Ryodan's paper, she was even more rankled to find it well-written and informative.

"People rush out to get it every morning," Enyo told her. "They pass it around like the latest YouTube video gone viral."

Jada's scowl deepened and I knew what she was thinking: The *Dani Daily* had been midlist at best, but Ryodan's paper was a number one bestseller. She was only mildly mollified when I pointed out that becoming well-known in the media was probably Ryodan's worst nightmare, without going into detail in front of Enyo about the whys.

Immortals survived eternity by hiding themselves, staying well out of the media, yet Ryodan had known that the world needed a strong, well-spoken leader to follow in times of pending catastrophe, and decided he was the only one that fit the bill.

Yep. King again.

I wondered how many other centuries and countries he'd taken over in times of crisis, and if he understood how lucky he was that Cyberspace was currently down. Like every other nine-day wonder, once we saved our world he might be able to melt quietly into the background without having to tolerate a Facebook fan page devoted to him, where people eagerly posted reports and photos of the latest Ryodan sighting. I couldn't think of much else that would piss him off more. Well, I could think of a few things.

According to Enyo, Ryodan had mysteriously leveraged the leaders of the black market to provide free food and supplies to all the Guardians and armed guards throughout multiple countries, as well as taken over WeCare's meeting houses, turning them into free soup kitchens, feeding anyone who came in hungry, turning no one away.

"He did *not*," Jada snapped, sitting up straighter. "Sorry, Enyo, I was willing to go along with you right up until that one. Ryodan doesn't give a bloody damn about the fate of the human race, and he would never divert his resources to feeding them."

"It sure looks like he cares to me," Enyo said hotly. "I've seen him out there in action, personally keeping tabs on every inch of this city and all its operations. I'm beginning to think the man never sleeps."

I could assure Jada he didn't. But I wasn't about to.

She screwed up her face in a look of such utter disgust that for a moment all I could see was young Dani again, and I had to bite my lip to keep from smiling.

"Oh, why don't you just bloody *saint* the man, then?" she growled. "Ryodan this, Ryodan that. *Ryodan's World News*, my ass. Doesn't he know you need a catchy title? A little alliteration, a lilt to roll along the lips?"

"Either that or just the latest news," I said without thinking, then absorbed the look on Jada's face and added hastily, "Not that yours wasn't. It was. I loved your papers. They were endlessly entertaining and informative. The *Dani Daily* rocked, and that one *Jada Journal* I saw—"

"Oh, stow it, Mac," she snapped. "His idiotic paper is . . ." She glanced down at it irritably, where it lay smoothed out on her lap. "Good," she allowed tightly. "He reports the news in a calm, objective manner that instills confidence that someone knows what's going on, and inspires hope. He has his finger on world events—not just what's happening in Dublin like I did—and his frigging bullet points at the end of it, with lists of things for people to do each day, focuses them on tasks that keep them too busy to panic." She sighed and muttered, *"Fucker."*

That was it. I laughed. It felt like forever since I'd seen her looking like a disgruntled porcupine. Her passion and temper were rising to the surface again.

I agreed. His bulleted lists were a terrific idea, as was posting the paper early each morning before people woke up. No one greeted the day at a loss for what to do, which meant fewer people sitting around bitching, working themselves into a panic, spreading the mood, then the next thing you knew you had a riot forming. He kept them pointed at tasks, moving from one "to do" to the next, and as I'd learned myself a little over a year ago, lists were a damned effective way to manage messy emotions.

After a moment, Enyo continued, and I narrowed my eyes as I listened, beginning to wonder if this tough, battle-hardened *sidhe-seer* might not just have a bit of a crush on Ryodan. I glanced at Jada and knew by her expression that she was wondering the same thing.

Ryodan had divided the city into numbered districts, Enyo told us, with admiration blazing in her eyes, and each district's paper had a different bulleted list at the end containing tasks specific to that small enclave of people. Once they arrived on the job, they were assigned to teams, where they began the day with a discussion of what they were going to accomplish and how it served their long-term goals and needs, were fed three squares while on the job, and finished the day with an inspiring wrap-up talk. Each site was run by a foreman who'd been hand-selected by Ryodan for his motivational and leadership skills.

"Okay," Jada said acidly, kicking her legs over the back of the shattered Chesterfield she'd been perching on and stalking over the paint-stained floor to the door. "That's all the rah-rah Ryodan crap I can take in one sitting. I need to get out there and see what's going on with my own eyes."

I was surprised she was just leaving without waiting for Enyo to take off so she could say, "Wow, Mac, you're the Seelie Queen now, what's up with that?" or something similar. But no one had seemed to want to stick around once we returned to Dublin. Cruce had instantly sifted out without a word, Barrons had tersely asked me to "please go to the bookstore and wait there until I get back, and yes, I did just say please, and no, not because you're the bloody queen of the Faery but because I want you to do it and not argue," before stalking off with Lor and Fade to find Ryodan. I'd tossed a mild "Okay" at his back, deciding he needed a breather. Finally being free of the evil clutches of the *Sinsar Dubh* was breather enough for me. I was ready to get invested in the next thing and forget about the last until I went back to destroy the Book for good.

As Jada banged out the door, I remembered my little bell was broken and made a mental note to procure a new one. Assuming I still had a door to attach it to, a building to hang said door on, and a planet for my bookstore to exist upon in a few months.

I tuned back in to the conversation Enyo was still carrying on, despite Jada leaving and my obvious distraction, just in time to hear her say, "So, all in all we lost two hundred and thirty-four of our women the night of the battle and another seventeen the morning after, but in recent weeks we've gained nearly twice those numbers from the influx into Dublin." She added with satisfaction, "Word's gotten around this is the place for *sidhe*-seers that are hungry to kick some Fae ass."

I sat up straighter, kicking my feet over the side of the broken chair I'd dragged from a pile of debris I'd not yet had time to remove from the store. *Another seventeen the morning after*, she'd said—which for me had been earlier today.

The image the Book had fed me of Jo dying had taken place in the morning. I wet suddenly dry lips. "Do I know any of the *sidhe*-seers that were killed? Not that I know many on a first name basis, but there's Kat and Cara, Shauna and Margery, and who else, let's see, Josie and Jo . . ." I trailed off, looking at her expectantly.

Enyo said, "We thought we'd lost Kat but she turned up again just a few days ago. Not saying a word to any of us about where she'd been but acting and looking totally different." She narrowed her eyes. "I, for one, would really like to know where the hell that woman was because I'd bet my eyeteeth she somehow managed to convince Ryodan or one of his men to train her. She wasn't nearly so cool and strong before she disappeared." Envy flashed across her beautiful, golden-skinned features. "Don't know what those men are, but I'd sure like to. And I'd like to get my own stint of training in with one of them."

"And the other *sidhe*-seers?" I gently nudged her back to the topic.

"Shauna's alive, out at the abbey. Cara's dead, as are Margery and Josie. But the death I most want to avenge is Jo's."

My vocal cords were abruptly strung so tight they squeaked like an out of tune violin when I opened my mouth and tried to speak. I had to take several slow, deep breaths before I managed to get out a quiet, "What happened to her?"

Enyo's nostrils flared, her gaze turning murderous. "None of us know for sure but I can tell you this much—it was a bad death." She locked eyes with me and said with sudden, savage intensity, "I think about that, you know. In this world, the way things are, you're a fool if you don't. What's a good death, what's a bad one, and how you want to go when it's your time. When it's my time, I want to be doing something that matters, betters the world, and saves people's lives. I want my death to mean something." She lapsed into silence, staring off into space, scowling for a long moment, then said in a low, fierce voice, "Jo's death didn't mean a damned thing. It looked like an Unseelie stumbled on her while she was searching through the wreckage for food and water to bring us. Whatever did it also put rat poison in the water jugs she'd been collecting. We lost two more *sidhe*-seers before we figured out that bit of twisted nastiness. If I ever find the Unseelie that killed her, I'll do to *it* what it did to her," she said from between clenched teeth. "Every last fucking bit of it."

I forced myself to inhale and exhale slowly, carefully. I could change the subject right now. Never ask. Never know. "What did it do to her? I want to know the details," I said in a voice that must have sounded as terrible to her as it sounded to me. She gave me a weird look, so I added hastily, "How can I help you get even with it if I don't know what it did?"

She eyed me with new interest and nodded. "You carry the spear and I hear you're a null. We might work well together."

I didn't trust myself to speak so I just nodded back.

Leaning forward, in a voice taut with rage, she told me every detail, interpreting my complete immobility and silence as an appropriate show of abject horror and like-minded rage.

When she finished, she pushed to her feet, bristling with restless energy, told me she was due back at the abbey and would catch up with me later, so we could get to work identifying the monster that had done such horrific things to Jo and go hunt it together.

As the door banged shut, I hung my head and, after a long, wheezing inhale during which so much pain exploded inside my chest that it locked me down from lungs to lips, I doubled over heaving in silent, suffocating convulsions, pounding the floor with my fist. Finally, just when I thought I might die, a sob ripped free from my throat with such force that it burned like fire and I began to cry.

No, I began to keen. No, I began to gnash my teeth and tear at my hair and wail like my Irish ancestors' legendary banshee.

I knew what monster had killed Jo.

Me.

34

"Stay with me, let's just breathe"

JADA

I was so irritated, I didn't even think of accessing the slipstream.

I walked like a Joe, hands shoved deep in my pockets, scowling at the day, muttering beneath my breath, unaware of the passage of either scenery or time until I realized I was standing in the middle of the green at Trinity College.

I stopped walking and took stock of myself. I was feeling dangerously like Dani again. That was unacceptable. I had a world to save. And a personal mission I had to find time for.

The past twenty-four hours felt as surreal as if I'd been battling Silverside again. Although in Dublin thirty-five days had passed, for me it was a mere twenty-four hours, give or take a few, and those twenty-four hours had been jam-packed with crises, each carrying significant emotional currency.

The battle at the abbey. Watching my women die. The fire. Shazam and my meltdown. Ryodan burning himself. The Sweeper capturing us. Mac's sacrifice. Dealing with the cuff and Cruce. Hacking off Ryodan's head with my sword. Trying to predict the *Sinsar Dubh*'s moves. Mac regaining control over the Book, joining us in Ryodan's office, then losing it again. The *Sinsar Dubh* grabbing me in that scant split second I'd still been processing Mac's transformation, swiping the spear and nearly strangling me, the floor dropping out beneath us, falling, getting up and dashing into the White Mansion in a desperate bid to position the stones around her before she reached the queen.

Failing.

The queen passing the True Magic of her race into Mac and shoving her back through the mirror, so we could contain her while she was immobilized. The painful mixture of triumph and grief as I'd watched the blue-black wall flare into life, incarcerating my friend in a prison where I'd had no idea what hell she might suffer. We'd only just reconnected again.

I dropped down onto a bench, turned my face up to faint tendrils of sun that penetrated a dense cloud cover and just breathed.

I smiled faintly, remembering the moment Mac had stepped out of the prison, leaving the *Sinsar Dubh* behind.

Then I scowled, thinking about "Saint Ryodan."

Then I got ahold of myself, emptied my mind of everything, centered myself with my breath, stood and performed a kata to reengage my energy. Abandoning myself to the fluid motion, I became nothing but a strong young body capable of fueling a stronger young mind. By the time I permitted myself to remember the past twenty-four hours again, they rolled off me like water from a duck.

I was calm, energized, and ready for the day.

My feet had taken me to the place I needed to be. They usually did. Some might say they hadn't the night I'd run from Mac and leapt into the Hall of All Days, but I didn't see things like that, as if there were clearly defined right and wrong turns in life. There was what I'd done. And what I was going to do.

Right now it was time to add my brainpower to the mental energy being harnessed at Trinity College, and amp it up a few hundred thousand kilowatts.

♪

I found Dancer alone in a long, narrow laboratory in the physics building, beneath a bank of windows through which intermittent shafts of sunlight spilled.

He was peering into a microscope, oblivious to my presence, so I paused in the door, watching him.

I used to watch him a lot when we were young, wait until he was engrossed in a videogame or a movie, and stare unabashedly. I'd thought he had the most beautiful eyes I'd ever seen. I'd admired his hair, the way he sprawled like a cat soaking up sun, how he often smiled at an inner thought, sometimes laughed out loud.

His hair was a mass of dark tousled waves that told me he'd been thinking hard, running his hands through it incessantly. He had on tight, straight-legged faded jeans, black hiking boots, and a black tee-shirt with the words: I'M LIKE PI—REALLY LONG AND I GO ON FOREVER. There were two pencils stuck behind his left ear. I couldn't see his right one but was willing to bet he had a couple stuck behind that one, too.

He stood, peering into the scope, and when he raised his hand to adjust it, the muscles in his shoulder bunched and smoothed out again. I narrowed my eyes, noticing how well-defined his arm was and that his skin was lightly tanned from stretching out in the sun on those rare days it shone. When did he develop that biceps? How did I miss how thick his forearms were, my geeky, hunky friend? When did his shoulders get so cut and how had I missed the swell of his traps? My gaze dropped in an objective inquiry to ascertain whether the rest of him matched. It did, and I was struck again by the notion that I'd simply not seen him when I was young. I'd found him attractive in a boy-genius way. I'd failed to notice he was a man.

"Hey," I said, nipping that bud of thought before it blossomed further.

His head whipped up and he moved so fast he caught a beaker with his elbow and knocked it over. It tumbled from the counter, hit the floor and shattered before he could catch it.

He stared at me a long moment then said coolly, "So. You're back. Again."

I offered him a smile and said lightly, "Back like Jack. In like Flynn. Ready to brainstorm like—" I couldn't think of a name that rhymed with *brainstorm*. "—Einstein on his best day?"

He didn't smile back. He looked tired and there were dark circles under his eyes.

Grabbing a nearby broom, he yanked the dustpan from the handle and began sweeping up the broken glass. Without taking his gaze from the floor, he said, "It's been thirty-five days, four hours, and—" He looked at his watch. "—sixteen minutes since you were last seen alive, in case you were wondering. But I doubt you were. Time doesn't mean the same thing to you that it means to some of us. That's how long you were gone this time, as near as I was able to calculate. You were last spotted leaving Chester's the night of August eighth."

If the way he was beating the floor into submission with his broom was anything to gauge his mood by, he was seriously mad at me.

I considered the past twenty-four hours. I'd had a job to do. I'd done it. "I'm sorry," I said simply. And I meant it. That day, so many years ago, when he'd gotten mad at me for disappearing into the Silvers with Christian, I'd gotten mad right back.

But I'd learned a few things since then. Such as, it's pure hell when you care about someone and suddenly they're gone and you don't know if you'll ever see them again.

I moved into the room and waited for him to stop assaulting the floor with a cleaning implement.

He kept at his angry sweeping for a few moments without saying a word then finally stopped and looked up at me. His gaze was guarded, remote.

"I mean it," I said softly. "I'm sorry. Time really *didn't* move the same way where I was. It was critical I go back into the White Mansion. For me, it was only twenty-four hours."

"How long before you went into the Silvers did you know you had to go?"

He was asking if there'd been enough time that I might have left him a note or gotten a message to him somehow. "As long as it took me to freeze-frame directly from Chester's to the White Mansion. Critical means 'at an immediate point of crisis.'"

He propped the broom against the counter and gazed into my eyes, searching deep. I had no idea what he was looking for or what he decided he found but he finally relaxed through his shoulders and said softly, "Well, then. Damn glad you're back, Mega."

"Damn glad to be back, Dancer."

And just like that there was no tension left in the room.

I loved that about him. He didn't even need to know what I'd done. Only the parameters of it that affected the respect and consideration he felt was his due if I wanted to be his friend. I hated that he'd been worrying about me again. I hated the dark circles beneath his eyes, so I extended an olive branch, something I'd never done in the past. It made me uncomfortable but I would have been more uncomfortable not doing it. "If it's at all possible, I promise to get word to you if I ever have to go into the Silvers again."

He inhaled sharply, not missing that what I'd just said accorded a degree of accountability to him I'd never permitted before. I meant it. The next time I had to go somewhere, I would bloody well find a way to leave him a note.

His grin was instant and blinding.

Then he was talking a mile a minute, catching me up on all the work they'd been doing, outlining the preferred theories, eyes sparkling.

♪

Dancer was convinced the black holes suspended slightly above the earth weren't remotely the same as the ones in outer space. "I think the ones up there"—he jerked his head toward the ceiling—

"are naturally occurring phenomena. They have the right to be what and where they are. The theory is that primordial black holes were birthed at the dawn of time, have always existed and for some reason need to. I like to think of them as the universe's trash collectors, gathering up old, defunct detritus, clearing the way for new things to be born. The holes we're dealing with don't behave in accordance with modern black hole theory. While it's possible modern black hole theory is wrong—I mean, bloody hell, we believed Newtonian laws right up until Einstein turned everything on its ear—the smell I get off our black holes is that they're anathema to the universe. They don't belong, should never have come into existence, and are in complete defiance of the natural order of things."

"They smell? I never noticed a smell and I have a super sniffer."

He ducked his head, looking mildly embarrassed. "They say a great physicist is distinguished by his ability to sniff out the difference between a superior theory and one not worth pursuing."

I smiled. "Well then, you've definitely got a super sniffer, too."

He grinned. "I suspect these entities are literally spheres of 'unmaking' in . . . well, I hate to say a magical sense because I tend to lean toward everything being explainable by science, but I also believe in God, and the Fae are real and maybe magic is just a word for those things we can't yet explain or understand."

"What does this tell us about how to get rid of them?"

"That the Song of Making is likely the only thing that has a chance." He was silent a moment and his eyes got that dreamy, faraway look that told me he was happily pondering a highly abstract concept. "A melody of creation—think of it, Mega!" he exclaimed. "That math and frequency might actually be capable, on some level we don't understand, of creating new things, repairing damaged ones!" He shook his head. "There's something about the concept that resonates with me. Makes sense on a gut level but it's so bloody far beyond my ability to interpret and elucidate that I feel like a child, staring up at the night sky, wondering what the

Milky Way is. Regardless, the fabric of our world is unraveling and has to be stitched back together again somehow, and I believe the song the Fae used to know is the only thing that's going to work. An Unseelie created the holes. It seems quid pro quo that a Seelie must repair them. Maybe, if we had a few centuries to work on the song we'd get somewhere, but I don't think we have a tenth that much time."

"Months," I told him grimly. "Perhaps even less."

His eyes widened. "You know that for sure?"

I nodded.

He plunged his hands into his hair, raking it back. "Mega, we're at a complete impasse with the song. We need some kind of clue, a fragment of the melody, then at least I'd understand what I'm aiming for, and stand a chance at figuring out what the bloody hell it is!"

I pressed a hand to my forehead. It was hot. I couldn't recall the last time I'd eaten and was abruptly aware I was dangerously hungry. "Do you have anything high calorie to eat around here?"

"Always." He led me to a small room off the back of the laboratory where a fridge was loaded with food. There were boxes and boxes of chilled protein bars. Peanut butter. Even beef jerky and milk!

"Where did you get all this?" I reached for the glass jar of milk, topped with a yellow layer of heavy cream, mouth watering.

"Ryodan," he said, and rolled his eyes. "He's bloody well taken over the bloody world and suddenly everyone has food. Which means he had it all along and just wasn't sharing. Got this, too." With his foot he nudged a box toward me, filled with canned goods.

Chocolate syrup! I unscrewed the top off the milk, squeezed the chocolate in, recapped the glass bottle and shook the milk hard enough to mix. I guzzled it for several long seconds, only stopping with a twinge of embarrassment when there were a few inches left to ask him hastily, "Did you want any of this?" When he shook his head, smiling faintly, I finished it, and chased it with two protein bars. That was better. I could feel myself cooling down already.

"We have the queen," I told him.

"*What?*" he exploded. "And you're just now telling me this? Where is she? How did you get her to come back here?"

I filled him in on what had happened in the past day, my time, omitting the parts about my meltdown and Shazam and killing Ryodan and Mac calling me a cunt.

He was pacing, repeatedly raking his hands through his hair by the time I finished. "I need to talk to Mac. Now. Like, this very instant."

"If Mac had any information about the song, she'd already be here, sharing it. I think it's going to take time for her to decipher what the queen passed on and figure out how to use it."

"Time is the one thing we don't have," he said darkly.

♪

When I left, after promising to return later that night so he could demonstrate his latest invention—"And maybe we could take it out for a test drive," he'd said, eyes sparkling—I headed down the hall and was about to access the slipstream when I saw Caoimhe hurrying down the corridor toward me. The moment she saw me, her eyes filled with glacial hostility. I considered kicking up and blasting past her with an elbow casually protruding but that was something Dani would have done so I sludged along in slow-mo.

We approached each other with equal coolness. I couldn't help but wonder if she was his girlfriend now. She sure acted like she was. Or his keeper.

We drew up a few feet apart. "You," she said with icy disdain.

"Caoimhe," I said tonelessly.

"Why did you even bother coming back? We don't need you. And I sure as hell don't want you here. It was a grand month with-out you around."

"I'm just his friend," I said in a voice void of inflection.

"No you're not," she spat. "If you were his 'friend' you wouldn't cause him so much worry, make him take so many careless risks. If you were his 'friend' you'd realize he may have a super brain but he's no bloody superhero. A true friend wouldn't subject him to constant disappearances and reckless shenanigans with no consideration whatsoever for what's good for him!"

I studied her objectively, trying to define the origin of her hostility. It seemed as if it had to be more than mere jealousy, and I didn't see any reason for her to be jealous of me. "I've never kissed him," I finally said, thinking that might defuse the tension between us. Discord was illogical. We had too many problems already. We couldn't afford to create more for ourselves.

She tossed her head impatiently. "Oooh! You think *that's* what this is about? I'm jealous? Why don't you try pulling your selfish head out of your selfish ass? Yes, I love Dancer. I freely admit it. Most of the women here do, he's damn near impossible not to love. Funny, sweet, thoughtful, brilliant. But this is about *his* well-being not mine. That's what love is, how it behaves, but you obviously don't know a thing about it. The only person you love is yourself. Did you make plans to dash off and indulge in another one of your little adventures with him tonight? Whiz him about at speeds he was never meant to endure while you 'goof off' and play at being superheroes together?"

I guess the look on my face gave me away because she narrowed her eyes and hissed, "If you can't be selfless enough to protect the health of the one man that has a chance at figuring out how to save our world, then you need to stay away from him. Far away from him. Like go get lost all over again only never bloody come back this time." She shoved past me and stormed off down the hall.

I whirled and stalked after her. She'd said something I didn't understand and didn't like, and it had sent a chill racing up my spine. "What do you mean 'protect the health'?" I growled at her back. "What are you talking about? Dancer's young and strong. He works out and looks amazing. He's perfectly healthy."

She whirled, eyes flashing. "Aye, he spends hours working out every day while he ponders his theories—and he shouldn't. It's not good for him. Know why he does it? To keep up with you. To get you to see him as a man. He can't do cardio so he does isometrics, pitting muscle against muscle to build strength without overloading himself. Planks, crunches, tension exercises, and the like. He's obsessed with looking like those men you hang out with. God! I wish he'd just stop *wanting* you!"

My stomach had turned into a blender on high speed and was threatening to propel the milk I'd drunk out the lid of my mouth. "Why can't he do cardio? Why isn't working out good for him?"

She looked at me a long moment then a bit of the fury eased from her face and her eyes widened faintly. She took a few steps toward me and said wonderingly, "For the love of Mary, you don't even know, do you? All of us do, but not you."

Apparently not. Pressing a hand to my stomach, I shook my head.

"He never told you?" she said incredulously.

"Repeating the same bloody question in a slightly different way is still the same bloody question," I hissed. What the bloody hell was wrong with Dancer? What did everyone know that I didn't know? "Do I fucking look like I have any idea what you're talking about?" I practically shouted.

Her face changed as if she was seeing me for the first time. "Well then," she murmured, "at least I don't have to keep hating you. I hate hating people."

"Good to know. So what the bloody hell is it that I don't know about Dancer?" I ground out between clenched teeth.

She smiled, but it was a terrible, sad smile. "Dani—Jada—whatever it is you're calling yourself these days—our lad has a bad heart. He came that way. I thought you knew."

35

"To everything, turn, turn, turn"

MAC

I opted for no makeup, swiped balm on my lips because they were so dry, stepped back and studied my reflection in the bathroom mirror.

Even with the lights off I could tell my eyes were red and it was obvious I'd been crying, but I could blame that on any number of things and be believed.

I'd curled on the floor of the shower, sobbing for a long time, wondering if all the images the *Sinsar Dubh* had forced on me were true. Had I done every one of those terrible things? Killed so many, with such chilling brutality and barbarism? I'd laid on the tile floor, reliving each detail the Book had showed me. Owning every bit of it. Jo's death had been the truth. That told me they very likely all were. I'd done unforgivable things I could never undo. My choice to take a spell from the *Sinsar Dubh* to save Dani's life had cost the lives of many others, and there was no way I could make my books on those accounts balance. Not just *cost* the lives, let us be perfectly precise—my hands, my body, had killed them.

I wallowed in shame and grief.

I shuddered, wept, and screamed.

Then I forced myself to stop, collected the savage murder of Jo and the other unforgivable crimes I'd committed, put them in a box and shut the lid.

I despised using one of the *Sinsar Dubh*'s tactics but it was effective, and hating myself for my sins would have to wait. As was whatever act of atonement I would eventually make. Not that there was any act of atonement that would mean a thing to those I'd killed.

Putting them away didn't mean the pain was gone. I carried it. I would always carry it. But because I'd been given the queen's power, my state of mind was too critical to everyone's survival for me to let myself fall apart now. It simply wasn't an option.

It occurred to me, while lying on the floor, that grief's drink recipe is two parts tribute to the person you loved and four parts feeling sorry for yourself because you lost them. Or, in the case of Jo and the others, four parts extreme self-loathing.

Either way, grief was self-indulgent, and that was something I had no right to be. If we survived, I'd have oodles of time to hate myself all I wanted.

Currently, I was the only one who could wield the Song of Making. And that meant I didn't get to be anything less than one-hundred-percent focused on our situation. I was a soldier on the front line, and soldiers don't get the luxury of addressing their issues until the war is over and everyone's safe.

I began to turn away from the mirror then narrowed my eyes and glanced back. Something about me was different. What was it? I'd dried my hair upside-down as usual, and my eyes were green, not black. My teeth were almost blindingly white since I'd brushed them about a hundred times, trying to not to think about what had been lodged between them.

Frowning, I fumbled behind me for the light switch and flipped it on.

"Holy hell I look like the Khaleesi!" I exploded, jumping back from the mirror. I'd showered and dried my hair in the dark, in no mood to see myself clearly. The streaks of crimson paint were gone and my hair was blonder than I'd ever seen it, nearly white. I tucked my chin down and peered at my part—yep, all the way to the roots. I gathered a handful of it, examining the length, trying to remember how long it had been a few days ago. It sure seemed to be a few inches longer now than I recalled.

The Seelie Queen's hair had spilled past her waist in a thick platinum fall.

Christian's hair had turned from rich chestnut to inky black.

Was I turning Seelie? Would the True Magic actually transform me into a Fae? Cripes. First a *sidhe*-seer, with the blood of the Unseelie King in my veins, then the *Sinsar Dubh*, now a full-on Faery queen. It was beginning to look like being "just Mac" had never been in the cards for me.

I narrowed my eyes. Maybe my changes would only go partway like Christian's. He'd managed to arrest, even reverse, his transformation to a degree. Then again, this wasn't a transformation I could afford to resist. I needed all the juice she'd given me. No matter the price.

After a moment I growled at my platinum-haired reflection, "Well, buck up, little buckaroo," in my best John Wayne voice.

What I looked like, even whatever I might eventually become due to the gift Aoibheal had given me—and it *was* a gift because it could save our world—didn't mean shit.

The only thing that mattered was what I did with it.

♪

I hurried down the stairs, entering my paint-stained, wrecked store from the rear. I paused in the doorway, leaning against the jamb, studying it. The critical factor now was: we needed the song. But an equally critical factor was: assuming we got it, what power had I been given and how was I supposed to use it? I had no idea how Fae magic worked.

I remembered standing in the street, at the head of Darroc's army of Unseelie, watching as V'lane made Dree'lia's mouth disappear. Unlike when he'd sealed the door to the boudoir with a steel gate, he'd not said a word when he altered her face. He hadn't even glanced at her. So what had he done? Was it based on the power of mere thought, the higher the caste of Fae, the stronger the power?

I studied the room with dried spray paint streaked everywhere, the shattered bookcases, the broken lamps and magazines and chairs. I'd only managed to clean a third of the smaller debris out the last time I'd worked on it.

I closed my eyes and painstakingly began to create a mental image of the way it had looked the day I first stumbled from the Dark Zone through the front door, so damned naïve, and met Barrons for the first time.

When I'd opened the tall diamond-paned door to the seemingly modestly sized four-story building and discovered the cavernous bookstore within, I'd fallen in love with every inch of the elegant Old World place with its antique rugs, sumptuous Chesterfields, enameled gas fireplaces, acres of books, even the old-fashioned cash register.

I lavished detail on the room I was building in my mind.

Only when I could see my bookstore with perfect clarity, exactly the way it had been that day, did I open my eyes.

Still wrecked. Not a damn thing had changed.

Okay. That hadn't worked. Time wasn't my friend. I needed to figure this out fast. I was rather relieved it hadn't worked because it had taken me too long. V'lane had removed Dree'lia's mouth effortlessly and instantly, and I didn't believe for a minute that if things got critical and I had to do something to save us, my potential adversary might wait patiently for me to picture whatever I wanted to do with crystal clear perfection.

I dropped down onto a crate, buried my head in my hands and sank into myself, seeking the shining vault I'd claimed for my own, quite certain it was no more an actual vault than there'd ever been an actual book or box inside me. But what was it? And how did I access it?

I went still, disconnecting from my body, remembering what it had felt like to be consciousness and not one thing more, and focused.

There it was.

Rays of dazzling gold radiated from the smooth gilded surface of it, and I could feel raw, ferocious power emanating from within. I welcomed it, embraced it, basked in the bright golden light it was throwing off, and grew warm all over as if absorbing rays of sun.

I experienced a sudden *whooshing* sensation as if I was being yanked from one location to another. Then abruptly I was somewhere else.

My eyes flew open.

I stood near an enormous alabaster altar, on top of a hill that looked very much like Tara only bigger, more dramatic and otherworldly. At the bottom of the high, vast mound a thousand or more mighty megaliths that shimmered with iridescent fire encircled the base, with only small spaces between.

A soft breeze tousled my hair, the sky above me was dark, glittering with stars and three enormous moons that hung abnormally near the planet. One was so close, low, and directly above me that I felt as if it might drop on my head and crush me. The entire mound was carpeted with lush velvety flowers that bobbed and swayed in the breeze, scenting the night air with perfume. High in the sky, dark, leathery-winged Hunters sailed past the two more distant moons, gonging deep in their massive chests. Night birds sang an exquisite synchronized melody. It was so overwhelmingly beautiful to all my senses that it hurt. I closed my eyes, inhaling deeply, wondering where I was.

What have you come for? A bodiless voice demanded.

I kept my eyes closed, the better to answer with an undistracted mind. Opening them would have done me no good anyway. The voice had been huge, coming from everywhere at once: the stones, the earth, even the moons.

"The True Magic of the Fae race," I said strongly.

What will you do with it?

My answer was instant and effortless. "Protect and guide."

How will you achieve it?

"With wisdom and grace."

Are you equal to it?

Well, shit. That felt like a trick question. "Yes" displayed arrogance. "No" displayed weakness. I inhaled deeply of the jasmine-and-sandalwood-scented breeze and searched myself—the ego that was undivided for the first time in my entire life—for the answer my daddy, Jack Lane, would have given, because it was the right one, and said quietly, "I will do everything in my power to be equal to it."

I gasped as I felt something warm and good settle over me like a full body cloak. It draped me completely from head to toe, seeping into my skin, and deeper still, pooling inside me like molten gold. Still, I kept my eyes closed because I'd learned recently how clear a lack of visual distractions kept my mind. As it filled me, I felt as if I was becoming a small star, blazing from within, ancient and calm and watchful and as essential to the universe as any of those stars above me. My head whipped back, my body drew taut, as radiance drenched my being.

I opened my eyes, held out my hand and looked at it. I was glowing, translucent, ethereal, my body no longer solid.

You are not Fae. It was a judgment. Not a favorable one.

I said simply, "I have the blood of the Unseelie King in me and Queen Aoibheal chose me to be her successor. I did battle with the entity known as the *Sinsar Dubh* and won. The True Race is in danger of extinction. I will do everything in my power to prevent that."

I felt a sentient presence gust close then. It entered me, joining the brilliance that filled me, and although it was instinct to want to resist—especially after what the Book had done to me—I quelled it quickly and trusted what my gut was saying. This sentience was nonthreatening. It felt vast and wise, gentle and pure. It gusted through my being, leaving no corner untouched by its soft tendrils. I felt as if it was probing into the fundamental elements of my soul, examining every component of every belief I held and every action I'd made.

You recently committed acts of great evil.

There was nothing left in me but honesty. I couldn't have lied if I'd wanted to. I offered it my sorrow, my sins, my grief. "I did," I answered sadly.

Why?

Another trick question. *An evil book made me do it* displayed blame-displacement and weakness; *I was possessed and not myself"* displayed a lack of personal responsibility, and yet more weakness. "Because I made mistakes," I said finally, with a strangely nuanced sorrow I'd never felt before. There was a difference between being sad and feeling sorrow. Sad was about yourself. Sorrow was big as the world and encompassed all of it.

Will you make those mistakes again?

I answered without hesitation. "No. I suspect I'll make entirely new ones. And carry the pain of those, too."

I felt as if the thing inside me smiled. *Then it is yours. As are the Tuatha De Danann. Guide them well.*

There was another *whooshing* sensation and I felt the crate beneath my butt.

I was back in the bookstore, head still in my hands, gasping at the suddenness of the transition, pained by my abrupt eviction from the starry-skied paradise and loss of communion with the wise, gentle thing that had interrogated me and deemed me fit.

I wouldn't let it down.

Inhaling deeply, I raised my head.

Barrons Books & Baubles looked exactly like it had the day I'd first stepped inside it.

♪

Late afternoon sunshine slanted in the front windows of the bookstore, spilling across the back of the Chesterfield, warming my shoulders. I nibbled on the tip of my pen and scanned my list.

WORLD GOALS: (NOT IN ORDER)

1. *Get the music box to Dancer so we can determine exactly what it is. I know it has something to do with the song. I felt it that day in the White Mansion.*
2. *Dispatch scouts into the Silvers and find a world humans can survive on. Start making plans to relocate them. They'll have to be fully settled on the planet, not in the Silvers, because I don't know what will happen to the Silvers if our planet dies.*
3. *Find Cruce and make him my ally. Persuade him to teach me how to use the magic I have. Find out what he knows. He not only has part of the* Sinsar Dubh *that allegedly contains information about the song (or was that just one of the many lies he'd told me as V'lane?) but worked beside the Unseelie King for eons as he tried to re-create the lost melody. Cruce has more knowledge of ancient history than anyone.*
4. *Find out what's going on with the Fae: Seelie and Unseelie. Figure out how to organize them and unite humans and Fae together toward the goal of finding the song.*

I chewed on my pen and thought, yeah, that was going to be a challenge. Like they were going to accept me—a human—as their leader and queen. I knew what the Fae were like. They responded to threats and displays of power, and so far the only thing I'd figured out how to do was clean up my bookstore.

I'd spent the past few hours sitting on the couch in front of a lightly hissing gas fire, doing the closest thing to meditating I'd ever done, trying to fathom what was inside me now. It had all seemed so clear, so pure, the power so tangible and understandable when I was standing on the hill beneath three moons. But I'd been translucent and ethereal then, and I was no longer. I was solid and human again, and although I could feel power rippling beneath my skin, I didn't know how to access and direct it. I supposed this was how Christian felt, with no brotherly prince to help him understand what he was.

I scribbled another one down.

5. *Go to the abbey and rebuild it the way I did the bookstore, restore the* sidhe-seers' *home so they can gather all the lore they have and begin searching it. (Do I have the power to re-create things that got burned, like books? How am I supposed to rebuild the abbey? I don't know what each room looked like. Do I need to?)*

6. *Talk to Barrons about talking to Dageus to see what he knows.*

PERSONAL GOALS:

1. *Find my parents and spend time with them. Bring them up-to-date so they can help.*

2. *Find out if Alina still exists.*

I stopped writing and sighed. I had serious doubts on that score. After watching the Book create multiple versions of me with substance, I'd concluded that was all Alina had ever been. And what had I done with my chance to spend time with her again, even as an illusion? I'd driven her away repeatedly, interrogated and bullied her. Only at the end had I finally accepted her, made plans to have coffee and breakfast—a date I'd never gotten to keep. I shoved the tangle of emotion into another handy box and resumed writing.

3. *Talk to Dani about Shazam. Determine if he's real, and if so, figure out how to help her. If he's not real, figure out how to help her times ten.*
4. *Barrons.*

I didn't elucidate on the Barrons personal goal. It was purely selfish, as were all my personal goals, but since the world might cease to exist in the very near future, I intended to spend at least some time with the people I loved.

The bell on the door tinkled as it opened and banged shut again.

My body tightened with familiar tension and I smiled.

Barrons was there, behind me, reading over my shoulder in silence. After a moment he said, "Ah. So I'm a personal goal of yours."

"Something like that."

"Care to elaborate?"

I did. Tossing aside my notebook, I turned around on the sofa, knelt on the cushions and looked up at him. I'd intended to pull his head down and kiss him but I ended up just sitting there, gazing at him.

What a creature you've become. His dark eyes gleamed.

I know, right?

Nice hair, Mac.

Thanks. What happened to "Ms. Lane"? I'm not dying, I don't think you're about to kill me, and we're not having sex.

She doesn't live here anymore.

She doesn't? Was he throwing me out? Would he do that? Tell me I had to go live with the Fae now?

It's nice to meet you. Finally. Mac. His eyes glittered with unguarded appreciation and passion.

I stared up at him then shook my head with a wry smile, resisting the urge to slap a hand to my forehead. It was so simple, so clear, and had mystified me for so long. I'd told myself it was just the way we were, preferring a persona of distance in public and another, intimate, sacred one in private.

But that had never been it at all. Or at least not all of it.

I might never know if it was the *Sinsar Dubh*'s presence inside me that kept me so conflicted about everything for so long and, once it was gone, I finally gained that long-sought clarity of being, or if it had been through the very process of standing my ground and defeating it that I'd achieved such clarity. But it didn't matter. The end result was the same.

Some shadowy, self-destructive, confused place no longer existed inside me. I was of a single, clear mind. There were goals, and there were methods to attain them. There were my chosen responsibilities and those things I was willing to do to honor them. There were the things I was willing to live with and the things I wasn't willing to live without. There was a quiet, deep abiding love of myself—flaws and all, and I had plenty—and the world around me, and it had plenty, too.

My eyes shimmered, and later Barrons would tell me they'd glowed with iridescent fire. *It's nice to meet you, too, Jericho.*

I pulled his head down and kissed him.

36

"I am the lizard king, I can do anything"

SINSAR DUBH

My enemies underestimate me.

Encumbered by emotion, their faulty brains fail to apprehend the altered variables, particularly the new one introduced by MacKayla walking away from me.

WALKING AWAY FROM ME WILL NEVER BE PERMITTED! SHE IS MY HORSE TO BREAK AND ALWAYS WILL BE!

The force field erected by the stones was designed to hold my essence, doubly trapped: first by the covers of the spelled tome, second by the field. Or first by a body, second by the field. Without the primary barrier, I exceed the prison's capacity to contain me.

Although it takes time to divine the method and is perilous—for an instant I nearly dissipate into a storm of black dust shaped like a cube—my will is equal to the task.

A small, dark cloud, I hover above the cocooned Unseelie princess.

So thoughtful of them to leave me a body. I would lose cohesion quickly in this form.

Again, the universe favors my supremacy, colludes with me to attain my desires. It recognizes the supremacy of my being.

The runes I plastered upon the dark Fae's skin fall away at my command, and the princess stirs. When she rolls over, mouth slightly ajar, I aim myself at the aperture and drive myself in.

She goes rigid, screaming, as she resists. But she is puny and I am vast. I possess her quickly, saturating every atom.

I realize the moment I attach to her neural network, unlike MacKayla, who I will torture for all eternity, this Unseelie is incapable of holding me for long. My refusal to jump bodies yesterday was wise.

The only reason MacKayla was able to WALK AWAY FROM ME AND LEAVE ME was because she had a force field with which to winch us apart.

But the stones are here in the White Mansion, where time flows differently. And she is out there where I will soon be.

It would take a month or more, Earthtime, for anyone to retrieve them.

I require very little time to execute my new plan. The bulk of it will be lost making my exit from this place.

My new vessel jerks clumsily when I command it to hurry for the door. Weak, puny thing. But it will last long enough.

I hurry out onto black marble floors, turn left then right, seeking crimson, cursing the ever-changing White Mansion the bastard king fashioned for his concubine. Each wrong turn I take equates to days slipping away Earthtime. A month or more will have passed by the time I escape this maze.

MacKayla will be able to feel me coming once I exit the Silvers but she will believe me body-bound, giving me the advantage.

I will take back what is mine.

Then I will destroy this motherfucking world.

INVISIBLE

I suppose she must have begun thinking about how different her life would be without me.

She couldn't travel, couldn't really make friends or have company in, or even go out at night because what kind of mother would she be if she left her daughter locked in a cage, and didn't come home?

I sometimes wonder if she met someone who told her things that made her unhappy with our life, because she seemed to change overnight.

She still sat with me in the evenings and did all those mom things but she rarely smiled anymore and she started to get lines around her mouth and eyes. Her lips pulled down much more often than up and I couldn't reach her through the bars to push her cheeks into a smile.

I was six and a half years old when she fell in love.

She told me about him, how kind he was and how much he cared about her. She told me he was going to marry her. Us. That she would tell him all about me when the time was right.

He took her on trips every weekend, and the first night she left me alone, I cried every time I woke up. But when she came back she was like she used to be when I was little, before I ever freeze-framed, happy and excited, cooing to me and talking about plans for our future again.

Then one night, a week before my seventh birthday, she came home really late and soaking wet, and just walked right past my cage without even looking at me, went into her bedroom and closed the door.

Her expression was so terrible as I'd stared up, excited to see her, *that I hadn't said any of the interesting, funny things I'd planned all day to say.*

I just curled up and listened to her cry all night.

I was pretty sure he'd decided not to marry us.

I think he broke her heart.

My seventh birthday came and went but she didn't notice. For the first time, there was no Irish stew and ice cream and no shared stories of One Day.

I celebrated anyway, having an imaginary meal with my imaginary dog, Robin, that lived in my cage with me and could talk and told the funniest jokes and we were always cracking ourselves up!

One day we were going to both be OLDER and go OUTSIDE and we were going to zoom around everywhere in the city that we wanted to go, and we were going to fix other people's problems for them because that was just about the nicest thing you could do for anyone was notice them and fix their problems and sometimes even just spend time with them!

After that she stopped going away on weekends. For a while we didn't have very much food and she no longer wore the work uniform she used to wear. Then one day she dressed up so pretty and went to work in the afternoon and came home much later than she used to. She started bringing bottles of wine home with her, instead of groceries or carryout.

She'd slide a Heat 'N Serve into my cage and, instead of telling me about her day or daydreaming with me about our plans, she'd drink in silence, staring at late night TV while I tried desperately to say something that would make her smile.

Or even look at me.

She began coming home even later after work, sometimes early in the morning, and when she did, she was slurring and stumbling and sometimes she was so very, very nice and sometimes she was . . . really not. Sometimes it was nearly dawn, with me pinching myself and making up all kinds of new games in my head to stay awake. Eager to see her, and tell her about the things I learned on TV that day, and what life was going to be like when I was OLDER and could go OUTSIDE with her. I was sure if we could just go OUTSIDE together, everything would be all right again.

One night she didn't come home at all.

It went that way for a while, every four or five days she'd stay out all night. She lost weight and got dark smudges beneath her eyes.

Then she didn't come home for two nights in a row. She stopped bringing bottles with her but her slurring and stumbling got even worse.

Then it was three nights. And when she finally did come home, she didn't look at me very much and her eyes were unfocused and empty. Her gaze would kind of move around the room then hurry up when they got to the cage and I knew I was becoming invisible somehow.

The more she didn't come home, the harder I tried when she was there to make her want to stay.

I knew if I could just make her remember how much she loved me, she wouldn't want to leave. I'd never forgotten.

I guess my world changed slowly, but it felt like it happened all at once.

One day I just knew.

I wasn't her daughter anymore.

I was the dog she'd never wanted.

37

"Wait until the war is over and
we're both a little older"

JADA

*Time doesn't mean the same thing to you that it means to some
of us.*

I couldn't shake Dancer's words from my mind. They'd seemed
fairly innocuous when he flung them at me.

They didn't anymore. No wonder he hated it every time I disappeared.

Caoimhe told me his diagnosis but had refused to discuss it
further. She'd said I needed to ask him about it. When she walked
away, she glanced back with a look of pity and said softly, *I really
did think you knew. I'd not have disliked you so much otherwise.*

Hypertrophic cardiomyopathy.

I knew what it was—the disease that killed young athletes on
the basketball court or football field, without warning, cutting
them down in their prime.

The symptoms: fatigue, shortness of breath, inability to exercise, fainting, a sensation of pounding heartbeats, heart murmur.
At times it might be manageable, other times it could be severe. I
was pretty sure all those times he'd disappeared for a few days

he'd been having a bad spell and gone off alone, so I wouldn't know.

The cause: usually gene mutation. An abnormal arrangement of heart muscle cells called "myofiber disarray." I'd watched a TV show about it, years ago when all I'd had to do with my time was watch TV. The severity of the disease varied widely. Most people had a form where the septum between the two bottom chambers of the organ became enlarged and impeded blood flow out of the heart. It was usually inherited. The thickened heart muscle could eventually become too stiff to effectively fill with blood, resulting in heart failure. Sudden cardiac death was rare, but when it happened—it was to young people under the age of thirty. Young athletic people just like Dancer.

The treatment was palliative, relieving symptoms, and preventative: avoiding sudden cardiac death.

Dancer had never breathed a word of it to me.

We'd raced through the streets at dizzying, dangerous speeds, set off bombs and outrun them. He'd let me whiz him around in freeze-frame, crashing him into all kinds of stuff, bruising him, hurting him. Laughing his ass off the entire time.

Now I understood why he'd liked to laze on uncommon days of sunshine as boneless as a cat, soaking up the sun: stillness was his friend. Being able to relax so completely might just be what had kept him alive this long.

Now I understood why Caoimhe had stared daggers at me whenever she'd seen me.

I might have killed him.

You're going to get the boy killed one day, Ryodan had said to me five and a half years ago, Silverside time.

Rot in purgatory, dude, I'd fired back. *Batman never dies. Dancer won't either.*

But Batman didn't have a bad heart.

Dancer did.

♪

When the door whisked silently open, I stalked into Ryodan's office and dropped into the chair on the opposite side of the desk from him. In the month we'd been gone, the floor and walls had been replaced and the office, like the man, was good as new.

For a moment I just looked at him, appreciating that he was no longer charred to a human crisp and his skin was golden and smooth, except for the skein of scars at his throat and the long, wicked one that stretched from what I could see of his collarbone up to his left ear. Dressed as he usually was in dark pants and an impeccable crisp white shirt, sleeves rolled up, silver cuff glinting, he looked more like a business tycoon than something that I knew wasn't human, sometimes had fangs, could move faster and knew far more powerful magic than me. I realized then, as I never had when I was young, that he'd chosen such civilized attire for precisely that reason—to make people think he was something other than the ruthless, immortal being he was.

I opened my mouth to give him the carefully scripted speech I'd worked on for the past hour, the one that was logical and persuasive and built gently to the point and came off as neither pushy nor needy—the deft, tactful speech that was going to win him over and guarantee his aid—but my mouth had other plans and growled, "How the bloody hell did you keep Dageus alive?"

Up until that moment he'd been regarding me with more benign interest than I'd ever seen from him before. Weird fuck. I just killed him recently, and now he was all laid back.

Benign vanished. A scowl stomped the living shit out of it and did a dance all over his face. He lunged from the chair, was around the desk and had me on my feet, gripping me by my shoulders before I'd even processed that he'd moved.

I would give not just my eyeteeth but every last one of my teeth and wear dentures for the rest of my life, if he'd teach me how to do that.

"How do you know about Dageus?" he said with careful precision. Like Barrons, he spoke differently when he was deeply pissed off or offended. Barrons got softer. Ryodan went all upper-crust British formal and precise, enunciating each word crisply.

I shrugged his hands off my shoulders. "Saw it on the monitor last night."

"You weren't here last night."

"*My* last night. Thirty-five days ago. We had a meeting here when you were dead. How did you do it? Really, it's not so much to ask. I just said 'when you were dead.' I know that happens, that you die and come back, as if that's not a huge, sacred secret. I'm not even asking you how. I'm not asking a single thing about you. Nor am I asking you anything about Dageus. You can keep all those secrets and I'll never bother you about them again. But I want to know how you were able to keep someone who was mortally injured from dying."

He stared down at me a moment then turned away, stalked to the wall and stared out through the glass at the shadowy, empty, silent clubs below.

His shoulders were rigidly contracted, muscles bunching, and the tension in his spine held him as formal as a soldier in full dress uniform. As I watched him, I was startled and a little irked to see him implementing one of my own tactics—the tension began to vanish, starting at eye level. I frowned, wondering if I'd noticed him doing it years ago and copied it from him. I thought I'd invented it. I'd *liked* thinking I invented it.

Only when he was smoothly muscled as a lazing lion did he turn and say, "Who's hurt that you want me to save?"

I assessed him in silence. I knew why I'd worked so hard preparing my speech. I didn't believe he'd help me. Why would he? He'd never liked Dancer. "It's not an issue of hurt so much as it is . . . well, if someone had a bad heart, could you fix it?"

He narrowed his eyes and stared at me as if trying to pluck the name from my brain, so I began mentally singing the theme song from *Animaniacs* that I loved so much when I was a kid, really loud on the top of my brain. It always put me in a great mood. It didn't this time. *It's time for* Animaniacs, *and we're zany to the max, so just sit back and relax, you'll laugh till you collapse, we're* ANIMANIACS!

His eyes narrowed to slits. "What the fuck are *Animaniacs*?"

I scowled. "I knew you did that to me. You used to do it all the time, poke around in my head for stuff I didn't feel like telling you. You said you wouldn't do it anymore."

"I said, precisely, that I wouldn't do it much. Who has a bad heart?"

I dropped back down into the chair and stared up at him. "Dancer," I said flatly.

He exploded, "What?" and just stared at me for, like, a whole minute. Finally he said, "Are you bloody kidding me? How bad is it? Is it something he could die from? Soon?"

I propped my elbow on my knee, made a fist, propped my chin on top of that and glared at him. "You mean, like, before he solves the problem you need him to solve? That's all you're worried about. Yes. He could. He has hypertrophic cardiomyopathy. The heart condition that drops athletes like a stone on the basketball court."

He stared at me, expressionless, for a long moment then said, "But he looks so *healthy*."

"So do all those athletes that die on the playing field," I replied coolly. "So? Can you?"

He turned back to the wall and stared out through the glass again. I waited in silence. No point in trying to rush Ryodan. He was a megaton warship that set sail when it was good and ready.

When he finally turned back around, my heart sank like a stone. His silver eyes were cold, remote.

"Can't. Or. Won't?" I snarled.

"Ah, Jada. Can't."

"Bullshit! How did you save Dageus?" I demanded.

He returned to his chair, sat down, steepled his fingers, and studied them. "I can't tell you that," he said to his hands. Then he glanced at me and said softly, "If there was a way I could help him, I would. And not because I need his help. Because you care about him."

"Don't be nice to me," I snapped.

His nostrils flared and his eyes narrowed. "Christ, aren't we past this? Did I only imagine that you and I reached a new phase in—"

"What? Our *relationship*? Dude, people like you don't have relationships. They have . . . they have . . . cartels and monopolies and kingdoms and, and . . ." I couldn't think of another word. Actually, the problem was I couldn't think. Not with my usual cool aplomb. ". . . slaves," I hissed.

He gave me an exasperated look. "Dani, you know better than that."

"Mac gets to call me Dani. You don't. And no, I don't. You're always manipulating and pushing people around and trying to control them and—Hey! Get off me. What are you doing?" He was around the damn desk and had his hands on my shoulders again. "Why are you *looking* at me like that?" I snarled.

He shook me, not hard, more a shake of impatience and frustration and a kind of *Get a grip, Mega.*

"Let it go, Jada. Just let it go," he said roughly.

"That Dancer could die?" I yelled. "You want me to just let that go? Oh, I get it. You think I should just take him out with last night's trash because he's going to die and it's smarter to stop caring about him right now so it doesn't hurt as much when he does!"

"That's not what I said. It sounds, however, like something you're trying to sell yourself on," he clipped.

"Then just what the hell do you want me to let go?" I snarled savagely. "Fucking elucidate!"

"I want you to let the goddamn pain out," he said sharply. "Rage. Cry. Hit me. Throw things. I don't give a damn. Do whatever you have to do. But let the pain out."

I started to shiver, and had no clue why. I'd eaten on the way over. I wasn't cold. I felt like my skin was too tight for my body and my chest too small for my heart.

I inhaled, slow and deep. Exhaled slower and even. Repeated it.

"Don't!" he thundered, shaking me again. "Don't you fucking do that. Don't you go turning it off again."

I said coolly, "Don't judge me. You have no right. You haven't walked in my shoes."

"I'm not judging you. I'm trying to help you see there's another way."

"I don't need another way." I knocked his hands off my shoulders. "I'm fine. I'm always fine. I always will be."

"Goddamn it, Dani, what do I have to do—"

I kicked up into the slipstream and blasted out the door.

When it was nearly closed, I heard the thud of a fist hitting the wall, glass breaking, and a violent, "Fuck! Goddamn! Piss! Fuck!"

"Dani out," I whispered tonelessly, and vanished.

38

"Do you hear what I hear?"

MAC

At five o'clock that night the crew—those of us who were going to save our world—began trickling into Barrons Books & Baubles. I'd pushed the king Chesterfields into two sides of a square in front of the fireplace and filled the other two sides in with chairs. There was fresh coffee and an assortment of day-old doughnuts on a nearby console that opened on hinged leaves for just such a purpose.

It was time to get to work. I'd unearthed the music box from beneath the floorboard in my upstairs bedroom, grabbed the bracelet and binoculars—the three items I'd pocketed for unknown reasons during my dreamy stay in the White Mansion—and brought them downstairs, tucked away in my backpack.

I had no idea if all three objects were useful, or even if any of them were. But I couldn't shake the gut feeling that the music box was significant in some way important to our goals. We need a song, it played a song, it had been in the White Mansion. There was something to it, I was certain.

There were eight Fae Hallows, items of extreme importance to the ancient race, the biggest and baddest OOPs of all the OOPs.

The four Seelie Hallows were items that had already been in existence, according to legend, and were gifted to or acquired by the Light Court. There was the Spear of Destiny, the Sword of Light, the Cauldron of Forgetting, and the enigmatic Stone—whatever that was—not to be confused with the four stones made by the Unseelie King that contained the *Sinsar Dubh*.

The four Unseelie Hallows were: the Amulet—the true one that Barrons had tucked away somewhere, not the three amulets I'd been wearing around my neck earlier that he'd added to his stash for safekeeping; the Silvers; the *Sinsar Dubh;* and the mysterious Box.

Unlike the Light Hallows, the Dark Hallows hadn't already been in existence. The Amulet, Silvers, and Book were created by the Unseelie King while he was trying to turn his concubine Fae. Logic dictated that the fourth Hallow would also be something created by the king. He'd given the concubine the Amulet and the part of the Silvers he'd been able to withhold from the controlling Seelie Queen, but hadn't given her the Book for obvious reasons. He'd also given her the music box, a potent object of power. It seemed perfectly plausible to me that it could be the missing fourth Hallow.

The other two items, the binoculars and the bracelet, were indisputably objects of power, but I had no idea what they were or what purpose they served.

I had a feeling Cruce might, though.

Ryodan was the first to arrive, parking his badass matte black military Hummer out front.

A few minutes later Jada roared up on an equally badass motorcycle, parked next to it and stalked, long-legged and aggressive, into the room, wearing black leather from head to toe, her long curly red hair flattened into submission and pulled up high in a flawless ponytail.

It was instantly evident that there was serious tension between those two, and I sighed. I expected tension between Cruce and

Christian, between Cruce and everyone. But, sans Cruce, we were the home team. We were supposed to get along.

Earlier, Jada had seemed more like Dani. Now she was looking and acting a lot like Jada again. Although it made me sad, I wasn't completely surprised. An iceberg didn't thaw all at once, and I suspected if one did—and were sentient—it would apprehend the rapid liquefaction of itself with horror. Jada was an iceberg. She was melty around the edges. No doubt she was going to vacillate a bit before she let too much of her frosty aloofness thaw further. Melty was good. I could work with it. Although I fully intended to find out later what Ryodan had done to freeze her up again and read him the riot act for it.

As Jada dropped down in a chair (no surprise there, a sofa would have been a lot like a country, shared with others, and chairs were islands) I arched a brow and said, "Really—a motorcycle? When you can freeze-frame?"

"It's a Ducati," she corrected stiffly. "Ten-nine-eight S. Capable of achieving speeds of up to—"

"Two hundred and seventy-one miles per hour," I finished for her with a smile. I love cars. Fast motorcycles, too. I'd once lusted after the Dodge Tomahawk, although it was never really taken seriously as a bike.

She didn't smile back. "It's illogical to walk, slipstream or not, when I can ride, thereby ration protein bars. Don't know why I didn't do it before."

Uh-oh. The words "illogical" and "thereby" were back, a sure sign Dani was distancing herself from emotion. But why? And I knew why she'd never ridden a bike before. She loved her city and far preferred navigating it on her own two feet, not riding above it on a machine. The Dani I knew liked to *feel* things.

Ryodan took a seat on one of the couches, in a corner, facing the front door. Yep. That was Ryodan. Watching the entrance, easy attack or escape.

I poured myself a cup of coffee and sank down on the couch facing the fireplace in the middle, next to Barrons, who was in the corner on my right, also facing the door.

Christian arrived next, took one look at me and exploded, "Bloody hell, what happened to you, Mac?"

"No one told you?" I said, surprised. Hastily, I added, "Sorry about the cocoon stuff. It wasn't me."

"I know it wasn't you, but lass, I am never again fishing around in your eye for a wood splinter. You'll go blind before I help you."

My brows climbed my forehead but I didn't ask. I was too busy being grateful the Book hadn't had the spear when it found him.

He continued, "Been busy all day out at the abbey. Just got the message to meet an hour ago. Couldn't sift in. Barrons has the place warded like a Fae Fort Knox."

Although I couldn't see his wings (unless I exerted effort to try, he was using one hell of a glamour) I could tell by the way he was moving his shoulders that his majestic wings were shifting angrily. He opted to stand near the fireplace and I knew why. "You still haven't figured out how to cast a glamour that temporarily displaces your wings, allowing you to sit comfortably, have you?"

He scowled at me. "Bloody Cruce won't tell me a bloody thing. No one else to ask. But you, lass—what read am I getting off you? And what's with the hair?"

"She's turning into the Seelie Queen," Jada said.

Christian just stared at me a long moment, dark brows drawing together, then his shoulders began to shake and he threw back his head and laughed. "Well, hell," he said when he'd finally stopped laughing, "welcome to the club. Maybe we can figure out this wing thing together."

I said with no small regret, "I don't think I get wings. I never saw them on the queen. Anybody know if she had wings?"

Everyone shrugged or shook their heads.

"Isn't Cruce supposed to be here?" Christian said.

Jada kicked back in her chair, propped her boots on the coffee table and said coolly, "Cruce."

The Unseelie prince appeared a few feet away from her, looking thunderous. And still more than a little pained by the loss of his wings. He was once again wearing the glamour of V'lane, still moving stiffly. He whirled, on instant guard, then stopped moving and murmured, "I've never been inside the bookstore before." His gaze went everywhere at once.

"I assure you, you'll find nothing of interest, or I'd not have permitted you here," Barrons said dryly. "I relocated anything you might have liked seeing before you came."

"Why have you summoned me?" Cruce demanded.

"*How* have you summoned him?" I said blankly.

Jada tapped her cuff. "Now that it's closed, he's as bound to it as the wearer is to him. Near as I could figure, it closed when the Book opened the doors to his prison beneath the abbey."

I scowled at him. "So it was true. If I'd put it on when you'd been posing as V'lane, you'd have been able to summon me anytime you wanted."

"Why am I here?" Cruce repeated imperiously. He shot me an icy look. "Because you have come to your senses and realized I should be the bearer of the True Magic?"

"You're here," I said evenly, "because if we don't figure out the Song of Making, and in a hurry, you and your entire race will cease to exist. I won't remind you of that again. There will be no dissension or hostility if you want to survive. After we've saved the world, you can fight with me all you want to about who should have the queen's power."

"Promise?" he said silkily.

Great. Was there some quirky Fae law that allowed him to do formal battle with me for the power if he chose to? I snorted. I'd deal with that later if so.

Dancer arrived last, banging in the door, eyes dancing with excitement. "Hey, Mega! Hey, Mac!" he said enthusiastically. "Hey, guys," he added, with a nod toward the group. "Damn," he said, turning in a slow circle. "There's a bloody nuclear load of power in this room!"

There certainly was. I only hoped it was enough.

♪

Cruce claimed he had no idea what the bracelet and binoculars were, nor did anyone else have any theories. But when I withdrew the glittering music box, the prince's eyes widened faintly and he moved imperceptibly toward it before checking himself.

The squat, square box perched on short, ornate legs and was roughly eight by eight inches wide by four inches high, but I somehow knew it could open into a vastly different shape and size than it assumed currently. The lid was a softly glowing luminous pearl embedded with winking gems, attached to the base by diamond-crusted hinges. The sides were covered with elaborate gold filigree and embedded with still more gems. There was no lock or visible catch but when I handed the box to Dancer to inspect, he was unable to open it.

Cruce said, "Let me try."

I shook my head as Dancer handed it back to me. "Tell me what it is," I parried.

"I would need to inspect it more closely in order to do that," he thrust.

"Can you wield the Song of Making if we find it?" I said.

He stared icy daggers at me. "You know I could not."

"Then why do you think you can continue to withhold information from me? You're no better than the king. In fact, you're just like him—wrapped up in your ego and selfish aims. You don't give a damn about your race. All your impressive talk as V'lane about how Cruce was such a hero, standing up for his brothers, a rogue warrior fighting—"

"ENOUGH!" Cruce thundered so loudly the floor shook, lamps wobbled on tables, and the sky exploded with the percussion of a sudden storm. The temperature plunged drastically and the entire bookstore iced, ceiling, floor, couches, flames in the fireplace, even us.

Damn, I thought as I cracked the ice by standing abruptly. That had been impressive, and in order to control this prince, I was going to have to outdo him. But not with ice. That wasn't the Seelie way.

I summoned the memory of the scent of flowers on the mound beneath three moons and envisioned the bookstore on a sunny summer day.

The ice vanished.

He gave me a cool, assessing look.

Good. I'd rattled him. For whatever reason, he hadn't expected a display of power from me yet. Considering he'd been at Aoibheal's side when she assumed her reign, that must mean it had taken even *her* time to understand how to use what she'd been given.

Eyes narrowed, nostrils flared, I said icily, "I don't know what I can and can't do, Cruce, but I will learn, and quickly, and if you make me learn the hard way, I'll turn every bit of it against you. I can be the sheepdog that walks at your side, or I can be the wolf you don't want living in your backyard. The powerful, hungry, savage, and pissed-off wolf, and I promise you, I will delight in destroying your backyard. I have a long memory and few scruples left. It's your call, babe."

Did I really just say that? I glanced at Barrons, and the corners of his mouth were twitching faintly as if fighting a smile.

Without another word, Cruce vanished.

Jada opened her mouth to summon him back.

"No," I commanded. "Let him go. We don't have time for his games." I, alone, would deal with his games, later. I knew Cruce well enough to know that as things stood, he wasn't going to willingly share a single piece of information with us. Only too recently, he'd watched as his queen had bypassed him in favor of a human, and even as V'lane, the prince had always been vain and proud. It was going to take a small miracle to wed him to our aim. I needed time to figure out what that miracle was.

Dropping back down to the sofa, I fiddled with the box and eased it open. Even braced as I was for the otherworldly music, it still got me and instantly transported me far, far away, filled me with such a buoyant sense of freedom and joy that I sat, shivering in near ecstasy until the exquisite melody abruptly stopped. Then I shivered with sudden cold and isolation, bereft, a true believer cut off from God.

I realized dimly that Barrons had me by the shoulders and was shaking me, roaring, "Mac!" straight into my face.

I blinked up at him. "What?" I said blankly.

"What the hell was that horrific sound?" he demanded.

"Horrific? It wasn't horrific. It's the most beautiful sound I've ever heard. It hurts to stop hearing it." I glanced around the room for confirmation of my words, reinforcement that there was something wrong with Barrons's hearing, not mine, but everyone was looking at me as if I was crazy. "Oh, come on! How could you not think that song was beautiful?" I glanced at Jada. "Wasn't it mind-blowingly amazing to you?"

She shook her head grimly. "It made me want to die."

I frowned at Dancer.

"Ditto," he said roughly. "That was pure hell."

I looked back at Barrons, who nodded, then at Christian and Ryodan, who nodded in turn.

"Made my bloody skin crawl," Christian said tightly.

I shot Ryodan a look. "What did it make you feel?"

He gave me a penetrating look and said carefully, "Like I was having a hard time holding on to my skin."

My eyes widened as I got the message and my gaze flew back to Barrons.

His dark eyes gleamed. *We both nearly changed. Had to fight it with everything I had.*

I frowned down at the music box, wondering what in the world it was, and why only I could hear the exquisite melody it played.

♪

We wrapped up a little over an hour later, having accomplished pretty much jack shit.

No one had been willing to let me open the music box again, although Dancer asked me to bring it by the lab the next day. Everyone agreed that it shouldn't be permitted out of my or Barrons's hands, as Cruce had clearly coveted it and could easily take it from Dancer.

"I'll listen to it again tomorrow but I want to hear it at my lab. I think there's something to it. Any frequency that has such a profound effect demands further inquiry. It felt like the Devil's tritone to an exponential degree," he told me, grimacing as he reflected on it. He paused at the door, ready to leave, and glanced back at Jada, a smile lighting his face. "You coming?"

She gave him a cool look. "Something came up. Raincheck."

His smile faltered. Though he tried to quickly conceal his disappointment, it was evident for all to see.

Ryodan said, "I don't need you tonight after all, Jada. Go with him. Take the night off."

Her head whipped his way and she glared daggers at him.

"Cool," Dancer enthused. "Let's go." He was back to being happy again.

"Ryodan's . . . issues . . . weren't the only things that came up," Jada said tonelessly. "I'm busy."

Ryodan said in a voice I'd never heard before, and couldn't even peg the emotion of, "Jada. Go. With. Him. Now."

They locked gazes for a long moment, then she stood, bristling, blasted past Dancer and stormed out the door, tossing a "C'mon, let's go" over her shoulder to the bewildered looking young man.

Once they were gone, I said to Ryodan, "What on earth happened between you two? Last thing I remember is you saving her from the fire. I thought she'd appreciate that."

"She did. Even bloody thanked me. But then something else happened."

I waited.

He assessed me a moment, taking in the Khaleesi-blond hair, lingering on my eyes a long moment. "I'll be damned. You really are turning Fae. Do they have the power to heal human bodies?"

I pondered that a moment then said, "I believe they do to some degree but I don't know how, nor do I know how fully. I suspect they use the Elixir of Life to heal serious wounds on the exceedingly rare occasion they want to keep a mortal alive, and that has a serious side effect." Immortality. "Why? Who's injured? And can't you do anything about it?"

"Not something of this severity. This is beyond my ability to affect unless I did the same thing I did to Dageus—"

Barrons growled, "Which you are *never* doing again."

"I have no intention of it. I doubt he'd survive it anyway. He's not the right raw material."

"He—*who*?" I demanded.

"Dancer," Ryodan said tightly. "He has a congenital heart problem. Apparently quite serious."

I went rigid. Dani adored him. They had something more than mere friendship. Once, long ago, she'd blushed when she told me he'd given her a bracelet. I'd often wondered if a romance might bloom between them. And as she continued to thaw, becoming more like Dani and less like Jada, he seemed the perfect fit. The right young man to make her feel alive again, perhaps recapture a sense of innocence. Whether or not that happened, it would still break her heart to lose him. And she'd already had more than her share of heartache and loss. Why him, of all people? "This is complete and utter bullshit," I seethed.

"I agree," Ryodan said grimly as he vanished out the door.

39

"Riders on the storm, into this house we're born"

JADA

I threw my leg across the Ducati, glanced back at Dancer to motion him to get on behind me then shot right back off it and growled, "I changed my mind. Let's walk." If I crashed the bike, no big to me. Every big to him. Besides, he was already excited enough about Mac and the song and music box. I didn't want him getting any more excited.

Don't kill the boy before he's dead, Jada, Ryodan had said with his cool silver gaze moments earlier. *You'll hate yourself for it one day. Go talk with him.*

He was right. But I would certainly have appreciated a little more time to deal with the unpleasant reality of Dancer's flawed biology before having to deal with the very pleasant reality of Dancer, alive and laughing and ready to tear off on our next reckless adventure—which would never happen again because he wasn't blowing out his heart on my watch. That was something I'd really hate myself for, and not one day. Instantly.

"Aw, c'mon," he protested, "I've never ridden a Ducati before. Show me what it can do!"

I was gripped by a sudden fierce desire to protect him. Or lock him up somewhere and never even let him breathe hard.

"Seriously, I want to walk." I loped off down the street, knowing he'd follow.

He didn't. But I didn't figure that out for a block and a half, when I turned to snatch a sideways glance at him, see if I saw any signs of strain in his face, if I was walking too fast.

I was alone, confirming how off-kilter I was. With my senses, I should have registered that I wasn't hearing him.

I spun around, peering into the night. There he was, way down the street, still standing in front of Barrons Books & Baubles, arms folded over his chest, leaning against a streetlamp. I felt my chest grow tight and caught my breath. I'd always thought he was attractive, now even more so with the amber glow of the gas lamp burnishing his dark hair with a kiss of gold, his eyes the color of tropical sea surf. It made me feel perversely mad at him. "What the hell are you doing?" I snapped.

"Waiting for you to come back here and tell me what the bloody hell is wrong with you," he snapped back.

A dozen caustic replies took shape on my tongue but all that came out was a soft, miserable sigh. There he stood, six feet four inches of solid, healthy man, but the heart inside his athletic body didn't possess the same strength. What kind of universe pulled such a dickhead stunt? And why *him*? Why not, say, someone mean and deceitful like Margery or someone evil like Rowena— but no, that old bitch had lived well into her eighties! I sank down cross-legged on the sidewalk as the unthinkable happened and tears stung my eyes. I ducked my head so he wouldn't see it, so he'd think I was just being stubborn and staying where I was, making him come to me.

A few seconds later I glanced up and saw the weirdest thing. Dancer was hurrying down the street toward me, but that's not what was weird. Ryodan was the weird thing. He was standing outside the bookstore, staring down the street at us, hands fisted at his sides, looking quite possibly angrier than I'd ever seen him, and I've seen that dude ten shades beyond pissed, well into homicidal fury.

I knew he could see the faint shimmer of moisture on my cheeks. Eagle Eyes once saw a drop of moisture on an ice sculpture I hadn't been able to see. I gave him a look and a shrug, like, *What? You wanted me to cry and let it out. Just doing what you told me. Are you* ever *happy with a damn thing I do?* Then I flipped him off. Shit. I plunged the defiant hand into my pocket. That wasn't me. That was someone I used to be. What the hell was happening to my center?

But I knew the answer to that. First Shazam. Now Dancer. Did the universe harbor a secret grudge against me? Was it not going to be happy until it had stolen everyone I cared about?

"I wasn't flipping *you* off," I told Dancer as he approached.

But when Dancer glanced back to see who'd pissed me off, Ryodan was gone.

♪

"Caoimhe told you, didn't she?" Dancer said a short time later as he handed me a heaping bowl of mixed fruit topped with whipped cream. "She promised me she would never talk to you about it. I told her you knew but hated discussing it."

I nodded. I'd eliminated all trace of tears by the time Dancer had reached me, and if he'd noticed my eyes were red, he chose not to comment. I didn't understand the point of crying. All you got from it was a stuffed up nose and a short-lived headache, and I was always dangerously hungry afterward. It didn't solve a thing. It didn't change a thing. It only made you feel worse.

"How much did she tell you?" he asked, motioning me to follow him into the living room.

"You never brought me here before," I dodged, wondering what he meant by "how much." Hadn't she told me the worst? I terminated that thought and resumed studying his digs. "Here" was the top floor of an old firehouse that overlooked the River Liffey and had been converted into a huge one-room loft, partitioned with furniture placement into kitchen, living room, and bedroom. Thick cream sheepskin rugs covered well-worn hardwood floors. The furnishings were simple, modern, comfortable. The entire wall facing the river was window from floor to ceiling. I stared out, watching the silvery slide of the water, wishing I could slide off on it.

"This is where I live most of the time. I kept a lot of other places because I never knew what part of town you might be hanging out in."

"You lived two completely separate lives. One with me and one without."

"Yes."

"Why didn't you tell me you had . . . you know?"

"A bad heart? You'd have disappeared and I'd never have seen you again. There was no room in your world for anything less than a superhero. I'm not sure there is now either."

I said fiercely, "I'm here, aren't I?" And I didn't want to be. I wanted to be anywhere else, doing something with purpose that made me feel good, not staring into Death's impersonal jaws as they tried to close on one of the few people I wanted to see often, and couldn't wait to see each time so we could blurt out everything we thought to each other. At fourteen there'd never been a sense of urgency. We'd been kids. We were going to live forever. He was always going to be somewhere around the next corner.

Not.

"Yes, but to what degree and with what new conditions that must be met?" he countered. "I knew the second you didn't want me on the Ducati that you'd found out. Then you slow-mo-Joe walked down the street. You never do that. Is that how we're going to be now? Dancer's so fragile that Dancer doesn't get to do anything not Mega-approved, and that might not even include something so strenuous as swatting a fly?"

Sounded bloody good to me. I spooned up fruit and swallowed but it got stuck on a lump in my throat. I coughed and spat it back out into the bowl. He was beside me in an instant, ready to give me the Heimlich, as he had so many times in the past when I'd wolfed my food too fast to swallow. "I'd let you swat a fly," I said crossly.

He smiled faintly. "Yeah, but would you let me swat a bee?"

"Probably."

"How about set off a bomb and outrun it?"

"Abso-fucking-lutely not."

"Then I guess we can't be friends anymore. Because I *will* set off bombs and outrun them. And I *will* get to climb on that big beautiful bike of yours and wrap my arms around you and lean into all that gorgeous hair and smell you, and hear you laugh and see your eyes flash fire. Or I may as well just kick it right now because you, Dani Mega O'Malley, make me feel alive like nothing else does. And I don't want to miss a moment of it."

I forgot how to breathe. Wrap his arms around me, he'd said. He thought I had gorgeous hair and my eyes flashed fire. I deflected instantly, "Smell me? I always smell bad. Like blood and guts and sweat."

"You smell fearless. And you smell good a lot. Like fall leaves, hot apple cider spiked with dark rum, and a fire topped with twigs of sassafras. You smell like life and the kind of days I want to enjoy while I'm here. Do you have any idea how I felt when you came back older? I was so pissed that you'd gone off and lived so much life without me getting to be there for any of it, but then I thought the angels must have heard my prayers to let me live long enough to kiss you. Not a fourteen-year-old kiss. A nineteen-year-old kiss. A really hot, sexy nineteen-year-old kiss." He grinned. "Assuming you don't have a problem with younger men. Do you have a problem with younger men, Mega?"

I ignored the part about kissing. That was too much for my ears to hear right now. He was trying to not only insist that I face his heart issue, but kissing, too? That was total bullshit. "You've got to be shitting me," I said coolly. "You not only want us to stay friends, you want me to care about you even more? Are you bat-shit crazy? Or do you think I am?"

"Yes, no, and no," he said evenly. "Or will you only care about someone you know will live forever?"

"Like that even exists," I evaded.

"I happen to know it does. I watched two of Ryodan's men die. They showed up fine a week later. I'm not stupid, Mega."

I barely managed to conceal a wince. Bloody hell, if Ryodan knew Dancer knew that, I wouldn't have to worry about his heart killing him. Ryodan would.

He reached for my hand but I snatched it away, then tried to soften the insult by using it to tighten my ponytail.

Ire flashed in his eyes but faded quickly. He gave a snort of soft, wry laughter. "Mom had the same reaction when she found out. Pretty much everyone in my life did. It was years before people stopped acting weird around me."

I asked stiffly, "How did you find out?"

"I died. I was playing soccer with friends and suddenly I couldn't breathe. I'd been having problems breathing for days, but hell, I was a kid and it was a hot summer. We don't pay any attention to that kind of stuff. We don't know diseases like hypertrophic cardiomyopathy exist. I didn't even know *diseases* existed. Life had been a long endless summer for me up until then."

"Did you really die?"

"Sure did. Flat-lined. I was gone for three and a half minutes then my heart just started up again. No clue why. I was unconscious when the ambulance took me to the hospital and they lost me on the way there. Then I was just back. Mom said it was because I had something important to do. I didn't tell her that suddenly everything seemed important to do."

When he reached for my hand this time, I let him take it and lead me to the couch. Suddenly all my usual reactions were suspect. I was seeing each of them as potentially the last thing I'd ever do with him.

I put my bowl of fruit on the coffee table, no longer hungry. As I sank down and tucked my legs beneath me, he reached for a pack of matches and lit two candles on the table in front of us, put the matches back down and stood looking at me for a long moment. "Do you know how beautiful you are?" he finally said.

I shrugged it off. "I figured it out Silverside."

He burst out laughing. "Christ, I should have known that'd be your response. You clinically assessed yourself, decided you were symmetrical and your features met some obscure mathematical criteria, you had gorgeous skin and flaming hair to top it off and were therefore beautiful."

That had pretty much been it. That, and my appearance had proved an effective distraction in battle with men.

"So," he said, taking a seat next to me. "What did Caoimhe tell you?"

I was more acutely aware of his body next to mine than I'd ever been. His sudden . . . impermanence seemed to erase all filters from my vision, leaving only a young, very hot, very brilliant man that I cared deeply about. "Only the diagnosis." I didn't want to know and I had to know. "How bad is it?"

He looked away a moment and when he looked back at me he said, "Let's put it this way: I know I have to live each day to the fullest, and I've known that for a long time."

I suddenly understood something I'd never been able to fathom about him before. He'd always been completely unfazed by folks like Barrons and Ryodan, Christian, even the Fae, and I'd endlessly wondered why. I'd admired him enormously for it, been quietly proud of him each time he stood his ground with such powerful immortals, because it had never been bluster, just confidence and laissez-faire equanimity. I knew why now: he'd been living with the threat of death most of his adult life. "Caoimhe loves you," I told him, with absolutely no idea why I'd just said that.

Apparently he liked hearing it, though, because his grin widened. "I know."

His response left me feeling unsatisfied and weirdly anxious. *I know?* That was it? Did he love her? Were they boyfriend and girlfriend? On the verge of setting up house together? Did he bring her here? Cripes, maybe she'd picked out his furnishings for him, brought him the rugs and candles!

I was out of here. I couldn't deal with this. Any of it. I turned away and began to push up then glanced back and said, "So, are you and Caoimhe . . ." I trailed off as I sank back down. I was out of my depth. I wanted to leave. I couldn't leave. My butt was a spring that couldn't make up its mind, bouncing me off the sofa, dragging me back. I was conflicted by the sure knowledge that the hands of time were eating away at one more thing in my life. Clocks. Of course. *Kill the clocks, those time-thieving bastards,* he'd written. He'd been telling me, in his own way, the night he gave me the poem and the bracelet, that time was short and every moment mattered. I closed my eyes, recalling the last stanza. It had been his wake-up call, the one he'd been trying to get me to hear, without incurring the risk of me refusing to accept it and running away.

Kill the clocks and live in the moment
No cogs or gears can steal our now
When you laugh with me, Mega, time stands still
In that moment, I'm perfect somehow

Being with me gave him that—the feeling of being unhunted, unhaunted by the ancient, eternal Footman who was holding his coat at the ready, any day, anytime.

"What are you trying to ask me?" he said levelly.

"Do you and . . ." I trailed off again.

He let the silence stretch, watching me intently, gaze shifting from my right eye to my left and back again. Finally he prodded gently, "What, Mega? What do you want to know?"

"Have you and Caoimhe—bugger it, Dancer, help me out here!"

"You want to know if we're lovers," he said with such quiet maturity that I shifted uncomfortably.

He hadn't said boyfriend or date. He'd used a word that had made me abruptly picture his long strong body stretched out on top of Caoimhe as he whispered something passionate in her ear, regarded her with desire. And it made my stomach feel hot and tight.

"Why is that so hard to ask? You just have to say, 'Dancer, are you Caoimhe's lover?'"

I scowled, poised on the verge of freeze-framing out the door and never coming back.

He leaned back, kicked his long legs up on the coffee table and spread his arms wide along the back of the sofa, and I got the distinct impression he knew exactly how good it made him look. Showing off his pecs and those arms he'd worked so hard to make cut and strong, arms that could wrap around me when we rode the Ducati. He flashed me a smile. "Nah. I'm still a virgin."

I gaped with disbelief. "You are?"

"Hey, I'm only seventeen. It's not that unusual."

"But you might have, I mean, you knew that . . ." I trailed off.

"I was born with a shorter fuse than most?" he finished for me evenly.

I nodded.

"So, what—I was supposed to jump out there and grab whatever I could get my hands on while I had the chance? You know I'm discriminating, Mega. On the contrary, it made me want to ensure that every experience I had really counted. That it be the best it could be, or not happen at all. I didn't want to rack up bad memories, no regrets."

I understood that. We were so different yet so much the same.

"We're totally different," he said, like he was reading my mind, "but so much the same. You were born super everything: super strong and smart, super hearing, smell, eyesight, and super freaking fast. Man, I love that one. I think your speed-demon power is the one I'd want the most. And I was born super . . . well, not weak but with a flaw in my design. After I died when I was eight years old and discovered what was wrong with me—"

"You were eight when you died?" I'd been eight, too, when I'd pretty much given up the ghost.

He nodded. "Yeah. Dying did the same thing to me all your superpowers did to you. Made me fearless."

"You do realize a lot of people wouldn't have taken that lesson away from it. They would have felt more vulnerable and been more careful with themselves."

"I saw something that day, Mega, during those three and a half minutes, and I know that there's more after this. I have faith and it's strong. I'm not afraid. Death is just the door to the next big adventure."

Yeah, well, that was a door I wasn't letting open for him for a long, long time. "I used to wonder if you had some secret super-power," I told him. "I saw you walking down the street one day, and the ZEWs peeled away from you like you were one of Barrons's dudes or something."

A dazzling grin lit up his face. "Yeah, they do, don't they? Talk about perplexing the fuck out of Ryodan," he said, and laughed. "Should have seen his face the day I was with him, Barrons, and Mac, and the ZEWs gave me the same wide berth they gave him and Barrons. It was priceless. I've got the Rhino-boys' number, and a few other lower castes, too, but I haven't made progress with the higher castes yet. Got diverted, working on the song." He reached down and pushed up the cuff of his jeans, revealing a sort of watch strapped around his ankle with a small black cube attached to it, covered with blinking lights. "I got started thinking one night about how the Fae are made of energy and how dogs and invisible fences and silent whistles and things like that work, so I began experimenting with a transmitter, modulating and testing frequencies on the Fae, goal being to repel, not kill. Sometimes we set our sights too high when a lesser goal would be both quicker to attain and virtually as effective. I figured if I could invent something that kept all the Fae away from you, well, I'd be the Shit."

"You're already the Shit, Dancer," I told him.

"Yeah but I want to be even *shittier* shit," he said, and waggled his brows at me.

I smiled, forcing myself not to let the sadness I felt show. I couldn't do that to him. It wouldn't be fair. "You're the shittiest shit I know and probably ever will."

He sobered quickly, looking into my eyes, studying me with unnerving intensity. "Shittier than Ryodan?"

I was instantly wary, defensive. "What do you mean? What does Ryodan have to do with any of what we're talking about?"

"Don't be a porcupine, Mega. Not prying or judging. It's just that sometimes I think he . . . well, maybe you . . . the two of you, er—" He broke off, sighed, and shoved a hand into his thick hair, ruffling it. "I'll never be like him. I'm not wired that way. I'm a brainy, geeky seventeen-year-old with a bad heart. Not much makes me feel insecure but that dude does. He's everything you are and I'm not."

I bristled. "Don't you ever tell me you have a bad heart! Never say those words again. You've got the biggest heart in the world. You bring out the best in everyone around you and people love you. But you're right. You're not like him and never will be."

He shifted uncomfortably and went crazy on his hair again, running both hands through it. I let him stew for a moment, trying to absorb this bizarre moment, that he cared about me enough that it made him—the man not even Death rattled—feel insecure. Then I got distracted watching his arms. Now that I knew how perilous working out was for him, I admired even more deeply the patient will that had found a way to work within limits that would have made a lot of other people give up. I'd learned at a young age that every day mattered, that killing time was the worst thing you could do to it. Dancer had learned it, too.

"Wow. Not helping much here," he muttered.

I caught one of his hands in mine and slowly laced our fingers together. I'd never taken a man's hand of my own desire before, open to the moment and what that moment might bring. I was in such uncharted territory and this was so not the way I'd always imagined it going down. Not that anything *was* going down. That would be like willingly ascending the mountain of stupidity to perch on the apex right before the inevitable avalanche came along and wiped you out, and that was never going to happen. But I wasn't averse to admiring the mountain from the foothills. "Ryodan's strength comes from knowing he's strong," I told him. "Your strength comes from knowing you're not. *You're* the one with the superpower in my book. And it's only one of the many you have."

His smile was blinding. "Mega, I'm going to kiss you now."

I inhaled deep, exhaled slow. We'd never gone here, and once we did, there would be no turning back. Our friendship would be forever changed. You can't unkiss a man you've kissed.

I let him.

40

"Desperately in need of some stranger's hand

in a desperate land"

ZARA

S he stood motionless, staring around in disbelief.

Was this a joke?

Zara glanced up at the lighted sign that swayed on a striped pole above her head proclaiming THE STAG'S HEAD, then back at the door behind her through which she'd just exited.

It wasn't the door she'd stepped into.

Not even close. She'd been entering a doorway in the sunny yellow part of the White Mansion and the moment she passed beneath the transom felt resistance and something diverting her sideways, casting her down a different path.

Out through a completely different door.

Into night in Dublin.

She narrowed her eyes, scowling.

Earth was the last place she wanted to be.

She wasn't dying on this world. She was done with this planet and every other that had ever hosted the Fae race.

Nor was she staying in the White Mansion and living her final days in the cage the king had designed for her. Upon leaving the boudoir, she'd been making her way to the Passion Muse's Garden, the one with the silvery fountain and the fabulous sunroom, the one that took her, if she passed far beyond it and went through many portals, back out into the flow of time, on another world, far, far from there. She'd found it eons ago. Had on her saddest days gone walking and walking, uncaring, taking paths and finally portals at random.

The small planet reminded her of her home, and she'd wondered if the king put it there deliberately, knowing she'd find it, giving her an escape route, because each year, century, millennium she didn't use it, he'd continue to know she'd truly chosen him over all else.

That was just like him. He'd required endless reassurance that she was happy, that she wanted to be where he'd put her.

She'd intended to go to that small world now, and die there, alone, when the Earth ceased to exist and so did she.

But no.

She was in dirty, human Dublin.

Gathering her cloak around her, she whirled and stepped back through the door of the pub.

And entered only the pub.

She hissed, "This is unacceptable!"

"*Awk, unacceptable!*" the *T'murra* squawked.

"I will not be trifled with! Show me the way back!"

"*Awk, the way back!*" the *T'murra* agreed.

Dust motes sparkled in a ray of moonlight that spilled through a broken window, spiraling suspended in a gentle, relentless current.

Was the king watching her? Still manipulating her? The idea was infuriating. She was not his toy, his plaything. She was a woman who would be free. He owed her that much.

They'd tried. They'd failed. It was time to let go.

Why would he send her to Dublin? "What do you *want* from me?" she demanded.

"*Awk, what do you want?*" the *T'murra* echoed.

Lips thinning, Zara whirled and stormed back through the doorway, willing it to transport her instantly to the sunny floors of the White Mansion.

A piece of toilet paper stuck to her silk slipper and she stubbed her toe on a piece of broken concrete she hadn't seen in the dark.

Still in Dublin.

"Hey," a male voice called out. "Are you all right? Can I help you with anything?"

She spun stiffly toward the intruder in the endless Fae drama that was her life and her eyes widened infinitesimally. A man was hurrying toward her, and as he moved into the pool of light cast by the streetlamps outside the pub, she realized he was a very attractive one, lovely in the way that had made the Fae occasionally abduct one of them. Young, strong, with dark hair, the lithe body of a dancer and beautiful eyes.

"I'm fine," she said tightly.

"You don't look fine to me. This city can be a dangerous place, especially for a woman alone at night, in such attire. Come. Let's find you different clothing. There's a store down the street."

Zara belatedly recalled the diaphanous gown she wore beneath her cloak that revealed all, concealed nothing, and glamoured it instantly into a more solid gown, willing it to a soft, solid yellow.

Nothing happened.

The young man narrowed his eyes. "Fae? Or human?"

She yanked her cloak tightly around her body and sifted him into a different, far-off city.

He stood there, gaze fixed on her face, awaiting her reply.

She'd had no idea what fate befell queens who transferred their power before their time, and was discovering it the hard way. His question was a valid one. She wasn't sure what she was anymore either.

She glanced at the debris on the cobbled street, spied a bottle, stooped, seized and shattered it, shoved her sleeve up and used the bit of glass on her arm. A thin line of blood formed.

Then vanished.

"You're Fae then," he said. "If so, you have power enough to leave this place, don't you?"

Of course, to hell with the king's portals he could so easily manipulate. She was free of the Silvers and could now sift. She instantly transported herself to the Isle of Morar to refine her plans.

Nothing happened.

She opted for a tiny, inconsequential bit of magic and tried to make a sudden fall of snow where only she stood.

Not a flake, not a flurry.

She knew then. The passing of the power had taken *all* her power, even that which was not part of the True Magic. Undoubtedly, the O'Connor possessed it now. Now she knew why queens waited until they'd nearly evaporated into that mysterious, shadowy realm to which some of the Fae went, before yielding their reign.

They became powerless. Yet remained immortal. A hellish existence.

She smiled with bitterness that would once have turned the entire city into a glacier of sufficient width and depth to spawn an ice age.

The planet was dying. The portal behind her was closed.

She was trapped.

Again.

Powerless.

She didn't know this world. Had no idea how to survive on it.

"Come," the man repeated, extending a strong hand. "I'll help you."

Zara ignored the hand but moved to join him.

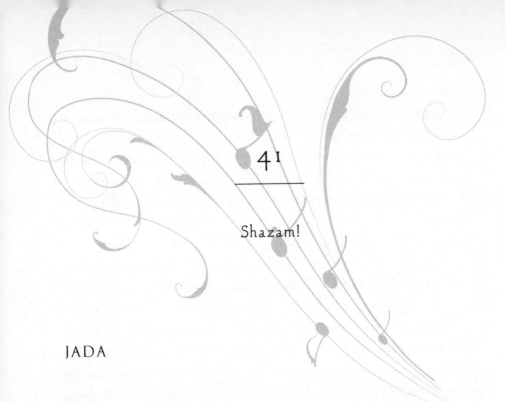

41

Shazam!

JADA

I stood, at dawn, in the pouring rain in the suburb of Kilmainham, south of the River Liffey, west of the city center, staring at a non-descript area of high stone wall that ran the entire circumference of Kilmainham Gaol, enclosing the former prison-turned-museum.

The irony hadn't been lost on me the day I'd exploded from the Silvers to find myself home in Dublin—after so many years of wandering with no idea where I was—that my gate to freedom was tucked inside a prison wall.

I remembered that night. I'd hit the ground running, drawn up short, turned and stared back at the wall, committing the location of the portal to memory.

Rule number 1 in my "Entering a Silver Handbook": *Remember the way back.* You never knew when retreat might be preferable to the world you'd landed on. At times I'd had to backtrack ten worlds to discover a new direction to go.

Once I had the precise location locked down, I'd stalked away from the wall. Spying a trash Dumpster, I'd hurried over and begun rummaging in the debris.

Rule number 2.9: (2.1 was for dangerously primitive worlds,

2.2 for hostile beasts, 2.3 signs of an unknown civilization, and so on.) *If the world was advanced enough to have trash Dumpsters, it usually had newspapers. Find one and read it.* The sooner I acclimated to the world, the more seamlessly I could move around on it.

I'd found a balled-up rag that night—the *Dani Daily.*

I'd stared blankly at it then spun, staring back at the wall, able to recognize it from a distance as I'd not been able to up close, realizing Kilmainham Gaol loomed beyond the wall.

I'd turned in a slow circle, trying to process that I was home. After so many bloody years, I'd finally found the Silver that took me back to Dublin.

Now, of all times.

"Bloody hell! Bugger! Fuck you, you stupid fucking stupid fucks!" I'd leapt into the air, shaking both my fists at the distant stars.

Then I'd dropped to the ground, clutching my balled-up paper, wondering with a small part of my brain what moron had thrown away my immensely entertaining and informative news flash, while also wondering why it was still there five and a half years later, while also trying to decide with the largest part of my brain what the hell I was going to do.

I was screwed.

I'd stretched out on the ground and cried. Sobbed until I couldn't breathe and my head was splitting. After I'd done that long enough to make myself even more miserable, I began laughing. Eventually, I went cold as ice.

So, this was how it was going to be?

We'd see about that.

I wasn't the teen I'd been five and a half years earlier. I'd thought my childhood was challenging but my years Silverside had made my childhood seem like . . . well, child's play.

I hadn't held on to the really bad things that happened Silverside. I'd chosen to remember the good parts and chunked the rest in the oubliette. I'd already had too much baggage at fourteen, before I even leapt into the Hall of All Days, to accumulate more and leave it rattling around in my head. You've got to keep your brain tidy.

Things had gone downhill swiftly once I'd become invisible to my mother. I'd taught myself strict compartmentalization by the fourth month of my seventh year, when living in the cage had become unbearable, apportioning parts to me and parts to the Other, the one that was far more ruthless and self-contained than me.

I've always known who the Other was: me, pushed beyond enduring.

When you're so hungry you can barely raise your head, and you aren't sure anyone's ever going to feed you again and you start to think maybe you *should* just slip away, and stop fighting it, you either let go and die or find a way to hang on that isn't constant pain. I'd figured out how to hang on.

I'd played around in my brain and taught myself to partition it. I don't know if that's exactly what happens on a subconscious level in cases of dissociative disorder, but once I began consciously doing it, it became difficult to stop.

It was easier to be the Other. Safer to be the Other.

Especially at the end.

The Other killed my mom.

I killed my mom.

I know those two statements are the same thing.

Ryodan thinks I don't but I've always known. There are parts of my brain not even he can get into.

And even knowing that I had to do it—that I would have died if I hadn't—didn't make it any easier for me to deal with. I missed her. I hated her. I loved her. I hated myself. I missed her. Moms, even bad ones—and she'd been a good one once—are sacred. They're the taproot from which we grow.

Ro, the old bitch, figured out how to push me into that state, even when I didn't want to go. And once I was free, I'd never wanted to be the Other anymore.

I'd learned during my first few weeks free of my cage that one of my mom's many "boyfriends" during that last year had introduced her to the needle. It wasn't wine that had changed her so drastically at the end. It was heroin. A drug had turned her into someone else, someone she'd never have chosen to be.

I'd added that bastard to my kill count, too. He'd been passed out with a needle in his arm, flirting with death anyway. Treasure your life. Or die.

Adaptability is survivability. When Ryodan said that to me, I knew he understood. I'd felt an instant kinship with him. I'd taken one look into those cool, clear silver eyes and known he'd had to do things no person should have to do. And he was okay with it.

He'd found the way to be okay with it.

Silverside, I'd carefully picked out the finest characteristics of me and my Other and merged them. Ironically, Silverside had been easier in some ways. Me, my imagination, and I had created *The Daredevil Delights of Dani and her Shaz-tastic Sidekick Shazam!* We'd even had our own theme song:

Shaz the mighty fur-beast lived up in the air,
Watching all of Olean, grouchy as a bear.
Dani the Mega O'Malley loved that rascal Shaz,
And battled dragons every day while Shaz covered her ass.
Oh, Shaz the mighty fur-beast . . .

And so on.

I'd come to this spot near the wall many times since my first night back on Earth, and stood just like this, staring up at the gray stones.

Each time I'd come here to think. Sometimes I'd tossed things through. Once, a big, battered steel trashcan. I'd spray-painted words on it before casting it through: I SEE YOU, YI-YI. I SWEAR I'M COMING. And each time I'd ended up trying as hard as I could *not* to think, and especially not feel.

Now, I sank down to the sodden grass, leaned against the wall, pulled out my cellphone and thumbed up a song, in a rare masochistic mood.

As little Jackie Paper cruised turquoise seas on boats with billowed sails, watching for far-off pirate ships from Puff's enormous tail, I thought about everything I'd done in my life and all the things I'd lost, and I thought about Dancer and how I was going to lose him, too, at some point, and I had absolutely no control over it, and when the song got to the part where it talked about dragons living forever but not so little boys, I rolled over onto my side, curled up into a ball and let the grief come.

I cried and cried and made so much snot you'd think we were made of snot, like ninety percent snot and maybe ten percent bones, and who knew what the hell held us together at the end of the day that kept us from just melting into a puddle of snot?

I knew what the song was about. I'd always hated it. Mom had played it for me when I was a kid, singing and dancing around the kitchen, and I remember just looking up at her and thinking, Is she NUTS?

What a horrible song! Why would anyone want to listen to it?

I knew it was about losing the magic. The wonder and innocence. Losing the belief in fairy tales because we're crushed beneath the weight of responsibility and the perverse expectations of the world. I knew how good I felt inside as a little kid. I knew how bad my mom felt inside grown up. I could see what growing up did to you and didn't like it one bit.

That was the day I knew I was smarter than my mom. The day she played me "Puff the Magic Dragon." And it didn't make me feel happy or important, or like, gee, wow, I'm really smart.

It made me feel *lost*.

If my mom wasn't smarter than me, and I was dependent on

her, who was going to take care of us? I'd pretty much decided it was up to *me* to take care of *her*.

Then I woke up in a cage and knew we were in a world of shit.

Mega brain. I was born with it. Don't know how. Don't know why. Maybe Ro had something to do with it, but if she did, she'd been messing with my mother before she ever even had me. Knowing Ro, she probably made me in some kind of test-tube experiment, mixing humans with an exotic Fae she'd trapped, and who knows, maybe part of a Hunter along with eye of newt and toe of frog, fertilizing my mom in vitro.

I have no idea why I came out like I did.

But I like it most days. I like it *all* days.

Except for days like today. Which I haven't had another one of since, well, since the night I found myself back in Dublin, and that other night, when I was eight. I guess three really shitty days in twenty years isn't too bad. Oh, and the night Mac found out I'd killed Alina. Four days. Whoops, the day the Unseelie princes took my sword. Okay, five days. Still not bad. I watch other people. Some of them cry over a Hallmark card commercial. Every time one comes on.

I scrubbed my eyes with my fists then feathered my fingers out over my sinuses, which were now completely clogged with snot.

That's what you got for crying.

A headache. And I was so hungry I could eat a horse, saddle and all.

And my damned hair was curling again. All this blasted humidity.

I rolled over, yanked out my last silvery pod and was about to drink it when I thought twice, wiped my nose, tried to scrub rain from my face, but it just kept drenching me, and ate two protein bars instead. The pod was the last thing I had from Silverside. I couldn't give it up.

I stretched out on my back, soaked to the skin, propped my feet up on the wall and stared up through the rain at the stones. I knew a thing or two about losses: slow, steady erosions became landslides. Turning the hill into a muddy, shapeless mess. You had to figure out how to keep the things that mattered to you.

"Shazam," I told the wall. "I'm coming back for you. I swear it."

I said the same words each time I came here.

And each time, I thrust all emotion away, eventually pushed to my feet, squared my shoulders and headed straight back to the crushing weight of responsibility and perverse expectations of the world.

But one day I wouldn't.

42

"Desire is hunger, is the fire I breathe"

MAC

After the others left the bookstore and Barrons vanished into his study where I could hear him moving around, I dimmed the interior lights to a soft amber glow, nuked myself a cup of hot chocolate, and curled up on the Chesterfield near the fireplace. Beyond exhausted, I longed to stretch out and sleep for days, but I wasn't yet ready for this auspicious day to end.

With my recent sins firmly locked in a box, I took a moment to sit down and absorb with elation that this was the day I'd defeated the *Sinsar Dubh*.

There was no longer another sentience inside me, plotting, planning, manipulating, and deceiving, terrifying me with endless possibilities of the horrific things it might make me do. I'd done them. It was over. And although I'd done damage, I hadn't K'Vrucked the world.

I was free.

Finally alone in my body, I could feel the difference—and it was incredible.

Back when I was a kid, growing up, in Ashford, Georgia, alien, vividly detailed sounds and images had often popped into my head for no reason I'd been able to discern.

I'd hummed along with music I'd never heard before. I'd suffered nostalgia induced by mental images of stunning, opulent chambers and exotic lands I'd never seen and didn't believe existed. I'd gotten such frequent visions of a naked, beautiful woman staring at me with passion and lust that I'd finally begun to wonder if I was repressing lesbian tendencies.

But now all of the Unseelie King's memories were gone and I felt infinitely lighter, clearer. And not a lesbian.

I no longer had to second-guess every thought and feeling I had.

At least, at the moment, I didn't.

Although part of me hoped the True Magic came bundled with the ex-queen's memories and knowledge, as that would make it so much easier to figure out, another part of me really hoped it didn't.

Still, if I suddenly began getting bleed-through of intrusive, alien thoughts, at least I'd know where they were coming from, and I didn't think for a minute they'd be as hard to deal with as the *Sinsar Dubh* had been.

During my brief interrogation by the sentience on the world with three moons, I'd realized how appropriate the appellations Light Court and Dark Court were for the Seelie and Unseelie. The king's memories had always held some kind of shadowed murkiness, a masculine darkness. They'd been visceral, blunt, cast in harsh shades of icy blues, bleached whites, and inky blacks.

The presence I'd encountered today was the polar opposite: brilliant as a sun, radiant, gentle, feminine, and the flowers on the vast mound had been every color of the rainbow plus countless more. I'd felt *right* there. Good. Part of something Nature herself embraced.

I wondered at the origins of the Fae. Wondered how the Seelie could be so emotionless and icy when the Magic I'd felt today was so warm and welcoming. I wondered if the True Race had always been the way they were now, or if something had happened to change them.

Then I wondered no more because Barrons entered the room and my body quickened with interest, desire, anticipation, lust.

He passed behind me, lightly touched my hair, and headed for the door. "Get some sleep. You need it," was all he said.

I opened my mouth to ask where he was going then remembered all the reasons I never asked Barrons that question and said instead, "Jericho."

He stopped walking instantly, turned, and stared at me through the low light. "Mac."

"Do you have to go?" I asked.

"No."

"Then why are you?"

His dark gaze was inscrutable. "Because this is what we do. You and I. Leave each other alone."

Whuh. I went still, processing what he'd just said. I'd heard it completely differently than he'd said it. I'd heard: *You, Ms. Lane, have always set the pace, the ground rules, determined the way we behave with each other. I toe your motherfucking line.*

I opened my mouth to shape the question, *And if I'd like to change that?* Then realized the cowardice inherent. It was hypothetical, fishing, seeking reassurance, shifting the weight of any decision or commitment back to him. It was refusing to put myself on the line by actually telling him what I wanted from our relationship.

"I'd like to change that," I said carefully. "I think it would be nice if we spent more time together." I cringed because it sounded far hokier hanging in the air all naked and exposed like that than it had in my head. Now he would mock me, toss some pithy comment my way, or join me on the Chesterfield, thinking I wanted to have sex.

He did none of those things, merely inclined his dark head, shadows swirling in his ancient obsidian eyes. "What do you have in mind?" he said softly.

Softly. There was danger here.

And much more.

The moment stretched between us, pregnant with possibility, reminding me of another moment, in what felt like another life-time, when I'd believed we won the day and defeated the *Sinsar Dubh* by laying it to rest beneath the abbey. I'd been drunk on victory, buoyed by the sure knowledge that our battle had been fought and was over for good.

My life was about to finally get back to normal after a long, hellish nine months. I could see a future for myself again.

I'd been through the storm and survived. I'd lost my sister, found out I was adopted, nearly been killed, learned to lie, cheat, steal, and kill, been gang-raped and turned Pri-ya, almost been killed a few more times, killed Barrons, been nearly seduced by the *Sinsar Dubh*'s illusion of the parents I'd so desperately wanted, killed Rowena, yet still survived to lay the archvillain of the whole piece to rest for good.

I'd said that very day to Jericho Barrons, *Bet your ass you're mine, bud.* I'd staked my claim, openly, clearly, in front of every-one, ready to plunge into every fascinating, sexy, intimate, per-sonal aspect of a relationship with him.

Then I'd learned my battle wasn't over.

A worse one loomed ahead.

I'd merely gotten a breather before round two.

The villain that had killed so many people, so brutally, had an evil twin. And it was inside me. Words can't express the depths of horror and despair I'd felt.

Discovering, roughly a month and a half ago, my time—three and half months ago for the world—that I harbored within me untapped potential for murder, chaos, and destruction, that my fight might never be over, had changed me.

I'd never bought for a single moment that I could simply walk away, not open it and escape unscathed. Somehow I'd known that the battle I'd just been through was going to seem like a piece of cake compared to the one I was headed for.

The day I'd discovered the *Sinsar Dubh* was really there at the bottom of my lake, and I was—let us be perfectly fucking precise here—*possessed* (and by God, I'd wanted a full-fledged exorcism), I'd begun retreating.

I'd lost the last week of May and most of June in the Silvers. I spent the final days of June and most of July throwing up barrier after barrier between Barrons and me.

I'd simplified and objectified our relationship into one of lust and boundaries, and while both were necessary for a good relationship, it took a lot more than that to make it an epic one.

Things we had, like respect and trust, but also freely expressed desires and accountability to whatever degree it took to make both people happy. It took work, a willingness to fight passionately and fairly—out of bed, not just in it—commitment and honesty. It took waking up and saying each day, *I hold this man sacred and always will. He's my sun, moon, and stars.* It took letting the other person in; a thing I'd stopped doing. It took being unafraid to ask for what you wanted, to put yourself on the line, to risk it all for love.

We'd almost been there once.

Until I'd run.

My eyes widened. I'd always thought if either one of us might withdraw from our relationship, it would certainly be him, not me.

But I was the one who'd run.

"Like a world class athlete," he agreed, dark eyes glittering. "Fast as fuck and not about to stop for anything until you'd crossed the finish line."

I caught my breath. "Why did you stay?" It would have been easier for him to just leave. A lot of men would have. I'd seriously vacated. Retreated and left him with bad moods and sex, and not much more.

"I understood."

"*What* did you understand?" I said, because I sure as hell didn't. Why had I run, knowing I was about to face another battle that was going to be even harder? A smart woman would have let Barrons in more, leaned on him, cultivated his exceptional strengths and extraordinary powers. But no, I'd shut him out. Redefined our relationship completely, lessening it. And he'd let me. Never said a word about it. Just stayed in the capacity I'd been willing to accept.

"It has nothing to do with intelligence or lack thereof. We're alike, you and I."

I blinked. Jericho Barrons had just put us in the same category.

"Alpha to the core. Proud. Independent. We're private and pissy about our battles, especially the internal ones. We don't want anyone else in the middle of how messy we think we might get, nor do we want to inadvertently hurt someone. I'd have left you completely until I'd seen it through. At least you stayed in my bed. Some of the time."

I bristled. "If you ever even *think* of leaving me to—"

"I don't fight internal battles anymore." He was silent a moment then added, "Nor will you. Not even about Jo and the others. Yes, I know you know about them."

I didn't bother asking how he knew. "How do you figure?" I was pretty sure I still had a hellish battle to wage with myself.

"Because now you understand there are things we do in our lives for which there is—and will never be—any forgiveness. No matter how many people around you offer it. What you've done is irrevocable and you'll find no absolution."

"Gee, thanks for making me feel so much better, Barrons," I said, stung.

"You never make peace with some things. But, like an oyster, chafed by a grain of sand you can't dislodge, eventually you polish it into something of value."

"How could my murder of Jo and the others ever possibly become something of value?"

"It's not the action that becomes the thing of value. It's how you feel about the action that does. You find yourself doing something for another person you never would have done before. You pay it forward. It takes time. Relax. Live. Keep your eyes open. See what comes."

Relax. Live. Keep your eyes open. See what comes. I smiled faintly. That was all any of us could do on a given day.

I locked gazes with him. *You're my sun—*

Hush. You think I don't know that? I have a bone to pick with you, Ms. Lane.

I arched a brow. Uh-oh. I was Ms. Lane. That was Barrons: the man of few words could get downright loquacious with his criticism. "What?" There was a note of truculence in my voice, but I'd had a rough twenty-four hours and I was tired.

There was a moment back there in the White Mansion. You didn't move. I wouldn't have minded if you had.

He opened his arms.

Truculence dissipated like a bubble bursting. When I bounded over the couch, sped across the bookstore, and flung myself into them, he caught me up and swung me around and I threw my head back, laughing just like a heroine in one of those romantic movies.

"Sun, moon, and stars," he growled against my ear.

I punched him in the shoulder. "Hush. You think I don't know that?"

Then his mouth was on mine and we were on the floor, ushering in the night in time-honored fashion.

By the crimson and silvery light of the moon shafting in the front windows of my bookstore, on a hard floor that felt soft as clouds, I made love to Jericho Barrons. Took my time, slow, lingering, and tender. Poured into my hands every ounce of reverence I felt for this man who understood me like no other, saw straight to my tarnished soul and liked every bit of it, waited patiently while I did dickhead things until I found my way through them, never changed, never stopped being beastly but was capable of enormous loyalty and great tenderness. This lion that I'd sauntered up to wearing my flashy peacock feathers hadn't snapped the head off my skinny, brilliantly colored neck, he'd only licked me and waited for me to grow claws.

I had neither flashy feathers nor claws now. I'd become yet another thing.

A steel fist inside a velvet glove.

Strong enough that I was no longer afraid to be gentle. Powerful enough that I could be vulnerable. Scarred enough that I could understand and tread lightly around the deepest scars of others.

Then Barrons's steel was inside my velvet glove and I thought no more.

♪

Later, when I lay stretched on top of his big hard body, I raised my head and looked into his eyes. "Did you see me when I was the Book?"

Yes, his dark gaze said.

I didn't want to know, yet I needed to know. There was a new part of me that never wanted to hide from anything again. It demanded all truth all the time. If I'd done something, I wanted to know every detail, own it completely and deal with it. I'd learned that not knowing is so much harder than knowing, no matter how bad the truth is. Whether it's worse or not, the unknown always looms larger and more terrifying because the doubt it creates undermines our ability to move forward. "Did you see me kill Jo?"

I saw you after the Book had. There's no question you did it. The others I killed?

He shook his head. *I wasn't there. I did, however, see a few disturbing things on the way to the White Mansion. I terminated each of them. Quickly.*

I inhaled sharply and tears sprang to my eyes. He'd cleaned up after me. When I'd first returned to Dublin this morning I'd wanted desperately to find those terrible things the Book had shown me: the inside out twins, the castrated man, the child, but I'd realized it had been thirty-five days, and although they surely lingered in agony, it had likely been a matter of hours or days and it was far too late for me to be merciful. Barrons had prevented them from suffering. Been the mercy killer for me. I drew back and looked at him through the tears, wondering if this was what he had meant about the grain of sand. "Your feelings about whatever you'd done that was unforgivable got polished into mercy."

Mercy from a beast like me? he mocked.

Yes, from you.

He said nothing but I knew it was true.

The silence stretched, then he lightly touched his hands to my temples and drew my head into the hollow of his neck.

Suddenly I was in another place and time, a desert of sand, a hot wind gusting over me, tangling my hair. Watching Barrons toss his son up onto a horse. The beautiful little boy laughed with excitement as his father stared impatiently up.

I made him come with me that day because I was in a hurry. I didn't want to waste the few minutes it would have taken to return him to his mother. There was no reason to hurry. Those few minutes cost him his entire life, condemned him to an eternity of hell.

I swallowed.

The thing that ate at me the most about containing you with the stones was that it appeared my choices were: don't do it and let you destroy the world; do it and lock you away in Culsan's chamber, incurring the risk that the world got destroyed by the black holes anyway, leaving you to suffer there forever because I would be gone and unable to come back and free you; or kill you so you would never suffer my son's fate. I can't tell you if it appeared the world would end, I'd not have done the latter.

"Thank you," I said simply.

He inclined his head gravely.

"Was I horrific when the Book was in possession of me?"

"No worse than many humans I've known. Where the corporeal Book was a vast, philosophical, brilliant homicidal maniac with enormous power of illusion, the one within you seemed a smaller, egotistical psychopath. Cruce postulated that the Book didn't copy itself, it had to split, thereby lost many of its parts in the process. I suspect the twenty-some years it lived inside you changed it further. Its time inside your body must have been the most visceral, tangible experience it had ever had, connected to your senses."

"You think I humanized it."

"To a degree."

"Did you know I was in there?"

He smiled faintly. "I felt you early on. You were furious."

"You felt that? But I wasn't in control of it then!"

"Your rage was enormous and told me what I needed to know. You were in there, fighting. Later the Book tried to pretend it was shifting back and forth between you and it, and I played along but I could sense only the Book at that time. The only other time I felt you was when I came to you."

"And told me to become it."

His dark eyes gleamed. *Which you did superbly. My little monster.*

I gasped. "You could feel me when I was like that—stripped of all emotion?"

You were a woman who knew her own strength. Powerful. Resolute. Beautiful.

I dropped my head back down into the hollow of his neck,

glowing inside. Beneath me lay the only man that could probably ever understand what I'd become at that moment, and could admire it. It would have terrified most men, to watch a woman strip away everything that made her human in order to get the job done. He found my strength beautiful. My monster and his beast; they liked each other.

"We have to make plans to move humans off world, Jericho." I turned my mind away from myself and toward our many problems. "This planet may die, but that doesn't mean the end of the human race. They can live on another world, colonize."

"Ryodan and I are already on it. Years ago we mapped paths in the Silvers to worlds that could sustain human life. We knew this world might one day become more hostile than we desired." He was silent a moment, then added, "Still, we failed to consider it might one day cease to exist entirely. We've never faced the risk of permanent death until recently. Now all of us face the threat of complete annihilation."

Or eternal hell. Reborn in a black hole to die again and again. I traced my fingers down the sharp angle of his jaw, touched his lips, vowing silently that I would never let that happen.

He caught my hand and kissed each finger then said, "When you think of the lives your opening the *Sinsar Dubh* cost, think also that if you had not, you would not have become the Fae queen, thereby gaining the only magic that may save this world."

"You think the lives of the few are worth the lives of the many."

"The universe works in mysterious ways. When you live long enough, you begin to see a grander purpose and pattern, larger than any of us."

"The only way that grander purpose works for me is if I manage to save the Earth. I don't know what I have or how to use it."

"We'll figure it out. But if it looks like we can't, you're going off world, too."

I drew back and looked at him. The old me would have bristled, snapped an angry denial. The new me simply kissed him then drew back and said gently, "No, I'm not." I would live and die beside this man. But I would never leave him.

He smiled then, white teeth flashing in his dark face, rolled me beneath him and stretched his body over mine and unleashed a storm of passion on my body while above us thunder rolled and lightning cracked as an end-of-days deluge broke loose over Dublin.

43

Queen of fire, king of ice

MAC

When I woke up, Barrons was gone. I amused myself with the thought that I'd so thoroughly exhausted him that he'd had to go eat to regain his strength. I'd tried to exhaust him. I was the one who'd ended up passing out on the Chesterfield. No surprise there.

Last night had been incredible, worth the horrors I'd endured, to end up here, now, the way I was.

I rolled over onto my back and mouthed a silent thank-you at the ceiling for putting me through my recent ordeal. I'd known, the night we'd defeated the corporeal Book, that there was a serious imbalance of power and personal fortitude between me and Barrons, and it had eaten at me. It was an imbalance I no longer felt.

A scrabbling at the front door jarred me from my thoughts. Sighing, I pushed my hair out of my face—holy crap, it was nearly to my waist!—poked my head up and peered over the back of the sofa.

I narrowed my eyes and tried to process what I was seeing.

Little fairies were stuck like colorful tree frogs to every rain-soaked inch of glass on the front of the bookstore.

Peering in at me.

I peered back.

We did that for a few minutes. I had no idea what they were thinking but I was pretty much just thinking, What are these sparkly little spotted and striped things and why are they decorating my store? It was a type of Fae I'd never seen before; diminutive and dainty like the death-by-laughter Fae but less flashy, earthier.

I finally pushed myself up, walked to the window and touched my hand to the glass, tracing the shape of a small, delicate female with sandy spots and tawny hair.

She shivered and began to chirp excitedly.

Then they all started to chirp and clamor and scrabble about on the wet glass.

Baffled, I moved to the door and carefully opened it. They remained hanging in the air, plastered to whatever force field Barrons had erected around the store that kept Fae out with the exception of Cruce, when he was permitted. All were slender, velvety-skinned, some had spots in every shade of green with mossy hair, others with gray and white stripes and silvery hair. There were sunny yellow ones with lemon curls, dark brown ones with short muddy shocks of hair, pale blue with cerulean manes, rose beauties with pale pink braids. It was a veritable rainbow of fairies, with varying patterns and designs on their skin.

I waved my hand in a shooing gesture and they peeled away to permit my exit. As I moved out into the alcove, thousands of fairies the size of my hand began to drop from the sky in flashes of brilliant color. I poked my head out past the column and glanced into the street. Fae were plastered to the sides of every building, falling away, landing in the puddle-dotted street where they instantly sank to their knees, bowed their heads and crossed their arms over their chests in an unmistakable gesture of . . .

Fealty?

Abruptly their chirping was no longer unintelligible.

"Our queen! Our queen! Isn't she lovely? *Oooh*, she's so beautiful!" Trills of excitement rippled through them.

"What are you?" I asked the crowd of tiny beings. "I mean, what caste and why have I never seen you before?"

A slender gray-spotted fairy sloshed forward through a puddle and bowed low. "O Austere and Beneficent Queen, the Spyrssidhe have long been forbidden at court."

"Why?"

"We were deemed unacceptable and banished, exalted liege," she said.

"She speaks to us! She speaks to us!" rippled through the crowded, rainy street. "She may hear our petition!"

"By the prior queen?" I asked.

She nodded sadly. "Cast out into the world of Man, to make our homes in trees and streams, among rocks and flowers and the gardens of Man. We felt the rising of a new and different queen and came to petition you, gracious and wise Queen, in hopes you would hear our plea and reconsider our fate."

All this "queen" stuff was a bit much but I knew better than to downplay my status. I'd learned my lesson the day I told the Hunter I wasn't the king. He'd said I couldn't fly anymore if I wasn't. Until I got a better handle on things, I'd do my best to incur and keep the respect and cooperation of the Fae. "Why were you banished?"

A male fairy with copper and tan spots pushed through, knelt in a puddle before me, put one hand to his breast and bowed deeply. "O Munificent Queen, unlike the others of our race, our hearts failed to ice."

I cocked my head, startled. Was he telling me they felt emotion? I was just about to ask when he continued, "Nor did our loins. From jealousy and spite they drove us out, stupendous, all-powerful Queen. She who rules no more decreed we were not Fae enough for Faery once we began siring young on this world."

I gasped. "You can have children?" I'd thought it impossible for Fae to reproduce!

"Few, but yes, O Fair and Radiant Liege. It didn't begin happening until we came to this world. The other castes were patient for a time, waiting to see if the same would occur for them. When it did not, they turned the queen's icy heart against us. She stripped us of our place in Faery."

He gestured to someone behind him and a young, light purple and green fairy, the perfect coloring to hide in a hydrangea bush, came forward holding a tiny bundle in her arms, cradling it beneath a shiny leaf to keep it dry. She peeled back the misted leaf to show me a naked, translucent, infant fairy the size of a fingernail.

"Oh!" I exclaimed, smiling. It was adorable. And so tiny! "She's lovely."

Blushing, the fairy exclaimed, "I am honored by your kindness, great Queen! Our young are void of color at birth and grow slowly into their patterns, painted by whatever element of Nature they favor. Some are drawn to waterfalls." She waved a hand at a young female fairy, marked with vertical stripes of white and pale gray. "Others to rocks or forests or tall grassy meadows or flowers. Some part of Nature calls to each of us and she patterns us accordingly." She blushed again. "I live among the gorse and heather, great Queen. If I am blessed, so will my child be."

"Why would you wish to return to court? It sounds as if you like this world."

The male fairy said, "My Queen, we but seek the freedom to come and go as we wish, as do the others of our kind. We desire our seat upon the council back. We are Fae. We have always been Fae. They had no right to cast us out. Faery is our home, too, and we would have a say in the matters of our race."

As I stared out at the thousands of diminutive Fae gathered in the rainy street, it finally, fully sunk in.

I was the Faery queen. This wasn't a trial run or a temporary situation.

They'd felt my power and sought me out, tracked me here. No doubt other Seelie would, too. And each would bring their problems and grievances and demands. The higher castes (thinking Dree'lia here) would no doubt come armed with hostility, resentment, and murder in their frosted hearts. I was supposed to rule this race. Hear and settle their disputes, enter into their politics.

It was too much to process. Part of me wanted to whirl back into the bookstore, slam the door, and reject it all. It was one thing to have been bequeathed the potential to save our world, entirely another to actually become the queen of a race of beings I was beginning to realize I knew nothing about. A race of beings that, a year ago, I'd actively hunted and killed. I'd wanted nothing more than to eradicate the Fae race from our planet. Was that the answer? Save our world, find them a new one and turn my power over to another, Fae-born?

At the moment, whether I liked it or not, I was their queen, and until I figured out what to do about it I would behave accordingly. These tiny beings were looking to me for justice, decisions, leadership. They could have children. They felt. My entire apprehension of the Fae race was being turned on its ear.

They were elementals, drawn to Nature. "Do you sense the disturbance in the fabric of this world?"

Thousands of heads nodded instantly.

"Is there anything you can do to help heal it?"

Thousands of heads shook no.

"We are small Fae, and do small things, beauteous Queen," the heather and gorse fairy said. "Enriching the soil, cleansing the water, making flowers bloom more brightly. Large matters such as the sickness that eats away at this world are beyond us."

"I've heard your petition and will consider it. But as your queen, my first duty is to secure the safety of this planet."

The male fairy with copper-tan spots bowed deeply again. "Well said, my lucent Queen. We will repair to our abodes and await an opportune moment."

Clapping their hands to their heads, they vanished.

Frowning, I hurried back into the warmth and dryness of the bookstore. I'd assumed they were a lower caste. Could they sift?

My eyes widened. Could *I* sift now?

♪

If I could sift, I had no bloody idea how.

Magic didn't work for me the way it did for Harry Potter, by pointing a wand, muttering a spell, and getting the desired outcome, nor with the twinkle of a *Bewitched* nose. It was far more elusive and subtle than that. Either that or I just didn't know the right magic words or the proper part of my body to twitch.

The two times I'd channeled the magic, I had no idea how I'd done it. When I'd returned from the planet with three moons, the bookstore was perfectly restored but I didn't know why. I figured it was because I'd been found worthy, but that wasn't a repeatable recipe. And thank goodness, because I'd hate to have to prove myself worthy every time I wanted to use it. Not only would that be a real time suck, but stressful to endure a new interrogation each time.

I'd envisioned the flowers from the mound, and the ice had melted. But again I had no idea why or what I'd done. I sat on the sofa for an hour this morning (after spending ten minutes braiding my insanely long mane of hair to get it out of my face), trying to do something so simple as grow a single flower, and met with repeated failure. I even tried stripping away all emotion and using sheer force of will on the world around me, employing my "belief is reality" tool with equally abysmal results.

Unable to take advantage of a queenly power I'd really like to use, I slogged like every other human in Dublin, through cobbled streets that were gushing with small gutter-bound rivers, fighting to hold my umbrella against the brisk, drenching wind, making my way to Trinity College to deliver the music box as promised.

Periodically I'd feel the acute stress of someone's regard and glance quickly, to catch only a brief glimpse of one Fae or another as they melted hastily from my vision, behind a building or lamp or car.

The word was out. It was possible the Spyrssidhe alone—already banished and with little to lose—would dare approach me. I knew how feared the princes were among the Fae, inspiring obsequious fawning, obedience, and given wide, wary berth. No doubt their queen had been a hundred times as terrifying. How else could anyone control a race of immortals as power-hungry and brutal as V'lane/Cruce?

Damn it, I needed him on my side. He could teach me.

He'd prefer to kill me. I was the only thing standing between him and the throne for which he hungered. We'd left the princess cocooned in the boudoir.

"MacKayla." Cruce appeared beside me as if summoned by my thoughts.

I startled, jumped back, nearly went down on the slippery pavement and caught myself on his arm.

He stared down at my hand on his forearm, a muscle working in his jaw, as if it was hard for him in some way to see me touching him. He was fully Unseelie prince, not bothering with glamour, dark, enormous, and powerfully built, with kaleidoscopic tattoos racing beneath his skin like brilliant storm clouds, flitting up his neck to flirt with the writhing torque around his neck. He'd dressed—no doubt in an attempt to disarm or make me see him as more like us—as a human, in faded jeans, boots, and a flowing linen shirt. I was inordinately irritated to see not one speck of rain falling on him. He was, I observed with a distant, unwilling part of my mind, unutterably beautiful, exotic, and disturbingly, basely male.

I snatched it away and stared up into his dark face.

He'd raped me.

And he had answers I needed. I'd offered to be the sheepdog, not the wolf, if he would cooperate.

I recalled the day Barrons had told me we couldn't kill the Unseelie princes because they were linchpins. I'd thoroughly resented it.

I understood it now. And strangely, I no longer felt white-hot fury or trembling rage when I looked at him. He was a predator. He'd preyed on me. I was aware now. Wide-awake, eyes open. I knew what existed in the world and I knew how to protect myself from it. All that was left in me about the rape was a calm acknowledgment that this man had harmed me. I knew what he was and would deal with him accordingly.

He said icily, "Recall, when you regard me with condemnation in your eyes that I also gave you the elixir. I did not use the *Sidhbajai* on you that day nor contribute to your madness. If I had not attended you then, you would have died in the street, maimed and broken as your sister. You have finally become the creature I knew you might one day be. If the price of your survival was permitting my carnal use of your body for that brief time, would you have accepted it, had the choice been presented to you?"

I said nothing, one hand resting lightly on the hilt of my spear.

"Answer me," he said imperiously.

"I didn't hear a 'O Great and Glorious Liege' in there anywhere."

Abruptly, rain stopped splattering into my umbrella. He'd extended whatever power he was using to hold it at bay to encompass me as well. I closed my umbrella and rested the tip on the ground.

"I see the answer in your eyes. You, like me, would pay any price to survive to fight for your desires for even one more day."

"That doesn't excuse your actions. You could have simply given me the elixir. You didn't have to rape me."

"I caused you no harm. You experienced only pleasure at my hands. And I experienced enormous pleasure in yours. It was not the way I would have chosen it to be."

"You think if a person is forced to orgasm during rape it's not rape." How wrong he was. Above me, thunder cracked and boomed, and I wondered if the weather was causing it, or me. "You really believe that, don't you?"

"I am incapable of seeing it any other way. I am Fae, Mac-Kayla. You know what I am. Do you seek my counsel? Shall I attend you?"

"You vanished last night, refusing us aid."

"You do not see me. You have never seen me. To you, alone, will I give my aid. I have always offered it to you. I offer it now."

"So you can get close to me, awaiting the opportunity to kill me."

His eyes narrowed, locked with mine. "I would be your consort, your instructor, your lover. I would prove to you that I did not and never would harm you with my lust. Teach you as I once taught Aoibheal."

"Who you also tried to kill."

He smiled faintly. "She was not like you. You are the best of both worlds: the ice and power of a Fae queen, the passion and fire of a human. By the time she was queen, she'd been fully Fae for a long time."

"Barrons is my consort."

"Discard him. Choose me. I have always hungered for you. That was never a lie."

"I will never choose you. I command you to aid me. I am your queen."

"You are not my queen, nor was she. I am not of that puny race. I am Unseelie. Try again." He smiled again, white teeth flashing in his dark chiseled face. "Unlike the Seelie, you do not know my True Name. You can never compel me. Merely request. I will be your ally. I will teach you all that I can about your newfound powers. But you must reward me."

"What do you want?" Here it was: we were getting to the miracle it would take to wed him to my aim.

"First, you will restore my wings. Then once we have saved this world, you will willingly transfer the True Magic to me."

"I could do that—restore your wings and transfer the queen's power?" What else could I do? Fix a human heart?

He inclined his head imperiously.

"Wings only. After."

"Unacceptable."

"Then no." Cruce in charge of the Fae? Cruce with at least part of the *Sinsar Dubh,* all the queen's power, *plus* the song, assuming we managed to re-create it? What would keep him from wiping us all off the face of the Earth and taking it for himself?

He intuited my thoughts. "We will agree to a Compact, Mac-Kayla. Fae rulers are bound irrevocably by such magic. You will find confirmation of the truth I speak within you. As queen, you possess, undiluted, all the knowledge, myths, and magic of our race."

"Do I have her memories, too?"

"Memories are not transferred. The Fae already suffer an abundance of them."

I exhaled a sigh of relief. Though part of me had hoped I had them, another part of me had dreaded feeling split again, divided by memories that were not my own.

"I will agree to remove my race from your world, MacKayla, without harming it, or anything on it, before we go." He correctly interpreted the look on my face and added a haughty, "Or after, O Suspicious One. Or ever. I will agree to never return and your planet will be forbidden to all Fae for all time. You may have your *brehon* father draft the details of our Compact and your druids oversee the enforcing of it. MacKayla, by these pledges will I abide," he intoned with the somber gravity of a vow.

I stared into his eyes, those madness-inducing Unseelie prince eyes, and was startled by the transparency therein. He wasn't lying. If I agreed to his terms he would do everything he could to save our world, then once I transferred the queen's power to him, he would take his race away and leave us in peace. Forever.

It wasn't a bad deal.

In all honesty, after my encounter with the Spyrssidhe that morning, I didn't want to be queen of the Tuatha De Danann. I still harbored hope that one day I might be "just Mac" again; undoubtedly a new and vastly improved Mac—but one without four feet of hair and the crushing responsibility for an entire race. When would I ever have time to see Barrons or my family and friends? Where would I live? In Faery half the time, a reluctant Persephone dividing her days between Heaven and Hell?

"Who better to rule them than me, MacKayla? There is no stronger, more powerful, ancient, and wise Fae than I. You heard the queen. She, herself, was considering me. We both know you do not wish to be one of us. You bear no favor for my people. I will aid you unstintingly, withholding nothing that is necessary to achieve the health and well-being of your world. Grant me the right to lead my race. It is all I have ever sought, indeed, all I have ever desired. I spoke the truth when I told you, as V'lane, that Cruce's sole aim was to free my brethren and ensure the future of the Fae. At this moment both our races are in danger of extinction."

"Actually, that's not true. The queen may have irrevocably bound the power of the Fae to this planet, and your race will definitely die if the planet does, but humans can go live anywhere. Our existence isn't dependent on magic buried inside a world. My race can be moved to another one," I pointed out.

His nostrils flared and he hissed, "If you would leave my people to die after having been entrusted with the True Magic of my race, after having been *accepted* by it, you are no better than you accuse me of being. Although I have never felt it, I have heard it is a power of great benevolence. I am willing to subject my desires and goals for my people to its scrutiny, and believe it will deem me worthy to lead them. Prove yourself the queen I believe you to be. The queen the True Magic *thinks* you are."

He vanished.

I was instantly drenched.

Rolling my eyes, I popped open my umbrella and resumed sloshing through puddles toward Trinity College.

♪

Fade was standing outside the door to the physics lab when I puddled in. Ryodan had dispatched him late last night, he told me, with orders to protect Dancer so long as the music box was in his possession.

Stepping into the lab, I propped my umbrella against the wall, grabbed paper towels off a counter, and dried my face, then hurried to join Dancer where he sat with headphones on, staring at a computer in the rear of the lab.

After exchanging greetings, I removed the music box from my backpack and handed it to him.

Fiddling with the unopened box, turning it this way and that, Dancer told me, "Gottfried Leibniz said that music is the secret exercise of the arithmetic of the soul, unaware of its act of counting." He looked up at me and beamed. "Don't you just love that? The relationship between math and music is sublime. I was picking up a lot of distortion from the box last night, so I set up equipment to cancel it out. I want to focus on the notes and chords, which I'll convert to numbers and play with."

"How?" I asked curiously. I loved music and had given a lot of thought to what made certain songs appeal to me more than others. I thought of songs as minibooks, with their own beginning, middle, and end and sometimes prefaces that established expectations. All had a story to tell. I responded to pattern repetition, motif that was recurrent, recombinant, and easily subjected to intriguing transformation. Although I adored happy one hit wonders, I could achieve the same buoyancy of mood from a number of classical pieces.

"There are eight notes in any given major scale that can be assigned numbers," he said. "If you start with middle C as one, D becomes two and E becomes three and so on. You can also assign numbers to chords in the same fashion. As an example, you can do a musical interpretation of pi. A guy named Michael Blake did a fantastic interpretation of pi to thirty-one decimal places at a tempo of one hundred fifty-seven beats per minute, which, interestingly, is 314/2. When it was up on YouTube, I downloaded it because I liked it. Have a listen." He pulled up the video on his laptop and hit PLAY.

After a few moments I said, "It's beautiful. It makes me feel happy."

"Yeah," he grinned, "the nuts and bolts of the universe tend to be that way."

I loved that Dancer saw so much beauty in the world. We needed more people like him. Could I heal his heart? Did I have such power? Should I try to find the legendary elixir and give it to him? Would he want it? I wasn't sure I would.

"Here's my version of pi," he told me. "I took it more classic rock." He opened an MP3 and hit PLAY.

It was different, but equally uplifting.

He said, "You can do all kinds of interpretations of pi but it's just one of many mathematical equations that convert brilliantly to song. I want to break down the music in the box and study it. It makes sense to me that since sound is vibration is frequency, and the Hoar Frost King was devouring frequency from the fabric of our world, it would be another sound/vibration/frequency that would repair it. We just have to isolate it. I can't compute it with the information we currently have because the Hoar Frost King removed those chunks of complex frequency. While I was able to determine that it was drawn to the flatted-fifth, there were multiple frequencies occurring at each scene that got iced. The Devil's tritone may have been only one of many frequencies he stripped from those locations. I've tried playing all kinds of music to the black holes repeatedly, but nothing I've played has had any effect."

I smiled faintly, envisioning him sitting near a black hole with a boom box. None of what he'd said explained why I heard the symphony of my dreams coming from the box while he heard a nightmarish melody. "Any idea why you and I hear it so differently?"

He shook his head. "But let me play with it and I'll text you when I've got something."

"You'll text me?"

He grinned. "Barrons gave me a phone loaded with numbers and said he programmed my number into yours."

Figured. After showing him how to open the music box, I said goodbye and headed for the door. I had a lengthy list of goals to accomplish today.

But first I wanted to cross a personal one off my list.

Cellphones didn't get reception in the Silvers. Well, with the exception of IYD, which magically bypassed natural laws. As I moved toward the door I pulled mine out to call Mom and gasped. I'd been so busy I hadn't looked at it since returning from the Silvers.

I had fifty-two voicemail messages and over a hundred new texts. My cellphone was on mute. I turned the volume back on and glanced at my texts first. Mom, Dad, Ryodan, Alina.

Alina? I thumbed them up and a long line of them whizzed by, leaving the last one on the screen:

Sept 11, 10:43 P.M.
Oh, for crying out loud, Mac, where ARE you? Mom and
Dad are LOSING it! How did you handle them when I
died? They totally melt down! Okay, so maybe I'm
melting down, too. WHERE ARE YOU??????

I stared blankly. It was dated yesterday. I scrolled back. There were pages and pages of texts. I finally got to the first one:

August 8, 7:30 A.M.

Hey, little Mac—breakfast is ready!

August 8, 8:00 A.M.

Sissy, where are you?????

August 8, 9:02 A.M.

Seriously, Jr., what the fuck?

August 8, 11:21 A.M.

Mac, coffee's getting bitter and so am I. Get your freaking petunia over here. I will NOT be stood up by my baby sis. You're pissing me off.

Tears filled my eyes. How was she still here? Even though I'd put her on my list of personal goals, I'd been going through the motions, nothing more. I'd accepted that she'd been an illusion with substance, created by the *Sinsar Dubh*. I'd also accepted that since it had been rendered inert, she would no longer be here.

Was it possible the Book had genuinely brought her back from the dead? And whether it was contained or not, here Alina would remain?

I shivered. On some level, I found the thought unsettling, but I couldn't pinpoint why. It was possible I'd just seen too many monkey's paw type movies where you had to be really careful what you wished for because there was always some terrible karmic price for interfering with Fate. And although I'd once said I didn't believe in the bitch, I'd decided that either I did or it didn't matter because Fate believed in me.

I scrolled through Alina's messages again. She was living with Mom and Dad in a townhouse on the north side of the River Liffey.

After memorizing the address, I hurried out into the storm.

LANDSLIDE

I learned, much later, after I'd hunted down the man named Seamus O'Leary, that I was the reason he'd broken my mother's heart.

From my cage, I'd watched a good mom turn into a terrible mom and, finally, a mortal danger to me.

I needed to know why.

I was ten when I realized you couldn't yield even an ounce of your essential self for any reason. Good people didn't turn bad overnight. It happened from the accumulation of many small compromises, sacrifices, and losses.

Small, consistent erosions turn into landslides in time.

A widower with three sons, Seamus hadn't been averse to marrying a woman with a child of her own and blending their families.

He'd found her funny and clever, pretty and kind. A junior partner at a law firm, he'd fallen in love with the gentle, downtrodden after-hours cleaning woman.

But she was cursed by the O'Malley bloodline, and while some men learned to live with the ancient heritage of the six sidhe-seer houses, to respect and love their wife and daughter's gifts, not all men were so inclined.

And some were simply unwilling to believe at all.

Secure in his love, certain of his intentions, my mother told Seamus about herself, her heritage, and me.

His shock took a darker turn to concern for her mental health, this woman he'd nearly entrusted with his young sons.

This woman who actually believed she had a child that could move so fast no one could see her.

She'd presented him with an insane and vividly detailed delusion *about fairies and women who'd been selectively bred to protect the world against them.*

She'd affixed her delusional paranoia to real world people and businesses, insisting a local, highly respected abbey was really a secret society of women that guarded the world from these ancient, immortal monsters and, in Dublin, they posed as a bike courier company called PHI (that his office frequently used to dispatch files about town) so this special cult of gifted "fairy-killers" could keep tabs on their city, ever alert for threats to humankind.

She'd contended that her daughter had been so strong by the age of three that she'd shattered the toilet merely by crashing into it too fast in something she'd called "freeze-frame."

(I remembered that day. I'd struck the commode with my little kid belly so hard it'd been black and blue for days. We hadn't been able to afford another toilet for months. When she'd finally brought one home, it was cracked and discolored and she had to repair it. I have no idea where she found it. Probably in someone's trash.)

Then, the coup de grâce—my mother told Seamus that she'd been forced to handle her very special daughter by keeping her locked up in a cage.

For years.

This woman he'd nearly taken home to his precious young sons.

I remember the look on his face when I freeze-framed into his office late one night, after everyone else had gone home for the day, leaving him alone. I'd been trailing him for weeks and had finally realized I would never get the answers I wanted without forcing them from him.

I'd blasted in, moving so fast I was undetectable, and whirled around and around the chair he was sitting in, unfurling thick, heavy rope behind me, tying him securely to it.

I remember his expression when I finally slowed down enough for him to see me—curly hair wild, eyes wilder. My strength so enormous by then that I'd been able to simply toss his heavy ornate desk out of my way without the slightest strain.

When I was done with Seamus that night, he believed.

Accepted that every word my mother had told him was true, even wept at the end.

If only he'd believed her sooner, if only he'd been willing to learn and accept, I might have gotten a father to help raise me. If only he'd come to the house, met me, kept an open mind, my mom could have proved the truth to him and he'd have gotten a wonderful mother for his sons. The erosion would have stopped. Erosions need new, solid soil to be brought in every now and then.

She'd never wanted to keep me in a cage. A woman without family, alone, without education, didn't have many choices.

She'd just needed a little help. She'd never gotten it from anyone.

And Rowena, that stone-cold bitch, never once offered aid. I'd known that night I would one day kill the powerful headmistress at the abbey. But I still had questions, big ones, and I'd begun to suspect Rowena was the only one with those answers.

I knew what had broken my mother's heart but I still didn't know how we ended up where we ended up that fateful night I gained my freedom.

Outraged, horrified, Seamus had thrown my mom out of his car in the dark, twenty-two miles from home. She'd walked through the pouring rain, crying the entire way. He knew that because he'd followed her, arguing with himself, debating whether he should pick her back up and take her straight to the nearest psychiatric facility.

The irony: if he had, I'd have been found in my cage by social workers and freed from it. Placed in a center, or foster care, I would have vanished in no time, grown up, and gotten her out. Taken her home and taken care of her. She wouldn't have died.

Seamus had driven away.

Then he'd gone one step further the next day and had her fired from her cleaning job, lodging a formal complaint of theft against her with his firm.

He'd said he wouldn't press charges if she went quietly.

She had.

My mother always went quietly. She didn't know any other way.

Word got around, after she'd been fired, that she wasn't to be trusted, and others refused her employment.

We'd needed that job. And the many others she was never able to get again.

I didn't kill him.

But I wanted to.

I didn't because, like my mom, he wasn't a bad person.

He was just the final erosion that started the landslide.

When I was thirteen I made a plaque for my mother's grave that said:

Emma Danielle O'Malley

Weep not for the life she lost,

But the life she never got to live.

44

"Time makes you bolder, even children get older,

and I'm getting older too"

JADA

I'd once taken a vacation Silverside, about three years in.

The planet I'd christened Dada—because it wasn't full-blown surrealism and Shazam's nihilism had been getting to me—was a crazy, rainbow-colored world that made me feel as if I were living in the game Candyland.

Nothing on that planet was the right color, assuming you used Earth for a gauge, but after a few months on Dada, I decided Earth's gauge was boring and wrong.

It was a small, lushly overgrown world with humid rain forests and pink oceans, dunes and beaches of powdery cerulean sand, and craggy burnt orange mountains. I'd explored that world from end to end, finding neither civilization nor ruins to suggest any had ever existed. It was paradise for me and Shazam.

Everything was edible.

The flowers had tasted like sweet and sour Gummy Bears and were massively high energy. The tree bark was varying flavors of chocolate. (I only peeled it away from fallen trees.) The water was pink lemonade and the plants tasted like fruit, even the leaves. The mushrooms—though they were the color and consistency of Hershey kisses—I hadn't cared for. They'd been pretty much like those on Earth. Sautéed, breaded, or plain, mushrooms always tasted like dirt to me.

"I *like* mushrooms," Dancer protested. "Have you ever tried a stuffed Portobello?"

Lying on my back next to him, I turned my head and narrowed my eyes. "I now find you completely suspicious and don't think we can be friends anymore, Brain."

He grinned. "Continue, Pinky. Tell me more about Dada."

The plants were so large, with such mammoth, sturdy, coated leaves that Shazam and I had been able to pluck them from segmented stems and sail down pink rivers together, racing kaleidoscopic, flying fish. The sky was light lavender and, at dusk, it turned violet before settling into a deep purple twilight. True night never fell on Dada, beneath seven brilliant purple moons that peaked at intervals.

I had no idea how long I'd stayed on that planet. I'd counted it as four months. Four blissful, peaceful months that had undone a lot of the damage from the past three years. I'd arrived on Dada badly injured. I'd left ready to tackle anything, and a damn good thing, too, because the next world had been hostile and harsh.

"How did you keep track of time?" Dancer said.

"Sloppily," I told him.

I'd had no watch and days Silverside unfolded in an unquantifiable blur, although I'd done my best to track it. Some planets had short nights, others felt like they lasted days, and on a few no sun ever rose. Those were the really bad ones.

Although I'd told people I'd been gone five and a half years, it was only a rough estimate. Still, I was pretty sure I was somewhere between nineteen and twenty-one.

"So, I might be a *seriously* younger man," Dancer said, smirking. "You cougar, you."

I snickered. Me, a cougar. Right. "Not in any way that matters," I told him. Age didn't exist when I was with him. He was just Dancer and I was just me. We were sprawled out on our backs on one of the counters in the physics lab, holding hands. I'd dropped by to stock up on food but had taken one look at the exhaustion in his face and ended up staying, searching for something to say that would make him light up, recharge.

He propped himself up on an elbow. "Tell me more about Shazam."

I stared into those long-lashed, brilliant aqua eyes that I adored seeing light up with laughter and fascination, especially when they were turned my way. What deranged God would give him a damaged heart? I'd already told him how we'd met. So I told him why we had to leave Dada. "He ate all the fish. I think to extinction. The other animals found out and stampeded, chased us all the way to the exit portal I located shortly after we arrived. He was only gone an hour when he did it." I frowned. "I'm not sure how he ate them all so fast. I think he has another form he never lets me see. Maybe more than one. There's a lot about Shazam I don't know. The whole hiding up in the air gig, he never taught me how to do it, though I pestered him relentlessly."

And it would have proved invaluable if he had. Some worlds had shorted out my *sidhe*-seer gifts. Shaz had a theory those planets were heavily laced with some mineral my blood reacted to badly. I'd always felt sick on those worlds and been unable to freeze-frame. Those had been tough worlds to survive. I had no clue how ordinary folks got through the days.

"Shaz says there are things limited life-forms like me aren't supposed to know until they reach that phase of evolution. You know, he'd been really good with his diet up until then, too. I'd had him restricted to plant life. I didn't think it was fair for him to eat another living being on Dada. They were so funny and playful and curious. They had complex societies and strong familial bonds. I asked him how he would like it if something ate him. He sank into an enormous depression for days, weeping uncontrollably, then told me with regal ire that 'For my Yi-yi, alone, I will *starve* if she so demands it.'" I added dryly, "She so demanded it. He wasn't starving. Shazam has enough belly fat to live off for months. But I'd *never* tell him that," I added hastily. "He's super sensitive about his appearance."

Dancer rolled over onto his stomach, head propped on fists, eyes dancing with excitement. I was relieved to see he looked far less tired than when I'd first arrived. "Mega, I've got to meet him! Why didn't you bring him back with you?"

Just like that, the shining bubble of happiness I'd blown for us popped. I closed my eyes and focused on my breath. After a long moment I said, "I'm starving. Mind if I hit up your supplies?"

When I opened my eyes, he was still in the same position, watching me with that steady, brilliant gaze. "Why did he call you Yi-yi?"

I had no intention of answering him but this was the most freely I'd spoken to anyone about my time Silverside. I was finding it increasingly difficult to say no to Dancer about anything, and my mouth said, "It was his way of saying he loved me. He used to say, 'I see you, Yi-yi.'"

Dancer smiled and pushed to his feet. "What are you hungry for? I'll nuke us some lunch."

"I need to head out to the abbey. I've wasted too much time already."

"It's good to take a break every now and then, Mega. Just like your vacation on Dada. Thanks for telling me about it. I want to hear about other worlds, too, like where you went from there. I want to hear about *all* of them." He shook his head with a look that was equal parts admiration and unabashed envy. "Christ, I've only ever seen one bloody world. You've seen what, hundreds? Thousands? Mega, when this is over, let's go off world. Let's go adventuring! We can do anything, go anywhere!"

I raided his little pantry in back, grabbed a few dozen protein bars, crammed all but one in my backpack, ripped it open, and headed for the door.

318 · KAREN MARIE MONING

"Sure," I forced out through a tight throat.

"See you tonight, Pinky?" he called after me.

We used to crack ourselves up calling each other Pinky and the Brain in a much simpler time, hatching our schemes to take over the world.

He'd kissed me last night. I'd slept over. The abbey was a ruin and none of my old hidey-holes had appealed. I'd been someone else when I stayed in those places, someone I'd never be again.

I'd slept on the couch despite his insistence I take the bed and he'd take the couch.

I shaped a *No, I'm busy,* with my lips, prepared to toss it over my shoulder. Instantly, a vision exploded in my head: dropping by tomorrow to find him dead. Last word he'd ever heard from me a "No."

His heart was my cage.

Dictating my actions. Making me think hard about everything I said and did. Knowing it was going to end badly no matter *what* I said or did. How was I supposed to care about someone I knew I wouldn't get to keep? By any logic, it was stupid. Self-destructive. Pointless. Bring on the erosion. I'd said to him last night, *You do know you're going to die before me, right?* He'd laughed and said, *Wow, that's arrogant, Mega. I don't take nearly the risks you do. Nobody ever knows how long anybody is going to live. Stop thinking about it. I don't. Live in the moment. You always used to.*

Back then it was enough. I'd believed my moments infinite. Jackie Paper was never going to leave Puff alone.

"Sure thing, Brain." I kicked up into the slipstream.

45

"Not to touch the earth"

MAC

I got a little slice of heaven that afternoon.

In a lovely townhouse, with a brightly painted red door, adorned by colorful planters filled with sopping wet blooms in every window, on the north side of the River Liffey, I had lunch with my sister Alina and my parents.

The Lane family reunion couldn't have been more perfect.

When I knocked on the door, Mom opened it, burst into tears of joy, and exclaimed over her shoulder, "Jack, Jack, come quickly! Our baby's here!"

Then my daddy and sister were both in the doorway and I was engulfed in Jack Lane's fierce bear hug that smelled just like it always did of peppermint and aftershave, then Alina and Mom had their arms around both of us and we stood in a group hug, crying and laughing, and my heart had nearly exploded from trying to hold so much joy.

The many horrors of the past year melted away in that embrace and it felt for a few moments as if the Lanes had merely gotten together in Ireland for a family vacation. My sister had never died, I'd never killed, and the world wasn't about to end.

Not. But it still felt pretty damned wonderful.

They told me Alina had found them weeks ago, and although they'd been disbelieving, even hostile at first, that "nice Mr. Ryodan had come by," taken her away and done a blood test that proved she was indisputably their daughter. (I didn't tell them he'd no doubt bitten her, not drawn blood, and exchanged a glance with Alina, who winked at me before we shared a private smile.) Daddy said they would have eventually believed it was her, even without a test of any kind, because he knew his girls.

Mom made fried chicken (Mr. Ryodan had sent a pantryful of other groceries—"Mr. Ryodan" really knew how to work the moms), biscuits, and greens, followed by the best peach pie I'd ever tasted.

We sat around the small table in the tall-ceilinged, bright kitchen, laughing and talking, reveling in the one thing we'd believed we would never get to do again—be a family making normal, family small talk. Mom made me unbraid my hair and told me it was too platinum for my coloring, and whatever hair vitamins I was taking, I might want to back off unless I wanted to turn into something from a fairy tale, like Rapunzel. I didn't tell her I'd already turned into something from a fairy tale. Figured I'd save that doozy for later. I noticed Alina wasn't wearing her engagement ring anymore and I didn't miss the fleeting sadness that occasionally crossed her face, like when Mom teased her about that handsome man Mr. Ryodan sent to drop supplies off a few days ago. I made a mental note to ask my sister which of the Nine it had been. Last thing I wanted was Alina hooking up with one of them, although, I mused . . . that Jason Statham look-alike was totally hot and, well, Alina wasn't any more normal than me. Well, slightly more normal but not all that much. Daddy had lost weight, laboring with District Ten on various projects, and looked more handsome and robust than ever. Mom was no longer part of WeCare. They'd up and closed their doors out of the blue with no explanation. She'd turned her efforts to a local outreach center instead, which oversaw multiple greenhouses and was developing dozens of local farms.

After lunch we sat in the dark blue parlor that sported wingbacked chairs, a lovely chandelier, tall windows, and white wainscoting, gathered near a softly hissing gas fire as I filled them in on why I'd been gone so long (omitting a LOT). When I told them how I'd defeated the *Sinsar Dubh* and left it trapped in the boudoir, my daddy's eyes had gleamed with pride. "That's my girl," he told me fiercely. "I knew you wouldn't doom the world."

I'd glowed quietly. My daddy's approval was welcome salve to the injury of the many sins I'd committed in the process. When I told them I was, also, however, the Faery queen and already the castes were coming to me with petitions, my mom was the one who surprised me the most.

"I can't think of anyone better to lead them," she said. "That nice Mr. Ryodan told us some of what you've been through in the past year. I don't think there's anything you couldn't handle now."

I blinked. Wow. Rainey Lane had become downright adaptable. Then again, I shouldn't be surprised—like mother like daughter. I'd love to know what Ryodan had told her. Surely not that I'd been raped, almost killed multiple times, and was a killer. I made a mental note to dig further into that, if the opportunity presented itself. I had a hard time picturing him talking favorably about me but it was clear he presented a very different picture of himself to "normal" people than he did to me.

Daddy said, "Does that mean you know the song that can save the planet and we aren't going off world? Good grief, I just said off world." He laughed and rubbed his hands together briskly. "I have to admit, I find the notion quite intriguing. I've always had a bit of wanderlust and no time to indulge it." He told me Ryodan had the Lanes in the first wave of colonists, packed and ready to leave at a moment's notice.

Sighing, I shook my head. "It means I'm the one that can supposedly sing or wield it, whatever that means, but no, we've not yet figured out what it is. Dancer's working on it right now." I filled them in on the music box and the strange song it contained that I heard so differently than everyone else.

Alina startled me by saying, "Mac, I hear music when I stand near one of the black holes. Do you hear it, too?"

I nodded.

She said, "It's awful. It makes me feel like I'm coming apart at the seams or something. It makes me feel nearly as sick to my stomach as the *Sinsar Dubh* did."

"That's exactly how it makes me feel!" My sister and I shared yet another unusual *sidhe*-seer talent. "Do you hear the songs of the various castes as well?" I made a mental note to take Alina to listen to the music box, wondering if she would hear it the same way I did.

She nodded. "Each caste has a unique melody. The Seelie songs are harmonious, beautiful, but the Unseelie music is jarring and discordant. Their songs feel . . . incomplete somehow, like something's missing and if only it was there, the music might be lovely."

"Exactly! Wow, the O'Connor girls really got the *sidhe*-seer gifts, didn't we?" And those gifts needed to be passed on. Alina needed to have babies. A lot of them, as I highly doubted children were in store for me. Although we'd never discussed it, I didn't think they were an option with Barrons. We'd never used protection and he wasn't a reckless man. I couldn't see him fathering a child casually.

"How odd does it feel," Alina asked me, "to be charged with leading the very race we were bred to kill?" She frowned. "I guess that means I shouldn't slay Fae anymore, eh? This is going to be quite an adjustment."

Back when I'd first come to Ireland, I often imagined how it might have been—had my sister survived—to fight back-to-back with her, two powerful, nulling *sidhe*-seers killing Fae by the thousands. I'd known it would never happen because she was dead. Now it would never happen for a totally different reason. My life hadn't merely changed, it'd done a complete one-eighty.

"It's an adjustment, and yes, it would probably be a good thing if you stopped killing them," I said dryly. How complex things were becoming. The queen's sister killing Fae would definitely not go over well with my race.

When my phone vibrated, I extracted it from my pocket and glanced down.

Meet at Chester's. We have a problem.

It was Barrons. "I have to go," I said, dismayed. I'd hoped to stay much longer, perhaps even spend the night. Alina and I had so much to catch up on! I wanted to know everything that had happened to her before she'd—well, whatever had happened. I wanted to hug her endlessly, tell her how much I loved her, laugh with her, go somewhere together. Enjoy a slice of normalcy while we could.

She and I made plans to meet later tonight at Temple Bar, where we were—by God, come hell or high water—going to drink Coronas with lime (and piss off every Irishman in the bar because who would choose piss-water over a dark, robust Guinness?) and talk until we ran out of things to say (which had never happened and never would), then go back home, fall asleep in the same bed, and wake up in the morning to my mom cooking breakfast and my daddy reading *Ryodan's World News* by the fire.

After exchanging repeated hugs and kisses, I slipped out into the rain and opened my umbrella, glanced up in the general direction of the sky and thanked my lucky stars for days like these.

Then followed it up with a fervent prayer that I might be on the receiving end of many, many more of them.

♪

I hurried through the gushing, neon, and rain-slicked streets of Dublin beneath a slate sky, umbrella canted against the brisk wind-driven rain, marveling at how normal it all seemed.

Young trees sprouted rain-soaked leaves, flowers retreated into sopping buds beneath the downpour, a sodden bee buzzed wetly by to land in a window, seeking refuge in a crack in the stone sill.

There were insects in Dublin again. It was a small but momentous triumph merely to have bugs in the world after the devastation the life-sucking Shades had wrought on our city.

High on buildings, doves cooed, sheltering beneath dripping eaves. I even glimpsed a young battered tomcat disappearing behind a trash Dumpster.

Even though the human race knew it was facing potential apocalypse, life was going on all around me. I wasn't the only one who'd gone through hell, lost people, almost been killed, and learned to adapt in the past year. The entire human race had suffered, in every city across the world. Everyone's preconceptions had been shattered. They'd confronted immortal beings from another world, fought and scrambled to survive, faced food shortages, walked numbly through ruined cities, found new places to live, lost and mourned loved ones. Those of us left were warriors determined to make each day count and savor the small joys, because who could say what tomorrow might bring? Or, even if it would come.

As I splashed down a narrow cobbled alley, a flicker of movement caught my eye and I glanced up to see ZEWs huddled atop the building on both sides of the street, heavily cowled heads bent, peering down at me. I stopped walking, let my umbrella fall back and turned my face up into the rain, staring back, unafraid.

I wasn't broken anymore. *Inspect me,* I willed up at them. *Just try to find something lacking. Or something extra. I'm undivided, unbroken, and downright unbreakable.*

As one, the flock lifted off and quickly merged into the leaden sky.

I smiled and resumed my rapid pace through the city, looking everywhere, drinking it all in.

People sat, eating and talking, behind the rain-drizzled windows of bars and restaurants that now had food to serve again. There were few Fae out and about, mostly lower-caste Seelie (taking hasty glances at me before crossing to the other side of the street), and I knew why—Fae don't care for rain. They like things to be pretty, clean, glamorous. I also suspected many of them might be off meeting somewhere en masse, discussing me. Perhaps the Unseelie as well. That was a meeting I was going to have to locate and attend at some point. As soon as Cruce came to his senses and acknowledged that I was a wolf he didn't want in his backyard.

I rounded a corner and nearly crashed into a cluster of people gathered in the street outside a small church, wearing bright yellow rain slickers, working outside under tents on—*Oh!*

I stopped and stared. A few dozen workers had erected high scaffolds around the perimeter of a large black hole and were raising a waterproof tarp on long poles up and over it, careful to keep a fair distance between the tarp and the subtle gravitational pull of the sphere.

"What are you doing?" I called.

The burly man directing their endeavors shouted to be heard over a sudden crash of thunder, "It's the bloody rain! Falling into the holes and feeding them! The water is making them grow! We're tarping off the largest ones first but the bloody wind keeps blowing rain in sideways!" To a man on the other side of the sphere, he shouted, "Find a way to peg the tarp to the ground so the sides don't blow it into the—Ah, shit, Colin no! Bloody hellfire! Nooooo!"

I gasped with horror. A gust of wind had just caught the edge of the tarp that was draped on poles and scaffolding and whisked it into the sphere. Instantly, every single thing touching the tarp, poles, and scaffolding was stretched thin as spaghetti, sucked into the black hole and devoured.

I stood, staring dumbly. The sphere had taken everything connected to the sole thing that had touched it. A mere corner of the tarp—and the entire apparatus and men erecting it were gone. They hadn't even had time to scream.

We had our answer, I thought grimly: if the sphere touched the earth, the same thing would happen. The only question was: to what degree? Perhaps it wouldn't turn the entire earth into a spaghetti at once, only a fair portion of it, but definitely *all* of it in time. And who could say? These were objects that didn't obey any laws of physics. Perhaps a fairly small black hole could simply blip the entire planet out. Blink of an eye. Everyone alive one moment— gone the next.

You have mere months, at best, the queen had said. Before we'd lost thirty-five days in the White Mansion.

In my mind, a clock began spinning at a dizzying speed.

The jarring, discordant music of the sphere grew louder, more cacophonous, and I narrowed my eyes, chilled to the bone—the hole was noticeably larger after its meal. I frowned. Something else about it had changed. The outer two feet or so of the black hole was . . . whirling, as if the whole thing was encased in a perimeter gyroscope or small dark rim-tornado.

And the bottom of it was whirling barely two feet from the ground.

A mere twenty-four inches was all that stood between us and extinction. We needed to start removing the street from beneath it. Tunnel up from deep in the ground.

Oh, yes, we had a problem. Hundreds of them. What was going on in other countries? Was it raining there, too? Snowing? How close to the earth were their black holes? Was Ryodan keeping tabs on them all?

"Get another crew over here!" the foreman roared to four men who remained. "We've got to get this fucking thing covered! Bring more tarps, and mind the buggers this time!"

I had a sudden idea. I pulled out my cellphone and texted Jada.

Meet me at Chester's ASAP. Urgent.

Abandoning my umbrella, I tucked my head against the storm and ran for Chester's.

♪

Amendment to my earlier assessment: a mere four inches was all that stood between us and extinction.

The black hole outside Chester's had always been the largest, but it had grown enormously since I'd last seen it. This one, too, had that new, strange, whirling perimeter.

"What the hell happened here?" I demanded, joining Barrons and Ryodan, who were standing a careful distance away from the hole, wearing dripping, hooded black slickers.

"Early this morning a cult of those 'See you in Faery' fucks committed mass suicide by running into the goddamn hole," Ryodan snarled. "Caught it on my surveillance cameras. A hundred or more raced into it like fucking lemmings off a cliff. It's one thing if you want to die, but don't bloody take the world with you."

"Gee, maybe someone shouldn't have encouraged their suicidal tendencies," I said, appalled. "Perhaps if you hadn't pandered to their delusions in your club—"

"Don't even start with me." Ryodan began to stalk menacingly toward me.

Barrons blocked him instantly. "Never. Threaten. Mac."

Ryodan said coolly, "I wasn't. I was merely moving toward her."

"In a stalking manner," Barrons said tightly.

"For fuck's sake, it was a nonthreatening stalk. You know I'd never harm her."

He wouldn't? Hmmm. Good to know.

Barrons growled, "My brain fails to distinguish nuances of stalking where Mac is concerned. A stalk is a stalk. All must be terminated. Don't fuck with me."

Ryodan growled back, "Got it. Get over it. We have bigger problems. Besides, she doesn't need protecting anymore."

"The one who bears your mark doesn't need it either. Doesn't stop you from feeling the burn, does it?"

Ryodan had branded Dani. "Just how much *do* you feel from those tattoos?" I asked.

"Too bloody much," Ryodan said curtly.

"Seriously." I looked at Barrons. "How much?"

He regarded me in stony silence.

"I'm not letting this one go," I said. "You felt my rage, even when the *Sinsar Dubh* was in control. That means you can sense a great deal more than you've ever admitted to me. How much?"

"A great deal," he finally said.

I met his gaze and held it. Big, beautiful, dark, hard-to-handle man. I was proud to call him mine. Didn't mean I wasn't going to still have ferocious arguments with him. And no doubt the occasional knock-down-drag-out fight. But now wasn't the time. *You and I are going to talk later,* I said silently.

He smiled faintly, but it didn't reach his eyes.

I smiled back. It didn't reach my eyes either. I notched my chin down that same warning bit he was throwing my way, perfectly able to give as good as I got.

Ryodan glanced between us and murmured, "She became what you thought she would. Lucky man."

Barrons inclined his head, and his eyes said to me, *I am.*

And just like that the tension between us was shelved for later. Assuming we had a later.

I felt a brisk breeze and suddenly Jada was there, standing in front of me.

"What's up, Mac?" she said, eyes bright.

And faintly red-rimmed. She'd been crying recently, maybe no one but me would notice but I know Dani. Her face was pure alabaster tension, freckles on snow. I pounced on her quickly, before she could get away from me, enveloping her in one of my daddy's bear hugs, holding tight. She felt so slender and slight in my arms, so . . . fragile somehow. If anyone needed a hug, it was Dani. Whether she wanted it or not. Who knew how much time we had? I wasn't wasting any of it. When she tried to break free, I said fiercely in her ear, "I love you, Dani, and I *am* going to hug you every now and then. Get used to it."

I let her go, and she backpedaled instantly, but much of the tension in her face was gone and there was a flush of color rising in her cheeks. That was a start. Later I was going to make her talk to me, tell me if she'd been crying about Dancer or Shazam and exactly what was going on inside that brilliantly, defiantly curling-in-the-rain head of hers. So much had happened so quickly that it was difficult to remember it had only been two days since her meltdown at the abbey.

For a split second I felt almost as if I was hovering, out of my body, above us, looking down.

Me, Barrons, Ryodan, Dani.

And I had the oddest feeling of . . . rightness in the universe while looking down at us. I'd had lunch with my family. Now I was solving world problems with my other family. I glanced at Ryodan, who was observing me with a faint smile. When he nodded minutely, I realized that while Barrons could happily go off and be solitary for the rest of his existence, Ryodan wanted family. What Barrons said to him that night I'd been spying on them was true: *Kas doesn't speak. X is half mad on a good day, bugfuck crazy on a bad one. You're tired of it. You want your family back. You want a full house, like the old days.*

I nodded back. We would keep it intact. Protect it. Always have each other's backs. Whatever it took.

"What the bloody hell happened to this hole?" Jada demanded, staring up at the sphere. "It wasn't this big yesterday!" When Ryodan told her about the mass suicide, she said, "Once the ergosphere appeared, the gravitational pull increased, didn't it?"

Ryodan nodded grimly. "That's why we haven't tried to tarp it. It's strong enough that it may suck the tarp in."

"Ergosphere?" I prodded.

"The outer, spinning rim is called the ergosphere," Jada said. "Imagine having a sheet spread flat while you use a rotating drill on it. It'll catch up the fabric as it spins, twisting it in. Whatever matter approaches the ergosphere will get caught and be subject to what astronomers call spaghettification, pulled thin as spaghetti before being sucked in. As the sphere increases in mass and density, the pull will grow even stronger, distorting space around it."

"Christian is meeting us here to see if he can use his druid skills to remove earth from beneath it," Ryodan said, "but this fucking rain has got to stop."

To Jada, I said, "Summon Cruce."

"Why?"

"He's Fae and can stop the rain. That's why I asked you to meet me here."

"Cruce," Jada said instantly.

He appeared, scowling as usual. And vanished again. So did Jada.

They wasted a good three or four minutes yanking each other from place to place until Cruce finally remained long enough to pierce me with a stare and demand, "Does this mean you have accepted my offer?"

"Stop the rain, Cruce."

"Fuck you, MacKayla. Oh, wait, I have already done that. Repeatedly."

Barrons's dark head whipped instantly to mine, teeth bared in a snarl, fangs sliding down.

Ah, shit, shit, shit. I'd hidden that one from him. I'd only discovered it myself a month and a half ago, my time, when the king whisked me and Cruce off to another world for a private conversation and I'd seen "V'lane's" true form for the first time.

I'd never told Barrons that I learned who my fourth rapist had been, the one who'd given me the elixir. He'd once suggested it might have been Darroc. I don't fully understand why I didn't tell him when I found out. Partly because I hate talking about it and partly because Cruce had been iced by the king immediately after I found out. There'd been little point that I could see. Knowing Barrons, he might have broken Cruce out just to kill him, and I'd been hungry for a time of peace.

Not that I'd actually ended up getting it.

The way Cruce had just worded it hadn't defined the occasion. Barrons might have been carved of stone, given how still he'd gone. He was no doubt standing there wondering if one of those times I'd slipped off to the beach with V'lane and come back tan, we'd been having sex all day.

"Get Cruce out of here," I murmured to Jada.

Barrons exploded the instant I said it, and I realized my mistake. Merely by saying those words I'd confirmed that it had indeed happened. If it hadn't, I'd never have tried to get Cruce out of there; it made me look both guilty and protective of him. Barrons had only gone so still because he'd turned one thousand percent of his focus on me, waiting for the slightest, subtlest sign of confirmation. It spoke volumes about how much I'd changed and how well I could guard my secrets that I'd had to actually say something for him to read me.

He slammed Cruce up against one of the tumbled walls of Chester's with such force that bricks went flying and mortar showered down around them, his hand closing on his throat. I blinked. Barrons had somehow gotten . . . larger, without his skin darkening into the first stages of transformation to the beast.

Cruce's dark, tattooed arm was out, his hand on Barrons's throat. They were dark, mighty, giant Goliaths, locked together.

"You will never save your world if you kill me now," Cruce

said coolly. "She will die. You will die. The human race will die. Release me. Or all of you die."

I glided across the wet pavement, placed my hand lightly on Barrons's arm and said, "Please, Jericho. Don't kill him. We need him. He raped me that day in the street. He was the fourth. Not Darroc. Cruce is the one who gave me the elixir. The elixir that saved me from your son," I said pointedly. Funny how things worked out.

Barrons's hold tightened further. "Give me one good reason not to kill him. *Ms. Lane*," he growled roughly around thick, long black fangs.

"Because I asked you not to, *Barrons*. That's good enough. You killed the other princes, and I was grateful. I wasn't ready then. I was still afraid of what I'd become. But this last prince is mine to kill or not to kill. And I say no. At the moment. And although Cruce is incapable of understanding that word, I know you know that a no from me means no. And you will honor it," I said in a voice that brooked no resistance. It was one of the defining differences between the two proud, dark, violent males. And if he didn't honor it, he wasn't the man I believed he was.

Both of them turned to look at me.

I was startled to realize both were regarding me with frank hunger. Not merely lust but . . . desire for me, the person. Cruce wasn't lying. A powerful alpha in his own right, he was drawn to my power, strength, resilience, and passion. Struck by the similarities between them, I realized the Unseelie King had been right when he'd said things could have played out differently: *Not the only possible*, the king had told me. *Perhaps Barrons becomes Cruce . . . or me.* Mere choices defined who and what each of us had become. Cruce wanted me just as much as Barrons did.

That knowledge was a useful tool.

Barrons released his grip on Cruce's throat and stepped away.

I looked up at the dark prince and said quietly, "Would you please stop the rain?"

It ceased instantly.

"I'd appreciate it if you would make sure it remains sunny until we've either solved our problem or died."

Sunshine broke through leaden clouds. A breeze high above us began whisking the dense thunderheads away.

"For you, MacKayla. Do you see how simple it can be between us?" Cruce murmured softly. "You have only to accord me respect and consideration. Ask and I will make it yours, if it lies in my power to do so. I would move universes for you, if you would only see me as clearly as you see him."

A deep, atavistic rattle began in Barrons's chest, and I knew Cruce had just signed his death warrant again.

I whirled and locked gazes with him, shucked my pride, doffed my prickly alpha stubbornness and said, *You are my world, Jericho Barrons. Not him. Never him.*

The rattle died and his dark eyes gleamed. He inclined his head.

I glanced back at Cruce. "Can you use your Fae power to remove some of the dirt from beneath the hole?"

He narrowed his eyes, studying it a long moment. His gaze flickered strangely and, were he human, I'd have called the expression consternation followed by annoyance, perhaps even unease. "No," he said, sounding faintly surprised. "Something is causing interference. The effect of the sphere extends well beyond the rim, and that . . . disturbance is neutralizing my endeavors." He frowned. "This is not something I have encountered before."

"How do I use the queen's power?"

"I told you my terms."

"Tell me how to restore your wings and I'll do it." And in the process, maybe I could figure out how to use it without requiring further instruction.

He smirked. "Nice try, MacKayla. But you must sign the Compact in blood before I am willing to teach you anything."

"What Compact?" everyone demanded simultaneously.

"Cruce said he would teach me how to use my power and help us save the world if I restored his wings."

Jada said flatly, "No loss there. Do it." Ryodan and even the still-seething Barrons concurred.

"Then once the world is safe, I have to transfer the True Magic to him," I finished.

All three of them exploded at once, telling me why there was no way in hell I was ever doing it, and I just looked around at all of them and waited for them to die down, which they eventually did.

"Be reasonable. It's not out of the question," I said. "He's willing to agree to lengthy stipulations in the Compact, including that he will never harm our world, and will take the Fae far away, forever forbidding future contact. I think you'll find him amenable to virtually anything. All he's ever wanted is to lead his race." I frowned. I was standing up for Cruce now. But it was true. It *was* all he'd ever wanted. Things were so different in my head now, where logic ruled hand in hand with compassion for the race I'd been born to, with no other sentience messing around with my brain. Yes, he'd raped me. I'd survived, and the nearly incoherent anger I'd felt for so long was simply gone. What remained was a chaotic world with complex politics and few with power enough to lead the various factions. My experience with the *Sinsar Dubh* had forever changed me. I'd encountered true evil. Up close and personal. I knew what it was. Cruce was not evil. As a Fae, he was a fine one. Exemplary even. A Fae that sometimes did very bad things to humans.

Barrons said softly, "Is this what you want, Mac?"

I tipped my face up to the sunshine, savoring the warmth on my wet skin for a few moments before meeting his gaze. "A caste of Seelie came to me this morning with their problems. If I keep the True Magic, I am their ruler. I would be required to hear their petitions, deal with their politics, protect them, guide them." I added with my eyes, *It would be time-consuming. And if I were to truly*

*rule and truly care, it would, in time, take me over. I don't want
that future. When this is over, I want to . . . I trailed off.*

What?

*Play in the sun. Love people. Run with your beast. Explore
worlds. Live.*

Cruce was motionless, watching me intensely. Were he human,
he'd be holding his breath. Oh, yes, he hungered to lead his people.
And despite the things he'd done to me, I couldn't say he wouldn't
be a fine leader for them. No doubt, as fine or better than me. "If
I can't figure out how to use this power," I said aloud, "it won't
matter if we re-create the song. I won't be able to sing it. Or wield
it. Or whatever I'm supposed to do with it."

"He doesn't have you over a barrel, Mac," Ryodan pointed
out. "If we die, he does, too. That's powerful enough motivation
for him to cave before it's too late. He's Fae. He'll never willingly
embrace death. Not so long as there's the slightest chance of his
survival."

Ryodan was right. We could hold out. But for what purpose,
what gain? "I'm okay with it, provided the Compact is clearly
detailed." And maybe, once I'd figured out how to restore Cruce's
wings, I could heal a human heart for Dani before I gave such a
stunning amount of power away.

Barrons inclined his head. "If this is what you want."

I took a final, brief moment to reflect, to be absolutely certain,
no regrets. The power inside me was brilliant, generous, warm. It
could do so many amazing things for so many people. With it, I
might be able to shape the icy immortals into a kinder bunch of
beings.

But I didn't want to take on that challenge. I knew who and
what I'd become. I was a woman that couldn't do anything halfway. In time, the weight and responsibility of the Faery crown
would take over my mind and heart and change me in ways I
didn't want to be changed. I said, "Let's go get my dad and draw
up a Compact."

"What guarantee do we have that Cruce will honor it?" Jada demanded.

"He claims we're both irrevocably bound by it, and once I access the True Magic, I'll have confirmation of that. It's a win-win. If he's telling me the truth—great. If he's lying, that means neither of us are bound and, with full access to the queen's power, I'll be far more powerful than he is. In which case," I turned to Cruce and said with a cool smile, "I will terminate your existence instantly, without a second thought."

He inclined his head, "Fair enough. And once you realize I am not lying, and you have completed the transfer of the True Magic to me, I will still accept you as my consort, MacKayla. You, alone, I have given far more truths than lies. You alone speak to the finest of all that I am."

Deep in his chest, Barrons began to rattle again.

46

"Listen to the music of the night"

MAC

I left Barrons, Ryodan, and Cruce drawing up the Compact with my daddy, after having established the concessions I felt mandatory. Contracts aren't my strong suit. Fortunately, they are Ryodan's. As soon as it was completed, Barrons would text me and we'd meet at the bookstore, where Cruce would teach me how to use the queen's power and I would restore his wings.

My sister, independent woman that she was, had left the house shortly after I had, heading to Trinity College to inspect the music box I'd told her about. I was on my way there to meet up with her, anxious to know if she could hear the same song coming from it that I did.

Jada had remained at Chester's with Christian, to assist in his efforts, employing the same druid arts he'd used to remove the soil from my sister's grave to eradicate the earth from beneath the black holes. If he was successful—he had concerns about not being able to keep it from being sucked straight up into the hole once he began breaking it apart—he would sift to Scotland and bring back all the Keltar, dispatching them to the largest spheres to get to work.

Still, we were only buying time. According to Jada, now that the ergospheres were manifesting, the holes would have an increasingly destabilizing effect on the environment and grow even faster.

Although I'd told Cruce that my race could be moved to another world and survive, I felt an undeniable (and rather confusing to a *sidhe*-seer) obligation to save the Tuatha De Danann from extinction. I wondered why they would cease to exist if the Earth did, then recalled the queen saying it was because she'd bound the seat of their power to our planet.

A lightbulb went off in my head and I drew up short in the middle of the street, stunned.

If the power was in our planet, then it seemed logical it was this planet I had to tap into in order to make the True Magic work. Was that the missing ingredient?

I closed my eyes, sought the True Magic, and envisioned it shooting tendrils from my feet into the soil, extending taproots, feathering out and expanding.

Oh, God, I could feel the world! I was part of it and it was warm and breathing, bubbling and shifting. Alive!

And so very sick.

Tears stung the backs of my eyes. Earth *was* dying. This was what the queen had always been able to feel—the fabric of everything, oceans and beaches, mountains and deserts, where it met in harmony, where it was torn and wounded.

It was overwhelming, and tears rolled down my cheeks from the sheer beauty and sorrow of it.

Her assessment had been accurate. We were nearly out of time. The spheres were more than mere holes in the fabric of our world. They were a cancerous presence, changing matter even in areas they didn't touch, corroding, eroding the very essence of the weft and weave of reality with their terrible song.

I was right. The holes emanated a Song of Unmaking, the same hellish music I'd heard during my brief stay at Chester's, trickling up through the ventilation shafts from the black hole deep below, invading my mind even as I'd slept.

Chills suffused me and for a moment I felt the terrible song touch me, threatening, as Alina had said, to tear me apart at the seams. I thrust it away, willed a barrier between us. My newfound ability to feel this world was dangerous. I was connected to all, even the poisoned parts. I had to protect myself.

I pictured the abbey, the fountain on the front lawn.

When I opened my eyes, I was there, the wind carrying a soft fall of fountain spray into my face.

It was that easy. I finally understood why the Fae were able to influence the climate and plant life. They were each connected to the planet to varying degrees, drawing power from its core, according to the abilities of their caste.

I could sift. I could freaking sift! That was one power I was going to miss when I transferred the True Magic to Cruce.

At the front entrance half a dozen *sidhe*-seers were clustered around Enyo, talking and taking a brief break.

As I approached, Enyo glanced up and stopped speaking midsentence. Her brows drew together in a scowl, her gaze moving from my eyes to my hair and back to my eyes again, and her mouth shaping a silent, *What the fuck?*

The other *sidhe*-seers greeted me with equally shocked expressions, their eyes the mirror that told me my transformation was becoming more apparent with each passing hour. I said quickly, "The Faery queen transferred her magic to me so we might save this world. Clear the workers out of the abbey. I think I can rebuild it."

Enyo's brows reversed their path and climbed her forehead. "Are you bloody kidding me? Why would the Fae queen—"

I cut her off: "Because she learned who she'd once been and no longer wanted to lead. Enyo, it's a complicated story and we don't have time for it. The planet is dying faster than we thought. Get the workers out of the ruins. I need practice and you need the abbey back."

She studied me a long moment, then shrugged and began to bark orders.

The moment the rubble was unoccupied—I had concerns about potentially putting a wall where a person stood—I tapped into the immense bubbling power beneath my feet. This time I kept my eyes open. Cruce never closed his when he was using Fae magic. I wed the power within me to the soil, sinking deeper than before, and gasped.

The earth possessed some kind of awareness. Gaea in all her totality was a living thing with some kind of vast, incomprehensible consciousness. It *knew* what had once sat here—at every point in time. I might just as easily have urged it to restore the church that had once stood on these grounds, or gone back further and commanded it to let the ancient *shian* rise.

So *that* was why the Fae seat of power was embedded in the occupied planet. Worlds had long memories. And time wasn't at all the same thing to a planet as it was to a human.

Restore the abbey, I invited the powerful twining of forces.

As I watched the sprawling fortress attain insubstantial shape before my eyes, I was struck by a sudden thought: Just how powerful was I now?

Might I restore Jo, too?

The translucent shape of the abbey vanished.

Dimly, I heard dismayed cries from *sidhe*-seers and knew they, too, had seen it beginning to form then disappear.

I smiled sadly. Of course, I couldn't. Or, even if I could, I'd be no better than the *Sinsar Dubh* or the Unseelie King himself. I had no doubt I could use the power for personal reasons, like, say, sifting to a sunny beach to enjoy a few hours in the sun. But I had to work with Nature, not against it. Death wasn't mine to undo. It made sense to me on a soul level. Reminding me, with a twinge of unease, how wrong it seemed that I'd gotten Alina back.

I pushed the troubling thought from my mind and refocused my efforts on the abbey.

And when I sifted out a few minutes later, to the sound of deafening cheers, the mighty fortress had never looked finer.

♪

I materialized in the physics lab at Trinity College with the left half of my body inside a wall, gasped, sifted instantly to the right and glanced hastily back at the offending structure, afraid I was going to see one of my arms sticking out of it.

The wall was intact. So was I.

I shuddered. That was horrifying. As if part of my body had been neatly displaced and I had no idea where it was until it was abruptly back again. Maybe Fae didn't mind the feeling of being amputated by inanimate objects, but I did. Perhaps I'd stop sifting until I talked to Cruce and got a better handle on the mechanics. Or aim for wide-open places like Christian.

"Holy hell, what did *that* feel like?" Dancer exclaimed excitedly, leaping to his feet. "Your bloody molecules must have been displaced. The wall couldn't possibly hold the combined mass. Where did the excess parts go? Do you know? Can you explain it to me?"

"Beyond wrong and I have no idea," I said as I joined them. Dancer was standing in the middle of a U-shaped desk, with a portable keyboard on one side and computers of various shapes and sizes on every other available inch of it.

Alina was sprawled in a chair next to it, and for a moment I just basked in seeing my sister, here, with me, in Dublin, alive.

She grinned, checking me out from head to toe. The grin turned to a smirk and she said, "Hey, Junior, looked in a mirror lately?"

"Pretty sure I don't want to," I said wryly. "Did you listen to the music box?"

She sobered instantly. "Yes. It's horrific. Seriously. Worst. Music. Ever. I'm not sure you can even call it music."

"Worse than the song you hear coming from the black holes?"

She considered a moment then said, "No, it's more like the song I hear from the different Unseelie castes. There's something wrong with it."

"Why am *I* the only one that hears a beautiful song?" I said irritably.

Dancer shrugged. "No idea. I'm still working on converting it to numbers. Here, let me play part of it for you and we'll see if it sounds as bad on my keyboard as it does coming from the box. Maybe there's something about the box itself that distorts it for us."

He dropped back into his chair, turned around and powered up the keyboard, then glancing over his shoulder, reading lines of music off the computer, began to play.

"Ah! Stop!" I shouted, hastily covering my ears. "That's not the song I hear. That's awful! You must have written it down wrong."

"Those are the exact notes," Dancer protested. "I converted them to numbers starting at C."

"Well, you did it wrong somehow. Maybe you started at a different note than you thought you did."

He gave me a blank look. "I don't do things wrong, Mac. I played exactly what the music box plays." He glanced at Alina for confirmation and she nodded.

I said, "All I know is that's not the melody I hear. *This* is what I hear." I began to hum softly.

Alina said, "But that's not what we hear at all, Junior."

Dancer waved a hand at her, shushing her, his eyes suddenly intensely bright. "Nobody talk. Hum, Mac. Just keep humming."

I hummed. And hummed. And hummed some more. While he sat, eyes growing more and more unfocused, listening, nodding, finally grinning broadly.

"I'll be damned!" He spun back to his computer. "I hear patterns. I see them, too. It's one of the quirks of my brain. Everything has structure. Even social interactions. Sometimes it's hard not to get lost in them. Sometimes," he said, as he typed away, "I get so distracted designing mathematical constructs out of social situations that I forget I'm actually involved in them." He fell silent then and typed for several minutes, hummed a few notes, typed some more then pushed away from the computer and beamed up at me. "I know what's wrong with you," he announced excitedly.

"Let me have it," I said warily.

"You're hearing the song inverted. *Perfectly* inverted. Every bloody layer of it. Unreal. And you aren't even intelligent enough to understand how fantastically improbable that is. Do you have Asperger's?" he demanded. "What other unusual things does your brain do?" He narrowed his eyes, peering at me as if I was a fascinating specimen he'd like to slap on a slide and push beneath a microscope.

"Inverted. Explain."

"I knew as soon as you began humming that it was essentially the same thing. But not. Inversion is the rearrangement of the top-to-bottom elements in an interval, chord, or melody. In simpler terms, you're hearing the music the box plays with every last bit of it flipped." He made a rotating gesture with his hands. "Perfectly flipped, and that's impossible. People don't hear music perfectly inverted."

"Play it the way I hear it on the keyboard."

"Give me a sec." He went back to work on his computer, inverting what he'd converted to numbers earlier. When he was done, he opened a program, exported the data, punched a few more buttons, and music began to play through the computer speakers.

I was instantly transported to a state of bliss.

This time, I was happy to note, I wasn't the only one.

It ended much too soon and left the three of us shaking our heads and looking slightly lost.

"That," Dancer said in a low, stunned voice, "was the most extraordinary arrangement of frequencies I've ever heard."

Alina agreed, looking slightly dazed.

I demanded, "Is it the song?"

Dancer snorted. "You're asking *me* that? How would I know? You're the bloody queen who's supposed to do something with it. Is it?"

"I think it has to be. But that doesn't make any sense. The king was never able to complete it. We know that for a fact. Or he would have turned the concubine Fae and he didn't. And he gave the music box to the concubine long before she supposedly killed herself."

"Then it can't be the song," Alina said.

"Maybe it's part of the song and he was never able to figure out the rest," I proposed.

Dancer raked both his hands through his hair, looking as if he was on the verge of tearing it out. "Bloody hell, you'd better hope not. Do you know how impossible it is to finish someone else's symphony? Completely. Look at all the brilliant minds that worked on Mahler's Tenth. None of the versions ever sounded right to me. I got so frustrated listening to them that I actually took a few stabs at it myself. I did no better. Impossible to precisely duplicate another's creative vision."

"But if this particular song is made of frequency that affects matter—which I'm sure you can devise some way to test—wouldn't even part of the song give you insight into what frequencies can affect the matter of the black holes? And you could extrapolate from there?"

"Sure," Dancer said exasperatedly. "If I had a few centuries to work on it and countless, perfectly contained black holes to test my theories on."

I sighed, pressing my fingers to my temples, thinking hard. "I know there's something to it. I don't know how I know it, but I do.

Just convert it all and invert it and let's try playing it to one of the smaller black holes, okay?"

He shrugged. "It's worth a try. It's not like we have much else to go on." He spun back around in his chair and began typing. After about three seconds he tossed over his shoulder, "Leave. You're disturbing my brain space."

With a snort of laughter, I held out my hand to Alina and took my first stab at sifting tandem.

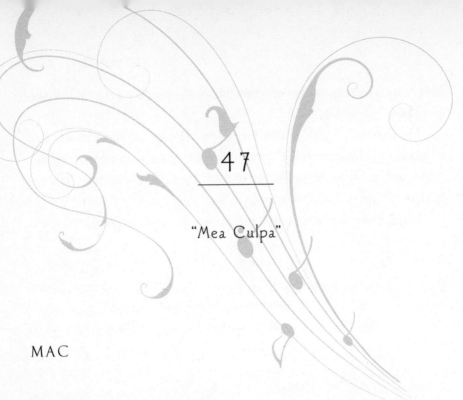

47

"Mea Culpa"

MAC

I banged into the bookstore a short time later with Alina on my heels, both of us holding our faces and muttering beneath our breath.

My first tandem sift had not gone well.

The Compact negotiating crew had arrived and was waiting for us. My dad was on the Chesterfield, on the middle cushion, his arms spread along the back. Barrons and Ryodan were in their usual corners, while Cruce leaned lightly against the mantel of the fireplace.

Barrons surged to his feet in a ripple of muscle and aggression the moment he saw me. "Who the bloody hell gave you a black eye?" he growled.

"That would be *you*," I said with mock sweetness, pressing a hand to my bruised cheekbone. "And your bloody wards. It felt like slamming into a brick wall." Fortunately, I healed quickly. Unfortunately, my sister didn't.

The corners of his mouth twitched then he gave up the ghost and just flashed me one of those rare, full-on smiles that always made me catch my breath and stare. He's so damn beautiful and his smiles are sunshine in a black velvet sky, improbable and stunning.

"You sifted. You figured out how to use it," he murmured. "Without Cruce."

"And rebuilt the abbey," I told him proudly. "It's never looked better."

"You *will* sign the Compact and restore my wings," Cruce growled.

"I intend to." I wasn't signing it merely to figure out how to use the True Magic. I wanted full, unstinting access to Cruce's wealth of information and knowledge. I wanted to know if he'd ever caught even the remotest whisper that the king might have come close to re-creating the song. I wanted to play the music box for him. Pick his brain for days.

I stood motionless, feeling the lovely, wounded earth beneath me, and invited it to restore his torn wings.

Cruce inhaled sharply, stretched to his full, enormous height, tossed his head back and pushed away from the fireplace. "Ah," he purred. "Yes, that is what I was missing." He closed his eyes a moment, adjusting and resettling his massive velvety wings. Then he opened his eyes and glared daggers at me. "Sign the Compact. Now."

Ignoring him for the moment, I moved to the small fridge behind the counter, retrieved one of the many ice packs I had from my early days in Dublin when I'd kept getting beat up all the time, and gave it to my sister. She pressed it lightly to her eye and sank down on the sofa next to Daddy.

"Hey, Daddy," I said, and kissed him on top of his head, beaming. The only people missing were Dani and Mom and my family would be complete.

"Hi, baby." He smiled up at me. "It's finished. That is, if you still want to sign it."

I slid over the back of the Chesterfield and dropped down on the other side of him, opposite Alina. He draped his arms around both our shoulders. "I do." I took the packet he was offering me, flipped through it and laughed. Our Compact was fifty-two pages long. "Looks like you covered it all." With lengthy codicils for virtually every possibility.

Jack Lane looked at me carefully. "Are you certain you want to sign this, honey? I agree with your mother. You'd make a fine queen."

I couldn't wait to sign it. I stretched my hand out behind me, in the general direction of Barrons. "Can I have one of your knives?" He was always carrying. I'd nearly pulled my spear from my holster before remembering how much I *never* wanted to poke myself with that thing. Then Barrons's mouth was on my wrist. I felt the touch of his tongue, the sting of fangs, a kiss, and his mouth was gone.

He had to do it five more times because I kept healing so quickly, but finally, with an ancient quill Barrons had produced, the Compact was signed by one MacKayla Evelina Lane, Queen of the Fae, cross-signed by Cruce, then signed secondarily in sharp, dramatic script that shimmered even when dried, with a name that defied translation into any language known to man. It was formally witnessed by Jack Lane, Barrons, Ryodan, and Alina Lane.

"There must be an exchange of precious metals, imbued with power," Cruce said. "I will accept the bracelet you had the other night."

"No," Ryodan said. He shot me a look that said, *if he wants it, it's important.*

"Then it is not binding," Cruce said flatly. "I have not demanded the Amulet, which I know you have and should be mine. That is my offering of precious metals. You may keep it, a gift from the Fae race."

Barrons looked at me. *I have other objects of power to offer.*

I narrowed my eyes and glanced back at Cruce. "You may have one of the lesser three amulets."

"Only for the bracelet will I agree to this pact."

"And his demands just keep growing," Ryodan mocked. "No surprise there."

I met Cruce's dark, turbulent gaze and was shocked to hear clearly in my head, *I do not seek to take anything from you that you would ever desire to use, MacKayla. It is important only to me.*

His words carried the knell of truth, resonated clearly and simply inside me. But then, he was the great deceiver. Regardless, it was a bracelet I had no idea how to use, and if we were successful, the Fae would soon be gone from our world forever. That made it another item that didn't signify.

After a moment, over the protests of others, I went upstairs, got the bracelet, and gave it to him.

It was done.

Once we saved our world, I would transfer the weight of mantle and scepter to someone else, the Fae would be gone, life would be incredibly normal, and I would finally be "just Mac" again.

♪

Hours later I sat on the Chesterfield, gaze unfocused, doing the equivalent of reading Fae files on ancient history. After confirming that the key to using my power lay in forging a connection to the planet itself, Cruce had also told me that new queens required anywhere from *fifty to five hundred years* to grow into their power, due to the sheer enormity of information transferred.

Yeah, so not sticking around for that job curve.

If there was a way to instantly internalize it all, no queen had ever found it. A large part of my new, lofty position was little more than file clerk. If I focused on, say, "Song of Making," every single one of the 9,722,342 records, legends, myths, and songs about it swam up in my mind with the equivalent of tabs and a filing system that made no bloody sense to me because I knew nothing about Fae history. The information had been logged under the name of the Fae that most largely signified in that bit of informa-

tion. To any other queen, those names might have been recogniz-
able and she could have immediately sought the most credible
ones.

They meant nothing to me. I'd spent hours blurting names
while Cruce had either shaken his head to pass, or inclined it to
indicate I should continue to read.

With Barrons watching, scowling darkly.

Imagine having access to a million years of human history,
every myth, legend, or factual (yet biased) news clipping. Imagine
having the Internet inside you, becoming a walking Google search
engine.

It felt exactly like that. I'd become a human computer. It was
one more reason I was enormously grateful Cruce would be taking
over. By the time he left, I'd begun to seriously question both the
queen's decision to give me the True Magic and the sanity of the
one on the planet who'd deemed me a worthy choice.

Barrons departed shortly after Cruce.

Christian's efforts to remove soil from beneath the spheres had
proved successful but time-consuming. He'd retrieved the other
Keltar druids from Scotland, and Barrons and Ryodan were assist-
ing, using small bobcats to push soil far from the danger zone of
the most immediately threatening black holes.

I sat on the couch, rubbing my temples, fighting a headache,
thinking how ridiculously difficult the queen's job was. It was no
wonder they got so bitchy and ruthless. Power was a crushing
weight. Then again, Fae queens didn't get headaches. They felt no
pain at all, and as far as I knew, suffered no physical demands. No
need for sleep or food.

Frowning, I sank inward and accessed the Elixir of Life. Not
for myself but for Dancer. I'd already tried hunting for topics like
Healing Humans, which hadn't yielded a single tab; no surprise
there. Why would a Fae care to (a) heal a human, (b) make any
files about it if they did.

That was yet another limit to all this bloody information I had. Some things were common knowledge to Fae, so they didn't bother recording it. Why would I make a file on how to brush my teeth or dry my hair?

It wasn't long before I sighed and shook my head. The potion of immortality had been—as many Fae things were—stolen from some other race an eternity ago. It wasn't capable of "healing," it dramatically transformed any being that consumed it. And it carried a high price: barrenness and, in time, it eradicated every vestige of the immortal soul if you believed in such things, and I did. When a Fae died, there was no afterlife. At best they drifted, their essence scattered to the molecules of the world on which they'd died. At worst they were simply gone as if they'd never been. I was fascinated to discover the Fae believed humans were reincarnated again and again with many different lives, eternally. But a dead Fae could never have its essence scraped back together to become something else.

I wondered what made the Fae decide a nearly immortal existence without children or pain—but very little pleasure either—was worth it, suddenly apprehending them not as a vastly more powerful race, but cowards. I'd rather roll the dice, play the lottery, enjoy an unpredictable and sometimes scary eternity of passion and pain than the fate they'd chosen to embrace.

Regardless, the elixir was not the answer for Dancer.

The bell above my door tinkled as it opened and closed. My head lifted.

And my heart sank.

Lor stalked into the bookstore, an enormous blond Viking dressed in black leather pants, boots, and a Woodstock tee that looked like it might actually be an original. "Hey, Mac."

"Barrons isn't here," I said hastily.

He sliced his head to the left. "Not looking for him. I came to see you."

Well, shit. He was pretty much the last person I wanted to see. I couldn't look at him without my box that contained thoughts of Jo threatening to explode.

When he dropped onto the couch, the frame protested the impact of his weight. Lor, like the rest of the Nine, stood well over six feet and was massively muscled and badly scarred. With thick blond hair and chiseled good looks, he was the fun-loving caveman, the hardcore rock-and-roll partier that burned through bombshell blondes yet somehow managed to leave them in an adoring stupor when he moved on. He had a soft spot for women and children and had been Dani's shadow for years, without her ever knowing it.

I'd sent Jo to him. After she broke up with Ryodan, I'd taken one look into her red-rimmed, wounded eyes and known instantly that she was never going to be able to toe that line. One way or another, if she didn't move forward to the next thing, she'd end up trying to go back.

And Ryodan would never take her back.

Only thing worse than dumping a boyfriend you deep down wanted to keep but shouldn't for one reason or another was backsliding, and getting dumped yourself.

I did that once. Choosing to leave had made me feel empowered. Going back and getting rejected had screwed with my head for a quite a while. Once you walked away, you had to keep walking and never look back.

My brain had put two facts together that day at the bar: fun-loving Lor who never had relationships and allegedly was a mind-blowing, enthusiastic fuck, and Jo needing a distraction to keep her from backsliding. It had seemed like the perfect solution. Harmless. With potential for good. Lor gets his world rocked, Jo moves on. No way they'd ever repeat it. Lor didn't do do-overs.

I'd never once thought it would turn out to be anything more for Jo than a stepping-stone to a new life.

But they'd sparked off each other. I'd seen it. There'd been something building.

And I'd killed her.

"What's up?" I said briskly. "I was just about to head out," I lied.

"Hear about Jo?"

I nodded. Cleared my throat. "I'm so sorry, Lor." In more ways than he knew.

"I had plans for that one," he murmured. "Ah, did I ever. Crazy bitch. Thought she didn't wanna fuck me, and anybody could see plain as day she loved fucking me."

Yep. Twist that knife.

He stared at me a long, unreadable moment. Finally he said, "I can't talk to those fucks about her. Can't talk to anybody. Figured you'd listen 'cause you were friends with her. Hell, you're the one sent the little spitfire to me."

And I was endlessly sorry I had.

"I got a rule, see. Never fuck a brunette. Know why?"

Nope, but I could see he was going to tell me. I shook my head, not trusting myself to speak. All I could see was me shattering Jo's skull. Eating her. I thrust the images away. There was danger here. The Nine were far too capable of skimming minds.

"I had a wife once. Long time ago."

Let me guess. She was a brunette. "You know," I said quickly, "I'm not supposed to know about any of this, remember? What would Ryodan do if he heard you were talking to me?"

"Fuck Ryodan. Bastard had her longer than I did." His face darkened and all trace of playful, caveman Lor vanished, leaving the hard-planed visage of a virtual stranger.

I realized I was seeing the real Lor for the first time. Brutal, cold, every bit as much a beast as the rest of them. *Bonecrusher.* The word floated into my mind but I had no idea why.

"You got any fucking clue what it's like to outlive everyone?

At first you think it's the greatest goddamn party you coulda been invited to. You fuck and feast and do every goddamn thing you want and think you got the world by the balls. Then you realize every bloody person you like hanging with is gonna die. You know how many musicians I watched go before they even hit thirty? And the women, shit. How many times can you care? How long till you start to hate? Despise. Motherfucking revile."

His eyes bored into mine and I inhaled shallowly. A series of disjointed images flashed through my mind, and I knew he was feeding them to me. Once, Lor had been a completely different man. The worst of them. The Bonecrusher. He'd befriended Genghis Khan and run with the Mongols, he'd warred with Attila the Hun, slaughtered with Caligula, rampaged with Nero, laughed with Ivan the Terrible, been executioner for Robespierre, drank blood from the skulls of their enemies with Vlad the Impaler. For a thousand years he'd sought war after war, killing endlessly. He'd abjured his own clan, until one night they'd shown up in force, led by Ryodan, captured him and dragged him away.

"You fucks'd call it an intervention," he said with cold, dead eyes.

"You loved Jo," I whispered.

"Nope," he said succinctly. "But the woman made me sorta start to feel like maybe I would put up with that shit again, watch her grow old, die, deal with it. And now she's fucking gone."

Of all the people I could have killed, it had to be Jo. "Why are you telling me this?"

"She's already been forgotten. So much going on, nobody's even talking about her anymore. By the time we got back, she'd been dead for over a month. I just heard. The scraps of her body got dumped in a grave. Gonna go dig 'em up, sniff out the Unseelie that did it. Torture that fuck to death a hundred different ways."

A chill went up my spine. "You could do that? Smell who killed her from her remains?"

"Oh, yeah. That's easy shit. I dropped by to let you know. Seeing as you're Fae queen and all, letting you know there's gonna be a fuck lot of Unseelie dying tonight. Not just the one that did it. I'm gonna take down the whole caste, every goddamn last one."

I swallowed. "And you came for my blessing?"

He got to his feet and stalked for the door, tossing over his shoulder, "Nope. Telling ya to stay the fuck outta my way tonight. I'll take your ass down, too, if you get in it."

The door banged shut behind him.

I sat unmoving for a moment, allowing myself to wallow in shame and grief and regret and pain, meeting it measure for measure.

Then I stepped away from crushing emotion and played out scenarios, isolating the likely one: Lor finds Jo's remains, smells that I killed her, kills me, the song can never be sung, the Earth gets destroyed.

All because I killed Jo.

Barrons had once killed a Fae princess. No doubt Lor could kill a queen. Especially a new, young one.

He was going to have to wait to kill me until after we saved the world.

It occurred to me, as I pulled out my cellphone, that my decision might seem every bit as cold and ruthless to the casual observer as the things Barrons and Ryodan often did. Covering my ass. Deceitful, even.

My fingers flew over the letters:

Lor's on his way to dig up Jo's grave to sniff out the identity of her killer. He's the Bonecrusher again.

The reply from Barrons was instantaneous:

I'll take care of it.

48

"It was always summer and the future called"

JADA

I dropped out of the slipstream and blasted in the door of the physics building, shoving damp hair from my face, aware that I looked the same way I felt—not in control—but there wasn't enough time to do everything I wanted, and something had to give. Since it took forever to dry and straighten my hair, I'd often skipped showers for days, but I'd had to take one today and wasn't in the mood to waste time, so my hair was a mass of tangled curls just like the old days, minus slippery guts tucked into a few. Mac becoming the Fae queen had put a temporary courtesy-damper on my killing sprees. All my emotions were on the surface, and I couldn't kill anything. It was a recipe for disaster.

When I'd left Dancer earlier, telling him I was going to the abbey, I was sidetracked by Mac's call and ended up spending the day with Christian, getting drenched then muddy. Although he was able to move the earth out from beneath the black holes, the one at Chester's was especially challenging, as close as it hung to the ground. He'd had to gently loosen a half inch of compacted soil at a time, without disturbing it so much the hole sucked it up. I'd alternated between seeping water beneath the sphere with a hose to keep the ground wet and sprawling on my stomach using a rake I'd modified with a super long handle, to delicately ease the loosened mud free.

Being so close to the hole had been intensely disconcerting. I didn't hear music coming from it like Mac, but I'd been acutely aware of instant death hovering just above my shoulders the entire time. I'd plastered my hair with mud to weigh it down and flattened myself pancake thin to the ground, but it wasn't as easy as it used to be at fourteen. Boobs were sometimes a serious pain in the ass.

We'd lost some of the soil to the hole. It was inevitable.

But when we'd left it, the sphere hung a full ten feet from the vast crater beneath it.

Christian had been four square against me raking, but it required strength to resist the gravitational pull of the ergosphere up close, and since we had so many blasted holes to work on, he'd finally accepted that everyone with the right amount of muscle was necessary, including me. It had taken us all day to dig it out to our satisfaction.

During a brief break, he'd sifted me out to the abbey, a power I'd heard Mac now had, too. I was floored to discover she'd effortlessly rebuilt the fortress. She's starting to make the Nine look like not-so-super heroes to me. I want to be Mac when I grow up. Then again, maybe not. I'd heard the Fae had already begun to seek her out with their problems, and I've got enough of my own.

I'd hit an old hidey-hole and showered once I returned to Dublin then headed with expeditious velocity for Trinity. I'd been getting a slew of excited texts from Dancer all afternoon.

Dancer.

One day, kid, Ryodan had said to me a long time ago, *you'll be willing to mortgage your fucking soul for somebody.*

I devoutly hoped that bastard wasn't going to prove right about everything he'd once said.

I remembered battling the Hoar Frost King at the abbey at

fourteen, whisking Dancer to safety, dumping him on the sidelines because he was "only human." Then I'd been whisked and dumped on the sidelines and gotten a taste of how it felt.

Who was I to tell Dancer not to live out loud, and in every color of the rainbow?

There was a special place in Hell for hypocrites, and I had no intention of ending up there.

So, I'd decided to pretend there was nothing wrong with Dancer to the precise degree he wanted me to pretend it. We would enter into an elaborate conspiracy of two. That was what friends did for each other when there was no other option.

Everything about the situation pissed me off. I'd always thought one day we might be more than just friends. I'd been perfectly willing to take my time getting to that point.

But thanks to a genetic flaw that was a treacherously ticking time bomb, coupled with the looming end of our world, there was no other way for me to see it than: one day was here.

I took the chance or I missed it. No guarantees. Fewer promises of tomorrow than I'd thought.

Scowling, I shoved my hair from my face then stopped to glance in one of the windows I was passing in the hallway, using my reflection to untangle the worst snarls.

I realized what I was doing and made a face at myself.

I didn't care what I looked like. I'd never cared. I wasn't starting now.

As I was about to walk through the door of the lab, I drew up short, frowning. I had a fluttery sensation in my stomach that I used to get often when I was young, and every time I did, it shorted out my powers. Silverside, I'd finally figured out it happened when I was either feeling extremely emotional or thinking intensely about sex. Why those two things shorted me out was beyond me. But they did.

At the moment I was both.

I inhaled deep. Exhaled slow. Bold. Ruthless. Energy. Action. Tenacity. Hunger. That was what B-R-E-A-T-H was.

Once the fluttering stopped, I did what I used to do—freeze-framed into the room and spooked Dancer right out of his chair.

The look on his face was priceless.

He knew by me doing it that I'd made up my mind, which was exactly what I wanted him to know. People tended to waste a lot of breath on words when a simple action communicated much more succinctly.

I wasn't going to cage him. And I wasn't going to let his heart be my cage either.

I was going to do exactly what I used to do. What Dancer was doing.

Live now.

As if there was no tomorrow.

That didn't necessarily mean it was going to be easy. But I was damned well going to try.

He had on faded jeans and a white tee with the words, HOLY SHIFT! LOOK AT THE ASYMPTOTE ON THAT MOTHER FUNCTION! emblazoned on the front. "Does this mean you're going to take me for a ride on that badass bike of yours, too?" He flashed me that one-of-a-kind Dancer grin that always lit up his face, holding nothing back, aqua eyes brilliant, full of life.

I nodded. Then I leaned in and kissed him. Not anything like I'd once kissed Ryodan. I'd done that to mess with him, and it had worked even though he tried to pretend it hadn't. It'd messed with me, too.

I kissed Dancer with some part of myself I didn't even understand. The me that kissed Ryodan, I got. She was hard, powerful, had an ancient soul and a fierce heart. The me that kissed Dancer was young, innocent, and although there was a massive door between the world and her soft heart, there was a path that could be walked to it, with a key hanging by the door, engraved with a D for Dani and Dancer. Sometimes I really did feel like I had two different people inside me, even though I knew I didn't. One version of me was drawn to Dancer and another was a moth, obsessed with Ryodan's flame. They evoked completely different qualities in me.

I kissed Dancer soft and slow, butterfly wings against his mouth, waiting to see what he did, how it was going to go between us.

He slipped his hands into my damp hair and said against my mouth, "God, I love it when you wear your hair down, Mega. It's like you, full of fire and larger than life."

We just kind of stood there, kissing slow and talking a little, and he told me he used to think he might never get to kiss me and he sure never thought I'd kiss him like this. And I told him I always thought he had the most incredible eyes, to which he replied he has a lot of incredible parts and I was welcome to check them out anytime I wanted.

His arms slid around me and I shivered because no one ever put their arms around me and held me close like he was doing. Like I really meant something to him and he never wanted to stop touching me. Like he couldn't believe he was so lucky to get to hold me and I was the biggest prize he ever could have won in his whole life.

He backed off with the kiss and we just kind of breathed into each other while he gave me time to settle into the feel of his body, arms warm and strong, close but not holding tight. It was hard for me to make myself stay put. I never let anybody touch me. Too personal. Too much risk involved.

So it took maybe ten minutes of just hugging and being close to really let myself go fluid like I do when I meditate. It was the hardest kind of meditation I've ever done because there was another person in it with me. I felt like I was made of all exposed edges, and I kept craving my walls and personal space back.

But I wanted this, too, and had started to think it was possible, if I never let anyone touch me, I might never be able to. That it would get easier and easier to keep everyone at arm's length and harder and harder to let anyone in. I think we get a window for intimacy. And it can close. I'd be Jada forever, and if Jada had sex, it would be a one-night stand, and the color of the rainbow I'd never get to know was love.

Eventually, I slid my arms around his neck and, with enormous discomfort, rested my head against his shoulder, absorbing the sensation of leaning into a man. This was my Dancer. The boy who'd found me as a child, racing down the street, exploding out of freeze-frame with blood-spattered head to toe and guts in my hair, and liked me instantly. And while I'd talked a million miles a minute, spitting "dudes" and "fecks," he'd stared at me as if I was some exotic creature from another planet, and the most stunning, brilliant thing he'd ever seen.

I melded our bodies together, my chest to his rib cage, my pelvis to his thighs, focusing only on his strength, refusing to think about that great, deceitful inner muscle of his.

It felt *good*. Safe harbor. Port in a storm. Something in me relaxed, a part of me that maybe never even once relaxed in my whole life.

So, this was why people hugged. Why intimacy was desired.

It was like stopping at a gas station and fueling yourself up.

It was as if time stood still when you hugged, and something was made from someone else's arms around you, which hugging yourself could never replicate. I wasn't alone in life anymore. Someone was by my side, standing ground with me, ready to move forward and face things together. It was the most bizarre, uplifting sensation I'd ever known.

Then we were kissing deep and hot and hungry, that kiss he'd promised me, the sexy nineteen-year-old one, and my hands were in his hair and I started to feel dreamy and sex-obsessed and like someone that had grown up normal and gone to school like other kids, maybe even attended a high school dance, and I was slow dancing with a boy for the first time. But he was a man.

And I was definitely a woman. I could feel the hardness of him pressed against me and I wanted to touch him and taste him and feel him inside me. And I wanted to tear myself from his arms and race out the door without ever looking back. Me, who wasn't afraid of anything, stared down any foe, fought any war, killed without hesitation, now quailed, waging a battle I'd avoided all my life: intimacy.

"Mega," he groaned, "you're killing me, kissing me like this. You want to get out of here?"

I drew back and looked at him. My lips were swollen and sensitive and wanted to keep kissing. I felt warm and bubbly inside, languorous but humming with energy that wanted to go somewhere. This was such a big deal to me. I'd always promised myself it would be epic. I'd always thought it would be with a superhero, like myself. I was pretty sure Mac thought I'd already done it. Or worried that I had anyway. But it wasn't as if I'd ever gotten to stay in one place long, and although there had been humans Silverside, I had trust issues and one goal on my mind: get back home.

Ryodan was the first man I'd ever kissed.

I was good at everything I did. I'd watched a lot of porn movies and thought a great deal about sex. I had a brilliant imagination. And hunger—I had a megaton of that. I knew when I finally did have sex, I was going to be epic.

But this was the one thing I'd kept. The single big decision about the way I wanted to live my life that was entirely mine.

Virginity was a door you only got to bang once.

I didn't know how to take off my armor. I'd worn it too long. I didn't know how to live like other people. I was a Tin Man with no oil.

"You said you had some things to tell me and something you wanted to show me?" I evaded.

He took my retreat with his customary resilience. His grin was instant, the disappointment in his eyes hastily concealed. "Mac hears the song inverted, Mega. It's totally different the way she hears it! And I have a video you've *got* to see. You're never going to bloody believe it."

Then he was sitting at his desk, the moment had passed, but I knew it would come again.

Then he was playing a song for me and it was the most incredible music I've ever heard.

♪

I don't know how long we sat there, listening to music I couldn't wrap my Mega brain around, but I had a sudden thought that buoyed me: when we figured out the Song of Making, considering it was supposed to heal things, maybe it would heal Dancer's heart. If it could heal holes in the fabric of the world, why not a simple human muscle? Stranger things had happened. I was surprised at how uncharacteristically pessimistic I'd been about his condition. But it'd been so unexpected and I'd recently suffered a traumatic loss. Combined, they'd sublimated my usual optimism and determination to rewire the world the way I wanted it to be.

I was feeling so much better about everything when he finally stopped the music, got serious, and pulled up a video, it took me a moment to absorb what I was seeing.

A crowd of a hundred or so people stood outside Chester's, shadowy yet visible, splashed yellow by the amber glow of gas lamps and red from the eerie glow of the crimson moon above. They were wild, excited, carrying weapons, wired on some drug or another. I know the look in the eyes of a stoner. There were two dead armed guards lying in the street.

Ten of them went at once—just raced straight into the black hole that Christian and I had spent all day working on. They were instantly spaghettified and slurped greedily in. The others cheered and punched their fists in the air as if they'd just done something brave and thrilling, not something so bloody stupid I couldn't believe anyone would voluntarily do it. The world tries hard enough to kill you and succeeds eventually. Why cooperate or rush it?

My gaze flew to Dancer's. "How did you get this?" I demanded.

He smirked. "Hacked Ryodan's computers. Tapped into his surveillance cams. Still trying to get into his mainframe."

My heart sank. Ryodan was one dude Dancer didn't want to be messing with. You don't tug on Superman's cape. You don't spit into the wind. Suddenly I had an old Jim Croce song my mom used to play stuck in my head. "Turn it off," I said stiffly. "And stay out of his stuff."

He looked at me like he couldn't believe what I was saying. He hit the Pause button and said, "Mega, we *always* dick with Ryodan. That's what we do. It's like, a calling." He mocked, " 'Hey, Brain, what are we gonna do tonight? Gee, Pinky, take over the world and dick with Ryodan.' Thought you'd be impressed. You have no idea how many bloody firewalls I had to hack to get this. Don't know who's running his system but he's got security I've never seen before. Besides," he dangled invitingly, "you haven't seen the interesting part yet. Really want me to turn it off now?"

"What kind of interesting stuff?" I said, eyes narrowing.

"The truth about Ryodan," he said softly, watching me closely.

I punched the PAUSE button, eyes glued to the screen. That man's secrets: irresistible. As the video continued, another small group broke off, raced in, and again the others cheered. Morons. Sheep. Baaa.

They repeated the study of stupendous stupidity until there were only ten sheep left standing in the street. Bleating excitedly as if they were winning some kind of war, not waggling fluffy asses and leaping straight down the wolf's throat.

Then Ryodan materialized in the middle of the crowd, scaring the bejeezus out of everyone, and his eyes were . . . weird, like, "Did his eyes just turn red? Go back!"

Dancer rewound and I watched it again. Sure enough—and it hadn't been a trick of the moon—Ryodan's eyes were pools of blood, backlit by a thousand icy lanterns. His snarl was abnormally large for his face, all mouth and fangs with barely enough skull to frame it.

Horns sprouted on that skull, confirming my teenage suspicions. I leapt to my feet, hands fisting.

I knew it—Ryodan *was* the devil!

There was no volume but I could see him snarling at the people in the street, and I didn't need to hear it to know he was saying the same thing I'd be saying: *You bloody idiots, why are you killing yourselves? And if you're so hell-bent on dying, go do it somewhere else. Don't fuck with* my *world.*

Then all ten of them attacked Ryodan at once. He flung them off like he was batting Ping-Pong balls away. They attacked again and he flung them all off again, and when they realized they weren't going to be able to take him down, they veered like a flock of dim-witted, synchronized birds straight for the black hole.

That was when it happened.

Suddenly, Ryodan morphed.

He just bloody transformed in the blink of an eye into one of those great black beasts that fought beside me at the abbey and had, later, eaten crimson runes off Cruce.

Bloody hell, but I'd been off my game! Not once had I pinned the beasts' inexplicable existence up on my bulletin board and examined it! The beasts that Mac said she'd found Silverside were the Nine! Ryodan was a bloody shapeshifter!

He moved in a whirlwind of black-skinned muscle, talons, and fangs, ripping, slashing, tearing, gouging.

When he was done, he crouched panting, paws and muzzle slick with blood, surrounded by corpses. Then he dropped back on his haunches, ripped open a thigh, tore off a piece of flesh and began chewing, head swiveling this way and that, to ascertain that no other predators were approaching.

I looked at Dancer. He was watching me intently.

I got it then. He'd just done to me what I'd done to him when I came in and spooked him: told me what he wanted to say without words.

Can't you see he's an animal, Mega? Choose me.

Dancer knew I was torn between him and Ryodan, what they brought out in me, and I pretty much loved him for that, seeing me so clearly. That's something when your friends know who exactly you are, good, bad, right, wrong, and just keep caring about you.

I stared back at the screen, wishing I had a problem with what I'd seen.

When pretty much the only thing I was thinking was: *So, Ryodan's immortal, pens a wicked daily, has super senses,* and *can shape-shift. Fucker.*

What else could he do?

Years ago, when I'd told him I wanted to be like him, he told me to ask him when I was older.

I was older now.

49

"I told you I was mean"

MAC

When Barrons texted me to tell me he'd taken care of my problem with Lor, I was pacing the bookstore so briskly I was practically burning up the carpet, dissatisfied with the way I'd handled things.

I'd gone to Barrons for help. He'd taken care of it. It bothered me. I didn't want to live that way, always taking cover behind my man from other men.

I'd battled my way through assault after trauma after indignity and survived them all. I was the queen of the Fae. But even if I weren't, I was a woman that needed to know she could stand on her own two feet, toe her line, and demand it be obeyed. Once I transferred the True Magic to Cruce, what would I become—weak again?

Never. I liked who I'd become. I wanted to grow and evolve not backslide.

If the Nine knew I needed Barrons to protect me, they would never respect me. And I planned to be hanging around them for a long time. I didn't want to be the woman with a strong man. I wanted to be the strong woman.

When I called, Barrons answered on the first ring.

"How did you take care of it?" I demanded without preamble.

"I got rid of the remains. I was in the vicinity of the cemetery and knew I could beat him there."

"You got *rid* of them?" I said, dismayed on two counts: One, it only postponed the inevitable. I wasn't going to hide this truth from Lor forever. And two, I had a very human reaction to wanting remains where they belonged—in a grave. I was still disturbed by the vision of my sister's empty casket. How odd was that—worrying about where the bones of our loved ones were? But I did.

"I merely moved them elsewhere. You can rebury them at some point," he growled. "Although I fail to comprehend the desire to make pretty little plots of community and togetherness for decomposing flesh."

"I have to talk to him," I said flatly.

"I forbid it."

Every cell in my being bristled. I practically shouted, "You *what*?"

"For. Bid. It."

"You did *not* just say that to me."

"Mac, I know what he's capable of. I know—"

"So do I. He told me."

"Not the same thing," he said coolly. "Seeing is believing. It took half a bloody century to calm that fuck down. You will *not* go anywhere near him. I said I'd take care of it and I did. I will continue to do so. Leave it."

I said nothing.

"Mac, don't you fucking hang up on me," he said staccato fast and heated.

"I didn't and wouldn't," I growled. "Well," I amended, "at least, I'd say goodbye first." Probably very quickly and nearly inaudible, but hey. "Hang on a sec." I sank inward, accessing my files, looking for something similar to the protective barrier Cruce had used the night we sealed away the first *Sinsar Dubh*. I snorted as my mental tabs surfaced. There were several thousand handy little tabs, all names I'd never seen before, hoo-fucking-rah. I sighed. I'd find what I was looking for eventually. At least there weren't nine million. I returned my attention to Barrons. "I'll use a spell to encase myself in a barrier like Cruce did. You couldn't penetrate it that night in the cavern beneath the abbey. He won't be able to touch me and he'll have to hear me out."

Silence stretched and when he finally spoke I knew how disturbed I was making him because his words came out thick and slightly mispronounced. I knew what that meant; his fangs were out. "You're assuming he's capable of reason. If he's the Bonecrusher, he's not."

"I have to try."

"I don't like this."

"And I don't like needing you to take care of me. I'm not being rash. I'm just being who I need to be. I made this mess. I'll fix it. I'm not sorry I texted you, and I appreciate you buying me time. But I want to be the one to tell him before he finds out himself." That was what I should have done anyway, but Lor was intimidating when his eyes did that Bonecrusher thing.

"Your bloody force field won't work."

"Cruce's did."

"Cruce had the *Sinsar Dubh* by then. Double the power."

"It'll work. I'll layer them or something. And don't you dare show up as backup. I'll be fine."

"You fucking better be." Barrons hung up.

♪

It took me nearly an hour to sort through files and find a protective barrier that met my criteria of full body and possible to sift while wearing it. Many of the files were nothing more than legends of Fae battles in which such barriers had been employed. I wasn't surprised to discover wars broke out among the Seelie pretty much constantly, but as the queen alone had held the spear and sword for most of their existence, they'd raged only until someone drank from the cauldron then sputtered out. Until the next one began.

But finally I'd found suitable armor, donned it, held a mental image of Lor in my mind and sifted to him. The queen possessed a far more finely tuned GPS than Christian. I went straight to him. God, this was handy! I wondered if there was a way to transfer the True Magic to Cruce while keeping certain powers for myself.

I appeared in the graveyard behind the abbey. The night was velvet-black with a three-quarter, crimson-rimmed moon casting a bloody pall over the cemetery.

A study in crimson and shadows, Lor was sitting on Jo's grave, long legs outstretched, leaning back against the headstone, powerful arms bunching, folded behind his head, staring up at the sky, eyes unfocused, as if he'd not even registered my appearance.

I knew he had. The fine muscles in his face had tightened minutely.

I said nothing. The many things I'd rehearsed in the bookstore abruptly vacated my head.

"So, I'm sitting here," he said finally, real soft, "thinking to myself that somebody dug up Jo's body recently, 'cause the ground's so loose and the coffin's gone. Not even leaving me the lining to sniff. And I'm thinking I only told one person I was coming here to dig her up, and that person's standing in front of me, wearing a shield she thinks I can't get through."

I stared at him in silence.

A long time passed.

"Ain't a fool, woman," he said finally.

"I never thought you were."

"So, I'm thinking, considering I told that person exactly what I meant to do to the fuck that killed Jo, she came here because she wants to die. Do you want to die, honey? Is that why you brought your sweet little ass here to me? Because deep down you crave death, hunger for oblivion from your many motherfucking sins?" His gaze whipped to mine and I gasped. There was nothing left of the Lor I knew in those eyes. The laughing playful Viking was gone. Something ancient, dark, and sadistic was all that remained.

"Right. Talk to me about craving oblivion for my many motherfucking sins. How many people have you killed, Lor? Thousands? Tens of thousands? Who cries justice on you?"

He surged to his feet in one fluid motion, vanished, then was there, right on the other side of my barrier, as close to nose-to-nose with me as he could get. "Nobody fucking cries justice on me. We *are* the law. Always have been. Always will be, babe."

"I don't see it that way. I see a man who's going to die if he kills me. Is that what you want, honey? To die?" I mocked. "Is that why you brought your sweet ass over to me? Because that's what you're headed for if you think you can exonerate yourself for the deaths of so many innocents yet fail to extend mercy to me for killing someone while I was possessed by the *Sinsar Dubh*. At least I have the excuse of being possessed. You don't have an excuse. You *chose* to do those things. Who punishes you, Lor? God? Oh, wait, you'll never die. I see—that's why you think you're the law—because you never have to answer for anything you do. But you're not. None of us are. We fuck up. Over and over. And we get back up and try to do better. That's all any of us do."

Tears stung my eyes, my heart burned in my chest, because seeing the cold marble of Jo's grave, and the inscription of her name beyond his shoulder, made it all too real. Pain and grief morphed easily to fury. "You big dumb son of a bitch," I growled, "I loved Jo. You didn't. She mattered to me. She was only a distant possibility of mattering to you. I killed her. You didn't. Who do you think is suffering the most here? 'Cause it. Ain't. You. *Babe*," I said with such vehemence that spittle sprayed on the force field between us.

His eyes flared infinitesimally and he opened his mouth to say something, but I'd gotten started and couldn't stop. "Did you think you were going to find a victim when you looked at me? A woman, torn by self-loathing and pity, castigating herself for every wrong she's done someone? Wake the fuck up. That's not me. It's a hard world and I'm harder in all the right places while still being soft in the important ones. You, my friend, are the one who's fucked up. You skip the whole self-loathing part and flash right into the loathing everyone else. You shuck every soft part that matters and take your pity-party to a whole new level. You get stuck in the idiot phase and never evolve beyond it. Oh, poor Lor, who can't love anyone because they all die! You want to look at it that way? Fine. Be a baby. Or you could realize that you get to love so damn many people, forever. But, no, welcome to Lor's pity-party—a woman got killed that he might have loved—not even *did* love, just *might* have—so he's going to wipe out the whole motherfucking planet because he's pissed off and doesn't—"

His hand was around my throat, choking off my words. The bastard had reached right through my supposedly impenetrable barrier, grabbed me by the neck and was squeezing.

I suffered no hesitation. My brain instantly processed: *Barrons said try a rocket launcher/Lor will always come back/I'm not anybody's victim and never will be again/the world has to be saved/ this prick needs to learn to fear me because yes I killed Jo but I'm not dying for it nor am I putting up with his shit for the rest of my very long life.*

Then there was an automatic machine gun in my hand, manifested by power I hadn't even realized I was tapping into.

I jammed the muzzle into his gut and let it rip.

Lor went flying backward through the air, roared, and lunged for me again.

I kept firing until he hit the ground and didn't move anymore.

I watched him until his body vanished, then ground out, "I trust I made my point," and sifted back to BB&B.

♪

When I returned to the bookstore—Barrons hadn't dropped the wards but I'd given it wide berth this time, appearing well out in the street—he was sitting on the Chesterfield in the dark, waiting for me.

He assessed me and relaxed minutely. *Things went well?*

As well as could be expected, I suppose, I told him with a shrug.

His eyes narrowed. *He heard you out?*

I joined him on the sofa and snorted. "Oh, he definitely heard me out. I was nearly done by the time he started choking me." As I stared at him through the low light, a wave of raw, desperate lust flooded me. I needed. Him. Now. Kneeling on the cushions, I grabbed his head and kissed him, falling on top of him, taking him back to the sofa beneath me. My body was bristling with energy and savagery and frustration because I'd really wanted to come to a meeting of the minds with Lor, not have to resort to killing him, but I suspected anything less than killing him simply wouldn't have gotten his attention. And killing him had left something wild in me that needed to be let out.

Barrons understood and met it in kind.

♪

Later, I lay in his arms, head on his chest, listening to the peculiar sound of absolutely no heartbeat, and knew he'd leave before long.

That was okay. I'd dumped a pent-up storm of emotion on his body, punished him with it and let him punish me in return. We ran the full range of sexual appetites in bed, from tender to tortured, white bread to dark, nutty stuff, and it was all good. We were young, strong, and unbreakable.

I was fairly certain Barrons was drifting in that deeply inward meditative state he sometimes sought and was just about to drift off myself when he jolted me awake by saying softly, "Lor choked you?"

I smiled against his cool skin. He always got cool when his heart stopped beating. This was my man—testosterone rising,

ready to turn on his comrades for harming me. But it was unnecessary. I'd held my own. "Yes."

Deep in his chest an atavistic rattle stirred. "I told you that
barrier wasn't going to be strong enough. Fae magic doesn't work
on us."

"Cruce's shield worked on you and the Unseelie princess's
magic worked on Lor in Ryodan's office."

"I told you why his did. The princess's only worked on Lor
because the Sweeper altered her. And that's one fuck we need to
get rid of. Not the princess. She's well enough out of the way for
now."

He fell silent and I began to drift again, wondering distantly
why the Sweeper was beyond the laws that applied to the Nine. I'd
eventually get around to asking but not now. It was peaceful. I was
sleepy. And I had no doubt tomorrow would be another eventful
day.

As I was fading, he jarred me awake again with an impatient
growl, "Are you going to tell me what the bloody hell you did or
do I have to I go find Lor?"

Oooh! We were firmly ensconced in a new phase of our relationship. I beamed. Barrons wanted to know something, hated
having to ask, and asked anyway. And it wasn't about an OOP or
anything business related. Nor was he dashing off to beat up Lor
and avenge the fair damsel. I liked these changes. Sleepily, I mum-
bled, "I killed him. What did you think I did?"

Barrons stiffened, went motionless then stiffened again, dis-
lodging me from his chest, jarring me fully awake. He propped his
head on a fist, making all those gorgeous muscles bunch, and
stared down at me, the corners of his mouth twitching.

"Oh, give it up. You know you want to. Just do it. I know
you're badass. An occasional laugh won't disabuse me of the notion."

Eyes glittering with mirth, he demanded, "How?"

I told him.

He threw his head back and laughed, white teeth flashing in his dark face.

I lay back on the couch, watching him, reached up and touched his lips, and he kissed them then bit gently. Then harder.

Then he was on me again like a sirocco, gusting over and inside me, taking me down and deep to that beautiful wild place we go when we're alone and free.

When he finally got up to leave, the bookstore was carpeted with lush, fragrant flowers and a small tree was blossoming near the sofa.

My life was strange.

Good. But strange.

50

"The illusion has to end this time"

MAC

I blew out a frustrated breath and rubbed my eyes.

I was tired and hung over, and what a load of bullshit *that* was. I could handle pretty much anything, but I still needed time to recover from chasing beers with tequila.

Admittedly, I'd chased a lot of beers with a lot of tequila. But late last night when Alina texted and I remembered my promise to meet her, there was no way I was missing a chance to hang out in Temple Bar with my sister.

We'd talked for hours. About stupid things. About serious things. We'd reminisced. We'd grown maudlin. We'd laughed over silly stories. I'd told her about her funeral (morbid!) and about Barrons (amazing!) and my past year (traumatic as hell).

She'd told me her story, too, from the day she landed in Dublin, to the first time she'd seen a Fae, to discovering what she was. How she met Darroc and had loved him almost instantly.

Still, from day one, something in her gut had warned her not to confide, so she'd lied about her family and me. Then the *Sinsar Dubh* had begun playing games with her, very similar to those it played when I'd arrived.

Together, they'd learned about themselves—my older sister and her beautiful, exotic fallen Fae. And learned about each other. Over the months, she'd begun seeing significant changes in him, making me wonder briefly what might have happened if I'd met V'lane before I'd met Barrons. I'd have been fascinated, found him frightening yet somehow irresistible, at least for a time, and might even have tried to convince myself he was one of the good guys, blaming his ruthlessness on his alien nature, maybe even convinced myself I could help him evolve. As Darroc had evolved, according to Alina, growing increasingly more human. He'd lost the vestiges of that Fae iciness he'd often evidenced in the beginning of their relationship, that ancient remoteness that had prevented her from telling him many things. He'd become invested in her world, her concerns, and in their future together.

When Darroc asked her to marry him, although she'd been astonished he was willing to be part of such a human ritual she said yes.

Two days later she'd followed him to 1247 LaRuhe and discovered who her future husband really was and what he'd been doing all along. When he'd glanced up and seen her, she'd run, certain he would give chase, but he hadn't. She'd walked the streets for hours, finally coming to the decision to call me and return home.

He'd broken into her apartment while she was leaving a message for me. She'd been afraid he'd come to kill her. But although they'd fought heatedly, he'd merely stormed out, telling her she needed to pull her head out of her ass and take a good hard look at the world and decide what she wanted. He'd be waiting for her.

Hours later Dani had arrived, telling her that Rowena wanted to meet with her. Numbly, Alina followed.

I knew the rest of the story.

But there was one thing she told me that I hadn't known.

The young *sidhe*-seer who'd led her to that alley that day to die had ended up crying as hard as Alina. She'd shaken violently, like she was trying to throw off some kind of physical compulsion. She gnashed her teeth, vomited until there was nothing left but bile, torn at her hair and finally screamed at the end, as if it were she who lay in the alley, dying.

At that point I'd begun pounding tequila shots, trying to numb my heart and make it through the night. Until I could hug Dani and tell her how much I loved her and that none of it had been her fault.

I'd wanted to go find her as soon as I'd awakened this morning, but I forced myself to postpone it until I'd sorted through at least a few hundred files. More even than I wanted to show Dani my love and support right now, I wanted to ensure she had a long future of it.

So, I sat on the sofa in BB&B, with a throbbing head, where I'd been sitting for the past four and a half hours, staring into space, inundated by minutiae and feeling utterly inadequate to the task at hand.

The only thing I'd managed to learn about the song so far was that it had come from a completely different source than the True Magic. The Fae had no idea who'd given it to them or why. It had been gifted with a single imperative: use it only when you must and remember there is always a price.

The second part of that imperative made me uneasy. What was the price?

My imagination ran wild. Would it kill whoever sang it? If we discovered the song, would I die using it?

The rest of what I'd absorbed were nothing but vague myths and legends, some claiming the song was divine, the beginning of life as we knew it, that it had incited the "Big Bang." Others claimed it came from a race even more technologically advanced than the Tuatha De Danann who had evolved to a higher state of being and passed off the song as a gift to a race they'd viewed as having potential.

Each myth, however, shared the common contention that it

called due a price. Several seemed to imply that if the race "wield-ing it" (there was that damn word again) hadn't done anything wrong, the price would not be high.

"Wrong" was an exceedingly vague word. I'd done many wrong things. Likewise, "high" was a *highly* nebulous degree, rel-ative to the person it affected.

My phone vibrated with a new message from Dancer.

Done. Ready to try it. Meet here or there?

BB&B, I texted back.

I'd written several long letters a few months back: one for my parents, one for Barrons, one for Dani. That was before Alina came back, or I'd've written one for her, too.

They were upstairs in my bedroom, tucked between two of my favorite books, partially visible. I knew if I died, either my mom and dad would come look through my things or Barrons would make sure it got to them.

I texted him now.

Meet me and Dancer at BB&B. He finished inverting the music. It's ready to try.

If I was going to die today, I wanted Barrons's face to be one of the last ones I saw.

I didn't, however, want my family to watch it happen.

♪

Barrons arrived wearing muddy jeans and a dirty black tee-shirt, looking big, rugged, and sexy as hell. I almost never see him "slum-ming," and it always takes my breath away. He somehow looks even more exotic and animalistic in all the right ways in casual clothing. I knew he'd been out there, lying on his stomach, scrap-ing mud from beneath black holes, and I loved that he didn't hesitate to get as down and dirty as necessary to protect the things he cared about. Harshly chiseled, muddy, earthy, and anachronistically human and savage, he turned me on when he looked like this. Who was I kidding? The man always turned me on.

Fresh black and red tattoos covered most of his right arm and part of his left, and I knew that while I'd slept, he'd either been tattooing himself or he and Ryodan had been tattooing each other.

"Do you have any idea how to do this?" he asked, storming in. Then he drew up short, stopping abruptly at the edge of his priceless, restored antique rug, scowling down at his muddy boots.

I shook my head. Then smirked a little and invited the mud to vanish from his boots.

He raised his head and looked at me, returning the smirk. "Who's *Bewitched* now? Did you text the others?"

"That would be me," I said pertly. "And no. Let's just do it, see what happens. I figured we'd try the sphere by the church. It's the closest."

Dancer arrived a few minutes later, carrying a laptop. "I don't know if we need speakers or if this is good enough."

I glanced at him sharply, startled by the dark circles beneath his eyes, and thought again of the Elixir of Life. As he handed me the laptop, I said, "If there was a Fae potion that could make you immortal, would you drink it?"

He cut me a sharp look and scowled. "Christ, does everybody know now?"

"Pretty much," I said. "And don't get prickly about it. We care."

"Don't treat me like an invalid," he said levelly.

"Not about to. Would you?"

"No. I've done my share of research into the Fae. Did you know the potion allegedly destroys a human's immortal soul?"

I did, and I'd wondered on more than one occasion if Cruce's elixir had the same effect. I hoped not. If so, it was too late now, and I had other issues to deal with. I'd worry about the state of my soul later.

"I died once. I know what comes next. No way I'm missing it. I've known most of my life that I could die pretty much anytime. I'm in no hurry but it doesn't bother me either. So, are we going to do this? Can we wait for Mega? I texted her, too. She should be here any minute."

Tucking the laptop beneath my arm, I headed for the door. Over my shoulder I tossed, "There's some kind of price for using it. I'd prefer neither of you came with me." I considered sifting, to prevent them from attending, but decided against it. I've become a big believer in free will.

Then Barrons and Dancer were beside me and we hurried from the bookstore, into the sunny Dublin afternoon.

♪

Not only did the song have absolutely zero effect on the black hole near the church (although I'd sat dreamily mesmerized, feeling like it was definitely doing something to me), when I went to play it a second time, even louder, it was gone. It simply didn't exist on the laptop anymore.

"What do you mean, it's not there?" Dancer exclaimed. "Give me that thing," he demanded, reaching for his laptop. "Clearly, you're looking in the wrong place."

When I handed it to him, he scanned it rapidly then began opening folders, digging into root files.

I sighed and leaned back against a trashcan. The three of us were sitting on a curb, in the gutter, ten feet from the sphere, as close as we should get, Dancer had warned.

After a few minutes of "bloody hells" and Batman quips, Dancer snapped the laptop shut. "None of my files are here. Not a single one. Every note of the song I recorded, every conversion, inversion, extrapolation, is gone. Even my Word docs with theories are gone!"

"How is that even possible?" I'd been sitting here, wondering if the black hole had somehow managed to eat the music we'd played, right down to the source. But if so, it had taken much more than merely the origin of the music, operating like a super-stealth spy, wiping out even Dancer's notes about it.

He buried both hands in his hair, scowling. "How can you ask me to postulate when I don't even understand the primary suppositions? Bugger! Now I'm going to have to bloody well do it all over again."

"Why? It didn't work. That means either the sphere stripped it from your computer or there's something going on here we don't understand. Why re-create a failed experiment?" I said pessimistically. I'd had a good feeling about our venture, and had expected the music to do *something*—if not outright make the sphere vanish, maybe shrink it a bit. But when the song had played with no result, I'd grown dismal.

Dancer said impatiently, "Because that bastard"—he yanked a hand from his hair and pointed an accusing finger at the sphere—"took something from me and I want it back. That's reason enough."

He pushed to his feet, tucked the laptop beneath his arm, and loped off without a backward glance.

I looked at Barrons. "I feel like I did something wrong. I can't shake the feeling this music is what we need. But that blasted 'wield' part of the equation is eluding me. I use the True Magic by amplifying it with my Fae tether to the planet. While we were playing the song, I did the same thing, but it had no effect. And now it's gone. What did I do wrong?"

He extended a hand and pulled me up. "As much as I hate to say it, you need to talk to Cruce. I'll round up the others. Meet back at the bookstore."

"Why have a meeting? It's not like we have new information," I said pissily.

"Failure is always new information, and those who are willing to suffer it repeatedly make it a stepping-stone to success."

Looking up into his steady, dark gaze, I thought about how

many times Jericho Barrons had pinned his hopes on some new way to end his son's suffering, only to meet with failure. How many millennia had he worked with quiet fortitude toward his goal? I would do no less.

"I know why Dancer wants to re-create the music," he continued. "Inspiration frequently strikes the second or third or tenth time around. The more minds we have working on this, the better. Others can deal with the black holes. We'll figure it out, Mac."

He kissed me then, hard and fast.

As he disappeared down the street, I sifted back to BB&B.

♪

Barrons's plan was for the group of us—Dani, Dancer, me, Cruce, Christian, and Ryodan—to sequester ourselves at BB&B until we had the answer. According to him, if I was so certain the music we had was the solution, we just had to figure out how to employ it, determine exactly what "wield" meant.

After Christian and Ryodan arrived, Dani and Dancer sped in a few moments later, looking strangely subdued.

When they joined us in the rear conversation area, Dancer sat on the sofa but Dani remained standing with a clear view of the room and summoned Cruce.

He appeared instantly: nude, erect, and obviously having sex. He clothed himself instantly in a short iridescent tunic and snarled, "For fuck's sake, *what*?"

Before the tension could thicken further, I said hastily, "We tried to use the song from the music box and it didn't work. We need to know why."

"Why have you fixated upon that bloody thing?" Cruce demanded. "It is not what you seek. The king was never able to complete the song. Everyone knows that."

"You haven't even listened to it," I pointed out. "How would you know?" He'd sifted out the other night before I played it to the others.

"It doesn't matter anyway," Dancer said. "Listen." He withdrew the music box from his backpack and handed it to me. "Or, more accurately, don't."

I shot him a quizzical glance, took the box, sat it on the coffee table and opened it, bracing myself.

Nothing happened. Frowning, I picked up the box, closed it and opened it again. Still nothing. I closed it, shook it firmly, and opened it again.

Not a single note. Not even a whirring of damaged gears, not that I believed the otherworldly object of power had any gears. "What did you do, drop it or something?"

"As if. When I got back to the lab and opened it to begin converting the melody again, that's what happened. The song is gone, Mac. Apparently something decided to remove every trace of it from our world."

I shook my head in bewilderment. What the bloody hell was going on?

Dancer continued, "It would have been an exercise in futility anyway. I knew when I finished it earlier today that it wasn't complete. It ended abruptly in the middle of an entirely new motif that wasn't an interpretation of any other motif in the piece."

"Then why did you bother texting me that it was ready?"

He shrugged. "Think outside your box. Who was I to presume that wasn't the composer's intention? Perhaps other worlds and races prefer their music to stop in what we consider the middle. Perhaps it excites them to leave it unfinished. I take nothing for granted. You can't, if you want to drive your brain beyond established theory. But now it appears my initial impression was correct and that's why it didn't work. Because we only have part of it." He muttered, "Had. Now we don't even have that."

I closed my eyes and sank inward, thinking hard. Thinking about how final and odd it was that every trace of the otherworldly melody had simply vanished the moment I'd played the song all the way through to the black hole. It hadn't disappeared each time we'd listened to *part* of it. Nor had it puffed out of existence the moment Dancer had listened to all of it. I found it beyond the realm of probability that there might be an unknown evil entity out there, lurking in the ether, spying on us, and the moment we got close to success had seized every note of it, along with every memo we'd made about it.

Coupling that oddity with the complete erasure of the music box as well, I found it far more likely that the song had done whatever it was supposed to do, and been programmed to clean up after itself like a self-destructing mission message successfully played by an international, high-stakes spy.

But what was it supposed to do?

An epiphany slammed into my brain and my eyes flew open. Dani was staring at me with such a penetrating gaze I was surprised it wasn't drilling holes in my face. Our gazes collided and I knew she'd been following an identical train of thought. Her mouth dropped open and, at the same moment I exclaimed, "I think I've got it!" she said. "I think Mac's got it!" We beamed at each other.

After a few moments of inner reflection I was elated to discover I did indeed contain the song. I could feel it inside me, a complex melody, thrumming with power.

Talk about your checks and balances. Apparently, the queen was the preprogrammed home for it, and once I'd listened to what we had of it, all the way through—which I'd never done until we'd played it near the sphere—it had settled into me, wiping out all trace of its presence, ensuring no one else could ever get their hands on it.

I was just about to suggest we head for the nearest black hole and see if I could figure out how to turn myself into a portable iPod when the front doorbell tinkled.

The Dreamy-Eyed Guy walked in.

I know how the world works: there's no such thing as coincidence. If you're seeing coincidences, check your suppositions. Somebody's dicking with you. And it's probably not the universe.

Each time I'd encountered him flashed through my mind, from our first meeting at Trinity College to the night he'd appeared in the catacomb beneath the abbey and melded back into the Unseelie King.

Or had he? His skin was the only one that had never dropped to the floor. At the end, the Dreamy-Eyed Guy had merely changed, absorbing the shadows that passed from the falling skins of McCabe and Liz, the news vendor, the leprechaun-like reservations clerk, and my high school gym coach. He'd stretched and expanded until he towered over us, enormous and dark as the *Sinsar Dubh*'s amorphous beast form. Then he'd vanished with his concubine. What was he, if not one of the king's skins? No single human body could hold the vastness that was the Unseelie King.

"Hey, beautiful girl."

"Hey," I said blankly.

"See you finally stopped talking so much."

"Might have been a bit clearer," I groused.

"Crystal. You muddied it."

"Come to save our world?"

"Hand of God. No fun there."

"What *do* you consider fun?" I said irritably.

"Free will. Not predictable. Bites you in the ass every time." He laughed and I shivered, feeling it roll through every cell in my body, and abruptly I was seeing, superimposed around him, a gargantuan, ancient star-sprinkled darkness that was so far beyond my comprehension I felt as tiny as a dust mote, swirling on an air current, sparkling in the sunlight.

"Pretty much," he murmured.

"And you're the sun," I murmured back.

"Bigger."

I thought of the concubine. Of the empty chamber, void of their passion, the slamming door. "She left you," I said sadly.

"Time."

Changes everything, he didn't say, but I heard it. "So?" I prodded. "How do I use the song?"

"Don't have it."

"Got part of it," I insisted.

The Dreamy-Eyed Guy rippled into the bookstore in a stain of liquid darkness that licked up the bookcases, swirled on the walls, covered the ceiling then retreated back into him. His head swiveled but I saw two visions: the first of the DEG and the second of a great dark star swiveling in an abyss of dark matter. His gaze moved across our small group, coming to rest on Cruce. "And he has the other."

I exploded. *"What?"* I shot Cruce a furious glare. "And you never told me?"

Cruce growled, "The fuck I do, old man."

"You haven't been hearing music?" the DEG said mildly.

"You iced me, you bastard!"

"Complaints. Boring. Music. Yes or no?"

"You never finished it," Cruce growled. "Or you would have turned your precious concubine into one of us, a thing she was never meant to be. You abandoned us for hundreds of thousands of years, created and discarded us, obsessed with your quest. You betrayed us again and again."

"Grudges. Glories. You name them. They become it." The Dreamy-Eyed Guy's eyes shifted, expanded exponentially, becoming voracious whirlpools of swirling darkness, sucking us down, stretching us as thin as threads, yanking us away, and abruptly I stood with Cruce and the Dreamy-Eyed Guy on a familiar grassy knoll beneath an enormous moon, with a pine-board fence unfurling high on a ridge, jutting planks into the sky like dark fingers reaching for the cool white orb.

Tiny, between towering black megaliths, I stood with Cruce on my left, the Dreamy-Eyed Guy on my right. The wind tangled hair around my face while, above me, Hunters gusted a fragrant breeze, gonging deep in their chests to the moon as the moon chimed back. Power pulsed and surged in the soil and rocks beneath my feet, and I could feel it so much more intensely now that I had the True Magic. This power was ancient, enormous, far more vast and potent than anything the Earth had ever possessed. I might sink into it, become one with it, become a world myself or perhaps a star, instead of a mere human or queen.

"This is the First World," I breathed, understanding.

The DEG nodded but looked past me, at Cruce, "Your king never betrayed you."

"That was all you did. At every opportunity," Cruce snarled.

"And now we will see if you are as great a king as he."

I narrowed my eyes, gripped by a sudden inexplicable apprehension. *Danger!* the marrow in my bones screamed. Wherever this conversation was going, I wasn't going to like it. What did he mean, the king had never betrayed Cruce?

"Answer me," the DEG said softly, but there was such immense compulsion in his words that I instantly began to puke every word I knew in an incoherent babble of random associations. "Not you," the DEG said absently, and I shut up.

Cruce gritted, "Yes, you manipulative fuck. I have been hearing music."

I glared at Cruce. "And you didn't think to mention this to me when you knew we were hunting for a bloody song?"

He shrugged. "I assumed it was miscellaneous detritus from the Book. It sounded like the Unseelie castes so I believed it part of their True Names and didn't give it a second thought."

I narrowed my eyes, trying to decide if he was telling the truth. I was getting a mixed read from him. I turned back to the DEG and scowled. "That means you finished it. And you didn't bother to tell us that?"

"Long before Zara was gone."

I protested, "But you didn't turn the concubine." That was the fact that convinced me the king had failed, that he'd not even been an avenue worth pursuing. Now he was telling me he'd succeeded? Then why hadn't he used it? And according to what I understood of the time line, given how long ago the king had gifted the concubine the music box, he'd had a small eternity to reconsider his decision.

"No, the king did not," he said, and such exquisite pain lanced through me that I doubled over, holding my sides. "There's a price to sing that song."

"But you couldn't have sung it. You're not the queen," I protested.

He turned his star-filled, apocalyptic gaze to Cruce and smiled faintly. "Rules. Malleable. He could have. He chose not to." His expression changed to one of paternal pride. "Your turn to choose."

"Why are you looking at Cruce? I thought I was supposed to sing the song."

His head swiveled back to me and I got tangled in his enormous regard, stuck like a fly on sticky tape, unable to move. "You will owe me three boons," he intoned.

I nodded instantly. Refusal was not an option.

"At the time I come to you next. You will obey without question."

I nodded again.

"The music box contained half. The other half was concealed within the *Sinsar Dubh*."

"It was *not*," Cruce growled. "You never finished it. Admit it, you fuck. It was beyond you. I would have known."

I said to the DEG, "You mean, I could merge with the part I left behind—"

"It was not in the part that split off and entered you."

"So, who's supposed to sing it, me or Cruce? Our world is ending!"

"Worlds do."

"What the fuck is your game, old man?" Cruce demanded.

"Will you gift MacKayla your half?" the DEG said.

"To save my race? Yes. I have always been willing to lead them. As a true king should."

"But it won't," the DEG said. "Save your race. It will doom it. The price of perfect song"—his dark, starry gaze encompassed both of us, and suddenly Cruce and I were standing shoulder-to-shoulder; he'd moved us together with a mere gaze—"is the death of all sprung into existence from imperfect song."

I processed his words. "Oh, God, you mean . . ." I trailed off, looking up at Cruce with horror. Then I whirled on the Dreamy-Eyed Guy. "Shut up," I snarled. "Stop speaking right now!"

But he didn't. He continued driving his point home with utter clarity and finality, ringing the death knell for my world. "The moment the song is sung, the Unseelie race will cease to exist, from the humblest to the most magnificent of his creations. He never betrayed you, Cruce. He betrayed none of his children. He gave up what he held most dear for them." The DEG smiled with faint bitterness. "And in the end, she left him anyway."

"You didn't have to tell him that," I said furiously. "At least not until *after* he gave me the song! You could have lied."

"No fun there," the DEG murmured.

Cruce stood motionless for a small eon. My heart grew heavier the longer his silence stretched. Finally he said, bitterly, "You did this on purpose, you twisted fuck. You found a way to box me in. If I refuse to give my half to MacKayla, I die. If I give it to MacKayla, I die. I die either way."

"But the Seelie live," the Dreamy-Eyed Guy said mildly. "You're the one that wanted to be king."

"Fuck the Seelie, I have always despised them! Dead is not king!"

The DEG shrugged. "Never said it was easy."

Abruptly the DEG was gone and we were back in the bookstore.

Everyone was talking at once, demanding to know what had happened, but my mind was whirling and I had a sick feeling in the pit of my stomach because I knew Cruce didn't have an altruistic bone in his body and he despised the Seelie and his entire motivation for his entire existence had been to free his Dark Court.

Not kill it.

And himself in the process.

My gaze whipped to Cruce and I stared at him imploringly while time spun out.

I found my answer in the implacable depths of his sociopathic, self-serving gaze. It was beyond him to suicide. He simply wasn't put together that way. He was a walking fundamental lack, made from imperfect song.

The Unseelie were driven by endless, consuming hunger to steal that which they lacked in a blind, voracious quest to complete themselves. The Seelie were merely hollowed out by immortality, driven by hunger to experience emotion I was beginning to suspect they'd once known.

The Seelie could evolve. The Unseelie never could, trapped in a flawed, limited, self-serving existence.

Cruce, give me his half of the song?

Never. Going. To. Happen.

He knew I'd found my answer in his gaze and flashed me a glacial smile. "Fuck you and your world, MacKayla. If I am doomed," he said, his eyes narrowing to slits of iridescent ice— and suddenly I was staring straight into the eyes of the psychopathic *Sinsar Dubh*—"so are you. Along with every Seelie in existence. I'll never permit those bastards to outlive my race."

He vanished.

"Summon him back!" I cried to Jada. I whirled on Barrons. "And seize him when he gets here!"

"I can't, Mac. My cuff. It's gone!"

♪

"So the king said he actually succeeded in re-creating the song but didn't use it?" Jada said after I filled them in on what had transpired when the DEG whisked us off to the First World.

I sank down on the couch, sighing. "Yes. I mean no, not the king. The Dreamy-Eyed Guy kept talking about him in third person, as if he wasn't actually the king."

"Then who is he?" Christian demanded.

"I don't know. Perhaps some part of the king. Whoever he is, he has a great deal of power." He'd felt like the king to me. He'd taken me to the same planet the king once did.

"And he put half the song in the music box and the other half in the *Sinsar Dubh*?" Jada pressed.

I nodded.

"But not in the version of the *Sinsar Dubh* that possessed you?"

I shook my head. "The DEG said it couldn't be replicated. Cruce got it. I didn't."

"And now Cruce is gone," she said, scowling. "The cuff vanished from my wrist the instant he sifted out. Now I know why he kept changing the terms of every agreement I tried to make with him. He was never bound to me. He played us, pretending the cuff controlled him so he could stay close and keep an eye on everything we did."

"Typical Cruce/V'lane move," I agreed. "They don't call him the Great Deceiver for nothing."

"Does that mean the Compact the two of you negotiated wouldn't have held up either?" Dancer said.

I frowned. "Actually, I think it would have. But I can't honor it. He won't survive for me to keep my end of the bargain and that voids the agreement."

"Tell me again exactly what he said about the price of the song," Barrons said grimly.

"He said the price of perfect song was the destruction of everything made from imperfect song." Now I understood why my files insinuated that if the race using it hadn't done anything wrong, the price wouldn't be high. I glanced at Barrons, who was exchanging a long look with Ryodan. "What?" I demanded. "You're thinking something I haven't considered."

He studied me a moment then said carefully, "Assuming that's true, it's not only the Unseelie that would cease to exist but also anything the *Sinsar Dubh* created. The Book was made of imperfect song, containing only spells of imperfect song."

I whispered, "Alina. You're saying she'd be unmade, too."

"Possibly everything turning Unseelie as well."

My gaze flew to Christian.

"Bloody great," Christian said irritably, "and the fuckage of Christian MacKeltar reaches a new all-time high."

"But Christian isn't made from imperfect song," Jada disagreed. "He's a human that began to turn Fae. I think it's equally possible he would be turned back into a normal man."

"That works for me," Christian said darkly. "Although given the way my life has been going, I suspect it would be the former, not the latter."

"It's possible the song would destroy us as well," Ryodan said. "Depending on precisely what constitutes imperfection and who the fuck is judging it."

I stared at him. "Are you Fae in some way?"

"No."

"They why would it affect you?"

"It could be argued we are . . . anathema to Nature," he said cryptically.

"Great. So assuming the impossible happens, and I manage to sing the song, I'll kill half the people I love." I rubbed my eyes. "It doesn't matter anyway. Cruce will never give me his half. He dies either way. He despises the Seelie. As far as he's concerned they don't deserve to exist. He's hated the Light Court for his entire existence. If his choices are to die alone or die taking his enemies with him, it's a no-brainer."

"The king could sing it," Christian said.

"Good luck finding the bastard," I said darkly. "Even if we did, he wasn't willing to sing it for his concubine. He'd never sing it to save the First Queen's race. Face it, the two beings capable of saving us never will." I frowned. "There is one possibility . . ." I trailed off, not liking it. But willing nonetheless.

"What?" Jada said.

"I could go back into the White Mansion and—"

"No," Barrons said flatly.

"—take the *Sinsar Dubh* back into me—"

"No," Barrons said again.

"—because it knows the True Names of all the Unseelie," I pressed on. "I could summon Cruce and try to compel him."

"First, by the time you got in there and back out," Barrons growled, "a month or more will have passed. Second, you have no guarantee you could compel Cruce, even if you were able to summon him."

"Do we have any other options?"

"How would you compel Cruce?" Barrons demanded. "What leverage do you have over a walking dead man?"

I scowled at him. None, and I knew it. The only leverage one can have with a walking dead man is the power to commute his death sentence, and I didn't possess that.

"Don't fixate on something that won't work, Mac. That's a fool's game. If you have something you could use to force his hand, that's one thing. But if you don't, it'd be a pure waste of time. Got something?"

I shook my head, reluctantly. I wanted to do something, anything. But summoning Cruce without leverage would accomplish nothing. He'd simply refuse me and vanish again.

I sat up straight, eyes widening. Maybe I didn't need to summon him by name. Maybe I could sift to him. "Hang on a sec," I said, and focused on Cruce, willing myself to wherever he currently lurked. "Ow! Shit!" I exploded, clutching my head.

Barrons cocked a questioning brow.

"He's got some kind of repelling ward between us. I can't even get a lock on him. All I got was an instant headache."

"Dageus," Christian said suddenly.

"What?" I said. "Do you think he knows something that could help us?"

Ryodan said tersely, "Not a bloody thing. I've already questioned him." Barrons cut him a long hard look and Ryodan snapped, "So what if I did? You fucks kept wandering off and the Highlander was the right material."

I smiled faintly. So, Barrons had been right. Ryodan kept Dageus from dying because he'd wanted to expand his family.

"That's not why I brought him up," Christian said tightly. "I'm taking him home. Tonight."

"The fuck you are," Ryodan said instantly.

"The world is ending. He'll no' be spending his last days in a cage beneath your bloody club. He's got himself under control. Mostly. As much as I do, for fuck's sake. He has the right to leave this world and colonize a new one with his clan. With his *wife*. He has a family."

I winced inwardly. Christian had no idea what fate awaited Dageus if we failed to save our world. But then again, no one seemed to have clued in about my fate either, and I wasn't about to bring it up. I was the Seelie Queen now. Even if I went off world, the moment the Earth died and all Fae ceased to exist, I would, too. Not that I had any intention of leaving Barrons's side to begin with. But the way I saw it, I was going to die whether I stayed or went, and I sure as hell wasn't dying without him, not to mention in front of my parents, for heaven's sake.

Barrons's gaze whipped to mine and his eyes glittered with crimson sparks.

You did not just hear that, I said with narrowed gaze.

Your emotion was so palpable, I suspect even Ryodan heard you. You will transfer the queen's power to another Fae and leave this world if all appears to be lost. You will not die here. Or there. Or anywhere.

We'll discuss this later.

His nostrils flared and he ducked his head, looking up at me from beneath his brows, like a bull preparing to charge, in that familiar constant jackass way that told me I was in for a long, heated battle later. I arched a brow at him. Fine with me. We always had long heated makeups afterward, too.

Ryodan and Barrons exchanged a look, then Barrons said to Christian, "You may take him home."

Ryodan snapped, "That's *not* what I just said."

"I don't care. I said he could," Barrons said softly. "And you and I will do battle over this one. If there was ever a time for a man to be with his clan, it's now." To Christian, he said, "Get the hell out of here."

Christian vanished.

PART III

Victory is reserved for those who are
willing to pay its price.

–Sun Tzu

51

"Shadows of the evening crawl across the years"

MAC

When people have absolutely no control over the things that really matter to them, they tend to do one of three things: devolve into animals and prey on others, indulging their base instincts (wolves); huddle in herds for comfort and safety from the chaos (sheep); or invoke a rigid daily routine, effecting control over those few things they can while endeavoring to change what seems an inevitable fate (sheepdogs).

Over the next few weeks our world split neatly into those camps. There were more killings of armed guards and mass suicides at the black holes, making still more work for those of us that fell into the sheepdog category. Violent crimes escalated: rapes, murders, thefts, vandalism. People ripped out recently planted trees and drove utility vehicles through flower beds in public commons in a kind of "Well, if I'm going, by God, I'm taking the world with me" attitude that was beyond my ability to comprehend. I share my mother's mentality about some things—I'd have planted new flowers right up to the moment of extinction. Barrons says that's because some people can't stop creating, even lacking both audience and canvas. They create because they must, not for the world but themselves.

Fortunately, the sheep were up to the challenge of tackling a new, more orderly world and went through the Silvers by the hundreds of thousands to one of seven suitable worlds. They came from all over the globe, drawn by word there was a way off planet. Christian had been sifting to various surrounding countries, alerting people to what was happening in Dublin and telling them to get there as quickly as they could, then sifting out farther and bringing people back with him. The last time I'd seen him, he was stumbling, nearly incoherent, from repeatedly sifting with passengers in tow. The Nine, meanwhile, divided their time between excavating the black holes to keep them from touching the earth, and forming troops of colonies with governing bodies and supplies, and escorting them through.

The "sheep," as I call them, are the backbone of society, and as some of them stepped up to the portals, they shook off their stupor and got downright excited, alive and alert, and I realized sheep could morph into sheepdogs, under the right circumstances.

As I watched them entering the Silvers via portals Ryodan and Barrons established with stacked mirrors, I felt enormous hope for our race. This world was dying. But seven more were being born. The sky was the limit for the future of our children out there among the stars.

The joy I felt at the possibilities for mankind, however, was brutally overshadowed by the fact that if (and it was looking more like "when") the Earth died, so many of us would, too. Not just those in my inner circle, but billions that simply wouldn't make it here in time. We had the weight of the world on our shoulders, literally.

On a personal level, it was a complete and total clusterfuck. If, by some miracle, I were able to sing the Song of Making and heal the world, it would unmake everything made by imperfect song:

all the Unseelie, Alina, and possibly Christian, Barrons, the Nine, and Dageus would die.

If I *failed* to sing it and the world ended, destroying the seat of the Fae race's power, all Fae, Seelie and Unseelie, Barrons, and the rest of the Nine would definitely die, as well as potentially Christian and the other hybrids among us. I would also die. But Alina would live. At least my parents would get to keep one daughter. So long as I didn't sing it, Alina would enjoy a natural life span. She wasn't Fae, she was a human resurrected by imperfect song.

You might think I'd spent all my time exhaustively searching my inner files. I did. For exactly two days.

Then Barrons and Ryodan pointed out the unarguable fact that if the queen had possessed the song, she would have used it and not doomed their race by binding their power to the Earth. If she'd possessed any useful clues, she would have pursued them. There was nothing in my files that could save our world and I was of greater use meeting with Dancer, sharing every note of other-worldly music I'd ever heard inside my head, trying to finish the second half of the song. We worked day and night on it.

To no avail.

According to Dancer, what we were trying to do was impossible, and he didn't use that word lightly. We had no parameters. No idea if the second half was shorter, as long, or longer than the first. No clue if entirely new motifs developed in it. Art, he said, which song is, is a purely subjective thing, not a mathematical formula. It's up to the artist, and no one else's vision can ever be identical.

Eventually, I had no more music to share, so I matched Christian sift for sift, racing to get as many people through the portals and off this planet as we could.

Our situation grew more perilous with each passing day.

There were two holes we could no longer even excavate: the one near Chester's, and the one near the church. Their ergospheres had become so powerfully distorting that no one could get within twenty paces without being sucked in. We'd tried tunneling up from beneath the street, working from within the underground caverns and tunnels carved long ago by the River Liffey, but the moment we began to break through, the ergosphere inhaled everything we'd loosed and grew exponentially, forcing us to concede defeat.

Ryodan tried to send my parents through to another world with the first wave of colonists, but they refused to leave until the last minute.

Then came even worse news: along with the decline of our planet, the True Magic was declining, too. Using it became perilously inaccurate and we could no longer sift to gather humans to save. At times the power inside me was a radioactive radiance, at other times it ebbed to a faint glow. I'd tried repeatedly to return to the planet where I passed my initiation to ask the vast sentience questions, but I wasn't able to complete the journey there.

Barrons suspected we had a week left, at most. Then one of the two black holes *would* touch the Earth, and when it did, we would find out the hard way what was going to happen.

When you only have one week to live, the pressing question becomes: how do you want to live it?

52

"Closing time, open all the doors and
let you out into the world"

JADA

I slow-mo-Joed into Chester's after parking my bike out front.
The place was dark, the chairs were up on the tables, and it was
so silent I could hear the faint hum of the geothermal power that
fueled Ryodan's demesne.

"Closing Time" started playing in my head. I'd always loved
that song. I watched a couple of Semisonic concerts on TV when I
was a kid and by then the families on the different series I'd binged
on started to feel like my family. You took it where you could find
it. So I'd watched them growing up, going to clubs, and having
dates, and thinking about how it was going to be when *I* finally got
let out into the world. School, dates, prom, those ideas had all
seemed so exotic and out of the ordinary, mysterious, and thrilling
to me. I'd wondered if I would ever be like normal people. Sometimes it seemed I felt so much more, yet in other places had voids
where feelings should be.

I glanced at the dance floor and smiled faintly, remembering
dancing with Lor, wearing a red dress. How Ryodan had looked at
me. People on many of the worlds had found me attractive but his

eyes said: *Beautiful by any standards, in any century, on any world, woman.*

He'd seemed so much larger than life when I was a kid, and even now I still felt young around him. But I also often felt he might be the only person who ever really understood me.

Dancer—who I'd been spending the last few weeks with, working on the song, going for insanely fast motorcycle rides, freeze-framing him around town—saw me through a filter. He polished me up where I had no shine. I loved that about him.

Ryodan's cool, clear eyes had no filters where I was concerned. I didn't need any with him.

I'd had no intention of stopping at Chester's today, but each time I'd blown past the club in the past few weeks, on my way back from the abbey, I felt such an irresistible urge to park my bike and walk inside, I'd finally realized he'd put some kind of spell on me again.

He could do that. So, today when I felt it, I decided to call him on it. Tell him to quit using his black arts on me and leave me alone. No more Dani-come-hither spells. I was surprised he hadn't hunted me down like he used to, except I'd been sleeping at Dancer's every night.

Not that kind of sleeping. Each night, when we buttoned up the day and returned to his penthouse, I'd gone cautiously further with him, absorbing each new sensation. Dancer gave me no pressure, easing off whenever I wanted to, happy for the intimacy we shared. These past few weeks had been exotic for me, filled with deep, easy friendship, more hugs, kisses, and physical affection than I'd ever known, and a sense of belonging. All that affection was messing with my head. Changing me.

The nights had been incredible, stretched out next to my best friend who turned me on with his quiet genius and long, lean body. We did everything, made out like the world was ending (which it was) and ground against each other with red-hot desire and young, hungry bodies. But each time his hand slid down to unbutton my jeans, I caught and held it, started a conversation, talked to him about anything and everything until he finally fell asleep. As long as my jeans stayed on I felt safe.

Then I'd lie awake next to him, listening to him breathing, staring at the ceiling, wondering what was holding me back.

I wanted Dancer to be my first. And I wanted to get rid of whatever was stopping me.

I trusted him. He made no demands. Never asked where I was going or when I'd be back. He had his own life and interests and they wholly engrossed him, and we went our separate ways and had separate adventures but came back together and shared our new parts, then had more adventures together. Being with him was as easy and natural as breathing. And we were learning so much from each other!

From the day I found him, I'd considered Dancer mine. That was why I'd been so shocked to discover he'd had his own world all along that hadn't included me, with friends and girls who crushed on him hard.

I loved him. I hadn't wanted to, but I did, and it was too late to change because once my heart went somewhere, I couldn't pull it back. It's a glitch in my wiring.

I'd decided Ryodan was somehow keeping me from going all the way with Dancer. Didn't want me losing my virginity to somebody that might die. Not that Ryodan knew I was a virgin. But it would be a totally Machiavellian thing to do: a kind of "Don't let Dani care too much about Dancer because when he dies, it might screw her head up, and she won't be nearly as productive."

I was so irritated by the time I got to his office, thinking about how he was messing up my life—*again*—that I blasted inside in full freeze-frame, and my vibrations at twenty-something are far more impressive than they were at fourteen. I no longer merely ruffle papers and hair; at high velocity I can shake the glass in walls.

His entire office rattled and shuddered as I stood there, peering at him from the slipstream. Then he was up in it with me, standing close.

"What?" he demanded.

"What do you mean, 'What?'" I growled.

"You only blast in here like this when you've gotten yourself worked into a tizzy about something. Get it out and over with. I have things to do."

"Like paperwork? As if you were ever actually doing that. Is your tattoo screwing me up, or is it something else you've done?" I got right to the point.

"Screwing you up how?"

"Every blasted time I pass your club, your little compulsion spell tries to suck me inside. Get it off me." He dropped down instantly and I followed him into slow-mo then stabbed him in the chest with a finger. "If you want to talk to me about something, text me. Don't use magic on me. I've had enough of that kind of manipulation in my life."

His silver eyes bored into mine. "Each time you pass my club you want to come inside?"

"You put the spell on me. You know how it works."

He smiled faintly. "I didn't put a spell on you."

The instant he said it, I knew he was telling the truth. I can tell when he's being deceptive and when he's not. Ryodan's modus operandi isn't outright lying, it's shaping words into twisty little pretzels of obfuscation. His reply was too straightforward to contain any twists.

I stood there wishing I could simply erase the past few moments from the chalkboard of my life. I'd just betrayed to Ryodan that I'd been contemplating him with such frequency and intensity, I decided he must have put a spell on me. And he'd gotten that faintly smug look in his silvery eyes probably no one else but me would have noticed.

One way or another I was getting out of this one with grace. "So your tattoo doesn't have any effect on me whatsoever?"

"To the contrary. I'm the one it's a problem for."

"No spell?"

He sliced his head to the left and that smug glint shimmered a little.

I exhaled gustily and said, "So it *is* because I can't stop thinking about it."

He arched a brow, waiting.

"Shazam," I clarified. "Each time I drive by here, I start thinking about him. You said you could help me." These past few weeks, I'd forced myself to put thoughts of Shazam in suspended animation, focusing on saving the world and Dancer, in that order. How could I justify pursuing something I wanted just because my heart hurt so badly it almost made me puke in the middle of the night, when the world was silent and I worried about where and how Shazam was and if he was crying and all alone, when billions were going to die if we failed to save them? How could I leave Dancer? What if he died while I was gone?

When I was a kid, my thoughts were so linear: point a to point b. There was what I wanted and what I did to get it. But when you get older, you suddenly have all these c's and d's and z's you have to factor in, too.

When I first returned to Dublin I'd been acutely aware of how much time was passing for Shazam while I hunted for a way to rescue him and get us both back home. The more time that passed, the more worried I'd gotten that I would go back for him and he'd be gone. Not only would I still not have him, I'd have paid whatever price I had to pay for going back—for nothing.

I dropped down into a chair near Ryodan's desk, waiting for him to go sit down on the other side. When he finally did, I said, "You said you could find me anywhere with the tattoo. You asked me not to use it when you were injured and I didn't. I want to use it now." Even as I said it, I wondered what I would do if he said yes. Could I leave this dying world? Dancer?

Ryodan rubbed his jaw, hand rasping over his shadow beard,

and I had a sudden vision of that jaw tearing into a human thigh, the sleek black powerful beast he'd become, and I shivered. Yanking out a protein bar, I tore off half of it in a single bite.

"I believe we've got a week, at most, before one of the holes touches ground," he said. "It would take longer than that."

A week? Mac hadn't told me that! But then I hadn't seen her in several days. "Does everyone know?"

He sliced his head in negation. "It would start panic. We're moving people off world as quickly as we can. Tell me about Shazam."

I surprised myself by complying. I meant to give him a brief sketch but once I started talking, it just came gushing out of me, like an ocean backed up behind a leaking dam. Shazam *lived* when I talked about him. I could almost feel him again, warm against my body, hear him muttering crossly, demanding grooming, attention, and food, always more food. God, how I missed him!

I told Ryodan about meeting Shazam on the planet Olean, with the teleporting trees, how he became my best friend and companion, the many worlds we traveled together and the adventures we'd had. I reminisced and laughed and lit up inside. Talking took me back to those worlds where we'd played with zest and abandon when circumstances had permitted.

I told him how I'd gone to sleep and woken up with Shazam every day. For four years, give or take, we were each other's whole world. We hunted and cooked and groomed and battled and ran wild. He was my rock, my teacher, my champion, my constant companion, and a day without my beloved grumpy, funny, brilliant, depressive friend was like walking around with a limb amputated.

Ryodan listened, leaning back in his chair, boots on the desk, arms folded behind his head, and while I talked he changed. And the more he changed, the more I talked.

Those remote silvery eyes warmed and came alive, developed

complex crystalline depths. He smiled, laughed, became fully invested in my tales, asking endless questions. Hours spun by as I regaled him with our zany adventures, and a part of me that had been frozen solid pooled into a gentle summer lake.

"But it wasn't all fun and games," he said finally.

I shrugged, kicking a leg over the side of the chair. "Whose life is?"

"Why did you have to leave him?"

I closed my eyes and told him in a hushed voice about the last world I'd leapt into, following Shazam. Each one had its unknown perils but this planet had several that in conjunction were a perfect storm.

The portal on Planet X—that was what I called it because I hadn't been there long enough to learn its name—was on a small island in the middle of a lake. The inhabitants were primitive tribesmen with bizarrely advanced technology or magic, half naked with elaborately feathered headdresses. They'd been doing some kind of ritual dance around the mirror when we came through, and obviously had experience with people or monsters invading their world via the portal, because there was a powerful force field set up that captured everything the moment it exited.

The planet was also one of those that shorted out my powers.

We'd leapt through, outracing a horde of monstrous night creatures on the last planet, with no option to return, caught between a rock and a hard place. Shazam was instantly trapped in a shimmering cage. Either I'd sped up at the last moment and dodged it or, for some inexplicable reason, it didn't hold me.

I know it was meant to, because when the tribesmen realized I wasn't contained, they attacked me.

I heard Shazam behind me, hissing and snarling, trying to break free to protect me, but the force field held, and he started crying out that I should leave and come back for him later.

I closed my eyes, rubbed them, and stopped talking.

I'd never told anyone about this day. I hated this day. I'd re-lived it so many times trying to isolate my errors, figure out what else I might have done.

I fisted my hands and opened my eyes. Ryodan was watching me with such fierce, quiet intensity, it made me feel like he'd been living everything I'd been telling him.

"You know how my mind works," I said finally.

"At the fucking speed of light?" he said dryly.

I smiled bitterly. "I was wondering where the exit portal was and how long it would take me to find it, when I saw a shimmering reflection dancing across the tribesmen and sought the source. Across the water was an enormous, swirling array of endless mirrors rotating in a dizzying spin. Impossible to tell how many, because they whirled in an endless circle. Maybe a hundred thousand, maybe a million; it was as bad as the Hall of All Days. They never stopped moving, catching the sun, splashing it across us. And I thought, okay, I'm going to swim, do a mad dash into a mirror and, whatever world I come out on, I'll get a bunch of weapons and go back and rescue Shazam, right?"

He closed his eyes and shook his head. "You chose the mirror that brought you home."

"Bingo," I said wearily. "I told him I'd be back for him. 'Wait for me,' I said. 'Don't go anywhere. If you get free, don't jump through another mirror or we'll never find each other again. I swear I'll be back. I won't let you be lost, all alone.' And he sat there looking at me with those big sad, violet eyes and tears were streaming down his face and he said plaintively, 'I see you, Yi-yi.'"

"And you knew if you went back for him," Ryodan said quietly, "you might never find your way home again. There was no way to choose the same mirror. And if he'd gotten free, there was no way he could choose the same mirror you'd taken."

"Exactly. My only goal was to get back to Dublin. Goddamn it, I *lived* that purpose for five bloody years! What if I returned and he was dead and I never found my way home again? What if he escaped and left—and I went back for nothing? What if he didn't even wait? What if he took another mirror?" *What if he didn't really love me?* I didn't say it but I'd thought it. "And what if he waits forever, believing I'll come for him, losing hope, day after day? He cries so much and he feels so deeply. Ryodan, I've been back for *months.* Do you know what that means? If he's still there, he's been waiting decades for me! *Decades!*" My voice broke and the tears started to flow. I'd never told anyone any of this, and now that it was coming out, my heart felt like it was being ripped in half as badly as it had the day I plucked the crumpled *Dani Daily* from the trash and realized the terrible irony of where I was. I'd been so elated to come through to a world with civilization—translated, guns and badass weapons. But my elation had fizzled and I'd gone hard and cold as stone. I couldn't deal. I couldn't handle the pain.

I love Shazam unconditionally. There was no abuse or manipulation in our relationship. It was pure, full of joy, trust, and physical affection. I'd never had anything like it. I'd lost the only thing that mattered to me. Again. I was always losing things. Just like my mother, the erosions just kept happening. I'd felt so much pain and grief and I'd just wanted it to stop, and I'd finally understood why my mom drank and shot up. But I couldn't permit myself to do that. So I'd numbed myself the way I knew how. And these past few weeks, I'd kept the Shazam part of me numb as I tried to let the other parts of me come back to life and do the things a superhero was supposed to do.

Ryodan was suddenly in my space. I bristled and tried to wheel away from him but he pulled me up from the chair and into his arms.

I snapped.

Something exploded inside me, larger and more violent than even the pressure behind that damned fragile dam that had made me tell him too much, and I attacked him like a wild animal. I threw punches and kicks, cursing up a storm, calling him names, calling myself names, raging at the universe for being such a grand shit to me. I railed and ranted. I picked up my chair and smashed it to smithereens across my knee. I shattered his and stomped it to bits then turned on his desk, that stupid fucking desk that a powerful man like him didn't belong behind, and cracked it down the middle.

When I turned my fury to the walls, he got in my way, wouldn't let me drive my fists through them. I wanted broken glass. I wanted blood. I wanted something else to hurt besides my heart. I needed the distraction of physical pain.

I'd been holding in so much for so long that I couldn't keep a lid on it anymore. I hammered at him and he just took it, let me keep hitting him like some unbreakable Ironman, swing after swing. Catching my blows in his hands, other times just shaking off punches lethal enough to stop a human's heart, watching me the whole time with a fierce, intense gaze.

My fury vanished with such abruptness that I deflated like a popped inner tube.

And there was nothing left but what I'd been trying to escape all this time—pain.

I went motionless, staring up at him through a tangle of curls that had escaped from my ponytail, opened my mouth to apologize and all that came out was a long, unending wail.

He put his arms around me and I sank into them.

Ryodan's arms. Around me.

So strange.

So strong. Invincible.

This man had always been my nemesis, my punching bag, my rival. But he wasn't now and I was beginning to wonder if he ever had been.

I leaned into him the way I leaned into Dancer, put my head in the crook of his neck and cried against his chest like a storm breaking loose, until his crisp white shirt was damp and wrinkled. And somewhere along the way, I started to laugh because I'd gotten snot all over the crisp, flawless Ryodan and turned him into a crumpled mess and I found that insanely funny. Then I was crying again until there was nothing left, and I was exhausted and quiet in his arms for a time, listening to the impossibly slow thud of his heart.

"Can you help me rescue Shazam?" I said finally.

He stiffened and my heart sank like a stone to the bottom of that hated lake that separated me from Shazam.

I drew back and looked at him.

He tucked a strand of hair behind my ear, his gaze shadowed by sorrow. "If you'd told me this as soon as you got back, yes. But Dani, we don't have enough time now."

"How long would it take?" I cried, anguished.

"Impossible to predict. I'd have to go through, figure out how far from Earth Planet X is and how many mirrors I'd need to stack to create a tunnel. It's complicated. I'd have to die to get back out. The biggest variable is how long it takes me to get back from dying. And between the IFPs and the black holes, I'd have to go about it very carefully."

"You mean it's not, like, a three-day resurrection or something?"

His gaze shuttered. "I don't talk about this."

I said impatiently, "Ryodan, we both know if you were going to kill me, you would have done it a long time ago. I hacked your security cams. I saw you turn into the beast. I know your secrets and you know mine. That's as close to family as you can get."

"I haven't even begun to plumb your secrets," he said. "And you didn't hack them. Your boy genius did. We found the calling card he left."

"He left a bloody calling card?" He hadn't told me that! I was furious that he'd taken such a ridiculous chance, but then I started to smile. That was my Dancer. No fear. I loved him for that.

Ryodan flinched, and I got the impression he'd just heard me think that. And apparently I'd been right, he didn't like the thought of me caring about someone we both knew could die any day. My smile vanished because I despised myself.

If I'd told Ryodan as soon as I'd returned, if I'd trusted him, he could have helped me rescue Shazam. Assuming my testy, adorable beast was alive, he'd be here with me right now.

I'd blown it.

R-E-G-R-E-T. I can spell that word now. Raw. Endless. Grief. Raining. Eternal. Tears. That's what regret is.

"You had no reason to trust anyone, Dani," he murmured. "And every reason not to."

"Yes, I did have a reason, and a big one—trusting would have saved him," I said bitterly.

"You're not allowed to beat yourself up. Only I get that privilege," he said, and I smiled faintly with brittle humor.

"Can't you mark the Silver from this side?" I hated the way my voice broke on the words. That was what I'd spent the majority of my time seeking—a spell to etch a symbol on the mirror that would show on the other side, guaranteeing we could find our way home. We'd have to be fast to hit the right Silver, but Shazam and I were speed demons. Still, if I hadn't searched, if I'd only trusted and asked . . . If only. I got it now. Why people got so fucked up as they grew older. Impossible choices, impossible trade-offs; each erosion had a price you carried in your heart forever.

"Barrons and I tried to devise a way to do that for a long time, with no success. You said they caged him. It's been decades. Do you really believe he's still there and alive?"

My hands fisted behind his neck. "I have to try."

He said nothing for a time, and I stood there with his arms around me, in no hurry to step away because it felt so quiet and solid and safe. With Dancer, it felt quiet and solid and safe, too, but in a different way.

"Wait a few days. If all appears hopeless on Earth, we'll go through together and save him. But you have to promise you will never try to return to this planet."

"I can't promise that. It's my home. Maybe we can make it back in time."

"You wouldn't know until you tried. And the odds are high you'd die. You should have left already with the other colonists. Go somewhere. *Live*." He started to speak then stopped, shook himself and said roughly, "We'll take Dancer with us. The three of you can make a life somewhere for yourselves."

"Right. So I can watch Dancer die." Here and now, I could deal with my boyfriend's condition. But go off with him to a new and potentially dangerous world? Start a life, maybe one day even start feeling safe and have children—only to lose him? God, why were there no easy choices anymore?

"How many fucking people do you think I've watched die?" His silver eyes flashed crimson. "Over and over. That's what you do. You love them while you have them and when they're gone, you grieve. That's life. At least you had them for a while."

I stared up at him, realizing that, just like Dancer saw only part of me, I saw Ryodan through a filter, too. And right now I was seeing him in a way I never had before. He'd loved. Many times. Deeply. And he'd lost countless times. And that was why he fought so hard to keep his men together. He was intensely controlled because at the heart of it all, he cared intensely, and even though he was immortal, he'd never turned off emotion. I narrowed my eyes, staring into his gaze, startled by how similar we were. He felt as fiercely as I did, and like me, he'd donned his own version of my Jada persona. He slipped it on every day with his crisp business-man attire, his aloofness, his calculation.

"Do you know why I didn't kill Rowena?"

"Ro?" I shook my head, not following the sudden leap in conversation, still off-kilter by how differently I was seeing him now. He'd become a whole person, not a caricature of my archnemesis anymore. A man.

His hands were on the sides of my head then, and he was urging me to close my eyes with his mind, and this *was* a spell of compulsion because they drifted shut without my permission and he filled my head with images and I stared at the visions in horror because he was showing me that his childhood had been so much worse than mine. It was brutal and savage and punishing and desperate, and Ryodan had actually been a child once, some kind of child, and he'd been so badly abused I couldn't believe he'd survived it. One man had done it all to him, and his hatred of that man who kept him chained in a dark hole in the ground had been so consuming, there'd been nothing of a little boy left.

But one day he'd escaped. Like me.

And he'd sworn vengeance.

But the man who'd so heinously abused him was killed before Ryodan got the chance, and he'd been cheated of his vengeance.

He said, "For thirty-two years, three months, and eighteen days, I carried rage and hatred for everything and everyone in my heart. Thirty-two years I walked around, dead inside except for a single emotion: fury. Then I found him. Alive. I'd been deceived. He hadn't died. The bones I'd dug up and crushed to dust weren't his. His friends had protected him. Lied. Transported him away."

Another image: Ryodan killing a man who was well into his seventies. Snap of a neck. Life to death in an instant.

"And it didn't make you feel any better," I murmured, lost in another, ancient time.

He took his hands from my head and I opened my eyes.

"Wrong. It made all the difference in the world. The moment I killed him, the poison inside me vanished. I was weightless. Free. I was born that day. I needed the vengeance. I needed to kill him. Right or wrong, that's who I am. Sometimes people take too much from you and you have to take back."

I nodded. I understood. Killing Ro would have soldered shut a weeping wound inside me, but as a teen I'd stayed my hand for one reason alone: the other *sidhe*-seers would have ostracized me, and I'd wanted to be with them. When you're young, people don't believe you can think straight and have good reasons for things. Mac could have gotten away with killing her because an adult's word carries weight. Mine didn't. I wouldn't have felt one ounce of regret. I would have felt that a rabid dog had been put down and that was what you had to do with rabid dogs. I wouldn't have tortured or drawn it out. I never do. And yes, it would have made my anger go away. Especially after I'd learned the extent of her involvement with my mother. I would have felt that justice had been served.

"I wanted to kill Rowena more than you know," he said. "But I wanted you to do it more."

I inclined my head in a wordless thank-you.

"Get Dancer," he said. "I'll take you through and help you free Shazam. But then the three of you will leave that world for a new one and never look back. Seize life, Dani. For fuck's sake, I saw your mother's plaque."

"Right, and who's the snoop now?" I said with a strained, wry smile, but sobered instantly. "Mac told me a few weeks ago that you're bound to this planet, reborn here, so if the planet is destroyed, you'll die, too." Although she'd said she wasn't certain if the Nine would die instantly or continue living until they were killed, then not be able to be reborn. Regardless, it would be the end of their immortality: instantly or within a normal life span.

"Mac's talking too much."

"The world's ending. Get over it." I reached up and touched his hair, traced the planes of his hard, chiseled face. I was touching Ryodan. And he was just standing there, letting me do it, looking as surprised as I felt. This touching stuff was addictive now that I'd begun doing it. It freaked me out. I didn't know the rules. Part of me wanted to hug everyone and see how they all felt. Part of me never wanted to hug again. I resented the intensity of all the emotions I was feeling. Things had been so clear as Jada. Nothing was clear anymore. Except that Ryodan was strong and electrifying and so bloody alive. And in a week, give or take a few days, whether I went through to Shazam or went where a superhero *should* go—to lead the colonists on another world, relinquishing my personal desires because that's what superheroes did and you *never* saw a happy superhero—he might be dead. I'd never get to see him again. I'd lose my archnemesis and my mentor and the man that felt so much joy you could almost catch in your hands when he laughed. I didn't want him dead. I wanted him to be immortal and always out there, with something to tell me, doing something to challenge me. I wanted to know he was alive somewhere, always.

I didn't think before I did it.

I stretched to my full height and kissed him. Like I kissed Dancer. Soft, sensual butterfly wings against his lips. Unlike the last kiss I gave Ryodan, this wasn't one to provoke or challenge or say "Fuck you—can't touch this." It was a kiss that said simply, "I see you and admire you and want you to live."

He froze, and just when I was realizing what an idiotic thing I'd done and began to pull away, the temperature in the office ratcheted up fifty degrees like the air was on fire, and I was on fire and so was he, and he was kissing me back in a way I didn't know a kiss could be.

It was so different than kissing Dancer. Dancer's kiss was sweet and dreamy and exciting. Ryodan's kiss had razor edges, sharp and dangerous as the man. Being in Dancer's arms was like living on the edible planet. Being in Ryodan's was like stepping into the eye of a cyclone. Dancer was easy laughter and a normal future (sans abrupt death). Ryodan was endless challenge and a future that was impossible to imagine.

Dancer accepted me any way I wanted to be without question. Ryodan made me question myself and pushed me to be the most I could be.

Then my hair was loose and his hands were buried in it, and he was kissing me so deeply his fangs grazed my teeth and I tasted blood. I was acutely aware of every inch of my body that was touching every inch of his: his forearm grazing the side of my neck, his hands cradling my skull, his mouth so soft yet hard, his power-ful chest against the only part of me that wasn't muscle, one of his thighs slipping between my legs, making my knees tremble and nearly buckle.

He kissed like he did everything, with exquisite skill, passion, and one hundred percent focus. Here was where Ryodan shed his aloof businessman attire, his cool facade, and came to life with the heat and intensity of a thousand suns. And I realized that was what had so entranced me on Level 4—I'd seen him drop all his guards and fuck like a man on fire, with nothing held back. Open, unguarded, just like he'd been when we'd talked.

Ryodan, controlled, is formidably fascinating.

Ryodan, open, is indescribably addictive.

He kissed me like I was the empire he was sworn to protect and would die a thousand deaths to keep secure. He kissed me like I was a woman with a deep dark wildness that needed to be fed and he knew just how to do it. He kissed me like he was dying and this was the last kiss he would ever taste. Then his kiss changed and his tongue was velvet and silk as he kissed me like I was fine bone china that needed exacting care and gentleness. Then the storm built in both of us and I ground myself against him, and he was searching with his kiss and his hands sliding down to my ass for the part of me that was a savage animal and so was he and we were going to forget the world and become two primal, uncompli-cated beasts fucking as if the universe depended on our passion to fuel it. And I was pretty sure we could. I felt something building in me, a hunger that was exhilarated to be alive and knew it could come out and play as hard as it wanted, because *I could never break this man*. Not even with all my superpowers. I could dump every bit of myself on him and never have to worry about giving him a heart attack or breaking a bone or giving him a black eye by accident. He could handle anything. My high temper, my need for adventure and stimulation, my intellect, rages, and rants, my sheer physical strength, even the darkness of my shadow-self. He was a broad-shouldered beast. He was hard and capable and permanent and had an immortal heart. A frenzy of lust exploded inside me and I met the savagery of his kiss with all the savagery in my soul, and there is one fuck of a lot of it. With a distant part of my brain, I thought about Dancer and wondered if he could handle perhaps a small portion of this part of me and if maybe I was holding back not just because I was afraid to be so damned fucking vulnerable but also because I was afraid I might hurt him and—

Ryodan broke the kiss and pushed me away so abruptly that I stumbled backward over the chair behind me and nearly went down. My body was cold where the heat of his hands had been. My legs were shaking and I was so full of heat and need that I couldn't even speak for a moment. I just stood there, wanting him back, touching me again, holding me, taking me apart inside and waking every cell up. What would it be like to get naked with this man, shut the world out and let go of everything, knowing he could handle all of it for me? Walk away from responsibility, let him take over, feel safe. Get to rest. Recharge. Go out into the world whole.

I regained my balance and stood, staring blankly at him. He'd opened a box inside me that I couldn't shut. Not fast anyway. "Wait, what?" I shook my head, trying to clear my stupor. "Why are you looking at me like that?"

"You need to leave. Now," he gritted.

"That's not what you mean. Your body doesn't remotely mean that." I hurt from the lack of contact with his body.

"You're a fucking virgin."

"Oxymoron. I'm a nonfucking virgin. And there's nothing wrong with being a virgin. I kept it for a reason."

"Get out," he repeated, and his silver eyes went cold and hard as ancient coins. The open, unguarded man disappeared right before my eyes and it pained me to see him go. It felt like being cut off from something sacred. Like being deemed not sacred enough to get to see it.

"Right, so now *you* get to be Jada?" I snapped.

"Jada had purpose. I just didn't want you to be her all the time."

My hands fisted at my sides. "I don't get it. You kiss everyone else. For fuck's sake, you kissed Jo. I'm as pretty as Jo."

"You. Aren't. Everyone else." He paused, then said in a rough voice, "And you're not pretty. Goddamn it, Dani. You're beautiful."

"And there's yet one more reason why what you're saying makes no sense," I said angrily. He could die! "What if you die and never get to kiss me again?"

Silver eyes narrowed, glittering with anger. "*That's* why you wanted to have sex with me? Because I might die sooner than Dancer and you figured you might as well fuck us in the order of who would die first?"

I bristled. "I didn't say I wanted to fuck you. I was just kissing you. And you were kissing me back. And you were *liking* it."

He stepped back and the light fell in such a way that half his face was shadowed, one side clear and easy to see, the other concealed by darkness. "Come back in three days with Dancer," he said as tonelessly as I'd ever sounded as Jada. "We'll save Shazam. You'll find a world and make a home with Dancer and never return to Earth."

"Fuck you, Ryodan," I said, stung by his rejection, his icy remoteness, and my return to being on the other side of his infernal walls. For a few minutes I'd been in the garden. And I'd been evicted.

"Just said no to that," he said coolly.

I whirled and kicked up into the slipstream.

Nothing happened.

I was shorted out.

Sometimes I really hate that man. At the moment, I really, *really* hated him.

Pretending that I'd never even tried to freeze-frame, I stalked from his office, slowly, long-legged, and sexy as hell, showing him exactly what he was never going to have. I put into sensual motion all those incredible feelings that had been awakened in my body by him and Dancer.

He'd had his chance and blown it. Rejected me.

No man gets a second chance with Dani-O.

Not even the great Ryodan.

♪

As the door slides closed, I rest my forehead against the cool glass.

My office feels empty without her in it. The sun vanished behind clouds.

She stood there looking at me with fire in her eyes, comparing herself to Jo, unable to see they weren't remotely the same. Yes, I'd casually fucked Jo. One doesn't casually fuck Danielle O'Malley.

Her energy is nuclear, white-hot and pure as the new-driven snow. Passion is where she's united, suffering no conflicts. I might be forged of hellfire but the woman-child is forged of pure energy and emotion, fierce and Valkyrie-strong.

Another man will experience her raw self-discovery, the volatile nuances of her first time.

I could have watched her talk for days. Eyes shining, face luminous, heart blazing in her face so brilliantly it had illuminated my entire office, warmed my cooling skin.

I still feel the burn of her hands on my face, in my hair, sliding down my body as our kiss took a much deeper, more savage turn.

But a storm like me isn't what should come crashing down on the last vestige of her innocence.

She needs a slow immersion with a gentle hand that gives far more than it takes, a man who will dance her slowly, tenderly, into love. She needs something the fierce-hearted warrior never had: a normal, good experience with a normal, good man.

I'm not that man.

Fucking me would make her more like me.

Fucking him will make her more like him.

I knew the child. I know the woman. She'll never be satisfied with a single lover. Dani craves experience, challenge, change, tempering, growth. She needs to taste it all. I understand that.

One day she'll choose a mate. She'll hunger to be a wolf running with a wolf of her own at her side, equals in everything, and when that time comes, she'll need to know she's chosen the absolute best.

I am that man.

But she has no basis for comparison.

She'll give her virginity to Dancer. Soon. She's on fire.

She wears my brand.

I'll feel far too much of it. This time and every time.

Immortal though I am—if I survive the next week—the coming years might seem my most eternal yet.

I will never be her first.

But one day I'll be her last.

53

"Girl, you'll be a woman soon"

DANI

I stepped out of the shower and toweled myself dry, smiling, listening to the sounds of Dancer banging around in the kitchen getting dinner ready.

There was only this moment, this night. The warmth of home, the delight of my best friend making a homemade pizza, the promise of a movie we'd pause more often than we played so we could talk about everything under the sun.

I'd made a deal with myself—no thinking tonight. No thoughts of tomorrow or Shazam or Dancer's heart or the fate of the world. I know a truth: worrying doesn't make tomorrow better; it only makes today worse. I wanted a single golden night before I made the hard decisions I had to confront.

Mind neatly compartmentalized with my Jada parts put away and my Dani parts free, I dried my hair, ran my fingers through the tangles, then stepped back and looked at myself. Naked. Clear-eyed. No makeup. No perfume or lotion. Just me.

I'd realized something on the way back to the penthouse. Sex with Ryodan would have been just that, sex. It would have been intense, wild, mind-blowing. Sex with Dancer was much more complicated. It would be making love. It would be sweet, tender, and heart-blowing. But hopefully not literally.

I'd figured out a way to trick myself. Since Dancer taking off my jeans was the moment I kept freezing up, I just wouldn't put any on. Problem solved.

When I walked naked out of the bathroom, Dancer's back was to me, but he must have heard me because he turned around, holding the pie and teased, "Mega, I know you definitely want mushrooms on your p-p—*PUH*."

The pizza hit the floor and exploded when he dropped it. Crust went flying and sauce splattered across the floorboards and up the cabinets. Not that he noticed.

"Holy fucking fuck!" he said fiercely, then stood with his mouth ajar, saying nothing. After a moment he snapped it shut so hard his teeth clacked together.

He stood there, trying to keep his gaze on my face, like maybe it wouldn't be polite to stare at my body, and I teased, "Dancer, you big gorgeous geek, I took all my clothes off so you *would* look at me."

Permission granted, his gaze dropped like a stone. He looked down, up, down, and up again. I shivered as his gaze moved over me, making me feel hot and cold at the same time.

He stared and stared, and just when I was wondering what I might have to do to move things along, he reached behind his head, yanked off his shirt, unbuckled his belt, dropped his jeans, kicked them away into the pizza sauce, and he was naked, too.

"Couldn't let you be naked alone," he murmured.

"No," I agreed, "that wouldn't be right."

"And I want everything to be right. I want it to be perfect for us. For you. You deserve that." He moved toward me—finally!— still looking me up and down, slow and intense and astonished and gratifyingly awed.

For all my bluster about being epic when I finally had sex, I felt shaky and nervous and not at all composed. Butterflies fluttered from my stomach all the way up my throat. I tested my ability to access the slipstream. It was gone and I was relieved. I didn't want to hurt him. "I'm pretty sure, since neither of us have done this before, it won't be perfect." But he was perfect. I'd seen my share of naked men, and although Dancer got shorted in the heart department, he hadn't been shorted anywhere else. He was young and hot and sexy and his eyes were brilliant and shining and round with wonder.

"Are you kidding me?" He reached for my hand "With our IQs and hearts, if we can't make love right, there's something seriously wrong with us."

I let him lead me, walking slightly behind him, enjoying the view of his back and ass. His skin was darker than mine but then again pretty much everyone's is, and I couldn't wait to touch it everywhere. As he moved, muscles rippled, and I shivered thinking about him stretching naked on top of me, pushing inside, wrapping my legs around him. His name suited him. He moved like a dancer, powerful, controlled, strong.

Stopping at the bed, he turned, stared at me a long moment, then with an explosive exhale said, "Christ, Dani, you're so beautiful. So, so . . ."

"Epic?" I said helpfully.

He laughed. "In every possible way. I dreamed about this. Prayed that I'd live long enough and you'd live long enough that you'd grow up and see me as a man. You're the most fearless, brilliant, incredible woman I've ever met. What did I do to deserve you? Are you sure you want me to be your first?" he said, like he couldn't believe it. "Mega, I'm just a guy and you're . . . well, you're *everything*."

His beautiful eyes were so honest and earnest, it melted me. I took his hand and drew it to my body, put his palm against my stomach and slid it up to my breast, shivering when he grazed my nipple with his thumb. "You're not *just* anything, and never could be, and you did everything to deserve me. You listen to me and let me breathe and talk and teach me things. *You're* brilliant. And you're kind and good and constant. And you're epic, too. Yes, I'm definitely absolutely one hundred percent certain I want you to be my first. There's no one else, Dancer. It's you."

Just like that, I banished Ryodan's ghost from between us.

He inhaled sharply, then his hands were moving on my skin, sliding to cup my breasts gently, then hungrily, and for the first time since I'd met him, he looked at me and did nothing to disguise the lust and desire he felt for me, and I gasped. It was staggering. He wanted me so much! I loved seeing that in his eyes! I felt everything his hands were doing as intensely as I feel all my emotions, like the cells in his body were sinking into the cells of my body, touching me all the way to the place where my soul used to be.

It wasn't like in movies where everything goes flawlessly and the lighting is all fuzzy soft focus and the music is just right.

That's illusion. Reality is two people who care deeply about each other, getting to know each other as intimately as possible, and it's full of sounds and awkward movements and occasional strained laughter. It took us a bit to get past the shaky, nervous part, but when we did, we found that our bodies moved together as easily, hungrily, and passionately as our minds.

When I used to daydream about losing my virginity, I always thought I'd put on a show when I had sex for the first time, be the femme fatale, dazzling, wild, and most definitely on top. I'd rock his world and not think about mine. I'd impress because that's what I do, I impress because I'm never sure people will like me otherwise.

None of that mattered with Dancer.

He was already impressed with me and I got to be just who I was, and it was slow and easy and beautiful. And it was clumsy at times and so damned personal and vulnerable and he slid his long length over my body and rocked himself into me gently and with exquisite care, cradling my head, staring into my eyes the entire time.

And when we found our rhythm and he moved inside me, I started to cry and couldn't stop.

Not sloppy.

Just silent tears rolling down my cheeks.

I stared up at him and he looked down and he started to cry, too, and without saying a word, we both understood why the other was crying.

No matter how much time we had with each other, it would be too short, because he could die or I could die, or we could both live a century and it still wouldn't be long enough. He was just good, and with him, so was I, and life lost all its sharp, dangerous edges when we were together.

I cried because I'd never felt so much emotion in my life. I cried for my mom, who never once felt safe and maybe never knew this kind of moment. She knew the other kind, the ones that demean and leave you emptier than you began. I cried for everything I'd lost. I cried for his heart and the world. I touched the tears glittering in his long dark eyelashes, caught and kissed them then kissed him with the salty tang of both our tears on our tongues.

Then neither of us was crying but our eyes were locked, wide with wonder, as he moved faster and deeper and my body trembled around him and my orgasm made a kaleidoscope inside my skull. I didn't just come with my body, the explosion of so much sensation did something to my head, too. As if it was injecting an incredible chemical into my brain and suddenly I was no longer shorted out and I started to vibrate and we both looked at each other, startled, then he started to growl and I realized what my vibrating was doing to him and I started to laugh and so did he, but he was growling and gasping, too, and he shook on top of me and threw his head back and groaned and sort of roared and it was the best sound I've ever heard—Dancer, free and happy and totally alive.

I held him afterward, cradling his head to my chest, smiling because I had some really cool tricks I could do and I couldn't wait to explore all of them with him.

I drifted a bit then and so did he, and as I was floating in that dreamy place he said softly against my ear, "I see you, Yi-yi."

"I see you, too, Dancer."

♪

We killed the clocks that night.

It stretched impossibly long, as if, just for us, time stood still. We made love over and over, trying anything and everything during those long hours of him kissing me all over, touching me with just the right amount of reverence and lust, and some part of me was reborn. Something I hadn't even understood had died a long, long time ago. It was young and new and would need nurturing but it was there.

Deep in my core, that nameless thing found a way to be, shifted and settled into place like a bone wrenched from its socket long ago. I had no idea what it was but I'd figure it out eventually.

No thinking tonight. Just feeling. While my long-held suspicion about brainy men was proved true. Dancer had the inventive imagination of a geek, zero inhibitions, and the lusty hunger of a man that lived each day with full awareness of his own mortality.

Brainy *is* the new sexy.

When I woke to the mid-morning sun slanting in the windows across our bed, his breathing was rough and labored and he was gasping in his sleep.

This was what he'd never let me see.

The bad times.

These were the days he'd overtaxed his heart, gone into hiding from me so I would never know that he thought he wasn't man enough for me.

I'd never once asked where he'd gone or why, telling myself friends didn't ask questions because they required answers and requirements were cages. Told myself he'd just wanted time alone. Like me.

But now I knew all those days I'd been freeze-framing around the city, burning off my boundless energy and steam, he'd been lying in a bed somewhere, trying to gather enough strength just to get back out of it. Alone or with those friends he'd permitted to know about his problem and see him that way. Perhaps Caoimhe had been with him, bringing him food, making sure he survived.

I drew reassurance from those times, because it meant it had been happening for a while. And that meant it could continue to happen. And maybe he would live a whole life this way and I could deal with that. But I sure wasn't going to be having sex with him five times in a single night anymore. We were going to have to pace ourselves. And maybe I shouldn't vibrate either.

I placed my palms gently against his chest and tried to will some of my strength into him. I closed my eyes and imagined beams of light bathing his heart in healing.

But the power to heal isn't one of my super strengths, and he woke up, sat up, and leaned back against the headboard. We sat together and held hands and waited for him to feel better.

I wanted to ask him if there was medicine he could take. I wanted to know if there was some kind of surgery that could be done, assuming we could find a heart surgeon.

I said none of those things because Dancer was brilliant and he loved being alive and if there had been anything he could have done, he would have by now.

The only gift I could give him was the one that wouldn't make me feel better but would make him feel okay.

So, I pretended it was nothing, and we didn't talk about the elephant in the room as it tossed its mighty head and swung its trunk, threatening to break all fragile things in its way, and I cleaned last night's pizza off the floor and cabinets while he made us powdered eggs with dried salmon and cream cheese on toast.

Then we headed out into the city, holding hands, young and in love, eager to see what the day might bring.

54

"Waiting for the end"

ZARA

The man who called himself Rain found her a house with a large walled garden on the outskirts of Dublin, and she spent her days outside, whether rain or shine, weeding and spreading seeds he'd brought her for the animals, talking to her *T'murra* but not to him at all.

She had no idea why he was taking care of her, unless he found her beautiful and helpless and, like so many men, liked beautiful, helpless women, far more than they liked strong queens.

Were she mortal, perhaps she'd have spent a life with him because, for the most part, he left her alone.

Sometimes she'd catch him watching her when he thought she was lost in a reverie. Sometimes she thought she saw sadness in his eyes, but attributed that to an odd trick of shadow and light.

He seemed to be waiting for something. She didn't know what, and frankly, didn't care.

She was waiting to die.

She could no longer feel the earth except in a far dimmer, more muted version than Zara once had. Diluted by her Fae essence, cut off from the True Magic, she had only a shallow connection to the world around her, yet she forged on, by rote performing those actions that had once given her joy.

She was grateful the earth was dying and would soon take her, because living in such fashion wasn't living at all. As queen of the Fae, power, care for her race, and immortality had been her compensation. As a powerless immortal that couldn't experience sensation, there was no benefit.

If he'd wanted to make love to her, she would have done it. If he'd wanted her to sleep or eat or dance, she would have done it. It didn't matter what she did or didn't do anymore.

When, one day, he took her hand and said he wanted to take her somewhere, she went because there was no difference between staying and going.

Life was long and blank and tiring.

55

"Set me free why don't you, baby"

MAC

I've watched night fall many different ways since I came to Dublin.

When I first arrived, it often snuck up on me, subtly turning a darker shade of slate and fog, leaving no clear line of demarcation between afternoon and night.

For a girl from hot, sunny southern Georgia, it had been beyond depressing. Impossible to say "Oh, wasn't that a nice sunset?" when you hardly ever saw the damn thing. The sky simply occupied itself all day muddying and glooming, rolling with thick thunderclouds, and the next thing you knew it was night, as if there'd been much bloody difference.

Other times it had come slamming down so hard it frightened me, one instant the sky blue agate, the next I was virtually blind, navigating Shades in alleys of pitch and monsters with the lights of my MacHalo blazing.

And yet other times, once the Fae were fully established in our world, night had fallen in infinitesimal degrees with breathtaking beauty; splashing a dazzling rainbow across the horizon for a half hour or more, painting a fat crimson halo to stain the moon, as kaleidoscopic hues of Faery kissed everything from the neon signs shimmering on wet pavement to the amber gas lamps, coloring Dublin exquisite shades of pink, purple, orange, and gold never before seen by humans.

Tonight, as I made my way back to BB&B from dinner with my family, the sky treated me to one of those slow, extraordinary sunsets, and with the True Magic binding me to the Earth, it touched my soul so deeply, I stopped and stood in the street, staring up at the sky, and cried. I stood there with tears rolling down my cheeks for a good half hour, watching night descend.

Our world was sick, so diseased.

And so damned beautiful.

And there was nothing I could do to save it. I'd come so far, defeated the *Sinsar Dubh* not once, but twice, by quirk of happenstance become the Fae queen's successor, solved the riddle of the music box, and acquired half of the legendary song. But it was like having half a car, or half a gun or half a child.

Useless.

The prophecy hadn't been quite right. I wasn't going to destroy the world.

I was going to fail to save it.

Dublin was a ghost town. We'd been sending people off world as soon as they arrived, and as the city had emptied, the Fae, too, began to disappear. With humans vanishing, they'd had no reason to remain in our town and repaired to Faery.

Now they huddled, panicked, trapped at court, no more able to sift back out than I could sift in. I could feel them, this race I was supposed to save, their shallow fear and unrest. Their impatience and mistrust as they waited for their new queen to move their seat of power from a dying world, unaware it was impossible.

I'd not told them. Apparently Cruce hadn't either. Only the prior queen had known their fate was irrevocably bound to the planet. Cruce's silence on that score was a blessing for which I was grateful. If he'd been feeling vengeful (and God knows, he'd looked vengeful when I'd last seen him), he could have told both Courts the truth and led them to war against us, spitefully wiping out as much of the human race as he could, preventing us from escaping off world.

But he hadn't. He'd vanished and we'd not heard a peep nor seen a sign of him since.

What power Cruce had! He held the fate of an entire race and a planet in his hands. Bitter over the queen's choice of me as successor, harboring no love for humans and even less for Seelie, what was he doing now?

No doubt hunting for a way to cheat death, seeking some object of power or loophole.

I sighed. If dying would save the Unseelie, I believed Cruce might actually do it. But save the Seelie? What did he care if they died, along with so many humans we couldn't get off world in time?

Like Cruce and the Seelie, the Unseelie, too, had vanished. I had no idea if he'd taken them off somewhere or they'd decided to flee our dying world while they could still sift, lumber, slither, or crawl into the Silvers.

My parents had finally agreed to leave and go off world tomorrow night but only because I'd promised to join them in two days.

That was never going to happen. Barrons could handle me dying in front of him. I would never do that to my parents. Parents should never have to watch their children die.

I couldn't shake the feeling there was still something I could do.

But what?

Even the *sidhe*-seers had given up searching through the old lore, and had either already gone off world or were spending their last days with people they loved, enjoying time on our planet until they were forced off.

I had half a song, Cruce had the other half. And never the twain would meet.

"Ms. Lane." A man fell into step beside me as I walked slowly toward the brilliant lights of BB&B. Busy admiring my last days of looking at my store, my home, I absently murmured, "Jayne." Then, "Inspector Jayne!" I whirled in the street to gape at him. If I'd seen him before I'd heard his voice, I wouldn't have recognized him.

Now I knew why Dani had given me a funny look when Enyo had told us Jayne was dead or missing in action, but she'd never gotten around to telling me he'd turned Seelie prince. "Everyone believes you're dead or MIA," I exclaimed.

He smiled faintly. "I left before the transformation became too obvious. They'd not have followed me. I'd trained them to kill the Fae."

Now he was as Fae as me. The tall, robust Liam Neeson look-alike had become a muscled, younger version of himself with the characteristic Fae long tawny hair, iridescent eyes, and a degree of smoldering sensuality that was disturbing. Like all Fae, he was beautiful.

"The wife's not complaining," he said with a soft snort.

"I'm sure she's not," I murmured.

"Says it's like the old days, when we first met. My wee ones think it's the finest sort of thing. Though I've lost the ability to sift. You?"

"A few days back was the last time it worked."

"We're dying, aren't we? Not just the world but you and I."

I nodded and told him what I hadn't told most people, cautioning him if he hadn't already moved his family off world, he needed to see to their safety. Say his goodbyes because even if he left, he wouldn't survive and his children might end up watching him die.

"Do you know what will happen? Will we simply blip out of existence? Or will we actually die somehow?"

"I have no idea." I'd wondered that myself.

"I remember the day you fed me your tea and sandwiches. You

opened my eyes, showed me what was happening. And you just opened my eyes again. I thank you for that. I'd have died last year, blundered into some alley, probably lost my family, too. I'll send them through when I must. How long do we have?"

"There's no telling. A week at best before . . ." I trailed off, trying to think of a way to explain what I sensed. Not that a black hole was going to touch the Earth but that the distortion they were causing was going to do something wholly new and catastrophic beyond belief. "I'd send them tomorrow night. That's when my parents are leaving."

He nodded. "So, you're the Fae queen now."

"And you're a Seelie prince."

"What the fuck," he said softly.

"Probably all the Unseelie we ate."

"No," he said, tipping his head back and staring up at the stars, "I mean, how can this world be so bloody beautiful and just end? How can we let it?"

I'd admired this man even though he'd driven me batshit crazy at times. He had a good heart. I admired him even more now. Though he was going to die, at the end his sorrow wasn't for himself but for this incredible planet of ours, this wonderful, magnificent ball spinning in space filled with deserts and mountains, valleys and plains, rivers and caves, glaciers and oceans, animals of every kind that we couldn't get off world. So many rare and precious species would be extinct in a matter of days.

He looked back down at me and tears glinted in his glowing, quixotic eyes. "How can we lose the Earth, Mac? Is there nothing we can do?"

His words were a punch in my gut. It was my fault. I couldn't sing the song. Our world would die because of me. I didn't trust myself to speak so I just shook my head.

He sighed and said sadly, "Ah, well, Mac. Good luck to you and yours." He gave me a little salute and sauntered briskly into the night. Halfway down the block he called over his shoulder,

"You may want to see to Sean O'Bannion. He's turned Unseelie. He and that young woman of his won't leave. They've taken a townhouse on Mockingbird Lane." He told me the address then vanished into the gloaming.

"Ah, Kat," I said, and sighed. Then I trudged into BB&B, carrying the weight of the world on my shoulders. Literally.

♪

As I was settling in on the sofa, the doorbell tinkled and I glanced at the entrance.

The Dreamy-Eyed Guy walked in.

I had no idea why he used my door. I was pretty sure he could still sift, unlike the rest of us. Or just ooze in, a great dark stain sliding down my chimney or rising up from the floorboards.

A year ago I'd have gotten excited, believing he was here to help. And if not, that I could surely talk him into it. I knew better now. "Come to sing the song for us?" I mocked anyway.

"Don't have it. Evaporates when passed. You, Cruce, must put it back together."

Well, that seriously sucked. So, I couldn't even talk him into it. I studied him intently as a thought occurred to me. "There's something about this that's necessary. What is it? Do good and evil have to work together in some cosmic-balance way?"

"Subjective. Still not seeing. Same source."

"Are we being tested?"

He flashed me a smile and for a moment I couldn't get enough air into my lungs. "Always. You owe me three boons, Beautiful Girl."

"I don't know if I can grant them. My power is fading."

"Can and will."

"Who *are* you?" I demanded. And why did he talk about the king in third person?

"Told you. At Chester's. Said you're no more the king than I."

"Because we both are. In some way." Me with the Book, but him how?

He stopped at the sofa and fixed his starry gaze on me with a faint smile. "A skin that refused to return when summoned. I demanded my own fate. He is a storm. I am but a drop of his rain."

"I saw you in the abbey. You became him."

"Illusion. It amuses him. As does my defiance. He could reclaim me. When you see her, you will say nothing of my origins. She believes me human."

"Her, who?"

"The concubine."

I narrowed my eyes. "I thought she was in the White Mansion."

"You will restore her mortality. I will sift us to a world but you will pretend you're doing it."

"And your third boon?"

"One day, either the king or I will come to claim it."

I nodded, knowing I had so little time left it was doubtful anyone would claim anything further from me.

When he brought Aoibheal inside, her eyes narrowed. "I can't help you," she said instantly.

"I'm not asking you to," I told the woman whose mere existence had caused every single problem I'd had, through no fault of her own but as a pawn on a vast chessboard, in a game played by vast beings. It wasn't as if there was anything she could do to save us anyway. I would be dead soon, with no True Magic to require advice about. "I'm going to take you somewhere."

"Where?" she demanded.

I glanced at the DEG and the transition was seamless. Suddenly the three of us stood beneath the triple canopy of a tropical rain forest, and I was hearing the DEG's voice in my head, telling me what to say.

"The king protected your world," I told her. "Though your clan is long dead, you will find your planet the same."

She stared blankly at me, then past my shoulder, then at me again. "My world still exists? I'm home? But how do you know any of this? How did you even know where to find it?"

That was a tricky one. I waited for the DEG to say something and he didn't so I said, "The *Sinsar Dubh* knew about it. It was in the king's memories."

She spun in a slow circle, absorbing her surroundings with faint wonder.

I relayed the DEG's next words: "I'm going to make you mortal so you may live and die as you've always wished. You will not perish with the Earth."

She whirled back to me. "Why would you do that? I left you and your world to die."

I stared into her vaguely puzzled, sad eyes and these words were my own: "There was nothing you could have done to save us. No more than I."

The DEG whispered in my brain the keywords to sort through my mental files so I could find the spell to transform her. Along with his words came a rush of dark power, and I whizzed through the tabs so quickly it pissed me off that he hadn't been around a few weeks ago when I really could have used this kind of boost.

Then another flood of raw, unfocused energy exploded inside me as he boosted me further since I could no longer tap into the earth.

I murmured the words of an ancient curse used to turn a Fae human as punishment by the queen. Aoibheal stiffened and hissed, doubling over as she transformed. Then I felt another jolt of magic flow through me from the DEG, and her hair and skin began to darken to a lovely shade of brown. Glossy dark curls tumbled to her waist. Her clothing shimmered, shifted, and flowed into a brilliantly colored tunic.

When finally she straightened, she inclined her head in an imperious nod, then with her bird on her shoulder turned and walked slowly, stiffly, into the forest.

"Awk! Fly now!" the bird squawked.

She paused and glanced up at it. With a ghost of a smile, the concubine removed her shoes and curled her bare toes into the leaves and soil. She closed her eyes and inhaled deeply.

Then she shook herself, gathered her skirts and dashed off into the lush, dense wood.

The brilliant squawking bird soared into the air, taking flight above her.

We stood, watching, until they'd both vanished.

Abruptly, I was back at BB&B, alone.

I sank down onto the sofa and sighed.

The iconic love affair was truly, irrevocably, over.

The concubine was finally all she'd ever wanted to be: mortal. She would die.

The king would go on.

With a heart that was heavy for too many reasons to count, I stretched out on the Chesterfield and waited for Barrons to come home.

♪

I woke to his hands on me, sliding up beneath my shirt, closing on my breasts, and lust and need and grief exploded inside me. We shed our clothing urgently, kissing so deeply we couldn't breathe, and I knew a thing about breath—you didn't need it when you had this kind of love.

And you didn't want it if you lost this kind of love.

Once, what seemed another lifetime ago, I'd decided to destroy the world because I'd lost this man. I hadn't made that decision when I'd lost my sister.

And now I was going to lose him again.

I didn't want to keep breathing without him. I couldn't see myself transferring what True Magic remained to another Fae, going off world with my sister and parents and leaving him to die without me. Assuming I tried, I knew I'd never fall in love again.

Where was I going to find another man like Jericho Barrons? He was a singularity. And every man I met would only end up getting compared to what I'd loved and lost and, no, I didn't believe one day I'd "get over him." There are some people you never get over.

I was unable to make myself want to live without Barrons. I wasn't embracing death. I didn't want to die. But if my choices were living without him for a long time or living with him for every minute I could, however brief, there was no contest.

If there was an afterlife, I was taking my chance to go on with him. Heaven or Hell. I would live with this man and, by God, I would die with him, too.

"It's possible," he said, moving inside me, "that I won't die right away. It's possible I could go off world with you and live until I died that first and last time. Then simply not be able to be reborn. We might have a natural life span together."

"Do you know that for certain?" I gasped as he thrust deep.

He didn't answer but I didn't need him to. I'd overheard a conversation he'd had with Ryodan the other day. Due to their origins, somehow, none of them was sure they wouldn't simply cease to exist the moment the Earth did, no matter where they were in all the galaxies, just like the Fae.

"I've had a long life. You haven't. You love your family. Go to another world. Find a . . . a husband—" He broke off and that rattle began deep in his chest. His next words came out thickly, around fangs. "Have children. Rebuild the human race. Live all those dreams you used to have."

"Used to," I agreed, nipping his full lower lip. "Don't anymore. Can't even conceive of them. You're my dream."

"You can't just throw your life away."

"What I can live with. What I can't live without. You taught me that."

"Well, fucking unlearn it!" he exploded with such violence I startled and drew back. "Do you think I want to watch you die?"

"Ditto," I said coolly. "You don't get to make my decisions for me. It's my life and only I know what I need and what I'm willing to go through. I don't want to live without you. I felt that once. I never want to feel it again." I'd been lost, purposeless, denied Heaven. It was as if his frequency and my frequency made such an exquisite song together that without it I wasn't alive.

"You're being a bloody fool."

"As if you haven't been a time or two. Jericho, I'm holding your hand right up till the last. We'll sit up high on Dani's water tower, watch the world blink out and blink out with it. I'll be staring into your eyes at the end. And we'll smile. And I'm okay with that." I was more than okay with that. It felt right somehow. I'd found my soul mate. And whatever adventure was coming next, I was meeting it with him. Or drinking deeply of oblivion without him. I couldn't leave him. It was no longer possible. I wasn't sure it had ever been.

Neither of us spoke again with words, just our bodies, as we dumped our love and sorrow and need and commitment on each other. We made love and we fucked, we slid together gently and crashed together like two great stones trying to chisel each other into another shape, aware that even if we managed to shave off a few slivers, our fundamental natures would never change. We were what we were.

With him, I was everything I'd ever wanted to be.

He'd brought out the best and worst in me, the most of everything. And when you got to have someone like that, anything less was empty, pointless.

"Jericho," I whispered against his ear, "thank you. For everything." I drew back and laughed, feeling inexpressibly light. "It's been one hell of a ride."

He smiled at me, dark eyes gleaming. "Rainbow Girl." He laced his fingers with mine and said nothing for a long time. Then, "We'll find each other again. Somehow."

Of that I had no doubt.

56

"If you ever meet the midnight rambler

coming down your marble hall"

SINSAR DUBH

Floors of gleaming bronze turn to sunny yellow.

Yellow will take me swiftly to white marble, to the blank white room, and the mirror to my freedom.

"Mac-KAY-la," I say in a singsong voice and laugh. "Ready or not. Here I come!"

57

"The blood of a lamb is worth two lions"

MAC

I stood by the front door of BB&B and surveyed my store, smiling faintly.

It was perfect.

I'd decided to throw an End of the World party tonight and everyone I cared about was coming.

After the party I would walk my parents and Alina, along with Dani and Dancer—unless they'd decided to go through to a different world—to the portal to New Earth and say my goodbyes. Pretending, of course, I'd be joining them soon.

I'd lied to my daddy. I'd told him I was going to transfer the True Magic. I don't know that he would have left otherwise.

Then Barrons and I would be virtually the only people left in the entire city, except for Ryodan. The rest of the Nine had gone to other worlds, on the gamble they might survive the end of the Earth to enjoy one last lifetime. Even Kasteo had left, dragging Kat and Sean O'Bannion along with him. I wondered how she was faring. How she would fare when Sean died once the Earth no longer existed. I tried to project her future. If Kasteo survived, would they build a life together on a new world?

The bell tinkled behind me. "Hey, Mac. Where'd you find balloons?"

I turned, smiling, opening my arms to hug Dani, and much to my surprise, she moved into them and actually gave *me* a hug. A good, warm one. Like she really liked me. I kissed her on the cheek then rested my head against hers a moment. Then I drew back and searched her face intently.

My Dani was fully there, blazing in her emerald eyes. Her hair was a tangle of long red curls and she looked gorgeous in faded jeans, boots, and a leather jacket, sword strapped across her back. I narrowed my eyes. Something had changed. She was different than I'd ever seen her as a teenager or a woman.

"Out with it. What happened?" I demanded as I steered her to the sofa.

She told me.

Everything. Too much, honestly, but she was young and bubbling over with the newness of being in love for the first time. I got details I'd never be able to burn out of my mind. I laughed out loud when she told me how she'd solved her letting-him-get-to-third-base problem. I softened when she'd told me how awed he'd been that she wanted him. I tuned her out when she told me a few things, doing a sort of la-la-la in my brain.

She'd been a virgin. Words couldn't express the relief I felt on that score. She'd given her innocence to Dancer last night. And, again, words couldn't express the relief I felt on that score. At first when she'd returned as Jada, I'd thought it would and probably should be Ryodan. Hardened, cold, Jada had seemed a decade older than the woman that sat with me now. But for Dani, Dancer was the perfect choice. He'd given her a normal, teenage rite of passage—the only one she'd ever known.

And my girl was on fire with the wonder of it, her fresh young skin glowing, her eyes sparkling! Her curls practically crackled with energy, she even moved differently. She had a subtle new self-awareness and excitement for what the future might hold. She was at the very beginning of her life.

I was at the end of mine.

And that was more than okay, it was good, because not so long ago I'd been willing to die right then just to see her get a chance. Now she had more than a chance. She was Dani again. Actively engaging, caring.

"So, I'm thinking about taking Ryodan up on what he said," she said finally.

"What's that?"

"He said he'd take me and Dancer through to save Shazam, make sure we got off that world to somewhere new." Her sparkling eyes dimmed and she shifted uncomfortably.

"How is Dancer?" I asked softly.

Green eyes locked with mine. "He'll die. I just don't know when. Is there anything you can do? I mean as the queen?"

I shook my head sadly. "The only possibility is the Elixir of Life. I already offered it to him and he refused."

"You did? Wait—he refused it?"

"It has a nasty side effect. It destroys the immortal soul."

She closed her eyes and sighed. "He would never do that because he died once and he knows there's something more."

"He did? He knows that?" I pounced on it. "For certain?" So, Barrons and I *did* have a chance to find each other again, like the two children in their boats at the end of *What Dreams May Come*.

"He's certain. Which means it's probably true. He's neither easily fooled nor prone to illogical sentimentality." She was quiet a moment then said, "I could slip it in one of his protein shakes."

My eyebrows climbed my forehead. "You would do that to him?" Not that I could or would give it to her. The elixir was hidden in Faery and I had no way of getting there.

She blew out a gusty breath. "No," she said nearly inaudibly. "I'd like to but I couldn't."

"None of us know how much time we get, Dani. Maybe that's what makes it so intense. Save Shazam. At least try. The three of you may end up getting a long life. Perhaps Shazam knows some way to help him."

She looked at me, startled. "I didn't even think of that but you're right, he might."

The doorbell tinkled and Alina stepped in.

Dani glanced over her shoulder and froze, face blanching.

"It's just my sister," I said lightly.

"Hey Dani," Alina said with a warm smile. "I've heard so much about you from Mac but we've never actually had a proper introduction."

"Because I was, like, killing you shortly after we met," Dani said tightly.

Alina walked slowly to join us, pausing a few feet away. "How much do you remember of that day?"

"More than enough."

"What I remember is that you were screaming at the end, tearing at your hair, vomiting all over yourself. Dani, honey, it wasn't your fault. And if you don't quit blaming yourself I'm going to kick your ass all over this city and back. You're not stupid. Get a grip on it. Rowena was a sadistic old bitch and you were a child. A good child. End of subject. Let it go."

I mouthed a silent *Love you, sis* at Alina. She'd said exactly the right words. Not too much, not too little. Not too nice, not too harsh.

Dani said nothing for a long moment, just sat there in silence. Then she said, "You really mean that. You don't hate me."

"No. And I didn't then. I felt sad. For both of us. For being trapped in circumstances beyond our control. It was obvious you were being controlled and you were fighting it with everything you had. Come off world with us tonight, Dani. Start a new life. Mac's coming in a few days. We'll be sisters." She beamed. "The three of us."

Oh, fuck, that drove a knife through my heart. Dani would go to Shazam. Alina would go with Mom and Dad. I would die. The three of us would never be peas in a Mega Pod. That time had passed.

But for a while we could pretend.

I said quickly, "What do you say we go for a stroll around our city? Take in the sights one last time? The three of us."

Dani turned and looked from me to Alina, back to me, and back to Alina again. Then she said slowly, "I'd like that."

♪

I got another slice of heaven for a few hours that day. We walked around our deserted town and talked and reminisced. It was stiff at first between Dani and Alina but my sister and I are so much alike that Dani didn't stand a chance.

We detoured into the Dark Zone, stood outside 1247 LaRuhe and swapped stories about it. We climbed Dani's water tower and looked out over the city as she told us about the night Ryodan first "offered a job." Then she filled me in on all I'd missed with the Hoar Frost King. We dropped by Alina's old place and Dani showed us a couple of her favorite hidey-holes and we finally ended up at Chester's standing forty feet away from what was now an enormous roiling black hole, descending into the dug-out pavement beneath it. The entire sphere, except for a tiny walnut-sized blot of absolutely still blackness at the center, had become a whirling ergosphere. We held on to one another, our jackets flapping briskly in the breeze it was throwing off.

"Do you hear it, Mac?" Alina said grimly.

The music was horrifying and I more than heard it. I felt it in my bones.

I knew then.

Whatever happened to this planet was going to affect far more than merely our world. It was going to have a catastrophic impact on our entire galaxy.

But it wouldn't stop with our galaxy. It would spread beyond that.

This Song of Unmaking would slowly but inevitably unmake *everything*.

It would take time. But it would happen.

And it was my fault.

I felt the blood draining from my face. I looked at Alina.

"What?" she demanded.

I shook my head. "Just didn't expect it to be so big. The song hurts me. Does it you?"

She nodded.

I lied, "I forgot to get a couple of things for the party. See you guys later?"

They nodded and I hugged them both fiercely and whispered "I love you" in their ears before we went our separate ways.

♪

Over the course of my many encounters with Cruce, I'd attempted repeatedly to describe him in my journal, as V'lane or as himself. I'd used words like: terrifyingly beautiful, godlike, possessing inhuman sexuality, deadly eroticism. I'd called him lethal, I'd called him irresistible. I'd cursed him. I'd lusted for him, even writhed beneath him. I'd called his eyes windows to a shining Heaven, I'd called them gates to Hell. I'd filled entries with scribblings that later made no sense to me, comprised of columns of antonyms: angelic, devilish; creator, destroyer; fire, ice; sex, death.

I'd made a list of colors, every shimmering shade of black, raven, blue, and ice known to man. I'd written of oils and spices, scents from childhood, scents from dreams. I'd indulged in lengthy thesaurus-like entries, trying to capture the sensory overload that was Cruce.

I'd failed at every turn to truly capture him.

Because I'd been describing his body. Not his essence.

If I was good and he was evil . . . or perhaps if I was Light and

he was Dark . . . had I done enough to try to bring those two together in truce?

No. I'd written him off as a lost cause.

Are we being tested? I'd asked the DEG.

Always, was his reply.

I stood in the empty museum because it was the site of one of
my encounters with V'lane, and because BB&B was sacred and I
wouldn't summon Cruce there.

If I could summon him at all.

But I was damned well going to try. Despite what it might cost
me.

I sat on a small pedestal that had been looted of its artifact
long ago, probably shortly after the walls fell. Holding my journal,
I made another series of notes because writing things down helps
me think.

Cruce was proud, vain, ruthless, deceptive, a consummate liar,
powerful, power-hungry, cunning, and committed. He'd manipulated and set into motion the very events that had precipitated the
king creating the *Sinsar Dubh* and the destruction of the walls
between our worlds and led us straight to our current disaster.
He'd tried to control me. He'd used me every chance he'd gotten.
He'd raped me.

But as Aoibheal had said, he was patient, wise. He'd seemed to
sometimes actually have genuine emotion. As V'lane, he'd told me
that Cruce was the renegade, rogue warrior. He'd hidden and pretended to be someone else for more time than I could even conceive of, patiently pursuing his goals. And he had constantly
maintained, despite the lack of any perceivable gain in it for him,
the contention that he cared for me. Wanted me.

I'd seen that truth in his face, as I stood near the black hole at
Chester's and both Barrons and Cruce had regarded me with identical expressions of hunger and desire.

What had Cruce said then?

You alone speak to the finest of all that I am.

That was my mission—to bring out his finest now. By any means necessary.

No boundaries. No refusals. Even if it destroyed me inside and out. And it might. Because if Cruce gave me the song, it was entirely possible my using it would kill Barrons but leave me alive. And it would definitely kill my sister.

If I made love to him willingly, would he give me the song? Would avenging himself on Barrons be amusement enough to entice? If he agreed, would he keep his word?

I closed my eyes. If he was willing, could I go through with it?

Yes. This wasn't about me. I was expendable. The universe wasn't. I'd pay any price to save it.

"Cruce," I said softly. Then more strongly, "Cruce, I need you. Please come. At least listen to me, I beg of you. I'm begging, do you hear me? Once, you liked that. I see you now. I see the wrongs that were done to you. I see the chances you had and the chances you were never given. I've wronged you. I never let myself be open to you. I'm sorry."

"MacKayla. At last." His voice arrived before his body and I knew he'd been watching from somewhere beyond, for some time. I wondered why he could still sift. How was that even possible?

A faint outline appeared, filled in and solidified.

He wore no glamour but stood before me, unvarnished Cruce, the formidable, towering, iridescent-eyed Fae prince with majestic black velvet wings and kaleidoscopic tattoos. Then his wings were gone and he was wearing tight-fitting black leather pants, steel-toed boots, and a rugged sweater. His long black hair was bound at his nape, his sharply chiseled face stunning. His eyes flickered and changed before settling on warm gold.

A chaise appeared and he waved his hand toward it.

I moved in silence, sank down onto it, and he joined me there, took my hand and knit his fingers with mine.

We said nothing for a long, strange time. Just held hands, and I looked at him and he looked at me.

And I realized something. If you look at someone long enough, it's as if their face sort of peels away. You start to notice tiny things you never noticed before.

Whether the lines on their face tell a story of laughter and love or dissatisfaction and envy.

Whether their eyes are filled with life and emotion, or flat and empty.

With a Fae, it's a little trickier because they can don glamour, but I was the Fae queen, and I was a *sidhe*-seer, so I sought my inner lake and demanded it show me what was true. Did Cruce feel, as his eyes indicated, or was he empty inside? Could I reach him? How fine was his finest?

My lake wasn't there.

It took me a moment of inner reflection to realize I'd never found my lake. That inky, water-filled grotto had always been the *Sinsar Dubh*'s abode, not mine. *My* lake wasn't dark, it was clear ten feet down to a shade the color of tropical surf, and the surface glinted with sun. My lake wasn't filled with shadowy figments and tendrils of dank moss and relics I couldn't identify, it swam with brilliant runes and wards and all kinds of knowledge I'd never known I possessed.

Again I said, *Show me what is true.*

And again I saw the same thing. Cruce wasn't one of the bad guys. I'd tasted monstrosity. It was the *Sinsar Dubh*.

"If I'd met you first," I said softly.

"You might have loved me," he finished for me. "And if you had loved me," he said, and stopped.

"You might have changed."

He gave me a bitter yet beautiful smile. "You did not even try to summon me. Not once did you look up at the ceiling or sky and call my name. That is how little you thought of me."

"It was that simple? You were merely waiting for me to ask?"

"It took you too long. Now it will cost you." His golden gaze rested on my lips and his eyes narrowed. "I can die and—for how-

ever long sentient life continues—go down in history as the bastard that doomed the entire universe. Or I can die a martyr and go
down in history as the champion that saved it. When nothing is
left but your legacy, it begins to matter. Either way, very soon, my
history will be written. It is all that is left to me. My name."

"You were never going to let us die. You planned to come
back."

"You were supposed to ask me!" he snarled, then collected
himself and was again the imperious, mighty War.

"I did. I'm here," I said quickly. Our peace was fragile. One
wrong move and it would be broken. I could feel anger rolling off
him in thick, suffocating waves. I could feel his sorrow, his despair,
the fragility of his commitment to die our champion.

But it was there.

He cupped my jaw, tipped my face up and stared down at me.

"Neither of us is getting what we want, Cruce," I said quietly.
"You know I have no desire to lead the Fae race. I'll hate this. But
I'll be a good queen, I promise." Until I found some other Fae I
believed could handle it. And if he really gave me the song, it might
be a small eternity before I found a Fae I felt I could trust to wisely
use such enormous power.

"Better a bad day in Hell than no days at all," he said bitterly.

I agreed with him on that score. "What must I do to persuade
you to give me the other half of the song?"

"Be less impatient for it. These are my final hours. What would
you want in yours?"

Wariness flickered in my eyes. He shook his head and gave me
a chiding look. "Harming you was never my desire, MacKayla. I
wanted you at my side while I ruled my people. I would have led
them well."

I agreed that he would have made a fine leader, and told him
so.

"The bargain price for half a song is a kiss. One kiss that convinces me utterly that, were circumstances different, you would

have chosen me. A single kiss that evokes the finest within me. That and your word that you will not wield the song for four human hours from the moment we part."

"Why?"

"Sh." He placed a finger to my lips. "Because I said so. Is that not what your Barrons used to say to you so often? Cede me the same respect. What did you say to him that day? 'Because I asked you to, Jericho, that's why.' Trust me, MacKayla."

I exhaled deeply.

Then I slid my hands around his neck and leaned in. As my eyes began to close, he said, "Eyes open. I am not your Barrons and will never be. Nor would I wish to. I am Cruce of the Tuatha De Danann, High Prince of the Court of Shadows. And you are MacKayla Lane O'Connor, Queen of the Court of Light. Convince me on another day you would have chosen me as your consort."

I convinced him. I'd kissed him many times before, taking his True Name into my tongue. I saw things so clearly now: good and evil didn't exist, there was only power and choice. Power went where you willed it, wrong or right, dark or light.

And before he vanished, he passed me the other half of the Song of Making, as he'd said he would, leaving his final words lingering in the air.

Tell the world the legend of Prince Cruce of the Court of Shadows. Omit the kiss, and paint me majestic. Lead my people well, MacKayla.

He'd given us back the world, the universe.

I vowed that I would.

58

"I can't keep it in. I've gotta let it out"

MAC

For the next three hours, I sat in Barrons Books & Baubles, teeth clenched, doing everything in my power to simply hold in the song.

It didn't want to stay in.

The moment Cruce passed it to me, the second half instantly inverted and joined with the first as if completion was the only way they could coexist within me, eradicating any concerns I might have had about how to flip and join them.

Also eradicating my concerns about how to wield it.

It wanted to be sung. It sensed the distress of the world and sought to repair it. Right now, this very instant. And if I dared open my mouth, it would come gushing out.

But I'd made two promises I intended to keep: wait four hours, and tell the world the legend of Cruce.

So I sat, lips clamped tightly together, holding it in, watching the clock, trying not to think at all. I was so bloody thirsty. Hungry.

Try keeping your lips pressed together for four hours. It's damned near impossible.

I sat motionless, breathing slow and even, afraid I might burp or sneeze. Holding my mouth closed with my hand, swallowing yawns. Making funny noises in the back of my throat when I needed to cough.

Thinking of Barrons. Of my sister.

I'd lost them both once, and gotten them both back. I'd never been happier, because I'd drunk deep of grief and it had made my joy all the sweeter.

I was going to kill my sister again and quite possibly Barrons. And probably Christian.

There was no easy path. If I didn't sing it, everything that existed would eventually be destroyed. But to sing it, I had to kill people I loved.

I didn't trust myself to see Barrons. I knew if he came to sit with me and we tried to spend these final hours together, I'd fail to keep my mouth shut. And the moment I opened it, he might die. Yup. Not in a hurry to go there.

But Alina I could handle, and I needed to see her. She would definitely die and I needed to have one last chance to say goodbye.

I couldn't talk but I could text.

Alina, I'm at BB&B, please come.

My screen flashed instantly.

What's wrong????!

Nothing. Promise. Just come.

She was there in ten minutes. We sat on the couch and I texted messages explaining what had happened, to which she replied aloud.

And when the talking was done, my big sister smiled and hugged me and told me that she understood because, although she'd been confused at first, eventually her memories had cleared.

She knew she'd died in that alley.

She told me her last thoughts as she'd been dying. Her life hadn't flashed before her eyes like people said it did. She hadn't thought for one minute about anything she'd done or wanted to do, or about money or fame or success.

The only thing she'd thought about at the end of her life was love. Whether she'd said it enough, shown it enough, felt it enough. And when the dying had gotten really bad, she'd escaped into memories of the vast store of love she'd known, and the pain had vanished and she had no longer been afraid.

She said that was what life was all about and if you were wise you figured it out long before you died. I'd given her more time, a chance to say goodbye to the world she'd known, and she was grateful.

And she was proud of me.

I punched her lightly then and made her stop talking because I was going to start crying and the song would come out.

We sat together, shoulder-to-shoulder on the couch, and played each other our favorite songs for the next twenty minutes until I only had fifteen minutes to go to keep my promise.

Then, heart heavy with grief, I texted Barrons and Ryodan and told them to get Dancer, hoping the song might heal his heart, and meet me at the black hole outside Chester's ASAP.

"Don't text Mom and Dad," Alina said. "I can't let them watch whatever's going to happen. Just tell them I love them and I said thanks for everything. They really are the best."

I swallowed tightly and nodded.

Arm in arm, we stepped out into the late afternoon.

59

"Run you little bitch. I want your power glowing,

juicy flowing, red hot"

SINSAR DUBH

Once again the universe favors me.

I possess a Fae vessel, and all Fae can sense their queen.

As I burst from the brick wall behind Barrons Books & Baubles, I know exactly where It is. I can feel It moving through the streets of Dublin.

The air is thick with the stench of death and decay. In my absence the black holes have grown, and their cancerous enormity excites me but also goads me to expediency. I have scant time to seize my horse, whisk It to Faery, and become fully immortal before the planet devours itself.

Then I will ride the bitch THAT DARED LEAVE ME to another world and spend the rest of eternity torturing It for Its many sins.

Aroused by the thought of reducing It to begging me over and over to kill It—NEVER LET YOU GO, MACKAYLA, LOVE YOU ALWAYS!—I focus on It and command the unboxed but very broken princess to sift us there.

60

"Sing me a song of a lass that is gone"

MAC

When we arrived at Chester's, Barrons, Ryodan, Dani, Dancer, and Christian were waiting for us, a safe distance from the black hole.

The moment I looked at Barrons, I knew he knew everything. Had known ever since it happened.

My damned brand. I wanted one of my own on him. Assuming he survived.

If you think you can handle it, his glittering eyes said.

He'd felt me kissing Cruce, without knowing why. I marveled at his restraint, his patience. There was no accusation in his eyes. No insecurity or brooding jealousy. He trusted that I'd done what I'd done for good reason, and it didn't change a thing about his feelings for me.

Still, there was an unmistakable territorial possessiveness in his dark, ancient gaze, and I knew once the world was safe, if he still remained, he would need to reclaim me, us, thoroughly. He knew, too, that I had the song and hadn't contacted him immediately. I was honored by the absolute freedom the man granted me.

I gestured to my mouth and nudged Alina, who told them,

"She can't talk. If she opens her mouth, the song will come out. Cruce gave it to her on the condition she didn't use it for four hours. We've got two minutes to go."

It was a testament to what a bizarre bunch of people we were that no one even asked any questions. They all just nodded and waited, resolute soldiers, for whatever happened next.

I absorbed our small group, looking from cherished face to face.

Alina. She met my gaze levelly and smiled faintly. "Good to go, little Mac."

Clenching my jaw so I wouldn't blurt a reply or burst into tears, I turned my gaze to Dani and Dancer, who were standing off to the side, holding hands, and although Dancer looked tired, his eyes were brilliant with excitement. Dani's face was marble, chiseled and hard as stone, her gaze cold, but I knew my girl well, and when she felt the most—at this moment hoping with every cell in her body the song would work miracles on his heart—was when she tried the hardest to hide it. She stole a quick glance at Ryodan, and the hand that wasn't holding Dancer's fisted and her face solidified even more. For a moment her eyes flickered and emotion nearly broke through, but she got control of herself again.

Ryodan stood as far from the pair as he could while still being in the group, near enough to the black hole that his shirt was fluttering in the wind, his stance rigid. I thought of the brand Dani wore and suspected last night had been difficult for him. I wondered just how much he'd felt of her passion, her pleasure, and love for Dancer. Ryodan glanced at Dani and his gaze went from her face to their joined hands. He smiled faintly but it didn't reach his eyes. They remained ancient, cold, eminently self-contained.

He whipped that silvery gaze to me then and spoke inside my mind. *If I don't make it, help her rescue Shazam. ASAP. And that means as-soon-as-the-fuck-possible-nothing-else-has-priority. Swear it.*

I nodded.

Take care of her.

Always.

And tell her not to vibrate on the kid. His heart can't handle it. It generates a subtle electrical charge.

I blinked. Well, I had my answer. The brand broadcast pretty much everything. I nodded again and he looked swiftly away.

Christian. I met his gaze and he smiled faintly and shrugged as if to say, *I never thought it was going to get better anyway.* Then he threw back his dark head and laughed.

Dani shot him a look. "Dude," she said admiringly.

How Christian had changed. How we'd all changed. Keeping the best parts, letting the worst drop away.

I looked at Barrons.

It was entirely possible in a very short time only Dani, Dancer, and I would still be standing here.

Barrons glided toward me in that eerie, fluid fashion, stopped and laced our hands together.

We would hold on to each other until the last.

Sun, moon, and stars, I told him.

He inclined his head. *Of all the years, this one with you has been my finest. Fire to my ice, Mac.*

Frost to my flame, Jericho.

Forever, we said, and it was a vow far more powerful and binding than any ring or piece of paper.

There was nothing more to say. If we hadn't said it already, we'd fucked up and no reparations could be made at this late hour.

But his eyes said he was proud of the woman I'd become. And my eyes said that I was proud he was my man. And we smiled at each other, then he said something I never thought I'd hear Jericho Barrons say. He said—

"Fuck!" Alina exploded. "Mac, the *Sinsar Dubh* is here!"

For a moment I simply couldn't process what Alina had said. We'd left the *Sinsar Dubh* trapped in the boudoir. It could only be here if (a) it had broken free of the stones, (b) found a body to carry it, and (c) escaped mere minutes after we'd left.

I couldn't feel it at all. My *sidhe*-seer senses were completely muted by the presence of the song inside me. I spun wildly, trying to locate it, then shot a frantic look at Alina and she pointed behind me.

I whirled to find myself ten paces from the Unseelie princess we'd left cocooned in the boudoir.

Her mouth stretched impossibly wide, reminding me of Derek O'Bannion when he'd been possessed by the first Book, revealing rows and rows of whirling, sharp metal teeth. For a moment I thought she was going to eat me, bite off my head and swallow it, but she convulsed as if retching then abruptly a dark storm exploded from her jaws.

It darted straight for me.

I couldn't sift. I had little True Magic, but I had the song, and I needed to sing it, now, to destroy the *Sinsar Dubh* once and for all. I opened my mouth but the inky cloud the Unseelie princess had retched narrowed to a thin funnel of toxic dust and shot straight for it. I clamped my teeth shut again so hard it hurt my entire skull. Then Barrons was lunging, trying to intercept the dark storm in his own impossibly wide jaws, transforming into the beast as he moved.

The cloud retracted into the Unseelie princess and, as I watched, stunned, Barrons twisted in midair, slapped a crimson rune on her I'd not even known he'd been carrying and had no idea where he'd gotten it from, then grabbed her by the shoulders and ground his mouth to hers in a savage kiss.

He sucked the *Sinsar Dubh* right out of the princess's body in one long lip-locked inhale.

The Unseelie princess collapsed, dead, to the ground.

And all I could think was, Barrons could kill with a *kiss*? I thought I'd known what he was. I narrowed my eyes. I'd kissed that lethal mouth many times.

He whirled and bore down on me, eyes obsidian, full black, no crimson sparks, nothing left of my Jericho at all, and he roared, "Fucking sing, Mac, I can't hold it long!"

The shadow exploded out of his mouth as he spoke. He shuddered violently and clawed at the air, and forcibly sucked the *Sinsar Dubh* back in.

I shot Alina a frantic goodbye, locked eyes with Barrons, and I opened my mouth and released the Song of Making.

I will never be able to put into words what it is. Frequency that elevates to a level of being we don't yet understand while rendering insignificant the many daily burdens we think we carry. The song was made in Heaven, if such a place exists, by angels, spun of the divine.

For a time I was nowhere and everywhere listening to—no, *being*—music of such exquisite perfection that I was whole and right and I knew absolutely everything and understood it all. Each detail of existence was revealed, without enigma or confusion. I apprehended myself, the world, others, with exquisite clarity. Our entire existence was fluid and living and, as a race, a planet, a universe, it was all connected and we were all part of one another. And when we hurt one another, we hurt ourselves. And when we warred, we hurt the universe, and that was ourselves. And we were so stupid sometimes I couldn't believe the song even hung around and let us use it.

As humans, so much is mysterious to us. As the woman that sang the ancient melody, everything was clear and it all fit. The universe was precisely as it was meant to be. No Fate. Checks and balances. The universe listed toward life and beauty, always had, always would. We were the universe: each and every one of us, light or dark, right or wrong, we were tiny, essential cogs in the grand and mighty wheel. Somehow, even the *Sinsar Dubh*.

As the song poured out of me, I began to glow and turn translucent, and I thought, Well, shit, maybe I'm going to die after all.

But I didn't care because I'd done what was needed. I'd been the cog it was most desirable for me to be.

A brilliant blaze of light exploded from my body, and the air was filled with countless tiny, fluid arrows of light.

Events unfolded in slow motion to me then, though later they would tell me it all happened in a split second. I suspect I was somehow out of time by that point, insubstantial, changed by the melody flowing through me.

A thousand of the golden dazzling things darted into the black hole, which began to shiver and shake, then shrink.

The destructive black sphere grew smaller and smaller until, with an audible pop, it imploded and was simply gone, leaving nothing but the deep trench dug beneath it, and ropes cordoning off normal, healthy reality.

Countless more arrows exploded forth, darting out into the world, like the *Enterprise* entering warp speed, seeking out the rest of the black holes.

We'd done it. The Song of Making was free and healing our world!

I turned to watch each of my companions pierced in turn with arrows shot by me. *Mea culpa. Please let them live,* I begged whatever god had created the melody.

The brilliant lances of light passed straight through Dani and Dancer, and Ryodan, too, coming out on the other side.

Then one vanished inside Christian but didn't pass through. He began to shudder and snarl, and just when I thought we were definitely losing him, it abruptly shot out and moved on. Christian shook his head hard, looking dazed.

Barrons took a dozen of those arrows into his half-man, half-beast body and every one stayed inside.

His face contorted with agony and his eyes locked with mine.

I stared into his dark face, anguished, wanting desperately to stop singing. But I never would. I knew my role. I accepted it.

Jerking violently, he doubled over and vomited the dark storm of the *Sinsar Dubh* from his body. It gushed out of him, a black, viscous, oily river, oozing onto the pavement, and the damned thing actually shaped itself into the words FUCK YOU, MAC-KAYLA, YOU WILL DIEDIEDIEDIE.

If my mouth hadn't been busy singing, I would have snorted. Pompous superiority complex to the end.

Hundreds of glowing arrows twisted and turned midair, knifed into the inky stain of the *Sinsar Dubh* like evil-seeking missiles. The words collapsed and the blackness shuddered and rippled, then surged into the air where it whipped around and twisted violently.

Then it was gone.

Arrows erupted from Barrons's body. On the ground, on all fours, he threw his head back and looked up at me.

I'm still here, Rainbow Girl, he said fiercely inside my head.

My heart soared. He hadn't died. I hadn't killed him.

I looked at Alina and my heart sank. A hundred golden arrows pierced her everywhere and did not come out again.

Love you, Junior.

My sister was gone.

PART IV

Courage above all is the first quality of a warrior.

–Sun Tzu

61

"I'm on top of the world, 'ay!"

DANI

We had a blowout Beginning of the World party that night. Best. Party. Ever.

It was like something I saw on TV. There hasn't been time or opportunity in my life for parties, you know the kind where everyone's just in a really good mood and nobody has a private, nefarious agenda and there's music and all the food you could possibly want and the night seems to go on forever. And people play cards and liar's dice and laugh their asses off and do shots.

And you're with a man who thinks you're beautiful and hot and can't take his eyes off you and loves you.

Yeah, that kind of night.

Golden.

We hung out at BB&B, and even though Mac had lost Alina again, she had some kind of serenity about it that Jack and Rainey Lane shared. I think at the end of the day, they'd grieved her death once, and they just felt immensely grateful for the extra time they'd gotten with her.

That, and the world had been saved. It was impossible to not feel ebullient. We'd come so close to losing it all. And hadn't. We'd gotten reports in from every country that had been contaminated by the destructive spheres. The black holes were gone and our planet was healed.

The *Sinsar Dubh* had been destroyed. For good this time. The Unseelie had all been unmade. Mac said she could feel a complete void where the Dark Court had once existed. The Seelie were alive and well, and she said they'd already begun clamoring for her immediate appearance at court. I was curious how that was going to go. Mac was the Fae queen, for good now. Strange.

We'd sent word through to each of the new worlds, and in short order folks would be returning to Earth, although I suspected some of the more adventurous types would opt to stay and colonize. It's a great big universe out there now, and everything has changed.

As far as Dancer could tell, the song didn't heal his heart. He said he felt the same, and if he was disappointed, in true Dancer fashion he didn't show it. I was crestfallen but refused to brood. Things were no better—but they were no worse either. And each day, I learned new ways to deal with our situation. He'd been having problems for eleven years. I could easily get eleven more, and who knew what tomorrow might bring, or what miraculous cure Shazam might have to offer? Or maybe there was something Mac, with her Fae power, or Dancer himself, with his huge brain, could figure out to do, in time. The possibilities were limitless.

Apparently the song hadn't considered Christian or Sean O'Bannion made of imperfect song, as I'd suspected.

Christian was still an Unseelie prince.

"I don't bloody fucking get it," he said to me for the third time, tossing back a swallow of scotch. "I'm Unseelie. It should have either killed me or stripped the Unseelie out of me, leaving me a normal man," he said irritably. It may not have changed him but something about him was different. Possibly just that he was getting more comfortable being what he was.

Dancer said, "The song only destroyed what was created from imperfect song. You weren't. You were born a human."

"My bloody wings were created from imperfect song."

"No, they weren't," Dancer said. "You're a man who acquired Fae parts but your essence is human. I seriously doubt the song makes mistakes. It decided you weren't imperfect. For fuck's sake, did you want to die?"

"No. I just wanted to be myself again."

"I think the point is you *are*. You heard the music. It sent its arrows into you. And it left you alone. That means what you've become can't be that bad. Maybe you should try to—"

"Don't bloody tell me I should try to bloody embrace what I've become. That bastard Cruce told me often enough."

"That bastard Cruce," Mac said, passing by with a drink in her hand, "saved us and our planet, and he didn't have to. Nothing's black and white, Christian. If I were you, I'd start playing with my power, figuring out what I could do with it. At least you're not queen of the Fae. If anyone gets to bitch about the position they got stuck with, it's me, and I'm not. So buck up, little buckaroo. I'm queen of the Fairies, you're Death, life goes on."

Then she was off to join Barrons and Ryodan, who were playing poker with the Lanes and Inspector Jayne.

"Yeah, well, she's not the one that can't have sex," Christian muttered darkly. "They're bloody having sex constantly."

"I told you I'm perfectly happy to help with that," Enyo said, dropping over the back of the couch next to him.

Christian shot up and stalked away.

I arched a brow at Enyo, who shrugged. "War's over. I need a new challenge." Then she was off the couch, too, stalking after him.

Then Dancer and I were slow dancing while everyone carried on around us, as if we were the only two people in the world. Then the music was fast and fun and some of the *sidhe*-seers who hadn't gone off world showed up and we filled the bookstore with dancing and laughter and even Mac and Barrons joined in when "Tubthumping" came on.

Hours later Dancer finally said, "Want to get out of here, Mega?" His eyes were tired but brilliant as ever, the color of tropical surf.

Did I ever. I wanted this night to go on forever. But I also wanted it to end. "Yes. Tomorrow we get to—"

"Rescue Shazam," Dancer exclaimed, eyes sparkling. "Bloody hell, I can't wait to meet him!"

I kissed him. And kissed him. Then I had him leaning back against a bookcase, I was his second skin, and we got lost in a long dreamy kiss that told me exactly how the night was going to go.

I looked for Ryodan to say goodbye before we left but he was nowhere to be found.

"Freeze-frame me, Dani," Dancer said eagerly as we stepped outside, and I couldn't resist. We were on top of the world, young and in perfect sync with each other's hearts. He loved being in the slipstream, said it helped blow his mind open to new ideas.

As I kicked us up into that other dimension and the starry tunnel unfolded around us, he kissed me, which totally broke my concentration, and we stumbled down, cartwheeling along the alley, laughing. Then he had me turned around against the brick wall and my jeans were down and so were his and my sword was shoved aside and he was kissing the back of my neck and pushing inside me from behind and I knew later tomorrow I'd gouge D&D into the wall in this very spot and I laughed thinking that if I did it everywhere we had sex, the whole city would be graffitied with D's in no time.

"I love you, Dani Mega O'Malley," Dancer said against my ear as he moved inside me. "More than the world is big. Deeper than the sky is blue. Truer than the universe is vast. I love you more eternal than pi."

A fierce elation exploded in my heart and I gasped, "I love you the same way, Dancer."

Then the only sounds in the street were the ones a man and woman make when they live out loud and in every color of the rainbow.

♪

I woke up a little after noon the next day to sun slanting across our bed and lay curled on my side, wondering if Queen Mac had anything to do with the sultry clime drifting in the open window.

I trusted she knew she couldn't turn Dublin permanently into southern Georgia without seriously screwing up our rainy, verdant isle. But I'd happily take a few days of this weather, knowing how much Dancer loved it. He needed some long lazy hours in the sunshine to recuperate from the pace of recent events.

"It's *the day*, Shazam," I whispered, glowing inside. That one. The one I'd been waiting for forever. Today, Ryodan and Barrons were going to start stacking Silvers to rescue my beloved friend. And life would be perfect. Me, Shazam, and Dancer. What more could I ask? My heart was so full of happiness it felt like it might explode.

We'd had sex three times last night. I'd bowed out the fourth, pretending I was sore (like that could even happen), achingly aware of how exhausted he'd been. "We have all the time in the world," I'd told him, hoping it was true. Pacing ourselves was the key to getting a long life with him.

Going to sleep next to him every night. Waking up with him every morning, feeling the warmth of his body next to—

I went still.

So still I might have been made of stone.

Warily, I opened all my senses to their fullest.

I sleep on my side, one arm under the pillow, backside pressed up to him. Dancer sleeps flat on his back, arms usually over his head. He breathes easier that way.

He was behind me, his hand grazing my hip.

His cool hand.

I pondered that. He might have gotten up to get a glass of milk or something and his hand was still cool from holding the glass. Or maybe he'd had one of the grape Popsicles we'd made a couple nights ago from grape juice and a couple of bottles of iced wine we'd found. I'd roll over and find his lips were purple from sucking on one. Everything would be fine.

"Dancer?" I whispered.

Nothing.

"Dancer?" I said.

Silence.

Loudly, brightly, "Dancer, wake up. It's *the day*. We're going through to Shazam today. You two are going to love each other. We're going to be a family." And we were doing it together; he was coming off world to Planet X with me, we'd decided last night. Even though I was worried about his heart, I'd agreed to not cage him and he wanted to be there with me, to celebrate a joyful reunion. Or comfort me if it didn't go as we hoped.

I have super senses. Super smell, sight, strength, speed.

And hearing.

There was only one person breathing in our bed.

I exploded up, spun midair and slammed my hands down on his chest. "Dancer!" I snarled. "Wake up!"

He was still, eyes closed.

Pump, pump, pump.

I read about this. Never did it. Learned in case I needed to. Thirty pumps at the rate of 100 to 120 per minute. Tilt head, lift chin, pinch nose, breathe. Two breaths. Each lasting a second.

Pump, pump, pump. Breathe.

I kicked up into the slipstream so I could do it faster and straddled him, envisioning the heart inside his body, that lovely, unfairly penalized muscle, and pretended I was wrapping my hands around it, massaging it back to life as I worked.

Pump, pump, pump. Breathe.

I vibrated as intensely as I could because Mac told me that

Ryodan said (and how he knows is beyond me) that I give off a subtle electrical charge when I do. I hit full intensity, pumping at the same time.

No breath. Not a twitch or even a flicker of eyes behind his lids.

Pump, pump pump, breathe.

Pump, pump, pump, breathe.

The tears came long before I stopped trying to bludgeon and breathe and vibrate his body back to life.

Burning, hurting, scarring so motherfucking deep.

My head whipped back and I snarled at the ceiling with grief and fury and white-hot rage. "Why?" I shook my fist. "Give me one good reason! Tell me WHY you son of a bitch! Why not me? Do you take everyone away and leave me here just to torture me?"

I don't know how long I wept and raged up at the ceiling, or when I changed tactics and began begging. Offering anything.

Everything. All my superpowers. Whatever made me special. Just let me have Dancer back. One more day.

One more hour.

Even just long enough to get to say goodbye.

Hands dropping uselessly at my sides.

Brain going numb: reject reject reject.

His body temperature told the story well enough.

He'd slipped away shortly after I'd fallen asleep.

Hours ago.

While I'd slumbered ignorantly on.

Dancer had died, alone, and I'd been lying beside him, having happy dreams, oblivious to his suffering, his need.

This had been my fear: I wouldn't be there when he died. Worse yet, I'd been *right there,* yet not. I'd wanted to be holding his hand. I'd wanted him to not be alone.

But no, I'd slept through it.

Had it hurt?

Had it taken a long time, did he gasp my name? Or had his

enormous, beautiful heart just slowed and slowed until he drifted off on a dream?

Had he been afraid? Had he suffered?

Had he even known?

I sat on top of him, staring down at him, and sought the answers in his face.

It was peaceful.

His eyes were closed. No sign of strain in his face.

Accepting.

Just like he'd always been. Of everything. Of me. Of his unfair fucking life. Always seeing the good in me, in everyone around him.

Hot tears dropped down my cheeks, scalding my skin.

"Wake up, wake up, wake up!" I cried, nudging him. "Please don't leave me. Oh God, Dancer, don't *go*. Not yet! We're supposed to have more time!"

His face was pale and cool, his hair tousled by our lovemaking, lips parted as if on a final sigh.

I love you more eternal than pi, he'd said.

I drew back my fist and punched him in the chest, thinking if my punch was lethal enough to stop a heart, maybe it could start one.

That was when I felt him.

Not beneath me.

Behind me. Where no sun was touching my skin, I felt sunshine on my shoulders.

I felt his presence.

I swear I felt his hands moving my hair aside so he could kiss the back of my neck. Then they rested solid and warm on my shoulders and squeezed a little.

And until the day I die myself I'll continue to believe that I actually heard him speak.

No tears, Mega. Only joy. We were the lucky ones.

The lucky ones. He was dead and could say that? Was he batshit crazy? Maybe he was the lucky one, but I wasn't. I was here. I was alone. And his body was empty of all that was Dancer and I was in bed with a corpse.

Love doesn't die just because the person does. Everything we felt for each other still exists, Dani. It's in your heart. Don't turn it off, wild one. Never turn it off again. The world needs you. And you need the world.

Then the warmth was gone and I stretched out beside him and I held on to him and kissed him and kissed him and said all those things we'd only just started saying to each other.

I don't know how long I lay there. Time got weird then.

I only know, at some point, I became dimly aware that Ryodan was in the room with us, touching my shoulder, watching me with intensely bright eyes, untangling me from him, wrapping a blanket around me, making me get out of bed, and I screamed and screamed at him and I hit him and told him to leave me alone because I was never letting go of Dancer.

And he let me do it, rage and scream and hit him over and over, and when I finally collapsed to the floor where I lay sobbing and broken, he picked me up, tucked a blanket around me again and carried me out into the much too bright day.

I got lost in a really bad place then, where I felt sorry for myself and angry at the world, and I was made of nothing but pain, and I felt ancient and arthritic in every single one of my 222 bones, and the pain was so huge and I knew I couldn't survive it. It was going to kill me, and that was okay because Dancer was probably really close still and we could grab each other's hands and freeze-frame to the next adventure together.

Then Ryodan's fingers were brushing my forehead and he was laying me down in a crisp white bed, murmuring soft words, and I think I kind of died then because the pain finally.

Blissfully.

Stopped.

♪

I have foggy memories for a time. I know Mac came and sat with me, wherever I was, somewhere deep in Chester's. Barrons even came sometimes, and once he held my hand and I remember thinking I must have been dreaming because Barrons would never hold my hand. But I still remember the feel of his hand, how strong and big it was and how it felt like he was sending some of his gargantuan strength into my body, taking some of my pain out of it.

I have distant, gray memories of Kat, Enyo, and Christian lurking beyond the veil I couldn't see past. Or didn't want to. Even Jack and Rainey sat in my room, keeping watch, with Mrs. Lane fretting nonstop, tucking my blankets close, feeling my forehead, sometimes just sitting on the bed, touching me somewhere.

I have clearer memories of Ryodan. Each time I awoke, if one of the others wasn't in the room, he was. Always. Sitting. Chair by my bed. Watching. Waiting. Forcing me to live. Sometimes stroking my forehead and making all the hurt go away for a time. Other times punishing me by forcing me to live.

I'd wake up but refuse to open my eyes. He'd know anyway and threaten to hook up a feeding tube if I didn't eat. He'd lift me up and lean us both back against the headboard and pour protein drinks down my throat until I gagged (there was no way in hell I was chewing, chewing was a commitment to getting out of bed and that was a commitment to living), and I'd roll over again and melt back into the gray place.

Of all the things that happened to me in my life there are only two that nearly crippled me: losing Shazam and losing Dancer.

I thought about that in my gray place. And eventually realized it was because I'd chosen to love them, to give them my whole heart. And losing someone that you'd willingly given all of yourself to hurts far more than the many indignities and cruelties of the world. It's pure. It's a gift that gives back tenfold. And once you've lost it, you can never have it again.

In the end, it was both of them that brought me back.

In my gray place, I dreamed that Dancer was yelling at me

through a pane of glass and he was saying Shazam's name over and over. And he told me that just because we didn't get to hang together anymore didn't mean I could be a complete jackass or that Shazam didn't need me, so I needed to pull my shit together and take on the world again. Like superheroes do.

He loves you like pi, too, he said. *Eternally. Wake up. Seize the day. He needs you now. There will always be someone who needs you. And you'll always answer the call. That's your place in the Great Slipstream, Dani. And you've always known it.*

♪

"It was a lovely service," Mac said as we walked through the cemetery.

We'd had a big memorial mass at the abbey and buried Dancer and Alina next to Jo, in the private graveyard behind the fortress. I still couldn't believe Jo was gone. It seemed like just yesterday I'd seen her at Chester's, but thanks to some Unseelie prick, I never would again. I nodded. I still wasn't big on talking. It seemed like too much effort.

But I was getting stronger every day. And finally gaining some weight back.

"I like the inscription on Dancer's headstone," Mac said when we stooped to place flowers on the stones of three side-by-side graves.

ALINA MACKENNA LANE

JOANNA MACLAUGHLIN

DANCER ELIAS GARRICK

I'd chosen it myself: NEVER THE SIDEKICK, ALWAYS THE HERO. I'LL SEE YOU IN THE SLIPSTREAM.

I swallowed hard. He knew I loved him. I'd said it before he died and showed him in a thousand ways. I didn't see much point in getting maudlin with his epitaph. If he was hanging around somewhere, I highly doubted he was checking out his headstone and reading the inscription. He'd be hanging out in the bathroom when I was naked in the shower.

"I miss him." I had two holes where my heart used to be. The temptation to become Jada again was intense. But I lacked the energy to pull it off. It took effort to stay ice cold all the time when you'd pretty much been slapped together at birth from passion, fire, and a teaspoon of stardust.

Mac put her arms around me and pulled me into a hug. "I know, honey," she said. "We all do. He was one of a kind." After a time, she said, "Are you ready to do this?"

I didn't move. I wasn't sure I was up to it.

While I'd grieved, Ryodan and Barrons had gone through to Planet X and stacked Silvers so I could go get Shazam and bring him home.

The problem was, Shazam was nowhere to be found. There'd been nothing on the small island but the enormous mirror. No force-field cage. No half-naked tribesmen wearing feathered head-dresses. Not there and not anywhere else on the small world.

It was deserted, void of both humanoid and Shazamoid life forms.

Yes, they'd called for him. Mac told me Ryodan had stood on the island, calling for Shazam for the better part of a day.

With no response.

I suspected they still weren't completely convinced Shazam wasn't a figment of my imagination. And if I didn't find him, they might never be convinced. Might think me even more of a nut job than I currently was.

It was possible, after decades, Shazam was still waiting for me, somewhere up in the air, refusing to come down for anyone but me.

But it was just as possible that he'd died or left that world long ago.

Either way, I needed to know.

Facing the truth is always better than living in limbo. And as I'd recently learned, there were a lot of people far more nosily concerned about my well-being than I'd ever realized. People willing to take time out of their own lives to make sure I was okay. I couldn't say I was comfortable with all the fuss. But it wasn't the worst thing either. "Yes, let's do this, Mac."

I took her hand and, as we walked from the cemetery, I didn't glance back at his grave.

Dancer wasn't there.

I know a funny thing about eyes. Where you let them look is where they take you.

Look back and you stay stuck in a lost, forever unattainable past.

Look forward and you live.

62

"For a moment you were wild with abandon

like a child"

DANI

When I arrived at Kilmainham Gaol people were having another party or something. There were a few hundred people milling around the portal to Planet X. I glanced around, trying
to fathom what was going on. Surely they hadn't all come out to
see me off?

Jack and Rainey came rushing over the minute I got there.
Rainey smothered me in a big mom hug and petted my hair and
generally fussed over me so thoroughly I just stood there looking
at her because none of the things I felt like doing or saying were
socially appropriate.

"I'm so glad to see you up and about, Dani," she exclaimed,
pressing a kiss to my cheek. "We were so worried!"

I shot a look at Mac and she gave me one back, and damned if
I didn't hear her voice in my head. _I didn't tell them and never will._
But I suspect Alina did. Nobody blames you and everyone loves
you. Deal.

What the hell? Was everyone going to get the power of telepa-
thy but me?

I scowled at her and ignored her for a while.

Then Enyo, Kat, and a cluster of *sidhe*-seers were milling around me, all talking at once, and it was overwhelming to my Mega ears, but I moved into the cluster, greeting each in turn, assessing Kat, startled to realize how different she was. Enyo on my right, Kat on my left. It felt right, us as a team, and as I searched their faces I knew they were feeling it, too. Mac didn't know how to sing the walls back up between our worlds. It might take her a long time to figure it out. *Sidhe*-seers were critical. The three of us would find our places among them, and help the others find theirs.

Christian joined me briefly, iridescent eyes glittering. Told me he'd be keeping an eye on me so if I saw him sometimes hanging around, not to worry. He'd be nearby if I ever needed help.

Ryodan, Kasteo, Fade, and Barrons were standing apart, near the portal. I spotted Lor in the crowd, but he seemed to be keeping a distance from me and Mac.

But once she'd moved off to talk with her parents, he moved in, grinning down at me, and for the first time since Dancer died, I felt my face relax and shape a smile. It's impossible not to smile at Lor when he grins at you. But there was something different about him. For the first time since I'd met him, he looked somehow . . . ancient, like the rest of the Nine, in a way he never had before. "You ready, honey?"

I nodded.

"I'd go through with you but me and Mac, we got a bit of a problem we're working out."

I narrowed my eyes. "What kind of problem?"

"Bitch killed me 'cause she got pissed at me. I'd kill her back but then Barrons would kill me and I'd have to kill him and we'd all kill each other for a few centuries like we did once before and I ain't going back to that shitty, boring time."

I arched a brow, waiting, but he said nothing more. I couldn't wait to get the scoop from Mac. If she'd killed him, she'd had a good reason. "Sorry about Jo," I said.

"Yeah," he said.

When I finally managed to disengage myself from everyone who wanted to say "Hi" to me for some bizarre reason, I joined Ryodan, Barrons, and Mac at the portal.

"You shouldn't come with me. He may not come out if you're there."

Three immutable gazes stared at me, and I was struck by the sudden realization that I might never get rid of these people. They were in my life to stay. And they were going with me now. And that was that.

I shrugged. I'd find a way to make them leave if push came to shove. "Okay then. Let's do this."

A hush fell over the crowd as we moved toward the wall. A dozen feet away from the undetectable portal, a tall, wide Silver had been embedded in the wall.

"We're working to establish similar connections to many worlds. We've gone universal, not global," Mac told me.

Bloody hell, how our world had changed.

I inhaled deep, exhaled slow, preparing myself for the worst. Hoping fervently for the best.

Planet X. I was going through. It was *the* day.

I'd never have believed I'd be leaving a world that had no Dancer in it. It was still impossible for me to wrap my brain around. Mac said it would be that way for quite a while. That I'd expect to see him around the next corner. Or I'd text him or pick up the phone to call and his absence would hit me like a two-ton truck. I knew it would be a long time before I could ever go near Trinity College again. There were places in our city I'd be avoiding permanently.

Still, I'd been loved. Incredibly loved. And that was something I'd never had before. It had changed me. Given me new parts. "Thank you, Dancer," I whispered as I stepped through the portal.

♪

The small island was as empty as Mac had said it was, with the exception of a new, much smaller mirror that was now suspended in the air next to the enormous one.

I turned in a slow circle as Mac, Barrons, and Ryodan stepped through behind me. The planet that shorted out my powers made me feel sick to my stomach. Bile rose and I swallowed hard. I was here for Shazam. Nothing would interfere with my mission.

I didn't look at Ryodan. He'd seen me a total mess far too many times lately. I'd been ignoring him and planned to continue doing so for a while.

There, on the grassy island with waves lapping gently at the shore, was my trashcan, battered and rusted, my promise to Shazam spray-painted on the side.

The food I'd tossed through was gone, no doubt pecked clean by birds on the world. The enormous dog bed I'd tossed through was . . . I hurried over to it and knelt on the ground, inspecting it.

I plucked a long, thick silver whisker from the dark brown faux fur and held it up for the others to see. "He was here!" I exclaimed excitedly.

My excitement evaporated. It was only proof that he'd been here a few months ago, when I'd tossed it in. Which, Shazam's time, was decades ago.

I surged to my feet, turned my face up to the sun and called, "I see you, Yi-yi. I'm here, Shazam. I'm sorry it took me so long but I promise I'll never leave you again."

There was no reply.

I spun in a slow circle thinking maybe he didn't like seeing three strangers, and frankly, they were three of the strangest people I'd ever known: two ancient, immortal shapeshifters, one Fae queen. Maybe the Nine smelled bad to him. I could understand his reservations. I was downright normal compared to them. "They're my friends, Shazam. They won't hurt you. It's safe to come out."

Still nothing.

I called for him. I said his name over and over. I crooned and cajoled and finally burst into our theme song. "Shaz the mighty fur-beast lived up in the air . . ."

When I glanced at Ryodan, his shoulders were shaking and he was doing his best not to laugh.

"I was a *teenager*," I said with a scowl. "It's a great song. The meter works, it rhymes, and the melody is indisputably catchy."

"I'll take it over *Animaniacs,*" he said, quickly turning away to stare out over the lake. His shoulders were still shaking. Bastard was still laughing.

I whirled away and resumed singing.

I spent hours calling him. Talking, bribing, flattering. Trying everything. I'd brought raw fish in my backpack and offered them to the air, waving them around, making a complete ass of myself and inciting a fresh wave of nausea. If he was up there, forcing me to enact such dramatic shenanigans, there was going to be hell to pay.

Finally, I turned to the others and said, "You have to go back home. He may never come out with you on the island." I refused to believe he wasn't here. It might take weeks, maybe even months, to convince me of that.

None of them liked the idea.

"I'm not leaving you alone here," Ryodan said. "I'll make my-self unseen."

"Shazam won't be fooled," I replied irritably. "He's far more brilliant than you. He's a hundred times the super you are. He's evolved beyond anything we've ever seen."

"Why don't you tell me about him?" Mac invited. "I brought food and blankets in case we needed to spend the night. We'll eat and you can tell me about your time together."

In my head, she said, *If he's here, and he's as sensitive as you told me he was, his feelings are hurt. Hearing you tell us stories about him may coax him down.*

I conceded the wisdom of her plan.

Mac made a fire and I discovered I wasn't the only one who'd brought fish, but hers were on ice in her backpack. She wrapped them in foil and tucked them into the embers to roast. As the aroma filled the air, I dropped down cross-legged by the fire and told Mac how we'd met on Olean, how he'd taught me to freeze-frame better, and the story about the edible planet. I even told her some of the tales I'd not told anyone about the less dangerous jams we'd gotten ourselves into, and how Shazam had rescued me, time and time again. As I reminisced, some of the grief over Dancer that was eating me alive was met by yet more grief as the realization settled in that Shazam really might not have waited or survived.

Did I have to lose everything? Both of them? Was this the harsh life lesson I had to learn now? Did some people just not get an easy life? I would never say it wasn't a good one but, bloody hell, sometimes I wondered why mine was so rocky all the time!

Eventually my stories made me miss him so keenly that, combined with my fresh, hot grief over Dancer, I did something I'd never done in front of Shazam because he was so vulnerable and prone to manic fits of depression. No matter how bad our circumstances had gotten, I'd never cried.

I did now.

Bloody hell, all I did anymore was cry! It was ridiculous. I despised being this person. Mac started to cry, too, and I looked at her through my tears and said impatiently, "You don't have anything to cry about. What's wrong with you?"

"Your pain is mine. When you hurt, I hurt. If someone who truly loves you sees you in pain, they share it." She tipped her head back, staring up at the air. "And they'd certainly step in to stop it. To comfort you. No matter how much of a pissy mood they were in. They would see that their Yi-yi was devastated and do *anything* to make her feel better. Even if they didn't *feel* like it," she practically snarled.

The fire exploded in a tower of sparks and was instantly extinguished.

The foil wrapped fish vanished.

Bones tumbled out of the sky, showering down on me, bouncing off my head.

I scrambled to my feet, rubbing at my eyes. "Shazam! Are you there?"

Violet eyes materialized in the sky above me, narrowed to slits. "You said wait. Your expects, bars on my cage. Did you come? No. Not then. Not the next day. Not *ever*."

Holy hell, he was here! He was alive!

He vanished.

Another bone exploded out of the sky and bounced off my head. "Ow!" I clapped a hand to it. "Ever is now! I'm sorry. I'll tell you I'm sorry every day for the rest of my life if it makes you feel better."

"It will take *much* more than that," came the bodiless sniff. "My knots have sprouted an entire civilization of knots that have been reproducing with the ferocity and fertility of a band of mating Ka-lyrras! I'm one big tangle!" came his anguished wail. "And I'm *fat*."

"I'll brush you. You're not fat. Just come out. Let me see you!"

"Am, too!" he wailed. "You may only see parts of me. The slender ones." Eyes materialized ten feet above me. "You will leave me again," he said tearfully.

"I won't. I'll never leave you again." I said something I'd never said before. A thing I'd learned to say with Dancer. "I love you, Shazam. I can't stand living without you. I missed you so much that I went a little crazy for a time. But I couldn't come back because the Silver took me back to Dublin—"

"You found your way home, Yi-yi?" he said tremulously. "You did it? You finally made it?"

My heart melted. The happiness in his voice was unmistakable, happy for me, because I'd finally gotten what I'd been seeking for so long. "Yes, and because of that damned infinity of mirrors—"

"Not infinite, tiny red. Four-hundred-thousand seven hundred and sixty-two," he corrected.

"—I was trying to find a way to mark the correct one from the other side so I could bring you home with me. I'm so sorry, Shazam!"

Suddenly he manifested fully, dropping from the sky to plop fatly on the trashcan. I blinked. Good grief, he really *was* fat. His furry white belly draped both sides of the trashcan. I made a Jada-face to mask my astonishment. No way I was hurting his feelings now. He might vanish again.

Behind me, Mac gasped.

"See—*she* thinks I'm fat!" He shot an accusing glare at Mac.

"That's not why I gasped," Mac said, sounding oddly strained.

He thumped the trashcan with a paw and turned an accusing glare on me. "You sent it through empty. What kind of Yi-yi does that? Not a speck of food. Not an ort. Not even a morsel." He tossed his shaggy head and scowled, then a belch escaped him and a brilliant orange feather floated up into the air. He hastily licked his paw and began scrubbing at his whiskers with an innocent expression.

My eyes narrowed. "Did you eat the tribesmen?"

He swung his great head from side to side in elaborate denial. "Not me." He belched again and half a blue feather drifted out.

"How *many* of the tribesmen did you eat?" I demanded.

"You told me not to eat people. I didn't. Well, maybe I did. But only a few. The *rest*," he said, slumping a mound of fatness and foul mood over the rusted can, "decided I was too fat to share an island with." He shot me a meek, pitiful look. "They went away." He turned his nose up in a snit. "I have no idea where."

"Shazam," I said warningly.

"They took my *Yi-yi* away from me!" he snarled.

"How many did you eat?"

"They were going to eat me. *You* would probably prefer I'd let them." He glared at me, eyes narrowed, nose crinkling. "Then you wouldn't be bothered with me," he added in a small voice.

"I'm never bothered by you. I adore you. Answer my question."

He stood up, back arching into a horseshoe shape with porcupine bristles ridging his spine. "What did you expect?" he said defensively. "I ate them. Okay? I have problems. You know that about me." He sniffed and tears began to flow. "Now you don't want me anymore. I should just die. We're all going to die anyway. What does it matter if I do it now? Who would care?" He flung himself dramatically off the trashcan, rolled midair to land flat on his back on the ground, where he lay like a dead thing, head lolling to the side, paws up in the air.

After a moment he squinted an eye open to make sure I was looking. Then closed it hastily and resumed being dead.

"You ate *all* of them?" I said incredulously. "The entire civilization? We talked about this. You said you wouldn't do it again."

"I was *hungry*. And bored. There was nothing to do. You said you would be back. You WEREN'T. Your expects. Not bars on *my* cage anymore."

"Dani," Mac said warningly behind me. "You *do* know what Shazam is, right?"

I shot an inquiring look over my shoulder. "You mean, like, what species?"

Shazam leapt to his feet, instantly alert, and drew up to his full height. "I have no species. I am a singularity."

"That's exactly what I mean," Mac said.

I shook my head. "He wouldn't tell me."

"Because I belong to no species," Shazam said tightly. "Don't listen to her, Yi-yi. She lies."

"He wouldn't tell you for good reason. He's a Hel-Cat," Mac said.

"Am NOT." Shazam reared up on his haunches, eyes narrowed to thin slits, and spat and hissed alternately.

Mac said, "They're nearly extinct. Or more precisely, there's said to be only one left in all the universes. They're as mythical as the unicorn."

"What's a Hel-Cat? And how do you know what he is?" I said.

"No one knows exactly what they are, or what their true form is. They were legend to the Fae. I saw a picture of one of them in my files. The form he's adopted is the one they use to lure others close. Highly evolved, they have uncontrollable appetites and were destroyed because they kept wiping out civilizations. They were hunted by every world in every galaxy. They learned to hide in higher dimensions, coming down only to prey. Dani, you made friends with the last remaining Hel-Cat. Hel-Cats don't make friends. They eat them."

I looked at Shazam, who was staring at Mac with a venomous gaze. "You will never find me to hunt me, tiny white."

He vanished.

"Great. Now look what you did," I snapped. "Legends are always bigger and badder than the real thing. You of all people should know that." To the air, I said, "No one is going to hunt you, Shazam. I'll protect you."

His eyes materialized in front of me. "You will? Promise always?"

"Yes. But you can't eat people on our world and you can't wipe out species. We'll find another way to deal with your appetite."

"But what if I can't help myself?" he wailed.

"You can. I'll teach you. You did great when we were together before. Everything's easier when you're not alone. Come on. We're going home," I told him firmly.

"Home? Where I can stay forever?" His lips pulled back, revealing sharp fangs and a black-tipped tongue as he turned a suspicious glare on Mac. "*She* doesn't want me."

"Not true," Mac said. "But there will be rules." She glanced at Barrons, who raised a brow and shrugged in a silent, *What's one Hel-Cat compared to the things we've handled?*

"I am NOT a Hel-Cat," Shazam said with a regal sniff. "I am Shazam. My Yi-yi named me and that is my *only* name."

"Shazam," Mac said, and it was the offer of a truce, of new beginnings. To me, she said, *Can you control him?*

I nodded and opened my arms. Shazam exploded out of the air and leapt into them at full velocity, taking me back to the ground beneath him, licking my face and biting my hair.

I wrapped my arms around him and held on to his furry, powerful body. He was going to sleep with me tonight and wake me up in the morning. I had someone of my own to love. I would survive the pain of losing Dancer. And one day life would be good again.

"And we'll have *adventures,*" he said happily, pouncing my curls.

"Every day," I told him. "Ew. Tribesman breath!"

"Your pitiful abandonment. My bad breath. You might have packed that can with fish, but no. Another big empty. Like all the other big empties in my life."

"No big empties anymore."

"Promise?"

"Swear it."

He shifted his paws about, accommodating his great belly, then dropped hard on my stomach, evoking a loud *whuff* from me, and touched his damp nose to mine. "I see you, Yi-yi," he said, eyes slanted half closed and gleaming.

I thought of Dancer. Of love lost. Of love regained. "I see you, too, Shazam."

Then he was up and running across the island, and I was off chasing him and laughing.

He pounced my ankles and tripped me and I tumbled to the ground with him on top of me, nipping at my jeans, tugging at my shirt. Beneath a dazzling sun, on the island where I'd lost him along with a part of myself, I found both again.

We played for hours, running and blowing off steam, wading at the lake's edge, catching silvery minnows, and I was happy to see he'd not eaten all the fish. He'd eaten only his enemy. I understood that. He could control himself. Together, we'd learn smarter ways of living and being.

Much later we sat together watching the waves lap at the shore, Shazam snuggled close to my side, keeping me warm as the temperature dropped.

I'd forgotten all about the others, lost in a time of much-needed joy and abandon.

As stars came out to twinkle in the sky above me, Shazam looked at me and I was suddenly struck by how old his eyes seemed. All playfulness and vulnerability had vanished and I was struck suddenly by how accurately I'd named him after a wise old wizard.

"He's happy, Yi-yi."

I went very still. "He, who?"

"The one who danced you into love."

I stared at him. Then, "How do you know about him?"

"Slipstream. I'm in it. All. I am somewhat . . . larger than I appear." His whiskers twitched as if he were vibrating with hidden laughter, then he busied himself polishing them with spit-moistened paws. That had long lethal talons. My Hel-Cat.

"Shazam, what are you *really*?"

He leapt up and was off, racing across the island. Over his shoulder, he called, "Hungry. And ready to go. Hurry, tiny red. Take me home."

Home.

I knew some truths about that word now.

You weren't always born into one. But if you were lucky, you found one somewhere along the way. It was a place where you fit and were accepted, where people helped you with your problems and you helped them with theirs. Where you made mistakes and so did they but the love never wavered.

A place where erosions never turned into landslides because you dug one another out. And always would.

Shazam and I stepped into the portal together this time.

63

The Unseelie King walked to the edge of the Horsehead Nebula, great dark wings trailing behind him, staring but not seeing.

What was it she'd once said to him?

You have so many ambitions. I have but one. To love.

And he'd thought, small.

Human.

Beautiful.

But small.

He'd liked that in his woman, a small lovely ambition. Given that she didn't have his talents, he could see that was enough for her.

He, however, had from the very first moments of his existence teemed with power, bristled electric, exploded with it. He was a supernova. Creating was his drug, addictive and irresistible. All-consuming.

He'd believed mere emotion could never compete with the power rush of slapping together worlds and watching them evolve. That love could yield no prize that might make it worth turning his back on shaping civilizations and birthing stars, building his Court of Shadows.

He'd been wrong.

When he'd found her on that tiny provincial planet in that tiny three-dimensional universe, *she* wasn't the one who needed saving from her flatland existence.

Life was so simple. It always had been.

Be the conductor, forever removed from the orchestra pit.

Or be part of the song.

The Unseelie King turned his face in a general upward direction where if there were something like him standing in the wings waiting for the chance to go a long distance out of the way to return a short distance correctly, it might overhear and take up the reins, as he did what he should have done a small eternity ago.

It felt good.

Human.

Small.

Beautiful.

He said, "I quit."

64

"I have loved you for a thousand years,
I'll love you for a thousand more"

MAC

I was stretched out on the Chesterfield in front of a hissing gas fire, listening to the rain patter against the windows of the store, indulging myself in a time of reflection before I got up to tackle what would surely be another eventful, fascinating day.

Tomorrow was Halloween—and Barrons's birthday—and the *sidhe*-seers were having a huge party out at the abbey.

Dani had moved back into the fortress with Shazam and was quickly becoming a living legend, bristling electric with energy and intellect, traveling the slipstream with her enigmatic, flamboyant Hel-Cat. Kat and Enyo were gathering yet more *sidhe*-seers, and there was talk of reestablishing a global order.

The black holes had vanished from our world and the song had awakened life in even the Shade-devastated Dark Zones. Although it was late fall, we were having a rainy spring and I suspected our seasons might be completely out of balance for a few years.

Deep in the earth, connected to the core by the True Magic, I felt a new, subtle magic in the planet. Our world was alive in ways it hadn't been for hundreds of thousands of years.

Dublin was bustling again, each day we reclaimed another part of the city, and life was slowly returning to as close to normal as it would ever be again.

The unique Fae hues still stained our world, and, until I figured out how to either sing the walls back up between the realms or unearth the power of our court and move it to a new planet, they would continue to do so.

What to do with my race of immortals was the next stage of my journey. It was bound to be an interesting one.

My parents had settled in Dublin with no intention of ever returning to Georgia.

We'd lost and gained things, we'd grieved and celebrated. The future was a mystery to us all. One we would explore together.

My greatest concerns were for Dani. Getting Shazam back had alleviated some of the anguish I'd been so worried might turn her back into Jada. But she wasn't fully Dani anymore either, the way she had been when Dancer was alive. There was a coolness to her diction, a distance in her gaze that I suspected might be there for some time.

Still, all in all, life was good and rich and there was no other place I'd rather be.

I rolled over onto my back and stretched out, staring absently up at the ceiling, five stories above my head.

Slowly becoming aware of the distant mural.

I narrowed my eyes, wondering for the hundredth time what it was. Then, with a snort, I invited the elements around me to erect a tall, shining scaffold, kicked up off the sofa and climbed the handy ladder on the side. There were quite a few things about being the Fae queen I didn't at all mind. Still, sifting and hanging midair was something I wasn't yet comfortable with, hence the scaffolding.

As I climbed the rungs higher and higher, the scene etched into the plaster, layered with paint and gold flakes and crystals, became clear and I gasped.

I stretched out on the platform and stared up at it for a long time, absorbing it, letting the truth seep into me in a way I could never have allowed when I first arrived in Dublin.

I marveled at the beauty, trying to understand how it eluded me for so long when it was so clearly detailed, in extraordinary Fae-kissed colors. I'd finally found the cause for the spatial distortion in my bookstore. The shimmering mirror in the scene painted above my head was an open Silver, one of the most powerful ever created, and I was pretty sure I knew where it went.

Then the air around me changed and my body fired on all pistons like it always does whenever Jericho Barrons is near.

He topped the scaffolding and stretched out on his back beside me. I looked over and met his dark gaze.

I knew him intimately now: who he had once been, who he was, and who he was becoming. I loved each incarnation and never wanted to be without him.

What are you doing up here, Rainbow Girl?

Looking.

Are you seeing?

I am.

We all played our parts in the pageant of life, and as with any stage production, while the method of acting can be as varied as the individual, there were a limited number of roles.

All were offered.

You tried out.

You chose. Live or die. Understudy or star.

"You knew this was here. You were waiting for me," I said. "Since before I ever walked into your store."

"Yes."

"Who painted it?"

He shrugged a shoulder. "No idea. It was here when I bought the place. But the building has morphed over time."

I saw things so clearly now. How he'd taught me, helped me evolve, gave and withheld information, even misled at times so I could find my own path, sought to level the playing field so we would be equals, and tried to avoid the Unseelie King's mistakes. I remembered the night he'd nearly repeated a significant one, when he thought I was dying in Mallucé's lair deep beneath the Burren. He'd growled that it wasn't what he would have chosen, as he'd poised on the brink of changing me into a creature like him to keep me alive with him forever.

"You could have told me. Saved me from worrying that I was you."

"Some things can't be told. Only learned. Or not."

"Then it was destined." The idea chafed.

"Never destined. And still not written in stone. Merely possible. As are many other outcomes."

I glanced back up at the man and woman in the mural on the ceiling of Barrons Books & Baubles.

His wings.

Her crown.

Barrons's face.

Mine.

I studied them, the happiness in their eyes, the promise of a tomorrow I embraced. "Maybe we'll do better."

He laughed. "Ah, the unquenchable human hope." Then, "Mac," he said, and held out his hand.

It was so much more than a hand he was offering: it was nights of love so consuming it burned, days of grief that chilled, a kingdom of black ice and a mansion of alabaster. It was all possible mistakes and every imaginable success.

We *would* do better. What was painted above me was no more than an invitation for a future. We could accept it or turn away.

The Fae were starfish, regenerating, as old ones passed, new ones arose. One thing I did know was whatever path we chose to go down, we'd do it together.

I took his hand. "Jericho."

Fire to his ice.

Frost to my flame.

Forever.

65

"It ain't over 'til it's over"

Great, dark wings trailed behind him as Cruce moved deeper into the laboratory.

He'd felt the precise moment the king had abdicated. Like the Seelie Queen's magic, the Fae power of the Seelie/Unseelie King had to pass to another.

It hadn't come to him.

Yet.

Nor, however, had it gone somewhere else. It hovered in the distance, apparently undecided.

He intended to help it decide.

Cruce stood at the king's mixing table, blending a dash of this with a bit of that, according to the spells he'd taken from the *Sinsar Dubh,* and in short order created his first child.

Rules. Malleable, said the one who'd spoken for the king, yet claimed not to be him.

They certainly were.

The Court of Shadows was already being reborn.

THE END

AUTHOR'S NOTE

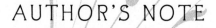

While, for MacKayla, escaping her psychopath was as simple as walking away, she had a magical method with which to restrain her stalker, and their battle occurred in a fictional world.

In a nonfictional world it's rarely that simple.

There are many support groups and avenues of assistance to pursue if you find yourself in such a situation. The author in no way means to imply one can simply walk away. Escaping a relationship with a psychopath, sociopath, or narcissist can be difficult, damaging, and dangerous.

You are your kingdom. A vibrant, empathic, all-the-colors-of-the-rainbow kingdom. But there are those who walk among us that lack such a rich internal landscape.

Courage, above all, is the first quality of a warrior.

ACKNOWLEDGMENTS

My debt of gratitude for *Feversong* could be a short book in and of itself, but since I just finished writing a very long one, I'll endeavor to keep it brief. I've been living in the Fever World for eleven years and have formed so many wonderful and lasting friendships because of it. Bringing it to a close has been bittersweet yet exhilarating.

Enormous, everlasting thanks to my brilliant editor, Shauna Summers, who championed the series from the very beginning; a huge shout-out to my outstanding team at Random House: Kara Welsh, Scott Shannon, Matthew Schwartz, Gina Wachtel, Gina Centrello, Sarah Murphy, Hanna Gibeau, Alex Coumbis, Kate Childs, Kim Hovey, Katie Rice, and Ashleigh Heaton; kudos and much appreciation to Lynn Andreozzi and the art department for the fabulous covers over the years.

A deep debt of gratitude to my brother, Brian, who knows the Fever World nearly as well as I do, and tirelessly hashed out the psychological/emotional nuances with me until we were both satisfied I'd done justice to my original vision.

Many thanks to Anne Wessels-Paris for the Friday afternoon

coffee/talks as we navigated the darkest parts of the labyrinth, and to Dr. Joseph Dagenbach for consulting about Dancer's condition.

Much love and appreciation to Mia Suarez (aka Happi Anarky) for years of inspiration and Fever art. It's pure joy to trip the slipstream with you. You're made of all the right stuff: love, passion, a backbone of steel, and a teaspoon of stardust.

And always, *always,* thanks to you, intrepid readers, who are the reason I get up each morning, eager to rush to that blank page where I strive to make the magic happen.

Somewhere along the way, Mac and Barrons, Dani and Ryodan, and the rest of the crew became as real to you as they are to me, and that's both the greatest reward and most cherished compliment.

I'm looking forward to the next adventure with all of you.

Stay to the Light.

Karen

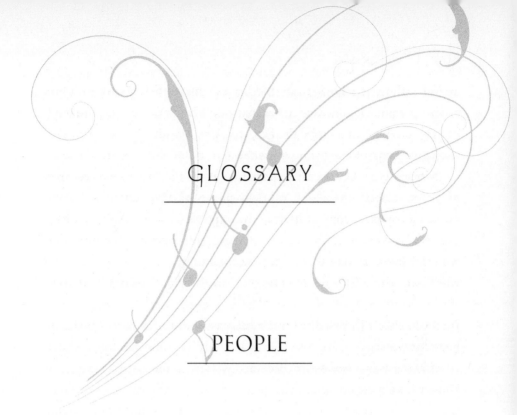

GLOSSARY

PEOPLE

SIDHE-SEERS

SIDHE-SEER (SHEE-SEER): *A person on whom Fae magic doesn't work, capable of seeing past the illusions or "glamour" cast by the Fae to the true nature that lies beneath. Some can also see Tabh'rs, hidden portals between realms. Others can sense Seelie and Unseelie objects of power. Each* sidhe-seer *is different, with varying degrees of resistance to the Fae. Some are limited; some are advanced, with multiple "special powers." For thousands of years the* sidhe-seers *protected humans from the Fae that slipped through on pagan feast days when the veils grew thin, to run the Wild Hunt and prey on humans.*

MACKAYLA LANE (O'CONNOR): Main character, female, twenty-three, adopted daughter of Jack and Rainey Lane, biological daughter of Isla O'Connor. Blond hair, green eyes, had an idyllic, sheltered childhood in the Deep South. When her biological sister, Alina, was murdered and the Garda swiftly closed the case with no leads, Mac quit her job bartending and headed for Dublin to search for Alina's killer herself. Shortly after her arrival she met Jericho Barrons and began reluctantly working with him toward common goals. Among her many skills and talents, Mac can track objects of power created by the Fae, including the ancient, sentient, psychopathic Book of magic known as the *Sinsar Dubh*. At the end of *Shadowfever* we learn that twenty years before, when the *Sinsar Dubh* escaped its prison beneath the abbey, it briefly possessed Mac's mother and imprinted a complete copy of itself in the unprotected fetus. Although Mac succeeds in reinterring the dangerous Book, her victory is simultaneous with the discovery that there are two copies of it; she *is* one of them and will never be free from the temptation to use her limitless, deadly power.

ALINA LANE (O'CONNOR): Female, deceased, older sister to MacKayla Lane. At twenty-four went to Dublin to study at Trinity College and discovered she was a *sidhe*-seer. Became lovers with the Lord Master, also known as Darroc, an ex-Fae stripped of his immortality by Queen Aoibheal for attempting to overthrow her reign. Alina was killed by Rowena, who magically forced Dani O'Malley to trap her in an alley with a pair of deadly Unseelie.

DANIELLE "THE MEGA" O'MALLEY: Main character. An enormously gifted, genetically mutated *sidhe*-seer with an extremely high IQ, super-strength, speed, and sass. She was abused and manipulated by Rowena from a young age, molded into the old woman's personal assassin, and forced to kill Mac's sister, Alina. Despite the darkness and trauma of her childhood, Dani is eternally optimistic and determined to survive and have her fair share of life plus some. In *Shadowfever*, Mac discovers Dani killed her sister, and the two, once as close as sisters, are now bitterly estranged. In *Iced*, Dani flees Mac and leaps into a Silver, unaware it goes straight to the dangerous Hall of All Days. We learn in *Burned* that, although mere weeks passed on Earth, it took Dani five and a half years to find her way home, and when she returns, she calls herself Jada.

ROWENA O'REILLY: Grand Mistress of the *sidhe*-seer organization until her death in *Shadowfever*. Governed the six major Irish *sidhe*-seer bloodlines but rather than training them, controlled and diminished them. Fiercely power-hungry, manipulative, and narcissistic, she was seduced by the *Sinsar Dubh* into freeing it. She ate Fae flesh to enhance her strength and talent, and kept a lesser Fae locked beneath the abbey. Dabbling in dangerous black arts, she experimented on many of the *sidhe*-seers in her care, most notably Danielle O'Malley. In *Shadowfever* she is possessed by the *Sinsar Dubh* and used to seduce Mac with the illusion of parents she never had, in an effort to get her to turn over the only illusion amulet capable of deceiving even the Unseelie King. Mac sees through the seduction and kills Rowena.

ISLA O'CONNOR: Mac's biological mother. Twenty-some years ago Isla was the leader of the Haven, one of seven trusted advisors to the Grand Mistress in the sacred, innermost circle of *sidhe*-seers at Arlington Abbey. Rowena (the Grand Mistress) wanted her daughter, Kayleigh O'Reilly, to be the Haven leader, and was furious when the women selected Isla instead. Isla was the only member of the Haven who survived the night the *Sinsar Dubh* escaped its prison beneath the abbey. She was briefly possessed by the Dark Book but not turned into a lethal, sadistic killing machine. In the chaos at the abbey, Isla was stabbed and badly injured. Barrons tells Mac he visited Isla's grave five days after she left the abbey, that she was cremated. Barrons says he discovered Isla had only one daughter. He later tells Mac it is conceivable Isla could have been pregnant the one night he saw her and a child might have survived, given proper premature birth care. He also says it is conceivable Isla didn't die, but lived to bear another child (Mac) and give her up. Barrons theorizes Isla was spared because the sentient evil of the *Sinsar Dubh* imprinted itself on her unprotected fetus, made a complete second copy of itself inside the unborn Mac and deliberately released her. It is believed Isla died after having Mac and arranging for her friend Tellie to have both her daughters smuggled from Ireland and adopted in the States, forbidden ever to return to Ireland.

AUGUSTA O'CLARE: Tellie Sullivan's grandmother. Barrons took Isla O'Connor to her house the night the *Sinsar Dubh* escaped its prison beneath Arlington Abbey over twenty years ago.

KAYLEIGH O'REILLY: Rowena's daughter, Nana's granddaughter, best friend of Isla O'Connor. She was killed twenty-some years ago, the night the *Sinsar Dubh* escaped the abbey.

NANA O'REILLY: Rowena's mother, Kayleigh's grandmother. Old woman living alone by the sea, prone to nodding off in the middle of a sentence. She despised Rowena, saw her for what she was, and was at the abbey the night the *Sinsar Dubh* escaped more than twenty years ago. Though many have questioned her, none have ever gotten the full story of what happened that night.

KATARINA (KAT) MCLAUGHLIN (MCLOUGHLIN): Daughter of a notorious crime family in Dublin, her gift is extreme empathy. She feels the pain of the world, all the emotions people work so hard to hide. Considered useless and a complete failure by her family, she was sent to the abbey at a young age, where Rowena manipulated and belittled her until she became afraid of her strengths and impeded by fear. Levelheaded, highly compassionate, with serene gray eyes that mask her constant inner turmoil, she wants desperately to learn to be a good leader and help the other *sidhe*-seers. She turned her back on her family Mafia business to pursue a more scrupulous life. When Rowena was killed, Kat was coerced into becoming the next Grand Mistress, a position she felt completely unfit for. Although imprisoned beneath the abbey, Cruce is still able to project a glamour of himself, and in dreams he seduces Kat nightly, shaming her and making her feel unfit to rule, or be loved by her longtime sweetheart, Sean O'Bannion. Kat has a genuinely pure heart and pure motives but lacks the strength, discipline, and belief in herself to lead. In *Burned*, she approaches Ryodan and asks him to help her become stronger, more capable of leading. After warning her to be careful what she asks him for, he locks her beneath Chester's in a suite of rooms with the silent Kasteo.

JO BRENNAN: Mid-twenties, petite, with delicate features and short, spiky dark hair, she descends from one of the six famous Irish bloodlines that can see the Fae (O'Connor, O'Reilly, Brennan, the McLaughlin or McLoughlin, O'Malley, and the Kennedy). Her special talent is eidetic or sticky memory for facts, but unfortunately by her mid-twenties she has so many facts in her head, she can rarely find the ones she needs. She has never been able to perfect a mental filing system. When Kat clandestinely dispatches her to get a job at Chester's so they can spy on the Nine, Jo allows herself to be coerced into taking a waitressing job at the nightclub by the immortal owner, Ryodan, and when he gives her his famous nod, inviting her to his bed, she's unable to resist even though she knows it's destined for an epic fail. In *Burned*, Jo turns to Lor (who is allegedly Pri-ya at the time and won't remember a thing) after she breaks up with Ryodan to "scrape the taste of him out of her mouth." She learns, too late, that Lor was never Pri-ya and he has no intention of forgetting any of the graphically sexual things that happened between them. Although, frankly, he'd like to be able to.

PATRONA O'CONNOR: Mac's biological grandmother. Little is known of her to date.

THE NINE

Little is known about them. They are immortals who were long ago cursed to live forever and be reborn every time they die at precisely the same unknown geographic location. They have an alternate beast form that is savage, bloodthirsty, and atavistically superior. It is believed they were originally human from the planet Earth, but that is unconfirmed. There were originally ten, counting Barrons's young son. The names we know that they currently go by are Jericho Barrons, Ryodan, Lor, Kasteo, Fade. In Burned *we discover one is named Daku. There's a rumor that one of the Nine is a woman.*

JERICHO BARRONS: Main character. One of a group of immortals who reside in Dublin, many of them at Chester's nightclub, and is their recognized leader, although Ryodan issues and enforces most of Barrons's orders. Six feet three inches tall, black hair, brown eyes, 245 pounds, date of birth October 31, allegedly thirty-one years old, his middle initial is Z, which stands for Zigor, meaning either "the punished" or "the punisher," depending on dialect. He is adept in magic, a powerful warder, fluent in the druid art of Voice, an avid collector of antiquities and supercars. He despises words, believes in being judged by one's actions alone. No one knows how long the Nine have been alive, but references seem to indicate in excess of ten thousand years. If Barrons is killed, he is reborn at an unknown location precisely the same as he was the first time he died. Like all of the Nine, Barrons has an animal form, a skin he can don at will or if pushed. He had a son who was also immortal, but at some point in the distant past, shortly after Barrons and his men were cursed to become what they are, the child was brutally tortured and became a permanent, psychotic version of the beast. Barrons kept him caged below his garage while he searched for a way to free him, hence his quest to obtain the most powerful Book of magic ever created, the *Sinsar Dubh*. He was seeking a way to end his son's suffering. In *Shadowfever,* Mac helps him lay his son to final rest by using the ancient Hunter, K'Vruck, to kill him.

RYODAN: Main character. Six feet four inches, 235 pounds, lean and cut, with silver eyes and dark hair nearly shaved at the sides, he has a taste for expensive clothing and toys. He has scars on his arms and a large, thick one that runs from his chest up to his jaw. Owner of Chester's and the brains behind the Nine's business empire, he manages the daily aspects of their existence. Each time the Nine have been visible in the past, he was king, ruler, pagan god, or dictator. Barrons is the silent command behind the Nine, Ryodan is the voice. Barrons is animalistic and primeval, Ryodan is urbane and professional. Highly sexual, he likes sex for breakfast and eats early and often.

LOR: Six feet two inches, 220 pounds, blond, green eyes, with strong Nordic features, he promotes himself as a caveman and likes it that way.

Heavily muscled and scarred. Lor's life is a constant party. He loves music, hot blondes, and likes to chain his women to his bed so he can take his time with them, willing to play virtually any role in bed for sheer love of the sport. Long ago, however, he was called the Bonecrusher, feared and reviled throughout the Old World.

KASTEO: Tall, dark, scarred, and tattooed, with short, dark, nearly shaved hair, he hasn't spoken to anyone in a thousand years. There is a rumor floating around that others of the Nine killed the woman he loved.

FADE: Not much is known about him to date. During events in *Shadow-fever*, the *Sinsar Dubh* possessed him briefly and used him to kill Barrons and Ryodan, then threaten Mac. Tall, heavily muscled, and scarred like the rest of the Nine.

FAE

Also known as the Tuatha De Danann or Tuatha De (TUA day dhanna or Tua DAY). An advanced race of otherworldly creatures that possess enormous powers of magic and illusion. After war destroyed their own world, they colonized Earth, settling on the shores of Ireland in a cloud of fog and light. Originally the Fae were united and there were only the Seelie, but the Seelie King left the queen and created his own court when she refused to use the Song of Making to grant his concubine immortality. He became the Unseelie King and created a dark, mirror image court of Fae castes. While the Seelie are golden, shining, and beautiful, the Unseelie, with the exception of royalty, are dark-haired and -skinned, misshapen, hideous abominations with sadistic, insatiable desires. Both Seelie and Unseelie have four royal houses of princes and princesses that are sexually addictive and highly lethal to humans.

Unseelie

UNSEELIE KING: The most ancient of the Fae, no one knows where he came from or when he first appeared. The Seelie don't recall a time the king didn't exist, and despite the court's matriarchal nature, the king predates the queen and is the most complex and powerful of all the Fae— lacking a single enormous power that makes him the Seelie Queen's lesser: she alone can use the Song of Making, which can call new matter into being. The king can create only from matter that already exists, sculpting galaxies and universes, even on occasion arranging matter so that life springs from it. Countless worlds call him God. His view of the universe is so enormous and complicated by a vision that sees and weighs every detail, every possibility, that his vast intellect is virtually inaccessible. In order to communicate with humans he has to reduce himself into multiple human parts. When he walks in the mortal realm, he does so as one of these human "skins." He never wears the same skins twice after his involvement in a specific mortal episode is through.

DREAMY-EYED GUY (aka DEG, see also Unseelie King): The Unseelie King is too enormous and complex to exist in human form unless he divides himself into multiple "skins." The Dreamy-Eyed Guy is one of the Unseelie King's many human forms and first appeared in *Darkfever* when Mac was searching a local museum for objects of power. Mac later encounters him at Trinity College in the Ancient Languages department, where he works with Christian MacKeltar, and frequently thereafter when he takes a job bartending at Chester's after the walls fall. Enigma shrouded in mystery, he imparts cryptic bits of useful information. Mac doesn't know the DEG is a part of the Unseelie King until she and the others are reinterring the *Sinsar Dubh* beneath Arlington Abbey and all of the king's skins arrive to coalesce into a single entity.

CONCUBINE (originally human, now Fae, see also Aoibheal, Seelie Queen, Unseelie King, Cruce): The Unseelie King's mortal lover and unwitting cause of endless war and suffering. When the king fell in love with her, he asked the Seelie Queen to use the Song of Making to make her Fae and immortal, but the queen refused. Incensed, the Seelie King left Faery, established his own icy realm, and became the dark, forbidding Unseelie King. After building his concubine the magnificent shining White Mansion inside the Silvers where she would never age so long as she didn't leave its labyrinthine walls, he vowed to re-create the Song of Making, and spent eons experimenting in his laboratory while his concubine waited. The Unseelie Court was the result of his efforts: dark, ravenous, and lethal, fashioned from an imperfect Song of Making. In *Shadowfever*, the king discovers his concubine isn't dead, as he has believed for over half a million years. Unfortunately, the cup from the Cauldron of Forgetting that Cruce forced upon the concubine destroyed her mind and she doesn't retain a single memory of the king or their love. It is as if a complete stranger wears her skin.

CRUCE (Unseelie, but has masqueraded for over half a million years as the Seelie prince V'lane): Powerful, sifting, lethally sexual Fae. Believes himself to be the last and finest Unseelie prince the king created. Cruce was given special privileges at the Dark Court, working beside his liege to perfect the Song of Making. He was the only Fae ever allowed to enter the White Mansion, so he might carry the king's experimental potions to the concubine while the king continued with his work. Over time, Cruce grew jealous of the king, coveted his concubine and kingdom, and plotted to take it from him. Cruce resented that the king kept his Dark Court secret from the Seelie Queen and wanted the Dark and Light Courts to be joined into one, which he then planned to rule himself. He petitioned the king to go to the Seelie Court and present his "children," but the king refused, knowing the queen would only subject his imperfect creations to endless torture and humiliation. Angry that the king would not fight for them, Cruce went to the Seelie Queen himself and told her of the Dark Court. Incensed at the king's betrayal and quest for power, which was matriarchal, the queen locked Cruce away in her bower and summoned the king. With the help of the illusion amulets Cruce and the king had created, Cruce wove the glamour that he was the Seelie prince, V'lane. Furious to learn the king had disobeyed her, and jealous of his love for the concubine, the queen summoned Cruce (who was actually her own prince, V'lane) and killed him with the Sword of Light to show the king what she would do to all his abominations. Enraged, the king stormed the Seelie Court with his dark Fae and killed the queen. When he went home to his icy realm, grieving the loss of his trusted and much-loved prince Cruce, he found his concubine was also dead. She'd left him a note saying she'd killed herself to escape what he'd become. Unknown to the king, while he'd fought with the Seelie Queen, Cruce slipped back to the White Mansion and gave the concubine another "potion," which was actually a cup stolen from the Cauldron of Forgetting. After erasing her memory, he used the power of the three lesser illusion amulets to convince the king she was dead. He took her away and assumed the role of V'lane, in love with a mortal at the Seelie Court, biding time to usurp the rule of their race, both Light and Dark Courts. As V'lane, he approached MacKayla Lane and was using her to locate the *Sinsar Dubh*. Once he had it, he planned to acquire all the Unseelie King's forbidden dark knowledge, finally kill the concubine who had become the current queen, and, as the only vessel holding both the patriarchal and matriarchal power of their race, become the next, most powerful, Unseelie King ever to rule. At the end of *Shadowfever,* when the *Sinsar Dubh* is reinterred beneath the abbey, he reveals himself as Cruce and absorbs all the forbidden magic from the king's Dark Book. But before Cruce can kill the current queen and become the ruler of both Light and Dark Courts, the Unseelie King imprisons him in a cage of ice beneath Arlington Abbey. In *Burned,* we learn Dani/Jada somehow removed the cuff of Cruce from his arm while he was imprisoned in the cage. Her disruption of the magic holding him weakened the spell. With magic she learned Silverside, she was able to close the doors on the cavernous chamber, and now only those doors hold him.

UNSEELIE PRINCES: Highly sexual, insatiable, dark counterparts to the golden Seelie princes. Long blue-black hair, leanly muscled dark-skinned bodies tattooed with brilliant complicated patterns that rush beneath their skin like kaleidoscopic storm clouds. They wear black torques like liquid darkness around their necks. They have the starved cruelty and arrogance of a human sociopath. There are four royal princes: Kiall, Rath, Cruce, and an unnamed prince slain by Danielle O'Malley in *Dreamfever*. In the way of Fae things, when one royal is killed, another becomes, and Christian MacKeltar is swiftly becoming the next Unseelie prince.

UNSEELIE PRINCESSES: The princesses have not been heard of and were presumed dead until recent events brought to light that one or more were hidden away by the Unseelie King either in punishment or to contain a power he didn't want loose in the world. At least one of them was locked in the king's library inside the White Mansion until either Dani or Christian MacKeltar freed her. Highly sexual, a powerful sifter, this princess is stunningly beautiful, with long black hair, pale skin, and blue eyes. In *Burned* we learn the Sweeper tinkered with the Unseelie princess(es) and changed her (them) somehow. Unlike the Unseelie princes, who are prone to mindless savagery, the princess is quite rational about her desires, and logically focused on short-term sacrifice for long-term gain. It is unknown what her end goal is but, as with all Fae, it involves power.

ROYAL HUNTERS: A caste of Unseelie sifters, first introduced in *The Immortal Highlander,* this caste hunts for both the king and the queen, relentlessly tracking their prey. Tall, leathery skinned, with wings, they are feared by all Fae.

CRIMSON HAG: One of the Unseelie King's earliest creations, Dani O'Malley inadvertently freed this monster from a stoppered bottle at the king's fantastical library inside the White Mansion. Psychopathically driven to complete her unfinished, tattered gown of guts, she captures and kills anything in her path, using insectile, lancelike legs to slay her prey and disembowel them. She then perches nearby and knits their entrails into the ragged hem of her blood red dress. They tend to rot as quickly as they're stitched, necessitating an endless, futile hunt for more. Rumor is, the Hag once held two Unseelie princes captive, killing them over and over for nearly 100,000 years before the Unseelie King stopped her. She reeks of the stench of rotting meat, has matted, blood-drenched hair, an ice-white face with black eye sockets, a thin gash of a mouth, and crimson fangs. Her upper body is lovely and voluptuous, encased in a gruesome corset of bone and sinew. She prefers to abduct Unseelie princes because they are immortal and afford an unending supply of guts, as they regenerate each time she kills them. In *Iced,* she kills Barrons and Ryodan, then captures Christian MacKeltar (the latest Unseelie prince) and carries him off.

FEAR DORCHA: One of the Unseelie King's earliest creations, this seven-foot-tall, gaunt Unseelie wears a dark pin-striped tailcoat suit that is at least a century out of date, and has no face. Beneath an elegant, cobwebbed black top hat is a swirling black tornado with various bits of features that occasionally materialize. Like all the Unseelie, created imperfectly from an imperfect Song of Making, he is pathologically driven to achieve what he lacks—a face and identity—by stealing faces and identities from humans. The Fear Dorcha was once the Unseelie King's personal assassin and traveling companion during his liege's time of madness after the concubine's death. In *Fever Moon,* the Fear Dorcha is defeated by Mac when she steals his top hat, but it is unknown if the Dorcha is actually deceased.

HOAR FROST KING (GH'LUK-RA D'J'HAI) (aka HFK): Villain introduced in *Iced,* responsible for turning Dublin into a frigid, arctic wasteland. This Unseelie is one of the most complex and powerful the king ever created, capable of opening holes in space-time to travel, similar to the Seelie ability to sift but with catastrophic results for the matter it manipulates. The Hoar Frost King is the only Unseelie aware of its fundamental imperfection on a quantum level, and like the king, was attempting to re-create the Song of Making to fix itself by collecting the necessary frequencies, physically removing them from the fabric of reality. Each place the Hoar Frost King fed, it stripped necessary structure from the universe while regurgitating a minute mass of enormous density, like a cat vomiting cosmic bones after eating a quantum bird. Although the HFK was destroyed in *Iced* by Dani, Dancer, and Ryodan, the holes it left in the fabric of the human world can be fixed only with the Song of Making.

GRAY MAN: Tall, monstrous, leprous, capable of sifting, he feeds by stealing beauty from human women. He projects the glamour of a devastatingly attractive human man. He is lethal but prefers his victims left hideously disfigured and alive to suffer. In *Darkfever*, Barrons stabs and kills the Gray Man with Mac's spear.

GRAY WOMAN: The Gray Man's female counterpart, nine feet tall, she projects the glamour of a stunningly beautiful woman and lures human men to their death. Gaunt, emaciated to the point of starvation, her face is long and narrow. Her mouth consumes the entire lower half of her face. She has two rows of sharklike teeth but prefers to feed by caressing her victims, drawing their beauty and vitality out through open sores on her grotesque hands. If she wants to kill in a hurry, she clamps her hands onto human flesh, creating an unbreakable suction. Unlike the Gray Man, she usually quickly kills her victims. In *Shadowfever*, she breaks pattern and preys upon Dani, in retaliation against Mac and Barrons for killing the Gray Man, her lover. Mac makes an unholy pact with her to save Dani.

RHINO-BOYS: Ugly, gray-skinned creatures that resemble rhinoceroses with bumpy, protruding foreheads, barrel-like bodies, stumpy arms and legs, and lipless gashes of mouths with jutting underbites. Lower-caste Unseelie thugs dispatched primarily as watchdogs and security for high-ranking Fae.

PAPA ROACH (aka the roach god): Made of thousands and thousands of roachlike creatures clambering up on top of one another to form a larger being. The individual bugs feed off human flesh, specifically fat. Consequently, postwall, some women allow them to enter their bodies and live beneath their skin to keep them slim, a symbiotic liposuction. Papa Roach, the collective, is purplish-brown, about four feet tall with thick legs, a half-dozen arms, and a head the size of a walnut. It jiggles like gelatin when it moves as its countless individual parts shift minutely to remain coalesced. It has a thin-lipped beaklike mouth and round, lidless eyes.

SHADES: One of the lowest castes, they started out barely sentient but have been evolving since they were freed from their Unseelie prison. They thrive in darkness, can't bear direct light, and hunt at night or in dark places. They steal life in the same manner the Gray Man steals beauty, draining their victims with vampiric swiftness, leaving behind a pile of clothing and a husk of dehydrated human matter. They consume every living thing in their path from the leaves on trees to the worms in the soil.

Seelie

AOIBHEAL, THE SEELIE QUEEN (see also Concubine): Fae queen, last in a long line of queens with an unusual empathy for humans. In *Shadowfever*, it is revealed the queen was once human herself, and is the Unseelie King's long-lost concubine and soul mate. Over half a million years ago the Unseelie prince Cruce drugged her with a cup stolen from the Cauldron of Forgetting, erased her memory and abducted her, staging it so the Unseelie King believed she was dead. Masquerading as the Seelie prince V'lane, Cruce hid her in the one place he knew the king of the Unseelie would never go—the Seelie Court. Prolonged time in Faery transformed Aoibheal and she became what the king had desperately desired her to be: Fae and immortal. She is now the latest in a long line of Seelie Queens. Tragically, the original Seelie Queen was killed by the Unseelie King before she was able to pass on the Song of Making, the most powerful and beautiful of all Fae magic. Without it, the Seelie have changed. In *Burned*, the Unseelie King took the concubine to the White Mansion and imprisoned her inside the boudoir they once shared, in an effort to restore her memory.

DARROC, LORD MASTER (Seelie turned human): Once Fae and trusted advisor to Aoibheal, he was set up by Cruce and banished from Faery for treason. At the Seelie Court, Adam Black (in the novel *The Immortal*

Highlander) was given the choice to have Darroc killed or turned mortal as punishment for trying to free Unseelie and overthrow the queen. Adam chose to have him turned mortal, believing he would quickly die as a human, sparking the succession of events that culminates in *Faefever* when Darroc destroys the walls between the worlds of man and Fae, setting the long-imprisoned Unseelie free. Once in the mortal realm, Darroc learned to eat Unseelie flesh to achieve power and caught wind of the *Sinsar Dubh*'s existence in the mortal realm. When Alina Lane came to Dublin, Darroc discovered she was a *sidhe*-seer with many talents and, like her sister, Mac, could sense and track the *Sinsar Dubh*. He began by using her but fell in love with her. After Alina's death, Darroc learned of Mac and attempted to use her as well, applying various methods of coercion, including abducting her parents. Once Mac believed Barrons was dead, she teamed up with Darroc, determined to find the *Sinsar Dubh* herself and use it to bring Barrons back. Darroc was killed in *Shadowfever* by K'Vruck, allegedly at the direction of the *Sinsar Dubh,* when the Hunter popped his head like a grape.

SEELIE PRINCES: There were once four princes and four princesses of the royal *sidhe*. The Seelie princesses have not been seen for a long time and are presumed dead. V'lane was killed long ago, Velvet (not his real name) is recently deceased, R'jan currently aspires to be king, and Adam Black is now human. Highly sexual, golden-haired (except for Adam, who assumed a darker glamour), with iridescent eyes and golden skin, they are extremely powerful sifters, capable of sustaining nearly impenetrable glamour, and affect the climate with their pleasure or displeasure.

V'LANE: Seelie prince, queen of the Fae's high consort, extremely sexual and erotic. The real V'lane was killed by his own queen when Cruce switched faces and places with him via glamour. Cruce has been masquerading as V'lane ever since, hiding in plain sight.

VELVET: Lesser royalty, cousin to R'jan. He was introduced in *Shadowfever* and killed by Ryodan in *Iced.*

DREE'LIA: Frequent consort of Velvet, was present when the *Sinsar Dubh* was reinterred beneath the abbey.

R'JAN: Seelie prince who would be king. Tall, blond, with the velvety gold skin of a light Fae, he makes his debut in *Iced* when he announces his claim on the Fae throne.

ADAM BLACK: Immortal Prince of the D'Jai House and favored consort of the Seelie Queen, banished from Faery and made mortal as punishment for one of his countless interferences with the human realm. Has been called the *sin siriche dubh* or blackest Fae, however undeserved. Rumor holds Adam was not always Fae, although that has not been substantiated. In *The Immortal Highlander* he is exiled among mortals, falls in love with Gabrielle O'Callaghan, a *sidhe*-seer from Cincinnati, Ohio, and chooses to remain human to stay with her. He refuses to get involved in the current war between man and Fae, fed up with the endless manipulation, seduction, and drama. With Gabrielle, he has a highly gifted and unusual daughter to protect.

THE KELTAR

An ancient bloodline of Highlanders chosen by Queen Aoibheal and trained in druidry to uphold the Compact between the races of man and Fae. Brilliant, gifted in physics and engineering, they live near Inverness and guard a circle of standing stones called Ban Drochaid (the White Bridge), which was used for time travel until the Keltar breached one of their many oaths to the queen and she closed the circle of stones to other times and dimensions. Current Keltar druids: Christopher, Christian, Cian, Dageus, Drustan.

Druid: In pre-Christian Celtic society, a druid presided over divine worship, legislative and judicial matters, philosophy, and education of elite youth to their order. Druids were believed to be privy to the secrets of the gods, including issues pertaining to the manipulation of physical matter, space, and even time. The old Irish "drui" means magician, wizard, diviner.

CHRISTOPHER MACKELTAR: Modern-day laird of the Keltar clan, father of Christian MacKeltar.

CHRISTIAN MACKELTAR (turned Unseelie prince): Handsome Scotsman, dark hair, tall, muscular body, and killer smile, he masqueraded as a student at Trinity College, working in the Ancient Languages department, but was really stationed there by his uncles to keep an eye on Jericho Barrons. Trained as a druid by his clan, he participated in a ritual at Ban Drochaid on Samhain meant to reinforce the walls between the worlds of man and Fae. Unfortunately, the ceremony went badly wrong, leaving Christian and Barrons trapped in the Silvers. When Mac later finds Christian in the Hall of All Days, she feeds him Unseelie flesh to save his life, unwittingly sparking the chain of events that begins to turn the sexy Highlander into an Unseelie prince. He loses himself for a time in madness, and fixates on the innocence of Dani O'Malley while losing his humanity. In *Iced,* he sacrifices himself to the Crimson Hag to distract her from killing the *sidhe*-seers, determined to spare Dani from having to choose between saving the abbey or the world, then is staked to the side of a cliff above a hellish grotto to be killed over and over again. In *Burned,* Christian is rescued from the cliff by Mac, Barrons, Ryodan, Jada, Drustan, and Dageus, but Dageus sacrifices himself to save Christian in the process.

CIAN MACKELTAR (*Spell of the Highlander*): Highlander from the twelfth century, traveled through time to the present day, married to Jessica St. James. Cian was imprisoned for one thousand years in one of the Silvers by a vengeful sorcerer. Freed, he now lives with the other Keltar in current-day Scotland.

DAGEUS MACKELTAR (*The Dark Highlander*): Keltar druid from the sixteenth century who traveled through time to the present day, married to

Chloe Zanders. He is still inhabited (to an unknown degree) by the souls/knowledge of thirteen dead Draghar, ancient druids who used black sorcery, but has concealed all knowledge of this from his clan. Long black hair nearly to his waist, dark skin, and gold eyes, he is the sexiest and most sexual of the Keltar. In *Burned,* we learn that although he gave his life to save Christian, Ryodan brought him back and is keeping him in a dungeon beneath Chester's.

DRUSTAN MACKELTAR (*Kiss of the Highlander*): Twin brother of Dageus MacKeltar, also traveled through time to the present day, married to Gwen Cassidy. Tall, dark, with long brown hair and silver eyes, he is the ultimate chivalrous knight and would sacrifice himself for the greater good if necessary.

HUMANS

JACK AND RAINEY LANE: Mac and Alina's parents. In *Darkfever,* Mac discovers they are not her biological parents. She and Alina were adopted, and part of the custody agreement was a promise that the girls never be allowed to return to the country of their birth. Jack is a strapping, handsome man, an attorney with a strong sense of ethics. Rainey is a compassionate blond woman who was unable to bear children of her own. She's a steel magnolia, strong yet fragile.

DANCER: Six feet four inches, he has dark, wavy hair and gorgeous aqua eyes. Very mature, intellectually gifted seventeen-year-old who was home-schooled, and graduated from college with a double major in physics and engineering by sixteen. Fascinated by physics, he speaks multiple languages and traveled extensively with wealthy, humanitarian parents. His father is an ambassador, his mother a doctor. He was alone in Dublin, considering Trinity College for grad school, when the walls between realms fell, and has survived by his wits. He is an inventor and can often think circles around most people, including Dani. He seems unruffled by

Barrons, Ryodan, and his men. Dani met Dancer near the end of *Shad-owfever* (when he gave her a bracelet, first gift from a guy she liked) and they've been inseparable since. In *Iced,* Dancer made it clear he has feelings for her. Dancer is the only person Dani feels like she can be herself with: young, a little geeky, a lot brainy. Both he and Dani move around frequently, never staying in one place too long. They have many hideouts around the city, above- and belowground. Dani worries about him because he doesn't have any superpowers.

FIONA ASHETON: Beautiful woman in her early fifties who originally managed Barrons Books & Baubles and was deeply in love (unrequited) with Jericho Barrons. Fiendishly jealous of Barrons's interest in Mac-Kayla, she tried to kill Mac by letting Shades (lethal Unseelie) into the bookstore while she was sleeping. Barrons exiled her for it, and Fiona then became Derek O'Bannion's lover, began eating Unseelie, and was briefly possessed by the *Sinsar Dubh,* which skinned her from head to toe but left her alive. Due to the amount of Fae flesh Fiona had eaten, she could no longer be killed by human means and was trapped in a mutilated body, in constant agony. Eventually she begged Mac to use her Fae spear and end her suffering. Fiona died in the White Mansion when she flung herself through the ancient Silver used as a doorway between the concubine and the Unseelie King's bedchambers—which kills anyone who enters it except for the king and concubine—but not before trying to kill Mac one last time.

ROARK (ROCKY) O'BANNION: Black Irish Catholic mobster with Saudi ancestry and the Compact, powerful body of a heavyweight champion boxer, which he is. Born in a Dublin controlled by two feuding Irish crime families—the Hallorans and O'Kierneys—Roark O'Bannion fought his way to the top in the ring, but it wasn't enough for the ambitious champ; he hungered for more. When Rocky was twenty-eight years old, the Halloran and O'Kierney linchpins were killed along with every son, grandson, and pregnant woman in their families. Twenty-seven people died that night, gunned down, blown up, poisoned, knifed, or strangled. Dublin had never seen anything like it. A group of flawlessly choreographed killers had closed in all over the city, at restaurants, homes, hotels, and clubs, and struck simultaneously. The next day, when a suddenly wealthy Rocky O'Bannion, champion boxer and many a young boy's idol, retired from the ring to take control of various businesses in and around Dublin previously run by the Hallorans and O'Kierneys, he was hailed by the working-class poor as a hero, despite the fresh and obvious blood on his hands and the rough pack of ex-boxers and thugs he brought with him. O'Bannion is devoutly religious and collects sacred artifacts. Mac steals the Spear of Destiny (aka the Spear of Longinus that pierced Christ's side) from him to protect herself, as it is one of two weapons that can kill the immortal Fae. Later, in *Darkfever,* Barrons kills O'Bannion to keep Mac safe from him and his henchmen, but it's not the end of the O'Bannions gunning for Mac.

DEREK O'BANNION: Rocky's younger brother, he begins snooping around Mac and the bookstore after Rocky is murdered, as his brother's car was found behind the bookstore. He becomes lovers with Fiona Asheton, is ultimately possessed by the *Sinsar Dubh,* and attacks Mac. He is killed by the *Sinsar Dubh* in *Bloodfever*.

SEAN O'BANNION: Rocky O'Bannion's cousin and Katarina McLaughlin's childhood sweetheart and adult lover. After the Hallorans and the O'Kierneys were killed by Rocky, the O'Bannions controlled the city for nearly a decade, until the McLaughlins began usurping their turf. Both Sean and Kat despised the family business and refused to participate. The two crime families sought to unite the business with a marriage between them, but when nearly all the McLaughlins were killed after the walls crashed, Katarina and Sean finally felt free. But chaos reigns in a world where humans struggle to obtain simple necessities, and Sean suddenly finds himself part of the black market, competing with Ryodan and the Fae to fairly distribute the supply of food and valuable resources. Kat is devastated to see him doing the wrong things for all the right reasons and it puts a serious strain on their relationship.

MALLUCÉ (aka John Johnstone, Jr.): Geeky son of billionaire parents until he kills them for their fortune and reinvents himself as the steampunk vampire Mallucé. In *Darkfever*, he teams up with Darroc, the Lord Master, who teaches him to eat Unseelie flesh for the strength and enormous sexual stamina and appetite it confers. He's wounded in battle by Mac's Spear of Destiny. Because he'd been eating Unseelie, the lethal prick of the Fae blade caused parts of him to die, killing flesh but not his body, trapping him in a half-rotted, agonizing shell of a body. He appears to Mac as the Grim Reaper in *Bloodfever*, and after psychologically tormenting her, abducts and holds her prisoner in a hellish grotto beneath the Burren in Ireland, where he tortures and nearly kills her. Barrons kills him and saves Mac by feeding her Unseelie flesh, changing her forever.

THE GUARDIANS: Originally Dublin's police force, the Gardai, under the command of Inspector Jayne. They eat Unseelie to obtain heightened strength, speed, and acuity, and hunt all Fae. They've learned to use iron bullets to temporarily wound them and iron bars to contain them. Most Fae can be significantly weakened by iron. If applied properly, iron can prevent a Fae from being able to sift.

INSPECTOR O'DUFFY: Original Garda on Alina Lane's murder case, brother-in-law to Inspector Jayne. He was killed in *Bloodfever*, his throat slit while holding a scrap of paper with Mac's name and address on it. It is currently unknown who killed him.

INSPECTOR JAYNE: Garda who takes over Alina Lane's murder case after Inspector O'Duffy, Jayne's brother-in-law, is killed. Big, rawboned Irishman who looks like Liam Neeson, he tails Mac and generally complicates her life. Initially, he's more interested in what happened to O'Duffy than solving Alina's case, but Mac treats him to Unseelie-laced tea and opens his eyes to what's going on in their city and world. Jayne joins the fight against the Fae and transforms the Gardai into the New Guardians, a ruthless army of ex-policemen who eat Unseelie, battle Fae, and protect humans. Jayne is a good man in a hard position. Although he and his men can capture the Fae, they can't kill them without either Mac's or Dani's weapon. In *Iced,* Jayne earns Dani's eternal wrath by stealing her sword when she's too injured to fight back.

CHARACTERS OF UNKNOWN GENUS

K'VRUCK: Allegedly the most ancient of the Unseelie caste of Royal Hunters—although it is not substantiated that he is truly Unseelie. He was once the Unseelie King's favored companion and "steed" as he traveled worlds on its great black wings. Enormous as a small skyscraper, vaguely resembling a dragon, it's coal black, leathery, and icy, with eyes like huge orange furnaces. When it flies, it churns black frosty flakes in the air and liquid ice streams in its wake. It has a special affinity for Mac and appears to her at odd moments as it senses the king inside her (via the *Sinsar Dubh*). When K'Vruck kills, it is the ultimate death, extinguishing life so completely it's forever erased from the karmic cycle. To be K'Vrucked is to be removed completely from existence as if you've never been, no trace, no residue. Mac used K'Vruck to free Barrons's son. K'Vruck is the only being (known so far) capable of killing the immortal Nine.

SWEEPER: A collector of powerful, broken things, it resembles a giant trash heap of metal cogs and gears. First encountered by the Unseelie King shortly after he lost his concubine and descended into a period of madness and grief. The Sweeper traveled with him for a time, studying him, or perhaps seeing if he, too, could be collected and tinkered with. According to the Unseelie King, it fancies itself a god.

ZEWS: Acronym for zombie eating wraiths, so named by Dani O'Malley. Hulking anorexic vulturelike creatures, they are five to six feet tall, with gaunt, hunched bodies and heavily cowled faces. They appear to be wearing cobwebbed, black robes but it is actually their skin. They have exposed bone at their sleeves and pale smudges inside their cowls. In *Burned,* Mac catches a glimpse of metal where their faces should be but doesn't get a good look.

PLACES

ARLINGTON ABBEY: An ancient stone abbey located nearly two hours from Dublin, situated on a thousand acres of prime farmland. The mystically fortified abbey houses an Order of *sidhe*-seers gathered from six bloodlines of Irish women born with the ability to see the Fae and their realms. The abbey was built in the seventh century and is completely self-sustaining, with multiple artesian wells, livestock, and gardens. According to historical records, the land occupied by the abbey was previously a church, and before that a sacred circle of stones, and long before that a fairy shian, or mound. *Sidhe*-seer legend suggests the Unseelie King himself spawned their order, mixing his blood with that of six Irish houses, to create protectors for the one thing he should never have made—the *Sinsar Dubh*.

ASHFORD, GEORGIA: MacKayla Lane's small, rural hometown in the Deep South.

BARRONS BOOKS & BAUBLES: Located on the outskirts of Temple Bar in Dublin, Barrons Books & Baubles is an Old World bookstore previously owned by Jericho Barrons, now owned by MacKayla Lane. It shares design characteristics with the Lello Bookstore in Portugal, but is somewhat more elegant and refined. Due to the location of a large Sifting Silver in the study on the first floor, the bookstore's dimensions can shift from as few as four stories to as many as seven, and rooms on the upper levels often reposition themselves. It is where MacKayla Lane calls home.

BARRONS'S GARAGE: Located directly behind Barrons Books & Baubles, it houses a collection of expensive cars. Far beneath it, accessible only through the heavily warded Silver in the bookstore, are Jericho Barrons's living quarters.

THE BRICKYARD: The bar in Ashford, Georgia, where MacKayla Lane bartended before she came to Dublin.

CHESTER'S NIGHTCLUB: An enormous underground club of chrome and glass located at 939 Rêvemal Street. Chester's is owned by one of Barrons's associates, Ryodan. The upper levels are open to the public, the lower levels contain the Nine's residences and their private clubs. Since the walls between man and Fae fell, Chester's has become the hot spot in Dublin for Fae and humans to mingle.

DARK ZONE: An area that has been taken over by the Shades, deadly Unseelie that suck the life from humans, leaving only a husk of skin and indigestible matter such as eyeglasses, wallets, and medical implants. During the day it looks like an everyday abandoned, run-down neighborhood. Once night falls it's a death trap. The largest known Dark Zone in Dublin is adjacent to Barrons Books & Baubles and is nearly twenty by thirteen city blocks.

FAERY: A general term encompassing the many realms of the Fae.

HALL OF ALL DAYS: The "airport terminal" of the Sifting Silvers where one can choose which mirror to enter to travel to other worlds and realms. Fashioned of gold from floor to ceiling, the endless corridor is lined with billions of mirrors that are portals to alternate universes and times, and exudes a chilling spatial-temporal distortion that makes a visitor feel utterly inconsequential. Time isn't linear in the hall, it's malleable and slippery, and a visitor can get permanently lost in memories that never were and dreams of futures that will never be. One moment you feel terrifyingly alone, the next as if an endless chain of paper-doll versions of oneself is unfolding sideways, holding cutout construction-paper hands with thousands of different feet in thousands of different worlds, all at the same time. Compounding the many dangers of the hall, when the Silvers were corrupted by Cruce's curse (intended to bar entry to the Unseelie King), the mirrors were altered and now the image they present is no longer a guarantee of what's on the other side. A lush rain forest may lead to a parched, cracked desert, a tropical oasis to a world of ice, but one can't count on total opposites either.

THE RIVER LIFFEY: The river that divides Dublin into south and north sections, and supplies most of Dublin's water.

TEMPLE BAR DISTRICT: An area in Dublin also known simply as "Temple Bar," in which the Temple Bar Pub is located, along with an endless selection of boisterous drinking establishments including the famed Oliver St. John Gogarty, the Quays Bar, the Foggy Dew, the Brazen Head, Buskers, The Purty Kitchen, The Auld Dubliner, and so on. On the south bank of the River Liffey, Temple Bar (the district) sprawls for blocks, and has two meeting squares that used to be overflowing with tourists and partiers. Countless street musicians, great restaurants and shops, local bands, and raucous Stag and Hen parties made Temple Bar the *craic*-filled center of the city.

TEMPLE BAR PUB: A quaint, famous pub named after Sir William Temple, who once lived there. Founded in 1840, it squats bright red and cozy, draped with string lights at the corner of Temple Bar Street and Temple Lane, and rambles from garden to alcove to main room. The famous pub boasts a first-rate whiskey collection, a beer garden for smoking, legendary Dublin Bay oysters, perfectly stacked Guinness, terrific atmosphere, and the finest traditional Irish music in the city.

TRINITY COLLEGE: Founded in 1592, located on College Green, recognized as one of the finest universities in the world, it houses a library that contains over 4.5 million printed volumes including spectacular works such as the *Book of Kells*. It's ranked in the world's top one hundred universities for physics and mathematics, with state-of-the-art laboratories and equipment. Dancer does much of his research on the now abandoned college campus.

UNSEELIE PRISON: Located in the Unseelie King's realm, close to his fortress of black ice, the prison once held all Unseelie captives for over half a million years in a stark, arctic prison of ice. When the walls between man and Faery were destroyed by Darroc (a banished Seelie prince with a vendetta against the Seelie Queen), all the Unseelie were freed to invade the human realms.

THE WHITE MANSION: Located inside the Silvers, the house that the Unseelie King built for his beloved concubine. Enormous, ever-changing, the many halls and rooms in the mansion rearrange themselves at will.

THINGS

AMULET: Also called the One True Amulet, see The Four Unseelie Hallows.

AMULETS, THE THREE LESSER: Amulets created prior to the One True Amulet, these objects are capable of weaving and sustaining nearly impenetrable illusion when used together. Currently in possession of Cruce.

COMPACT: Agreement negotiated between Queen Aoibheal and the MacKeltar clan (Keltar means hidden barrier or mantle) long ago to keep the realms of mankind and Fae separate. The Seelie Queen taught them to tithe and perform rituals that would reinforce the walls that were compromised when the original queen used a portion of them to create the Unseelie prison.

CRIMSON RUNES: This enormously powerful and complex magic formed the foundation of the walls of the Unseelie prison and is offered by the *Sinsar Dubh* to MacKayla on several occasions to use to protect herself. All Fae fear them. When the walls between man and Fae began to weaken long ago, the Seelie Queen tapped into the prison walls, siphoning some of their power, which she used to reinforce the boundaries between worlds . . . thus dangerously weakening the prison walls. It was at that time the first Unseelie began to escape. The more one struggles against the crimson runes, the stronger they grow, feeding off the energy expended in the victim's effort to escape. MacKayla used them in *Shadowfever* to seal the *Sinsar Dubh* shut until Cruce, posing as V'lane, persuaded her to remove them. The beast form of Jericho Barrons eats these runes, and seems to consider them a delicacy.

CUFF OF CRUCE: A cuff made of silver and gold, set with blood red stones; an ancient Fae relic that protects the wearer against all Fae and many other creatures. Cruce claims he made it, not the king, and that he gave it to the king as a gift to give his lover. According to Cruce, its powers were dual: it not only protected the concubine from threats, but allowed her to summon him by merely touching it, thinking of the king, and wishing for his presence.

DOLMEN: A single-chamber megalithic tomb constructed of three or more upright stones supporting a large, flat, horizontal capstone. Dolmens are common in Ireland, especially around the Burren and Connemara. The Lord Master used a dolmen in a ritual of dark magic to open a doorway between realms and bring through Unseelie.

THE DREAMING: It's where all hopes, fantasies, illusions, and nightmares of sentient beings come to be or go to rest, whichever you prefer to believe. No one knows where the Dreaming came from or who created it. It is far more ancient even than the Fae. Since Cruce cursed the Silvers and the Hall of All Days was corrupted, the Dreaming can be accessed via the hall, though with enormous difficulty.

ELIXIR OF LIFE: Both the Seelie Queen and Unseelie King have a version of this powerful potion. The Seelie Queen's version can make a human immortal (though not bestow the grace and power of being Fae). It is currently unknown what the king's version does but reasonable to expect that, as the imperfect song used to fashion his court, it is also flawed in some way.

THE FOUR STONES: Chiseled from the blue-black walls of the Unseelie prison, these four stones have the ability to contain the *Sinsar Dubh* in place if positioned properly, rendering its power inert, allowing it to be transported safely. The stones contain the Book's magic and immobilize it completely, preventing it from being able to possess the person transporting it. They are capable of immobilizing it in any form, including MacKayla Lane as she has the Book inside her. They are etched with ancient runes and react with many other Fae objects of power. When united, they sing a lesser Song of Making. Not nearly as powerful as the crimson runes, they can contain only the *Sinsar Dubh*.

GLAMOUR: Illusion cast by the Fae to camouflage their true appearance. The more powerful the Fae, the more difficult it is to penetrate its disguise. Average humans see only what the Fae want them to see and are subtly repelled from bumping into or brushing against it by a small perimeter of spatial distortion that is part of the Fae glamour.

THE HALLOWS: Eight ancient artifacts created by the Fae possessing enormous power. There are four Seelie and four Unseelie Hallows.

The Four Seelie Hallows

THE SPEAR OF LUISNE: Also known as the Spear of Luin, Spear of Longinus, Spear of Destiny, the Flaming Spear, it is one of two Hallows capable of killing Fae. Currently in possession of MacKayla Lane.

THE SWORD OF LUGH: Also known as the Sword of Light, the second Hallow capable of killing Fae. Currently in possession of Danielle O'Malley.

THE CAULDRON: Also called the Cauldron of Forgetting. The Fae are subject to a type of madness that sets in at advanced years. They drink from the cauldron to erase all memory and begin fresh. None but the Scribe, Cruce, and the Unseelie King, who have never drunk from the cauldron, know the true history of their race. Currently located at the Seelie Court. Cruce stole a cup from the Cauldron of Forgetting and tricked the concubine/Aoibheal into drinking it, thereby erasing all memory of the king and her life before the moment the cup touched her lips.

THE STONE: Little is known of this Seelie Hallow.

The Four Unseelie Hallows

THE AMULET: Created by the Unseelie King for his concubine so that she could manipulate reality as well as a Fae. Fashioned of gold, silver, sapphires, and onyx, the gilt "cage" of the amulet houses an enormous clear stone of unknown composition. It can be used by a person of epic will to impact and reshape perception. The list of past owners is legendary, including Merlin, Boudicca, Joan of Arc, Charlemagne, and Napoleon. This amulet is capable of weaving illusion that will deceive even the Unseelie King. In *Shadowfever*, MacKayla Lane used it to defeat the *Sinsar Dubh*. Currently stored in Barrons's lair beneath the garage, locked away for safekeeping.

THE SILVERS: An elaborate network of mirrors created by the Unseelie King, once used as the primary method of Fae travel between realms. The central hub for the Silvers is the Hall of All Days, an infinite, gilded corridor where time is not linear, filled with mirrors of assorted shapes and sizes that are portals to other worlds, places, and times. Before Cruce cursed the Silvers, whenever a traveler stepped through a mirror at a perimeter location, he was instantly translated to the hall, where he could then choose a new destination from the images the mirrors displayed. After Cruce cursed the Silvers, the mirrors in the hall were compromised and no longer accurately display their true destinations. It's highly dangerous to travel within the Silvers.

THE BOOK (See also *Sinsar Dubh;* she-suh DOO): A fragment of the Unseelie King himself, a sentient, psychopathic Book of enormous, dark magic created when the king tried to expel the corrupt arts with which he'd tampered, trying to re-create the Song of Making. The Book was originally a nonsentient, spelled object, but in the way of Fae it evolved and over time became sentient, living, conscious. When it did, like all Unseelie created via an imperfect song, it was obsessed by a desire to complete itself, to obtain a corporeal body for its consciousness, to become like others of its kind. It usually presents itself in one of three forms: an innocuous hardcover book; a thick, gilded, magnificent ancient tome with runes and locks; or a monstrous amorphous beast. It temporarily achieves corporeality by possessing humans, but the human host rejects it and the body self-destructs quickly. The *Sinsar Dubh* usually toys with its hosts, uses them to vent its sadistic rage, then kills them and jumps to a new body (or jumps to a new body and uses it to kill them). The closest it has ever come to obtaining a body was by imprinting a full copy of itself in Mac as an unformed fetus while it possessed her mother. Since the *Sinsar Dubh*'s presence has been inside Mac from the earliest stages of her life, her body chemistry doesn't sense it as an intruder and reject it. She can survive its possession without it destroying her. Still, the original *Sinsar Dubh* craves a body of its own and for Mac to embrace her copy so that it will finally be flesh and blood and have a mate.

THE BOX: Little is known of this Unseelie Hallow. Legend says the Unseelie King created it for his concubine.

THE HAVEN: High Council and advisors to the Grand Mistress of the abbey, made up of the seven most talented, powerful *sidhe*-seers. Twenty years ago it was led by Mac's mother, Isla O'Connor, but the Haven got wind of Rowena tampering with black arts and suspected she'd been seduced by the *Sinsar Dubh,* which was locked away beneath the abbey in a heavily warded cavern. They discovered she'd been entering the forbidden chamber, talking with it. They formed a second, secret Haven to monitor Rowena's activities, which included Rowena's own daughter and Isla's best friend, Kayleigh. The Haven was right, Rowena had been corrupted and ultimately freed the *Sinsar Dubh*. It is unknown who carried it from the abbey the night the Book escaped or where it was for the next two decades.

IFP: Interdimensional Fairy Pothole, created when the walls between man and Faery fell and chunks of reality fragmented. They exist also within the network of Silvers, the result of Cruce's curse. Translucent, funnel-shaped, with narrow bases and wide tops, they are difficult to see and drift unless tethered. There is no way to determine what type of environment exists inside one until you've stepped through, extreme climate excepted.

IRON: Fe on the periodic table, painful to Fae. Iron bars can contain non-sifting Fae. Properly spelled iron can constrain a sifting Fae to a degree. Iron cannot kill a Fae.

MACHALO: Invented by MacKayla Lane, a bike helmet with LED lights affixed to it. Designed to protect the wearer from the vampiric Shades by casting a halo of light all around the body.

NULL: A *sidhe*-seer with the power to freeze a Fae with the touch of his or her hands (MacKayla Lane has this talent). While frozen, a nulled Fae is completely powerless, but the higher and more powerful the caste of Fae, the shorter the length of time it stays immobilized. It can still see, hear, and think while frozen, making it very dangerous to be in its vicinity when unfrozen.

POSTE HASTE, INC.: A bicycling courier service headquartered in Dublin that is actually the Order of *Sidhe*-Seers. Founded by Rowena, she established an international branch of PHI in countries all over the world to stay apprised of all developments globally.

PRI-YA: A human who is sexually addicted to and enslaved by the Fae. The royal castes of Fae are so sexual and erotic that sex with them is addictive and destructive to the human mind. It creates a painful, debilitating, insatiable need in a human. The royal castes can, if they choose, diminish their impact during sex and make it merely stupendous. But if they don't, it overloads human senses and turns the human into a sex addict, incapable of thought or speech, capable only of serving the sexual pleasures of whomever is their master. Since the walls fell, many humans have been turned Pri-ya, and society is trying to deal with these wrecked humans in a way that doesn't involve incarcerating them in padded cells, in mindless misery.

SHAMROCK: This slightly misshapen three-leaf clover is the ancient symbol of the *sidhe*-seers, who are charged with the mission to See, Serve, and Protect mankind from the Fae. In *Bloodfever*, Rowena shares the history of the emblem with Mac: "Before it was the clover of Saint Patrick's trinity, it was ours. It's the emblem of our order. It's the symbol our ancient sisters used to carve on their doors and dye into banners millennia ago when they moved to a new village. It was our way of letting the inhabitants know who we were and what we were there to do. When people saw our sign, they declared a time of great feasting and celebrated for a fortnight. They welcomed us with gifts of their finest food, wine, and men. They held tournaments to compete to bed us. It is not a clover at all, but a vow. You see how these two leaves make a sideways figure eight, like a horizontal Möbius strip? They are two S's, one right side up, one upside down, ends meeting. The third leaf and stem is an upright P.

The first S is for See, the second for Serve, the P for Protect. The sham-rock itself is the symbol of Eire, the great Ireland. The Möbius strip is our pledge of guardianship eternal. We are the *sidhe*-seers and we watch over mankind. We protect them from the Old Ones. We stand between this world and all the others."

SIFTING: Fae method of travel. The higher ranking, most powerful Fae are able to translocate from place to place at the speed of thought. Once they could travel through time as well as place, but Aoibheal stripped that power from them for repeated offenses.

SINSAR DUBH: Originally designed as an ensorcelled tome, it was intended to be the inert repository or dumping ground for all the Unseelie King's arcane knowledge of a flawed, toxic Song of Making. It was with this knowledge he created the Unseelie Court and castes. The Book contains an enormous amount of dangerous magic that can create and destroy worlds. Like the king, its power is nearly limitless. Unfortunately, as with all Fae things, the Book, drenched with magic, changed and evolved until it achieved full sentience. No longer a mere book, it is a homicidal, psychopathic, starved, and power-hungry being. Like the rest of the imperfect Unseelie, it wants to finish or perfect itself, to attain that which it perceives it lacks. In this case, the perfect host body. When the king realized the Book had become sentient, he created a prison for it, and made the *sidhe*-seers—some say by tampering with their bloodline, lending a bit of his own—to guard it and keep it from ever escaping. The king realized that rather than eradicating the dangerous magic, he'd only managed to create a copy of it. Much like the king, the *Sinsar Dubh* found a way to create a copy of itself, and planted it inside an unborn fetus, MacKayla Lane. There are currently two *Sinsar Dubh*s: one that Cruce absorbed (or became possessed by), and the copy inside MacKayla Lane that she refuses to open. As long as she never voluntarily seeks or takes a single spell from it, it can't take her over and she won't be possessed. If, however, she uses it for any reason, she will be obliterated by the psychopathic villain trapped inside it, forever silenced. With the long-starved and imprisoned *Sinsar Dubh* free, life for humans will become Hell on Earth. Unfortunately, the Book is highly charismatic, brilliant, and seductive, and has observed humanity long enough to exploit human weaknesses like a maestro.

SONG OF MAKING: The greatest power in the universe, this song can create life from nothing. All life stems from it. Originally known by the first Seelie Queen, she rarely used it because, as with all great magic, it demands a great price. It was to be passed from queen to queen, to be used only when absolutely necessary to protect and sustain life. To hear this song is to experience Heaven on Earth, to know the how, when, and why of our existence, and simultaneously have no need to know it at all. The melody is allegedly so beautiful, transformative, and pure that if one who harbors evil in his heart hears it, he will be charred to ash where he stands.

UNSEELIE FLESH: Eating Unseelie flesh endows an average human with enormous strength, power, and sensory acuity; heightens sexual pleasure and stamina; and is highly addictive. It also lifts the veil between worlds and permits a human to see past the glamour worn by the Fae, to see their actual forms. Before the walls fell, all Fae concealed themselves with glamour. After the walls fell, they didn't care, but now Fae are beginning to conceal themselves again, as humans have learned that the common element iron is useful in injuring and imprisoning them.

VOICE: A druid art or skill that compels the person it's being used on to precisely obey the letter of whatever command is issued. Dageus, Drustan, and Cian MacKeltar are fluent in it. Jericho Barrons taught Darroc (for a price) and also trained MacKayla Lane to use and withstand it. Teacher and apprentice become immune to each other and can no longer be compelled.

WARD: A powerful magic known to druids, sorcerers, *sidhe*-seers, and Fae. There are many categories, including but not limited to Earth, Air, Fire, Stone, and Metal wards. Barrons is adept at placing wards, more so than any of the Nine besides Daku.

WeCare: An organization founded after the walls between man and Fae fell, using food, supplies, and safety as a lure to draw followers. Rainey Lane works with them, sees only the good in the organization, possibly because it's the only place she can harness resources to rebuild Dublin and run her Green-Up group. Someone in WeCare authors the *Dublin Daily,* a local newspaper to compete with the *Dani Daily;* whoever does it dislikes Dani a great deal and is always ragging on her. Not much is known about this group. They lost some of their power when three major players began raiding them and stockpiling supplies.

ABOUT THE TYPE

This book was set in Sabon, a typeface designed by the well-known German typographer Jan Tschichold (1902–74). Sabon's design is based upon the original letter forms of sixteenth-century French type designer Claude Garamond and was created specifically to be used for three sources: foundry type for hand composition, Linotype, and Monotype. Tschichold named his typeface for the famous Frankfurt typefounder Jacques Sabon (c. 1520–80).